also by
PAUL GUERNSEY
UNHALLOWED GROUND
ANGEL FALLS

AMERICAN GHOST

a novel by
PAUL GUERNSEY

talos
press
new york

Talos Press books may be purchased in bulk at special discounts for sales promotion, corporate gifts, fund-raising, or educational purposes. Special editions can also be created to specifications. For details, contact the Special Sales Department, Talos Press, 307 West 36th Street, 11th Floor, New York, NY 10018 or info@skyhorsepublishing.com.

Talos Press® is a registered trademark of Skyhorse Publishing, Inc.®, a Delaware corporation.

Visit our website at www.talospress.com.

10 9 8 7 6 5 4 3 2 1

Library of Congress Cataloging-in-Publication Data

Names: Guernsey, Paul, author.
Title: American ghost / by Paul Guernsey.
Description: New York : Talos Press, [2017]
Identifiers: LCCN 2017006577| ISBN 9781940456904 (hardback) | ISBN 9781940456928 (ebook)
Subjects: | BISAC: FICTION / Fantasy / Contemporary. | FICTION / Ghost. | FICTION / Occult & Supernatural. | FICTION / Fantasy / General.
Classification: LCC PS3557.U335 A83 2017 | DDC 813/.54--dc23
LC record available at https://lccn.loc.gov/2017006577

Cover design by Claudia Noble

Printed in the United States of America

For Zander,
Don't let anything boo you

ACKNOWLEDGEMENTS

As promised in Chapter 12, special thanks to Daniel "Thumb" Rivera and Benjamin LeBlanc for the roles they played in the creation of this work. Deep appreciation to my editor, Cory Allyn, for his vision, insight, and guidance. And much gratitude to my generous and encouraging early readers: Wendy Higgins, Victoria Woollen-Danner, Bruce Guernsey, David Gallipoli, and my wife, Maryann. Finally, I would be remiss in failing to acknowledge the contribution of my late cousin, Jim "Hobo" Millard, who over the years shared with me a great deal of his first-hand knowledge concerning biker customs and culture.

"Dude, I drank too much wine and fell asleep on Circe's roof top
And when I woke up and decided to get down, I forgot to use the ladder
I stepped off into thin air, fell to the ground, and broke my stupid neck
And my spirit came down here to the House of Hades."
—*Elpenor, explaining himself to Odysseus*
near the entrance to the Underworld

CHAPTER 1

Once you're dead, ghosts are everywhere. The first time one of them whispers to you from out of the darkness, you imagine your blood turning to slush just as it would if you were alive. You want to scream and run—but you are forbidden to make a mortal sound and there is nowhere you can go.

A few days before I haunted the informal gathering of family and friends that followed my memorial service, as I toppled in the underground river where we dead spend so much of our time, a voice reached me across the currents like someone speaking in a dream. For a moment I thought it might be my father—I had been thinking about him—but then I realized it was a spirit I did not know and I was afraid. I tried to swim faster, to get away. But escape was impossible and the voice clung to me as if the words were those of the water itself. He or she—I couldn't tell which—sounded like the slow stirring of stones in the depths of the river.

"Thumb Rivera. Do you hear me?"

When I didn't answer it said, "You won't escape, you know. I'll be with you forever, if that's what it takes. I'll cover you like a skin." A moment later, when I still hadn't replied, the ghost added, "Forever is a long time, Thumb."

"I *hear* you! What do you want?" I was only thinking these words, but the ghost clearly caught them.

"I wouldn't ordinarily talk to the likes of you—a criminal—but I've been given a message for you."

"Who are you?"

"I'm no one you would know."

I had no idea what to make of this voice, whether to believe it, or trust it, who—or whatever—it belonged to. No telling what it might really want from me, or want to do *to* me. Yet I was alone, in despair, and I seemed to have no choice but to listen, and try to understand.

I said, "Who's the message from?" I felt a surge of hope as I imagined the possibility of forgiveness from—I did not know exactly. From whoever mattered here in the world of the dead. Of course there was a lot I'd done that needed forgiving; I was under no illusions about that. But maybe my situation wasn't hopeless.

"Right now you are in the first circle of the spirit world. But your time here is limited. You can either move up, or fall below. Either way, you will not stay where you are."

"Move up to where? Fall below to *what*?"

"If you fall below, it's a much blacker death than this. You will never see a face. You will never hear a voice, or music. There is only night."

"So . . . is it *nothing*, then?" The thought of oblivion was less frightening than many other possibilities.

But the voice gave a gravelly laugh and said, "Not nothing, no. Because you will know that you are there. For eternity you will feel the crawl of every moment."

Once again I visualized my blood, thickened with crimson needles of ice. "All right. So . . . what then? Tell me."

"You were murdered." Although I'd figured this out, it was still a horrible thing to hear.

"I already guessed."

"In the coldest of blood."

Without a body, I could no longer shudder. But as the ghost spoke these words, I *imagined* myself shuddering.

"Yours was a complicated death. It left other lives in great disorder. To set things right, you first will need to learn exactly how and why you died. All the parts of the puzzle. You will need to connect those bones and make sense of the creature you construct."

I was silent for a while, my suspicions flaring anew. Finally, my outburst: "A *puzzle*? Like in a mystery novel, or a movie? Like, even though I'm dead I'm supposed to be a detective, or a character in a video game? Why? Who, exactly, in any kind of serious afterlife, would want me to do that? Who are *you*, really, and how do I know you're not just fucking with me?"

After a pause of its own, the spirit answered, "I'm just a messenger, and I have no further answers. You are free to believe whatever you want. It makes no difference to me."

There was another long silence during which I began to fear the spirit had gone away. In a voice that might have quavered had I still been alive, I said, "Why the dramatic setup, anyway? Won't it all just come back to me? Naturally, I mean, the facts of my murder? I was there, after all—and my memories about other things have started to return."

A moment later I added, "Hello? Are you there? Hey . . . messenger . . . "

"You've got a difficult journey ahead of you. But remember the consequences of failure. You will need to find a way to accomplish it. And finally, you will need to come to terms with what you've learned."

"So if I succeed? What happens then? Where do I go?"

"I have not gotten there myself."

"And coming to terms. Tell me what that means. Does it mean giving up on vengeance? Or do I have to forgive? Or do I have to *carry out* my revenge somehow?"

"You will have some choices. If you choose correctly, you might move on from here. If not, you will sink."

I already felt as if I were sinking. "And how am I supposed to get this done? I'm just a ghost. I have no power to do *anything*. I can't even leave the house I'm haunting. I'm a fucking *ghost*." But he or she did not speak again. The river ghost was gone—and I felt more forsaken than ever.

Much later—nearly *two years* later, after I'd learned not only that my first, frightening messenger had been telling the truth, more or less, but also what I needed to know about my death, although I was still far from "coming to terms" with it—I heard from yet another messenger, one of many I'd spoken to deep in that watery lightlessness. This ghost had a voice like the rush and gurgle of the river current.

"Thumb Rivera. You are giving thought to murdering a man."

By then I was no longer afraid of unfamiliar spirits. On several occasions, I'd served as a messenger myself. I said, "I'm only a ghost. I can't fire a gun. I can't light a fire. You know I can't murder anyone."

"Don't play games, you stupid boy. You *are* a ghost—and you've got the power to create fury and terrible fear."

After a moment I admitted, "I've been considering it."

"I've been told to warn you. If you cause a death out of revenge, you will remain a ghost forever. A solitary ghost who sits in the dark."

I said, "Thanks for your warning, spirit. But it's a sentence I might be willing to serve."

*

Ghost story. Murder story. Love story. The mystery at the heart of each is my own killing, all details of which, for long weeks following my first, incomplete illumination as a ghost, I was completely unable to remember. In fact, it was through hazy deduction rather than by hard evidence that I eventually concluded I had probably died violently, at the intentional hands of others. My first, obvious inference: At twenty-two years of age and in excellent health, I was far too young to have launched out on so abrupt and final a trip without having had help in packing my bags. Nor had I been in the habit of doing dumb things like playing with firearms or driving recklessly while under the influence—although I'd be a liar if I claimed I was never, or even infrequently, under the influence. Also there was the broadly circumstantial fact that, in having given over every bit of my time and attention to the first-hand research of the book I planned to write, I ended up willingly and even eagerly immersing myself in an environment and a way of living that had brought countless other risky lives, including that of my own father, to an early end.

The similarity to my father's fate was no mere coincidence: During the two years that preceded my death, I had more or less intentionally followed a parallel though far less glamorous course to the one my old man had navigated over a decade before—a life's journey that stopped short the day he and the stripped-down, twin-engine Beechcraft he was piloting, along with his cargo of Colombian cocaine, had all disappeared together and forever somewhere over the blue Caribbean Sea.

*

At this point, there are a couple of things I need to tell you. The first is that my full name is Daniel Starbird Rivera—though even in death I go by the road name of "Thumb." Rivera, of course, is Spanish; my long-gone, drug-smuggling old man came from Venezuela. He spoke perfect English, but with a staccato *Caraqueño* accent that made him sound impatient. The Starbird part comes from my mother's family name, that of a clan, all but extinct now that I'm dead, which for nearly two centuries clung like seaweed to the rocky midcoast of Maine. My parents met in Florida, which is where I was born and grew up until I left to attend an expensive college in a small Maine city I'll call Riverside. It's the same school at which my late Grandfather Starbird, a third-generation alum, had spent thirty years teaching mathematics.

College was fine; college was a pimped-out cage of whitebread privilege. Yeah, I guess that's my ultimate excuse for the slide I took to the criminal side: From my father I'd inherited the inflammable legacy of a risk-taking gene, and it was the absolute, suffocating safety and predictability of life at school that became the match to light the flame. Anyway, for the longest time things at college went normally for me. I was a biology major with a minor in English; my grades were satisfactory, and I had a smart, loyal girlfriend along with a handful of close college buddies who, I can say without exaggeration, all loved me. Then late one night a little over halfway through my college career I was lying awake and staring at shadows when in my imagination I heard my long-dead father speaking to me from out of the darkness. "*Hijo, qué verguenza,*" he said. "What a shame. You don't even know who you are."

A few nights later, as the headlights of cars swooped and stalled along my bedroom walls, I thought of him again. This time I could almost see him standing at the foot of my bed in his creased canvas pants and his leather flying coat and his teardrop sunglasses. I imagined him saying, "Daniel, *Qué te pasa*? You're not living your life like a man. Stop being afraid. Get up and take your fate in your hands. Do something bold."

After that I grew so restless that I found it impossible to quit imagining myself as an overfed jaguar in a zoo, pathetically longing for the sight of moonlight stabbing in bright blades across the damp leaf-litter of the forest floor. Even while wide awake I began to hear my father's call in the sound of every wind-driven rain. As if by predestination, I met Chef in one of the seedy clubs down along the broad river that divided Riverside. The bar was a spot of darkness where other students seldom went. Chef was a fellow southerner, a slow-talking, heavy-set biker boy from Alabama who was looking to get something going; he was hoping to join one of the three outlaw motorcycle gangs operating in the state or, failing to spark enthusiasm as a biker-club prospect, he planned on assembling his own little unaffiliated outfit and starting to make a living—at weed cultivation, on a little methamphetamine production, on some repackaging of prescription medications. The usual petty-criminal bullshit.

Chef had Cricket with him then. I remember how she stood next to his barstool with her fingers saddled over the shoulder of his jacket, saying little and looking from one to the other of us as we conducted a conversation punctuated by the crack of billiard balls. Although she wasn't a girl who at first glance struck you as smoking, when Cricket smiled—which she did infrequently—she would blow you away with her sudden bloom. The other thing about her was that, although she had a pale complexion and an Anglo last name and had grown up in some backwater potato town up along the Canadian border, there was something to her—some indefinable quality like an aura or an aroma—that told me there was no way she was not at least part Latina.

At some point later that night, when Chef's attention had been drawn elsewhere, I spoke a few words to her—So, Cricket . . . *te gusta bailar?*—and she smiled. It was obvious from her eyes that she had no idea what I'd said to her, but nonetheless her gaze rested on mine, and after a moment we both looked away as if we'd been seared to the backs of our skulls.

No, dude, I cautioned myself. *There's no future in that.* But as always, I had difficulty following my own wise advice.

*

After you die, and before you become fully illuminated as a ghost, you start out as a kind of ghost larva. You are no bigger than a fleck of dust, and formless. You don't know where you are, and you no longer see or hear in the usual ways. At first you can't remember much of anything, including your own name. You have to relearn almost everything.

At the outset there is also an awful sense of isolation and abandonment. You find yourself fantasizing that you might somehow be still alive—in a coma, maybe, or merely having a nightmare. Then, when denial temporarily fades, you wonder if you might not actually be in hell. But after your mind finally begins to clear and you are able to string together a few coherent thoughts, you tell yourself, *No, hell is not like this. Hell is a howling man in a red suit and tights. Hell is giant spiders and prison rapists. Real hell is being a child and left for an interminable weekend in the resentful "care" of Tiabuela—your Venezuelan great aunt—while your dad is off on a "business" trip.* However, you are also aware that when it comes to defining what hell really is or is not, you have no idea what in hell you're talking about.

A further facet to the whole post-death experience is a helpless, out-of-control toppling and tumbling that you eventually decide would be like what a body might feel as it was being dragged by a strong current along the murky bottom of a river, caroming off rocks and the waterlogged trunks of trees. So I wondered, shortly after the first few, feeble thoughts began to congeal in my mind, whether I might have died by accidental drowning. But this, as I soon would learn, was wrong.

My mortal memory began to resurface piece by shattered piece through that subterranean river of disorientation and confusion. How long did it all take? It was hard to tell. Time, though it still ticks on after death, is very different to us, the dead. Sometimes it moves in both or even multiple directions at once, like an eddy in the middle of an ocean, complete with boils and undercurrents—but this is something that you, as a linear, living person, are probably better off not even trying to wrap your mind around.

In any case, all at once "my eyes opened"—just a metaphor, since I no longer had real eyes—and my fully conscious and freaked-out essence found itself suspended at the exact point where three vast, gray planes came together. As my perspective began to adjust, I imagined—accurately, as it turned out—that I was either hanging or floating in a corner where two walls supported a ceiling. I was the size of a spark and everything else was so huge as to be almost unrecognizable. All around me, a dozen or more weightless gray streamers seemingly miles in length rippled through space like ribbons of greasy smoke, and these, I eventually understood, were the tatters of a dusty cobweb dancing in a current of air.

At first there was silence, and just as I'd begun to wonder whether I was deaf for all eternity, I heard the familiar sound of a car hissing past on a nearby street. I could tell the pavement was wet. Just afterward, I heard a rumbling commotion that drew my attention to a blur of motion far below; it looked like a storm-filled cloudbank or a mountain surfing on the wave of an earthquake and it was barreling toward me at a scary speed. The rolling peak or boiling thunderhead closed the distance between us until, with a siren-like yet also plaintive whine it shifted shape and settled directly beneath my dusty corner. Then it startled me further by seeming to lift its lid, and suddenly it was looking up at me with an unmistakable pair of eyes that my mother, when I was much younger, and when she still was speaking to me, would have described as being "big as millstones." After a moment I realized that these were the eyes of my own dog, Tigre—a huge, brindle-colored pit bull and bullmastiff cross, and by the way they focused on my corner I could tell he somehow knew I was there. From above, his severely cropped ears looked like giant horns. Once I recognized Tigre—*Tee*-gray is how it's pronounced, although I always called him Tigger when we were among people who lacked my love of Hispanic language and culture—further memories and realizations began hitting me like shots of lightning. My own name was one of the first things that came jolting back.

And, since this was my dog, I figured that the place where I found myself must also be my own—it was the house I shared with Chef and . . . two other bikers whose faces and various tattoos returned to me long moments before their names trickled back to whatever it was my mind had become. Mantis was one of the men,

Dirt the other. This partial recovery of my identity and associations temporarily filled me with the cruel illusion that I might actually be returning to my natural life. Nevertheless, what a relief it was to know Tigre sensed my presence up there in that corner, a dimple in space surrounded by the dusty festoons of a former spider's web! It was welcome proof that, despite the apparent fact that I was dead, something real remained of me. I experienced an emotion that might have made me cry, if I still had eyes.

Tigre: probably the only companion I ever had, aside from my mother, whose heart had never held even the tiniest taint of treachery. I then felt the first real hope of my afterlife: Maybe it would be possible for me to speak to my dog. But no sooner did this thought occur than I began to feel, for want of a better word, *faint*. I didn't know it yet, but I was on the verge of being cosmically smacked down merely for *thinking* about breaking the most important of the many "rules" new ghosts are always stumbling over like tripwires. No sooner did my mind hatch this forbidden thought than light and color faded around me and that dark underground river began tugging me back to its depths. Tigre also seemed to sense a change. He whined again, more softly this time, and with a heartbreaking absence of expectation, after which he lowered his head, wheeled clumsily away from my corner and began his thunderous trot back down what I now knew was the short front hallway to my house, headed, no doubt, to his special spot on the braided rug in the bedroom he and I shared.

Had shared.

Out of desperation, I tried to call him back. But my effort had the effect of immediately snuffing my senses of vision and hearing and violently dragging me back to the currents of the dark and infinite river where I toppled and tumbled and was uncertain of anything except that I was *somewhere*, and wherever that vague place might be, it was very far from heaven.

CHAPTER 2

So I met Chef, I met Cricket, and not long afterward I left college to enter their shadowy world of rebellion and risk. I justified this reckless plunge by telling myself that I was gathering experience for a novel or a movie script, and that in due time I would retrace my steps to the light of my ordinary life. But the truth was, I had found a fascinating flame and I wanted to see how long I could hold my hand in it.

I was no biker, but I had been growing pot on a miniature scale since my Florida high school days, and I had a gift for inspiring the best in a bud. Within two months of that first night in the bar along the river, Chef and I had rented our rundown rural ranch house. Although it stood but a twenty-minute drive from the center of Riverside, the place had no close neighbors, and it contained a cellar roomy enough to raise a modest clandestine crop. Across the street from the house, there was nothing but a stretch of coastal swamp where the tassels of marsh grass waved in the wind. Behind us, beyond the wooden fence that surrounded our new backyard—and set about thirty yards into the woods past the boundary of our landlord's property—sat an abandoned mobile home that Chef could convert into a methamphetamine kitchen. It was a perfect setup.

Chef was a competent hack chemist and a halfway decent motor-cycle mechanic, but completely hopeless with a carpenter's hammer in his sweaty, pink ham of a hand. As soon as the lease was signed, almost entirely by myself I pounded together a ventilated, sound-proof shed in the backyard, guided in my work by a set of plans I had found in a particularly useful issue of *High Times* Magazine. The job took almost two weeks, and when the building was finished, we dragged in a brand-new, five-thousand-watt Honda generator. The purposes for this private power source were to cable juice to Chef's trailer whenever it came time for him to don his vinyl elf suit and his respirator and brew us up a batch, and also to amp up my energy-intensive basement grow room, thereby avoiding the public power grid, where our consumption levels and telltale patterns of usage were apt to attract the unwanted attentions of the law.

Once the shed was up and the generator installed, Chef and I got down to business. I outfitted the basement with banks of grow lights, a powerful ventilation system, an irrigation network, and a state-of-the-art, temperature-controlled drying closet. I sowed our first crop, which consisted of several cannabis strains whose array of magical properties had fired my curiosity. Then I acquired Tigre, half-grown at the time, and began training him as our chief of security. I also took time to establish an elaborate bird-feeding station in the backyard: I'd always been a birder, and in college, as a budding biologist, I had given serious thought to specializing in ornithology.

To my surprise, Cricket did not immediately move in with us; instead, she spent no more than three or four nights a week at the house and behind the closed door of Chef's bedroom. But we did soon bring in another housemate—a greasy worm of a biker named Dirt whom Chef dragged home from the bars one night, insisting that he would make an ideal and unquestioning helper and deliv-eryman for both of us. And that he mostly was—though on several occasions we almost kicked him out for dipping into the crystal. Our number one household policy was that any of us could smoke all the weed he wanted, but touching the crank—even just to "taste" it—was out of bounds. It's no secret that meth fucks people up; not only does it turn tweakers into gargoyles, but it makes them do irrational and dangerous things. Chef and I certainly did not want anything like that going on around us.

One time when Dirt had been tweaking and did something I considered especially destructive and stupid, I beat the shit out of him for it, and wound up knocking a tooth right out of his dumb skull. He was lucky I didn't kill him. But more about that later.

*

About a year into our operation, we took on yet another associate and this completed our crew. The new dude was a tall, bearded, and seemingly capable biker named Mantis who had come to us from Arizona after abruptly resigning his membership, under circumstances he refused to discuss, in a chapter of one of the big, one-percenter clubs. All he would tell us about his flight from the Southwest was that he had been a chapter officer, and that there had been some accounting errors for which he was unfairly held responsible. Although it was strongly rumored that to become a member of Mantis's former club you had to have intentionally killed somebody, when he first presented himself to Chef and me, his demeanor was mild, almost meek, and we decided what the hell, anyone deserved forgiveness and a second chance.

From the time of his arrival it was apparent that Mantis also had eyes for Cricket. But by then Cricket had already made the jump from Chef's futon to my bed. When it happened—after she broke the news to Chef as gently as she could—I really did expect that everything we'd built would fall apart. I'd been prepared for threats, breakage, and maybe even some actual, wild violence. To be honest, I was excited about the prospect.

But Chef merely disappeared for a little more than a week, and after he came back, he carried on as always. The only hint of how badly he was hurting was that it took several days before he was able to look either of us in the eye. Later, Cricket and I concluded that he had reacted with such a surprising lack of drama because, not only did he have nowhere else to go, but from the start he'd understood that his luck with her would likely never last. All along, he'd been braced to see her swap him out for someone more like me.

*

The second time I returned to the land of the living, I found myself back up in that dusty corner above the front door to my house. The same cobwebs undulated before me and the empty hallway gaped below. I could "see" down the hallway into the living room and through the window curtains into the fenced-in backyard; in fact, when I concentrated, I could peer right through all the surrounding walls as if they were panes of dirty glass, a superpower I employed at once to locate Tigre, who was sleeping in my bedroom. Still far from fully illuminated as a ghost, I remained without arms, legs, or head. I wondered whether I might at least be able to leave my corner and motor to some other part of the house. Wondering led to effort, effort led to successful movement, and soon I set out on a slow, firefly-like flight.

I navigated into the kitchen, where I had already sensed that things had been screwed with. Sure enough, gone was Chef's alchemical assortment of methamphetamine manufacturing supplies, most of which, between his visits to the trailer, he had stored in cardboard boxes and bags on our kitchen floor and counters. The missing stuff included the mounds of bubble-packaged, pseudoephedrine-based cold and allergy remedies Chef used as a primary ingredient, as well as the gallon and half-gallon containers of ammonia, muriatic acid, paint thinner, Red Devil lye, and Drano, along with the smaller bottles of such explosive or corrosive chemicals as starter fluid, brake fluid, lighter fluid, and hydrochloric acid.

Also gone were the veterinary-size bottles of iodine tincture, the neat boxes of highway flares waiting to be broken apart for the red phosphorous they contained, all the laboratory gear, including the flasks and mason jars and other glassware, the coils of transparent tubing, the three-burner portable gas stove, and Chef's assortment of plastic tubs, buckets, and bottles.

I guessed that everything had been taken away as a precautionary measure. Either that or the house had been raided by someone—by the cops or a group of our business rivals. But of the two possibilities I thought precaution was the better bet, since there was no evidence of an invasion: no disorder, breakage, or rust-colored traces of blood. In fact, the kitchen looked tidier than usual, not only because the meth-lab inventory was gone, but also because our meager assortment of plates and bowls was stacked in the cupboards rather than piled in the sink, soaking in a greasy slick of water.

As I hovered there midway between the ceiling and the floor, Tigre thundered into the kitchen from the hallway that led down to the three bedrooms and the bathroom. He searched for me, whining and turning himself around, his thick black claws clicking against the linoleum. Clearly, he had no idea where, exactly, I was, and maybe did not yet even know *who* I was; he may merely have sensed a disturbance and been seeking its source. In any case, right then I had no time for him, because the absence of Chef's gear made it likely that they had also taken things that belonged to *me*.

Tigre made a nearly subsonic rumble in his throat as he followed me to the basement door. Of course, I couldn't turn the doorknob—but no longer was that door, or any door, a barrier to me: I passed right through it with no resistance save for a vague, overall prickling sensation that brought back a vivid childhood memory of pushing headlong through a wool curtain pregnant with static electricity. I found myself at the top of the wooden cellar stairway—Tigre barking behind me now with a growing alarm that was edging toward hysteria—and immersed in what would have been total darkness if I still had eyes. In a slow, dream-like beeline, I followed those stairs into the basement room where, ever since quitting college nearly two years before, I had spent most of my days conducting an all-female orchestra of various cannabis strains, each of them superbly bred, trained, and groomed to play her own special melody in the human imagination.

But now the cellar was empty not only of my strings and woodwinds and brass—my oboes and my clarinets, my cellos, violins, and xylophones, my tympani, all of which comprised the individual, distinctive voices of my sweet, beautiful, large-budded ladies—but also of every scrap of hardware and any other hint that I myself had ever existed. Not a screw or coupling or speck of planting medium remained; it was clear that they had carefully swept the concrete floor in order to obliterate every last, incriminating particle. This large portion of my life's work—my vineyard, my orchard—had been uprooted, burned over, and plowed under, and with it a major part of the person I had been.

I hovered there until I began to feel pathetic and then, without having to turn around I retraced my path up the stairs and through the door. I could as easily have ascended directly between the ceiling joists and through the plywood floor, but stairs were still a habit.

Tigre quit his barking as soon as I rejoined him. He whined and seemed to look directly at me as I passed like Tinkerbell above his wet boulder of a nose, and I was gripped by an almost irresistible urge to speak to him. But I did not dare: not only did I remember the unpleasant result of my last flirtation with this idea, but just the thought of causing the air to vibrate with the sound of my voice scared me to the point of blacking out.

I prickled my way through the rear wall of the house and into the fenced-in yard that contained, along with a few scattered and toppled plastic lawn chairs, Tigre's exercise equipment, my ambitious array of birdfeeders—all of them empty, and abandoned by the birds—and my generator shed. The wind was blowing, rain threatened, and the dry leaves of red maples cartwheeled through the air, each one making a *tick* as it touched the grass. It bothered me to learn that the strong wind had absolutely no effect on me; I could sense it only through the life I saw it give to objects such as leaves, and could feel neither its force nor its chill.

I knew the generator shed would be empty; they'd have dragged off my powerful Honda along with everything else. No reason to strain myself by peering through the wall. However, the shed did hold something else I valued: Over the course of two years, between scribbled columns of coded business notes, I had penciled several dozen poems on the shed's naked sheetrock walls. I was about to pass through the wall and reread them all when a whine from Tigre, followed by the sound of a familiar car turning into the driveway, drew me back to the house.

Tigre was standing before the front door, the stump of his tail twitching in excitement. A moment later the lock turned, the front door swung open, and my beautiful girl, Cricket, stepped in and dropped to one knee to hug my dog and murmur something into his neck just above the nasty spikes of his collar. Then she was on her feet again and her birdlike legs went scissoring into my bedroom, which she had sometimes shared with me, and where she now began tossing her way through the drawers in my two dressers. Each time she finished with one drawer, she slammed it shut and moved on to the next.

As I watched her work, I was happy to find that I could still feel many human things: I was glowing with nostalgia and affection mixed with some regret. What Cricket and I had most in common— had *had* most in common—was our mutual dedication to downward mobility. In another life, her name was Claire, and she was the daughter of a dentist—the *adopted* daughter of a dentist, as she was often quick to point out. In addition, I believed—based on intuition rather than evidence—that she, like me, was part Hispanic, though Cricket herself had been unable to say for certain what her heritage was.

Tigre barked, and I heard the rumble of Mantis's Harley-Davidson Softail coasting into the driveway. Cricket heard it too; she stiffened, shoved the last drawer shut, and hurried out to the living room, where she dropped onto the couch and began feeling around in the pockets of her leather jacket. After a moment, she produced a crumpled pack of cigarettes and tossed it onto the coffee table.

Tigre growled at Mantis in the doorway.

"Shut up," said Mantis quietly, and Tigre fell silent. A moment later he said, "Fucking dog's got to go." He looked up at Cricket, the two of them silently and expressionlessly locking eyes for a long moment before Mantis broke away and clumped around into the kitchen and down the hall to my room, where he conducted his own, more thorough, though apparently just as fruitless, search of my earthly possessions. Unlike Cricket's almost respectful rifling, Mantis scattered my clothes onto the floor, and he sent the vacant drawers crashing.

After he was finished, he returned to the living room, plunged his lanky frame into the couch next to Cricket, and kicked his heavy, black boots onto the coffee table. After a moment he rested his elbow on the back of the couch, pressed a tattooed fist into his beard, and stared at her in a way he would never have dared when I was alive.

"So, like, what were you looking for?" Cricket's voice was a note higher than normal.

Instead of answering, Mantis mimicked her tone, saying, "So, like, what are you *doing* here?"

Cricket drew a Bic lighter from within her jacket, her pale hand trembling slightly. Then she picked up the cigarette pack as if she were about to shake one out. Instead, she seemed to reconsider and ended up setting both the lighter and the cigarettes back onto the tabletop. She told Mantis, "The cops came to see me at work today. Spent a half hour talking to me down in the parking lot."

"Well, ain't that a coincidence? They came to look for me at Pete's. They weren't friendly, either. They did not seem sorry for our loss."

Cricket took up the lighter again and turned it over and over in her fingers before giving it a couple of idle flicks. "I don't get it. Why don't they just come and search the house? Get it over with?"

"No corpse yet, I guess," said Mantis. "That's what they're waiting for, I bet. Nothing but his empty truck, burned up in a quarry. Those three photos of him lying there dead that turned up online; maybe they're thinking that blood was ketchup and that he faked his own death, or something. If they ever find a body, I bet they'll be here in an hour."

Cricket nodded slowly, and I was gratified to see a wet line creeping down from one nostril. Almost angrily, she scrubbed it away with the back of her hand, then she reached into her jacket pocket and came out with a dense, dark chunk of a cannabis bud in a zip-lock plastic sandwich bag. She said, "This is the last of what he gave me for my birthday."

"*That's* what he gave you? Dope? For your birthday?"

She narrowed her eyes at him. "He said it was the most perfect small bud he'd ever grown. He said it reminded him of me."

Mantis said, "Well, if anybody could grow a perfect bud." Then he threw an obvious card on the table: "And he was right; if anybody's *like* a perfect little bud . . . " But she quickly brushed him off.

"It was sweet," she said, and rubbed her nose again. "Let's smoke some."

"What'll we do if the cops decide to bust in here right now with that search warrant?"

Cricket almost smiled. "I can swallow pretty fast."

She opened the bag and drew it to her nose for a moment, inhaling deeply with her eyes closed. Then she reached in and pinched a piece off of that gorgeous fragment of bud. Holding her hand above the table, she rolled the nugget between the balls of her thumb and slender forefinger to crumble it into resinous flakes, after which she packed it into the bowl of the little brass pipe that Mantis offered to her after pulling it from the pocket of his greasy jeans. Thick smoke rose languidly once the pipe was lit; I longed to catch a whiff of it, but, apparently, I no longer had a sense of smell. Maybe I really was in hell.

Mantis ended up smoking nearly the entire bowl by himself. Cricket took just one little toke, which was unusual for her—she may not have even inhaled—and after that, she waved him off every time he offered her the pipe.

When they were finished smoking my stuff, they settled back into the couch. They were silent for a long while, then Mantis started moving his tongue around the inside of his mouth in an experimental manner before finally sliding his reddened eyes in Cricket's direction. In a croaking voice, he began, "So, Crick, whadya say? You wanna . . . "

If I'd had a heart, it would have skipped a beat.

"No," she said, cutting him off.

I was afraid he might decide to press the issue—what would I do then? What *could* I do?—but he just shrugged and slumped.

After a minute Cricket said, "So, in his room, what *were* you looking for?"

Mantis shrugged again. "Whatever we might have missed the first time around. Any little scrap of his that could connect us to the business. The tone the cops were taking when I talked to them made me paranoid, I guess." He looked at her. "What about you?"

"Same," Cricket said, after a pause. A moment later, she added, "If they're coming, I think the shed might be a problem. He wrote stuff on the walls."

"Yeah? Does it mean anything? I always thought that was just a bunch of his usual crazy-genius bullshit, scribbled all up in there. Stuff about birds, maybe."

"Some of it was poems and stuff," Cricket confirmed. "One of them he said was all about how he felt about me. But there was other stuff too; he put it in code, and I think it was about how much fuel the generator was using, and maybe notes about different types of smoke he was growing. You know how some of them had, like, girls' names, and some were musical instruments? But I think cops could figure all that out if they wanted to."

"Fuckin' *Thumb*," said Mantis. I was touched to detect a note of wistful affection in his voice. Then he gave Cricket a direct look and smiled. "A poem on how he felt about *you*. How'd that one go?"

Cricket shrugged. When she spoke, it was with a slight catch in her voice. "I don't know. I'd go out there and try to read it sometimes, but I couldn't understand it. I don't think he really wanted me to."

After a moment Cricket took an audible breath and continued, "So I think maybe we should paint those walls out there."

"Nope. Won't work, and will just look suspicious. If they want to know what's under the paint, they can get it off easy enough. If you're really worried about it, the shed should probably just burn down."

She reached and settled her hand on the inside of his thigh. He slitted his eyes, slid them to the hand that was resting on his leg, and then widened them at her.

"Well then, why don't you take care of that for us?" she said. "For all of us, Thumb included?"

"Okay," he said slowly, and nodded. She gave his leg a gentle double squeeze.

"I mean, you should check with Chef first, but I think it's the thing to do."

"All right."

"Make sure you get a fire permit from the town office, though. Otherwise, we'll have the fire department here, not to mention the sheriff. If they ask, tell them we want to burn some construction debris."

"Not a problem, Sugar. She burns before the sun sets."

Quite willingly, even eagerly, I retreated to my corner above the door. In fact, I dove right through into that darkness on the other side.

CHAPTER 3

In both of the college writing classes I took, the instructors told me, "Write what you know." As I've mentioned, that's part of the reason I left college to live and work with Chef, grow weed, and hang out with bikers: I wanted to *know* something aside from the second-hand glory of my father's abbreviated criminal career and my own life as a privileged student. And maybe the book I wrote as a result would have been a decent one. But now that I'm dead, I've got a story that's much more appealing than that, and so I've switched my focus. What I now know gives me the unique opportunity to be the first person ever to write a book from beyond the grave. That's important, because one of the things that haunts me the most is the fact that, in twenty-two years on planet earth, there's nothing else I really accomplished. I'd like my life (and death) to have had some meaning.

As for discovering the missing details of my murder, not only is this something I've apparently got to accomplish in order to move on in the afterlife, but along with my natural curiosity about how it all went down—wouldn't you want to know what happened, if it happened to *you*?—it will help give some narrative shape to the otherwise shapeless experience of being dead.

All of this leads to something else I need to talk about at this point, because you've undoubtedly heard that dead men tell no tales, and you're doubtlessly wondering how it is that I'm able to tell you mine. Well, there's an answer, but it's a little complicated. In fact, the voice you're hearing right now as you read this is not entirely mine. In order to write my account from beyond the grave, I've had to work with a couple of living people—a kind of ghostwriting team. The first of these people I will tell you about is Ben, a spiritual medium a little younger than myself who often gets confused about what, exactly, I've dictated to him.

When things are going well, this is the way we work: Ben sits with his pudgy fingers resting on a Ouija board planchette, the Ouija board planchette on the Ouija board, the Ouija board itself on the cluttered card table in his little bedroom at the back of his grandmother's trailer, and he waits for me to spell my story, which he then enters sentence by sentence into a spiral-bound composition book. Of course, spelling everything out completely would take a God-awful amount of time—Ben might die of old age before we finished—so we've worked out a system to make it go faster. We use phonetics as well as first and last letters for names and frequently used words, and in dictation I drop out most of the vowels, which Ben fills in afterward; but there's more to it than that. We've developed a code that is a sloppy stew of familiar text-messaging acronyms and abbreviations combined with pidgin English and our own idiosyncratic set of shortcuts.

You probably remember that "official" Parker Brothers or Hasbro Ouija board from your childhood: The alphabet; a row of numbers, zero to nine; "Yes" in the upper left; "No" in the upper right; "Good Bye" at the bottom. A heart-shaped plastic table with a round window in the middle—the planchette—which glides around the board on little felt feet. In our work, Ben and I use "Good Bye" like a space bar on a keyboard; it separates words, which is especially important when you're employing severe abbreviations which otherwise would make no sense.

For instance, the letter G by itself stands for "ghost;" GS is the plural. DD is dead. AFL is "Afterlife." "MC": motorcycle.

"Cricket" is CCT; "Thumb" is "TM;" "Mantis," MTS; "Dirt," DRT. "Harley-Davidson": HD. "Ben" is just "B." And Fred—you'll hear more about him later—is "F."

As for the smaller, frequently used words, T is "the." "HR" and "TR": "here" and "there." N does double duty as "in" and "and." Z is "is," and S stands for "said," or "says." Just as in text-messaging, R is "are" or "our," and YR is "your" or "you're."

Regarding punctuation, other than two quick "Good Byes"—a bounce of the planchette at the bottom of the board—to end a sentence, there is none, and it's one of many problems we won't solve for a while. Three Good Byes is my way of asking Ben to start a new paragraph, which he sometimes does, and sometimes doesn't do. Another problem is that when I'm dictating an especially long sentence, Ben will sometimes forget the beginning before I've reached then end. Then he'll take the liberty of writing his own inferior approximation in the blue-lined notebook, forcing me to let it stand, or insist that he start all over.

Here's a brief example of how it comes together when it's going well. Say I dictate the following to Ben:

1S (Good Bye) YR (Good Bye) DD (Good Bye) GS (Good Bye) R (Good Bye) EVRYWR (Good Bye) (Good Bye)

On that second Good Bye—"Bye" is what I actually say to him—Ben picks up a pen and in our blue-lined composition notebook scribbles, "Once yr dead ghosts r everywhere," the opening line to this story.

Although it's still not a fast system in spite of our shortcuts, once we get warmed up and in synch, we can move along more rapidly than you might think.

*

Ben: a twenty-year-old rural Maine dude who, apart from his exotic ability to communicate with a dead guy—me—is a fairly typical product of his time, setting, and circumstances. A few decades back, by this point in his life he probably would've been working more or less contentedly in a shoe factory or a paper mill. But Maine mills of any kind now are almost extinct, and dependable employment for guys like Ben is hard to come by. He did manage to graduate from high school a couple of years ago, and if either of his long-divorced parents had any money he'd probably be enrolled with others of his kind in some third-rate college somewhere. As is, he lives in his grandmother's trailer along a stretch of winding, backwoods road, works with enthusiasm whenever work is available, and to his credit, never gives up hope that he one day will luck into a gig that enriches him enough to buy a car, move out on his own, maybe have a live-in girlfriend. He even entertains a few vague dreams that are grander than all that.

Ben spends a little of his time each week wandering the county like a dogged wraith as he hunts for the permanent job he probably never will find. Most potential employers barely give him a look before dismissing him as a lost cause—a country loser without even a car he can call his own. Once a month or so, he'll hook up with a team of amateur "paranormal investigators," a group of misfit nerds that travels northern New England in a van trying to capture electronic evidence of supernatural occurrences. In fact, it was during one of these dorky ghost-hunting missions that he and I first connected.

However, in spite of his frequent forays, whenever I'm looking for him odds are I'll find him holed up in his room at the back of his grandmother's trailer, where he plays endless fantasy-based video games on his laptop computer. Over time I've decided that it is these games and his passion for them that are the key to who Ben really is—by which I mean the person he *imagines* himself to be, and fantasizes he will one day become, just as soon as a handful of favorable

circumstances rains from the sky to shower him in silver coins waiting to be spent. Ben views his video games as preparation for the
real challenges he often dreams of facing, and in these games he
invariably casts himself as the hero he believes lies trapped beneath
his doughy skin. The roles he chooses are those of a man—decisive,
swift, agile with a sword—who is able to rescue beautiful women
from terrible men and monsters. In his games he is an invariable
righter of wrongs, a changer-for-the-better of other people's lives, a
man worthy of great respect. On the computer screen, as well as in
the future he imagines for himself, Ben *matters*.

I know all this not only because I've been able to observe him
closely in his most unguarded moments—when we're not working
with his Ouija board, he often forgets that I might be there—but
also because he will sometimes tell me things that he might never
confide in anyone else. Of these probably the most important is
that he's got a couple of young twin half-siblings, a boy and girl,
three years old and living in another state, whom he worries about
a great deal because of a series of awful experiences—he's disclosed
some of these to me, but refuses to let me share them with you—
that he'd had as a child with one or both of their parents. Of all
his heroic fantasies, undoubtedly the most practical is to move
closer to these kids in order to shield them from the sorts of abuses
that had happened to him. And to do that he needs some money, a
working, road-worthy vehicle, and a little more of just about everything than he now has.

I think that, even as the novelty of having me for an invisible friend begins to wear off, and in spite of his general misgiv-
ings about taking dictation from a ghost, these distant hopes and
unformed ambitions are what keep him working with me. He's
smart enough to realize that my brand of enchantment, dark and
soiled as it is, probably constitutes the only real magic that will
ever come his way, and as such, even though he can't quite imagine when and how his payoff will arrive, may well represent his

one chance to realize his full, heroic potential. In Ben's own wise words: "I don't know where I'm going, but I seem to be getting there."

Here I have to add that Ben's pretensions to heroism, while in general useful to me, occasionally impede my progress, because instead of sticking with my narrative, which is all I need him to do, he sometimes will argue about what could, would, should be, or should have been done about something I've been telling him. He even second-guesses some of my actions that aren't what he imagines he himself would do. For one example, when I first told Ben about the ghost girl who one day reached out to me in the underground river, he became agitated. He started to nag me about her. He thought we should "help."

That ghost girl: there I was, toppling in the darkness of the underground river when out of nowhere she seemed to spiral all around me. Otherwise invisible, she arrived in shifting ribbons of light like the aurora borealis, and she was so close I imagined her wet skin brushing against me. I could sense that, like me, she'd died young. But in spite of being lonely past the point of anguish, I dreaded hearing what she had to say. I assumed that as a messenger she carried some harsh new warning I had to heed; either that or there was a grim job I was expected to do under pain of an even deeper damnation.

It was at least a small relief that she spoke in an ordinary woman's voice rather than one that echoed death with the sound of gurgling water or the rasping of rocks. She said, "Thumb! Is it you? Is your name Thumb?"

"Who are you?"

"I'm Angelfish. I need your help."

"Help to do what?"

"You're the one who can do it! You're the only one! *Thumb!*" She sounded frantic, and her dancing lights were beginning to fade.

"What is it? I don't think I can do anything. What can I do?"

"Look for me! Keep looking! I'm *Angelfish*!" And with that she was gone, seemingly swept far past me in the river, which in her wake returned to blackness.

At this point in my narration, Ben sat up straight, his face flushed and his eyes wide, and he took his hands from the planchette. The romance of a hot girl in desperate need of help—even a dead girl—had obviously inflamed his imagination, and perhaps other parts of him as well. He said, "*Angel*fish. Would that be a biker chick's name?" He put his fingers back on the planchette.

CD B NO IDEA

"Did you end up helping her?"

HW CD I SH WNT AWA
(How could I she went away)

"Dude, so you never heard from her again?" Ben sounded upset. I hesitated before spelling.

NO I HRD 2S MO FM HR LTS GT BK 2 WRK
(No I heard twice more from her let's get back to work)

"Really? So what happened? What did she say? What trouble was she in?"

SH S
(She said)

. . . then I reconsidered and began again.

B STP
W HV 2 RT EVRYTG N T RT ORDR R MY STRY WL GT FCKD UP

(Ben stop. We have to write everything in the right order or my story will get fucked up.)

"Yeah. Okay. But just tell me what she told you. I really want to know."

B SHS A G N WV GT LTS MO GS 2 RT ABT 1ST
(Ben she's a ghost and we've got lots more ghosts to write about first)

"It wouldn't *kill* you to tell me," Ben said in a petulant tone, his hands now tucked beneath his armpits. "I wouldn't even need to write it until later." I was tempted to tell him about the other two underwater encounters I'd had with Angelfish, just to make him happy. But finally I decided against taking the chance of having those episodes shuffled into my book in the wrong places, thereby screwing everything up, so I just stayed silent until he quit sulking and was ready to move on.

*

After seeing Cricket and Mantis, the next time I returned from the Great Wherever I found the house empty again except for Tigre, who was snoring on the floor in my recently rifled bedroom. Nothing remained of my generator shed but a mound of ashes and blackened debris. The many words I had scribbled on those walls—all the things I'd thought of and dreamt—might as well never have been written, or dreamed. The sun was shining, but I could neither feel its rays nor sense how warm the air might be; it was now clear that I was completely cut off from the heat of life itself, a fact that I found dispiriting to the point of despair. Out of a desperate urge for rebellion—although rebellion against whom or what, I was not sure—I decided then that I would make a run for it, right through the high, wooden fence that separated our backyard from the woods and the abandoned trailer that had served as Chef's kitchen and, beyond where the trees ended, a desolate hayfield. Where I would go after that, I didn't know; escape itself was my only goal.

I never made it even as far as the fence. Each time I flew beyond a certain distance from the house, I would find myself back up in my corner among the cobwebs. On my last and most desperate attempt at getting away, the force that held me to the house sucked me right through the eye of the cobweb corner and hurled me into the dark river on the other side.

On a later visitation to the house, while I hovered in the living room steeping in my regrets, a human hand suddenly took shape in the air before me. I almost yelled in fear as I fled to my bedroom—and the hand flew right along beside me as if it knew where I was headed. Back and forth it chased me between the front hallway and my room; finally I went out through the wall and into the yard. I traveled as far as I could go without getting dragged back to my spot among the cobwebs, and that was when the hand cornered me, its fingers drawn into a fist. After a moment, when it hadn't tried to hit me, I realized that the ghostly hand was my own, and that I could make it open, close, and stick up its middle finger. I recovered from my surprise and took my "new" hand all around the inside of the house, swiping and grabbing at things—and was disappointed to find that it went through objects with only a crackle of seeming static, and without affecting them in any other way. Nor was I able to feel the texture or temperature of anything I tried to touch. The one, small breach in my otherwise seamless inability to affect the material world had to do with Tigre, who, when I passed that hand over him, stirred from his sleep with the hair standing stiff on the back of his neck. After a moment, he woke up, looked around, and whined.

Before long the rest of my ghostly "body" took shape. My other hand appeared with a little imagination on my part, as did my arms, legs, head, and torso. Although my completed avatar produced no reflection in the bathroom mirror, I was nonetheless able to "see" all of myself including my face because my sense of "sight" now consisted of many more dimensions than when it had been restricted by the physical limitations of actual eyes. I could even change my appearance at will, or take another shape—a bird, say, or a flowerpot. But I was satisfied to look more or less the same as I had in life—though with two exceptions. The first exception had to do with my body art—a set of tropically colored tattoos that included:

A jaguar clawing its way up the outside of my left arm, the spotted tail winding nearly to my wrist, and

On my right shoulder, the head of a harpy eagle (*Harpia harpyja*) with its crest raised and its beak gaping as if frozen in midscream, and

Over my heart, a life-size *caribe*, a ferocious little fish that the non-Venezuelan world knows as the red-bellied piranha, and

A bright green marijuana leaf on my right calf, and

A portrait of the Liberator, don Simón Bolívar, on my left calf, and

Taking up most of my back, a bare-chested Maria Lionza—a Venezuelan Indian goddess—wearing a crown of jungle flowers and riding a tapir, and

Finally, on the back of my neck, some inky blue Chinese calligraphy. (What that exotic and incongruous writing supposedly said, never mind; the message is meaningless now.)

These tats did not automatically reappear with the reconstruction of my bodily form, and rather than recreating them, which I easily could have done, I was relieved to be rid of them. Their loss made me feel less desperate to cloak myself in an identity that could never entirely be my own.

The second exception was that, as I am sure almost any man would do, I took advantage of the opportunity to make one part of myself a little larger than it had been in life. I momentarily got carried away with this enhancement before deciding I looked ridiculous, and dialing back a little from what had begun to resemble a baby elephant's trunk. But *just* a little.

Then, because I felt weird standing naked in the middle of the living room, I covered my invisible, illusory body with invisible, illusory clothing. I dreamed up a pair of jeans, along with work boots, a black t-shirt, and a blue-checked flannel shirt—all the things I would have worn in life. Only after that, and despite the fact that I could feel no actual clothes touching my nonexistent skin, did I feel complete.

I was then as whole as a ghost could be. I was illuminated.

*

The next time the river spit me out into the front hallway of the house—it might have been hours later, or days, I have no clear idea—I was in full, disembodied, bodily form, clothing and all. I could see right away that things in the house had been moved around, even cleaned up a little more, since my last visitation, but that once again no one was home except for Tigre. I decided then to push through the closed front door for the first time since my death. Shoulder first, as if breaking the door down, I prickled my way between the molecules of the wooden panels and emerged into the autumn sunlight that fell on the cast-concrete stairway leading up to the door. Across the road stretched that familiar, lonesome lagoon of coastal wetland, alive with the hypnotic wind-dance of marsh grass. Looking out over those waving tassels toward the horizon, I wondered whether it might be possible, now that I once again had a more or less human form, for me just to walk away from the house; there were a few places I was eager to visit in order to get started on investigating my murder. To be specific, I thought I could learn a lot by eavesdropping in all of my housemates' regular haunts. But I was not sure what my rules might be—if I were allowed to leave at all, where exactly could I go, and how long could I stay there? Too much about this ghostly new life was still a mystery to me.

Between the shoulder of the road and the edge of the marsh a pair of wooden electric-power poles stood planted side by side. One pole was whole and the other was broken, consisting of little more than a tall stump as a result of having been cracked the previous winter by the sideways impact of an automobile that had spun out of control as it rounded the icy ribbon of road. Five feet to one side or the other, and the car would have vaulted the snow bank and gone off into the marsh, probably leaving the driver unhurt except for wet legs from breaking through the ice and a few bruises from the punch of his airbag. As it was, the pole had stopped him hard, snapping his head sideways against the top of the doorframe and clean through the closed window. Suspended in air by snow that had been mounded by the road plow, the car's wheels were still spinning madly when I had arrived to look inside. I felt the driver's throat; he had no pulse. I'd considered pulling him out, stretching him across the snow, and pounding on his chest. Perhaps it would have made a difference if I'd done that, and also shared a breath or two with him—but probably not. Anyway, I'd decided to go back into the house and call 911 instead. He had been a professor at the college—a man around sixty years of age. Afterward, rather than uprooting the cracked pole, the utility company had merely sawed it off at the point where it was broken—about six feet above the ground—and left the rest of it standing. They set the new one in right next to it. Shortly afterward, someone sneaked in under cover of darkness and, from a nail near the top of the truncated pole, had hung a heart-shaped wreath woven of grapevines and flowers.

Although the remains of the wreath were still hanging, the flowers had long since withered and crumbled to dust, and the twisted vines were no longer recognizable as a heart; nearly a year's worth of weather had unraveled them from the wire around which they were wrapped and eroded them to a ragged brown oval that now reminded me of a gaping mouth.

I mention all of this because suddenly I saw the figure of a man standing by those two utility poles. There was an eerie, translucent luminosity to his appearance, and I could tell right away that, like me, he was not a physical person at all. In fact, he looked a lot like the professor of African-American literature whose compact and lifeless body I had watched the paramedics solemnly extract from that smashed vehicle. The man—or ghost, I guess I should call him—was looking not at me but at the hanging hoop of dried vines that had once made up a heart-shaped wreath. Round, gold-framed glasses shimmering on his face and dessicated marsh grass swaying behind and through him, he seemed to be shaking his stylishly hairless head at the waste of it all. I remembered his name—Virgil Shallow—because he was the first and only freshly dead person I had ever seen.

I was scared—I'd never seen a ghost before—and at first I just wanted to slip back into the house and hide. At the same time I was afraid of moving and drawing his attention, so I remained frozen in my place and watched him. Then, as he continued to ignore me and to stare at the ruined wreath, it occurred to me that there would be no barrier between the two of us the way there now was between my ghostly self and living beings. I might be able to talk to him. And maybe, as an older sprit, he would take me under his wing.

Just as I had made up my mind to risk calling out to him, the dead professor snapped his head in my direction. He was frowning deeply, and at once I felt sure he knew the circumstances of our previous encounter and that he blamed me for his death. That he faulted me for not saving him and for his becoming a ghost. After a moment I lifted my palm to him; I wanted to explain that I would have dragged him from his car if I'd thought it would help. I wanted to apologize. But at my movement, his eyes began to glow behind his glasses like a pair of embers. His eyes grew and they glowed, and then as I stood watching in horrified fascination I saw odd waves of motion surging back and forth beneath his clothes. Those strange tides rippled across him until thousands of twitching white worms burst from his jacket sleeves and the collar of his shirt and spilled down from the cuffs of his pants. The worms poured from him and fell to the ground and soon strips of flesh began to peel from him as well. The worms and the flesh continued to fall and to vanish until there was nothing left of the professor but a clothed skeleton with fiery eyes. Then the bones themselves lost their hold on one another and collapsed to the pavement, their collective clatter muffled by his clothing, after which his horrifying time-lapse decay was complete save for that pair of monstrous eyes that remained hovering in space, afire with fury.

I drew back into the house, turned to the cobweb corner, and retreated to the underground river. I hoped he couldn't follow me there.

CHAPTER 4

The house was different the next time I returned. The kitchen table, covered with a respectable cloth for the first time since New Year's Eve, was loaded with a spread that obviously had come from a caterer: platters of bread and rolled cold cuts, several salads, a steaming, glass-topped electric crock filled with what looked to be sausages and peppers, an array of condiments, a stack of disposable plates, a fan of plastic flatware neatly swaddled in paper napkins. At the center of it all stood a modest vase of white carnations, with a few wispy ferns mixed in. Also, Tigre was gone. I was immediately worried then about who might have him and what they might have done with him. I could not discount the possibility that someone had dragged him to a "shelter"—a fate which, for a business-minded, poker-faced, one-man monster like Mr. Tigger, would probably amount to a death sentence.

I went to the front door when I heard vehicles rolling into the driveway, followed by the sound of slamming car doors and voices. Through the door and the wall I could see them all, including my mother, dressed almost entirely in black, who was being helped from the rear seat of a rental sedan by Cricket and Chef. Cricket, in a long dress and white sweater that hid every one of her pretty tattoos, looked exactly like the young dental hygienist she might have become if she'd made some different decisions. Chef, for his part, had on a clean pair of blue jeans, a white shirt with actual buttons and sleeves, and his "dress-up" leather biker vest. His hair was pulled back in a stubby blonde ponytail, and it looked to have recently been washed.

On the other side of the car, Mantis and Dirt were removing their sunglasses and climbing off of their bikes. Mantis had on his old biker "cut" which, though stripped of all insignia that would have associated him with his former club, still bore the unfaded silhouettes of the missing patches, along with a few tatters of left-over stitching. Beneath the piebald denim, he wore not only a button-down shirt, but also a tie, which was a touch I found touching.

Dirt, on the other hand, looked just like Dirt always did: unshaven, and dressed in generic-looking "unaffiliated" colors heavily stained with motor oil and shot with burn holes from splashes of battery acid. Under the open denim vest, he wore a t-shirt decorated with an advertisement for his latest favorite fad beverage, Twisted Tea, and on his head, a greasy black bandana from which his dreadlocks struggled to escape.

Another car pulled in behind the one Chef had chauffeured my mother and Cricket in. Four nicely dressed younger people stepped out—three dudes and a girl, who after a moment I recognized as friends from the long-lost world of my two-and-a-half-year college career. One of the guys had been my roommate during our first two semesters, another had been our next-door neighbor in the dorm, and the third was a lonely Mexican kid from Des Moines, Iowa, whom I'd met in our first-semester composition class, and who used to insist on reading me his bilingual poetry. The chick was someone whose heart I'd broken, though not on purpose. She had been a passionate but serious girl, a reader of "important" books and, if she'd ever had the chance to meet her while I was alive, would have very much impressed my mother, a high school English teacher.

My four college friends, all of whom would, or should, be graduating by the end of spring, looked bewildered and a little scared to be standing there at the bottom of the driveway to a bikers' lair. Noticing this, Cricket, in as cheerful a voice as she could manage, called out, "Come on in, you guys! There's food." When they still hesitated, Chef walked back to them, gathered their shoulders in his huge arms and, speaking soothing words in his Alabama accent, gently herded them toward the front door. Cricket then wrapped an arm around my mother and the two of them followed the other five in, with Mantis and Dirt bringing up the rear.

So this was it then: The wind-down from some sort of mumbling memorial service intended to close, formally and forever, the brief book of my life. I was certain Cricket had planned it all; there was no one else who would have taken the trouble. She had undoubtedly made all the arrangements and convinced my mother to book the flight from Florida, assuring her as she did so that she had nothing to fear from the rough men I'd shared my home with. She would have contacted my former roommate, whom she had met once before, and begged him to bring anyone else who had known me.

To be honest, I was surprised at the extent of her efforts. Although I did not doubt she would miss me at least for a while, Cricket was one of the least sentimental women I'd ever known, and—especially in light of the way I'd seen her act around Mantis—I had imagined that she would move on directly with her life, never looking back. In addition, Cricket had never seen or spoken to my mother and so had no real reason to reach out to her in the wake of my passing. In any case, and regardless of whatever impulses had impelled her, I was grateful.

The ceremony they'd all attended no doubt was the sort of thing I'd often heard referred to as a "celebration of life," although no one here looked in the least bit celebratory. Certainly not my mother, who was walking with a noticeable bend to her upper back, and who, in spite of being not yet fifty, was suddenly seeming frail. Her mouth was set in a grim line, and behind the wire frames of her glasses her blue eyes snapped with what I recognized as anger.

Despite the fact that I no longer had either a beating heart or a churning stomach to serve as vessels for my emotions, I still managed to feel awful for her, as well as terribly guilty.

At the same time, in addition to my strong feelings about my mother, Cricket, and even the smart and broken-hearted college girl, I was on fire with the urgency of unanswered questions:

Had they finally found my body in order to burn or bury it? (I doubted they had, because, as Mantis had told Cricket, with my corpse in hand as evidence, the cops would have torn our house apart.)

Would anyone here today let slip a clue about who had killed me, and how it had been done?

And, where was my damn dog?

Inside the house, everyone at first congregated in the kitchen. Chef was describing the catered food as if he'd cooked it himself, and urging everyone to eat some of it, while Mantis had opened the refrigerator and with both hands was handing out cans of beer and bottles of Twisted Tea. Dirt stood nearby muttering, "There's hard stuff, there's real booze, if anybody wants some, tequila and stuff," but no one paid him any attention or gave any sign that they had even heard him. With wordless murmurs of thanks, my college friends all grabbed beverage containers and held them in front of their faces like masks at an old-fashioned costume ball.

Cricket waved off the beer that Mantis pushed at her, merely shrugging when he gave her a questioning look. After a minute, she took my mother's arm and guided her down the hall to my bedroom. Of course, I drifted along behind them.

"This is Danny's room," Cricket told her, with emphasis on the name my mother knew me by. I was glad to see that someone had picked up all of my things that Mantis had thrown onto the floor. The drawers, looking worse for the wear, had at least been placed back into the dressers.

There was a long moment of silence while my mother, her mouth pinched even more tightly than before, turned a trembling head from side to side as she took it all in. I could easily imagine what she was thinking. In her youth, she had been not only a beautiful woman, but a brilliant and uncommonly levelheaded one as well, with a bright and limitless future stretching ahead of her. Her one error, the first and only step she'd ever made beyond the boundaries of the prudence, and maybe the prudishness, that had defined her entire, previous life, had been her helpless fascination with my father. As an educated New England girl whose roots ran back to the Mayflower, she could not have chosen a lover more different than herself. He also could hardly have been handsomer or more self-confident, which never hurts a guy's chances. But I think the real key that both unlocked and unraveled her was that, as a pilot and a good-natured gangster, he could not have been more *exciting*. By the time she'd reached the age of twenty-three, Mom had already read a lifetime's worth of books about other people's passions, and one morning—or so it seemed—she suddenly awoke feeling more than ready for something exciting that was both real and entirely her own. That passion, that adventure, that something thrilling ended up being my charming and rope-muscled old man, who, complete down to his pencil-thin moustache, reminded Mom of a swashbuckling, Latino version of Rhett Butler from *Gone with the Wind*, a book she had read more than once. She actually dismissed quite a number of more "suitable" suitors in her headlong and heedless new addiction to life on the edge, and one night the story reached its climax in a wild elopement—a manic nuptial flight to Cancún in my father's plane—followed immediately by a prolonged estrangement from her family, and still later, by me.

By Mom's account, there were two lotus-like years before she slowly emerged from her trance and realized the mess she'd gotten herself into. There were a few more years during which she tried to improvise a sensible life with my father. Finally, after the logical and practical parts of her mind returned from their long exile—never, even for a moment, to leave again—she opted for a decisive separation, and immediately hurled herself into rebuilding her life—new education, new career as an involved and affectionate teacher, a few new men, none of whom ever held her attention for very long, and every other spare moment spent volunteering at a women's shelter. Around that time she started sending me to spend weekends and school vacations at my old man's apartment, in spite of the fact that he wasn't always around. While Papa himself invariably provided me with a blast of refreshing irresponsibility, too often, when my visit coincided with one of his frequent "business" trips, he would drop me off for the duration at Tiabuela's house, which he claimed was good for me in any case because she would teach me my culture. Culture notwithstanding, the old woman had no patience for me, and in fact seemed not to like her little half-gringo grand-nephew in the least, and I certainly *hated* her. Whenever I complained about this to my mother, she only echoed the thing about "learning my culture" and suggested that I needed to toughen up.

Well, no one can argue that I didn't grow tougher—and I now wondered whether mom ever felt bad about that advice, or any of the rest of it. Not that I necessarily *wanted* her to feel bad. . . .

I was twelve when my father disappeared. Tiabuela confirmed that he was dead, but claimed to know none of the details. Months later, "friends" of his got word to us that the U.S. military had shot him down over the Caribbean, but we were never truly certain. For all we knew, his associates themselves were responsible.

No matter; he was gone. And now, more than a decade later, as she commemorated the conclusion to her only child's life, I was certain the eerie parallels between my passing and his would not be lost on my mother. The circumstances of my death, the uncertainty included, added up to a downscale and far less romantic reenactment of my father's disappearance and demise, and this was something I knew had to be haunting her.

Cricket and Mom were holding hands now. Cricket said, "We were engaged." We hadn't been, but I was glad she'd thought to say it.

"Oh," my mother said, almost seeming to believe.

"He was going to tell you soon, if he didn't already."

"No, he hadn't."

"Well, he was. And, I don't know if he told you this either, but my dad's a dentist, and I was studying to be a hygienist."

"You are, or you *were*?" my mother asked, with an edge to her voice.

"I've been on a break. But I'm going back to it."

"Well, I hope you do," my mother said. "You are clearly better than all of this." As she spoke, she made a circling motion with her head to circumscribe her surroundings, both material and human.

Cricket should have stopped then, while she was ahead. But it was at that point that she became entirely too creative to be convincing to a person as perceptive, and as used to being lied to, as my mother.

"Thumb—Danny—was going to help me. Our plan was for both of us to work and save money all this winter and summer, and then I'd go back to school in the fall. And then *Danny* was going to start school again, too. Maybe next spring, if we could afford it."

Disappointment clouded my mother's eyes as she realized she'd been hearing a fairy tale. She shook her head. "Oh, my dear," was all she said. She gave Cricket's hand a squeeze and then let go of it.

After a strained minute had passed, Cricket took a different tack. "We've got some of his things for you. Personal stuff and things he wrote. Poetry . . . things. Would you like to take them home with you?"

Mom gave her a tight smile. "How about if I leave you with a check? Then you or one of the young men could just ship them to me down in Florida?"

"All right. Sure. We can do that." My mother nodded and had started to turn to leave my bedroom when Cricket blurted, as if allowing some dark and final secret to escape, "He had a dog."

Had? What did you bastards do with my dog?

My mother looked at her, and she continued, "I have him now. His name is Tigger, but Th*hh*—*Danny*—had another name for him.

The Spanish word for tiger, I think. I'll take care of him if you'd like." This, of course, was a huge relief to me—even though I wasn't sure she was telling the truth.

"What kind of dog?" my mother asked.

At this, Cricket seemed at a loss for words. "Part bull mastiff, I think," she said after a moment. "He's *very* good looking; he's got stripes in his fur. Danny spent a lot of time with him, training him and everything. He loved that dog. So, he's really well behaved, the best-behaved dog I've ever seen because of all the training and attention he got from Danny, and no trouble at all. Very protective."

"A *large* dog, then?"

"Yes, he's big."

"Well then, yes. Why don't you hang onto him? I'm sure Danny would want you to have him."

"Okay." Then, her voice brightening, Cricket added, "You can see him if you want."

"No," said my mother. "Thank you. I don't need to see him. It's not as if he's a child."

Their awkward conversation was interrupted by Chef, who had shuffled down the hallway to stand outside my bedroom with a stricken expression on his face. Cricket and my mother stared at him in grim anticipation and, in a near whisper, looking only at Cricket as he spoke, he said, "They, uh, want to say goodbye. To Thumb's mom."

At this, my mother drew herself up and brushed past Chef to stalk up the hallway to the kitchen. In an almost masculine manner, she thrust her hand out to my old college roommate, and when he, looking startled, took it in his own, she said, "Thank you so much for coming." She lifted her eyes and looked at each of my other college friends in turn. "Thank you all. It's meant a great deal to me. God bless you all."

My old roommate murmured, "I'm very sorry; I'll miss him. I hope, I certainly hope . . . " At that he bobbed his head, let go of her hand, and took a step back.

My mother pursed her lips and nodded vigorously as if not only understanding what he'd meant to say, but agreeing with him as well. A moment later my old next-door neighbor stepped forward and took her hand. "I'm sorry," he said. He stepped back.

Next came the Mexican poet. "Daniel was my friend," he said. He gave my mother a hug. "I'll never forget him." Then, with his lips close to her ear, he whispered, "*Cuídese bien, Señora. Dios te bendiga.*"

That left the girl with whose heart I had been so careless. Watching the others, she had suffered a meltdown, and now tears poured down her face and little convulsive gasps were bursting from her mouth. She was shaking, and seemed entirely powerless to take those necessary and final steps toward my mother.

Mom stared at her for a moment, then the furious look I'd seen earlier returned. She snatched a tissue from her jacket pocket and moved forward to press it into the girl's hand. "Use this," she ordered. "Use it now." The girl took a shuddering breath, nodded, and began to blot her eyes.

"Now, listen," my mother said, standing close to the girl and placing a hand on the side of her face while all the rest of them stared. "This is not worth any more of your life. Do you understand me?" After a moment, the girl blew her nose and nodded again.

"*Forget*," my mother insisted. "*Do* something. *Become* something." After she and the girl had embraced, Mom stepped back and drew out another tissue, which she used to make a couple of impatient swipes at her own eyes.

When my four college friends were gone, they left behind a vacuum that my housemates and Cricket seemed desperate to fill with upbeat chatter. They confabulated stories about clever things I had supposedly said, and thoughtful or mildly heroic things I had supposedly done, and they were visibly relieved beyond all measure when my mother finally agreed to accept three fingers of cheap wine in a water glass. After she'd taken the first sip, Mom looked at

Chef and said, "You all keep calling him 'Thumb.' It seems an odd nickname for such a tall boy; where did it come from?"

Chef said, "Ma'am, his road name used to be '*Green*thumb' until it got shortened. Because of his way with, you know, plant life."

Mom looked displeased, though not surprised. "*Plant* life?" she echoed. Dirt started to snicker and cough from around his bottle of Twisted Tea, but he cut it short when Mantis gave him a look of warning.

"Yes, ma'am," Chef said. "What I mean is, *anything* that was alive and either breathing or growing, he had a way with it. It was just phenomenal, his knack for botany and so forth."

Mantis elected to join Chef at the barricade. "We had a garden here every year, and Thumb made it grow," he said.

Chef nodded in vehement agreement. "Beautiful tomatoes," he confirmed. "*This* darn big around, some of them." His trembling hands curved before him to suggest a vegetable the diameter of a small pumpkin.

"And, you should see the lawn here, in summer," Mantis said. "If Thumb's sitting in the backyard and he spots a single dandelion off in the distance someplace, he gets right up . . . "

My mother, finally, could stand it no longer. In a matter-of-fact voice, she broke in by saying, "It would appear Danny never mentioned to any of you that his father was a smuggler of cocaine and marijuana for an international cartel?" They all stared at her in stunned silence. After a moment she added, "Well, yes; perhaps you are all a little too young to remember, but we used to have to *import* most of our illegal drugs before we learned to grow or manufacture a few of them here. So, I wonder if maybe some of Danny's horticultural talents might not have been employed in that direction as well?"

When no one answered, or could even manage to look at her, she added, with her voice rising a bit now, "And do you know what?

His father also disappeared under similarly mysterious circumstances, never to return. So, let that be a warning to the rest of you."

A minute later, just as the conversation had begun to sputter back to life, a distant buzz from some indefinite point beyond the house suddenly resolved itself into the unmistakable growl of an approaching Harley-Davidson motorcycle, which at its loudest is a combination of throaty rumble and sustained, earsplitting fart. To a biker, the sound of an individual motorcycle can be as recognizable as a voice, and my housemates and Cricket all fell silent once again, listening with apprehension as the machine drew closer, while my mother looked from one to the other of them with troubled and questioning eyes. The machine coasted to a stop across from our house, where it sat like some sort of apex predator, rumbling and giving off an occasional roar as if announcing a territorial claim to others of its kind.

Following the second, insistent roar, Chef, with almost theatrical reluctance, spread the blinds covering the kitchen window and peered out in order to verify what I am sure he must have strongly suspected and I already knew, owing to my ability to see through walls.

"It's Scratch," he said, without surprise. Scratch was the president of a club chapter that had established its state headquarters in Riverside about a year before. They were a new branch of the Blood Eagles, an up-and-coming national organization that had won its right to exist by surviving prolonged warfare against most of the older, established outlaw clubs, and were therefore a bunch of people with whom an informal, unaffiliated outfit like ours needed to be on good terms—or else steer completely clear of.

Scratch's name, after it had fallen from Chef's mouth, had a strange effect on me. I felt faint the way I did when I had either traveled too far from my corner above the front door, or was giving serious thought to making an actual sound or trying to move something or otherwise considered changing the physical world in a way that was forbidden to a ghost. At the same time, and in spite of the fact that I no longer had a sense of smell, I was almost overwhelmed by a powerful olfactory memory of something that reminded me of nothing so much as the interior of a brand-new automobile.

The motorcycle bellowed again. Mantis, with unconvincing breeziness, said, "I guess I'll go see what old Scratchy wants."

As he went out to talk to Scratch, I faded from the world even further, so close to falling into the underground river that I could hear it rippling through timeless time and spaceless space, and when I finally returned after what must have been a minute or so, not only was I still suffocating in that new-car smell, but I was trailing a memory of having been on my way to visit Scratch at his clubhouse. It seemed likely this was my most recent, and therefore my last, recollection as a living man, prior to darkness and rebirth as a spirit.

With irritation in her voice, my mother was asking, "Who is this 'Scratch' person?"

"He's just a friend, ma'am," said Chef, who was still using two fingers to spread the blinds above the kitchen sink. I could see the dark figure of Scratch as he straddled his idling Super Glide on the edge of the road opposite our house. Mantis had crossed over and stood talking to him.

"If he's a friend, why are you all afraid of him?"

Dirt answered, "He's one of those guys who's just kind of a *scary* friend." My mother gave him a look of contempt, and Cricket, after making sure my mom was not watching her, rolled her eyes at him.

Cricket said, "It's just that he's got some anger issues, and we know how upset he is about Thumb. Mantis is probably trying to calm him down."

My mother said, "If he's a *friend*, why doesn't he come in?"

Chef turned from the window to answer her. "Probably because he knows you're in here with us, ma'am. As Dirt tried to mention, he *is* a bit scary to some people; he's a big old boy, for one thing, and he has a haircut that he knows might seem somewhat strange to you, and he's also got some fairly prominent tattoos on his face that he understands might make him a bit frightening to a regular citizen like yourself. And then, there's the anger thing Cricket spoke about, which is a very real issue with him; he probably doesn't trust whatever might come out of his mouth in your vicinity."

Mom's eyebrows rose above the frames of her glasses. "So, this is all out of concern for my delicate sensibilities?"

"Yes, ma'am," Chef confirmed. "Beyond that, he's probably here because he wants to pay his respects—though in the words that come most naturally to him, which are not necessarily the words most of us would choose."

My mother's eyes traveled from Chef to Cricket and back again. In a quiet voice she said, "What do you suppose 'Scratch' knows about my son's disappearance?" But at that moment, we heard the front door open and Mantis was back among us.

His face expressionless, Mantis entered the kitchen, glanced at Chef and said, "He wants to talk to you." Then he opened the refrigerator, popped open a can of beer, and took a long, gurgling chug. Chef pulled his fingers from the blinds, excused himself to my mother, and headed out; I tried to follow him, but the strange exhaustion that had settled over me at the first mention of Scratch's name remained with me, making it impossible for me to squeeze my way through the front door once Chef had closed it behind him.

I returned to the kitchen as my mother was saying to Mantis, "I was just asking them what this 'Scratch' might know about my son."

Mantis blinked but held her gaze. "He knows Thumb is gone," Mantis said. "And he's wicked pissed about it. He *liked* Thumb."

Mom looked at Cricket, who nodded once and turned her gaze to the floor, biting her lip. Mom said, "You know, I don't believe that. And I don't believe *you* believe it."

After a moment Mantis said, "Hard to know how to answer you, except to say I'm sorry."

Chef returned after he'd been outside for only a couple of minutes. He and Mantis exchanged a brief but meaningful look, then Chef lifted his chin at Dirt and said, "Dude."

"*Me?*" Dirt said, with what seemed to be genuine surprise. "I don't want to." Facing the floor and seeming to pretend that his bottle of Twisted Tea was a microphone, he said, "Just tell me what he told you and that'll be good enough." Outside, the bike roared briefly, as if with impatience.

Chef shrugged and gave a snort. "Up to you," he said.

Dirt's prominent Adam's apple bounced, and from deep within his throat there came an involuntary noise, almost a whimper. He turned abruptly and left the kitchen to head out to the street. After he'd been gone a few seconds, my mother suddenly bared her teeth, nearly bumped Chef as she stalked to the window, and used both hands to spread the metal blinds with a crashing sound. Watching as Dirt slouched across the road toward the seated silhouette on the other side, she declared in a raised and slightly quavering voice, "*I may go talk to Scratch.*"

"*No!*" Cricket, Mantis, and Chef all barked at once.

She turned back to them with an open mouth, clearly startled if not shaken by their reaction. When she had recovered sufficiently, she gave a single nod. "I see," she said, in a quiet tone that nevertheless suggested all her suspicions had been confirmed. She almost smiled.

Dirt returned, pale beneath the dark stubble on his face, and went directly for his Twisted Tea, which he raised to his mouth with a shaking hand. After a moment, he turned to say something to Cricket—but Cricket was already gone. I tried to follow her, was desperate to do so in fact, but just as when I had been following Chef, I lacked the ghostly strength to push myself through the front door.

Anyway, I probably would not have learned much because a minute later, Scratch's bike gave a series of powerful, throat-clearing coughs before popping into gear, carving a muttering U on the blacktop, and exploding back down the road toward Riverside.

Cricket returned to the house wearing her best Sunday smile. "Now," she said. "*That's* over with. And, where were we?"

Everyone, including my mother, seemed to relax after that. Cigarettes were lit, fresh drinks were opened, and my mother's cloudy water glass was refilled with wine. The strange stench of fresh vinyl released its grip on my memory. When Chef made up something funny I'd supposedly said, there was relieved laughter all around. My housemates filled plates with food and ate ravenously, as if they'd been through some grueling physical ordeal. Even Mom stabbed a rolled slice of turkey with a plastic fork and nibbled on it.

At one point, while the five of them were still milling about the kitchen, eating, drinking and talking, Mantis passed behind Cricket and gave her ass a secret squeeze. Cricket remained expressionless, but she rocked her hips almost imperceptibly to show that his touch was not entirely unwelcome. This sight was so painful to me that, if my mother hadn't been there, and had I not been worried that I might never see her again, I would have fled back to the watery underworld.

After the feeding frenzy was over, Cricket took my mother by the arm and led her through the living room to the double windows that overlooked the backyard. She said, "I just want to remind you that *Danny* did have a real love for certain things." She waved a finger at the miniature ghost town of my bird-feeding station, some components of which had been blown from their hangers by the wind and were now lying among the fallen leaves. Unburdened by the weight of seeds and suet, many of the hanger posts leaned at drunken angles, and without a single bird in attendance the collection of weathered plastic dispensers was a sorry sight. Still, Cricket was obviously hoping my mother's imagination would allow her to envision the bygone glory. "Do you *see* all those birdfeeders?" she said, forcing a tone of wonder into her voice.

But Mom's eye had been caught by something else. "Why, there *is* a child here!" she exclaimed. "Or, there *was*. Whose is it?"

"What?" said Cricket, giving her a puzzled smile. "I don't understand."

"That small tire, hanging from the tree. Danny had a tire-swing just like it when he was little. His father put it up for him."

"Oh. No. Thumb put it up there, but it was for Tigger. To exercise on."

Mom gave her an incredulous look. "The *dog* used a swing?"

Dirt, holding a cigarette and a fresh bottle of Twisted Tea, had come up from behind and was standing near them now. "Well, he don't *sit* in it," Dirt said, and laughed. "Only a cartoon dog can do *that*. It's for jaw strength and endurance. What Tig'd do is he'd leap up, clamp onto that tire with his mouth, and then just hang there till Thumb told him he could get down.

"Sometimes Thumb would put him up there and then come back into the house and leave him there for a half-hour or so. Every so often he'd open one of these windows right here and he'd yell out, '*Shake* it, boy! Give it a shake!' and then it'd be the funniest damn thing you ever saw: Tigger'd start dancing and singing and twisting all around in midair like a fish on a line, and whining away like he thought he stood a actual chance at tearing a piece out of that steel-belted tire."

Mom asked, "And what was the purpose of all this, again?"

"Well, that's just how you train a fighting dog," said Dirt. "That and road work. Some of your more hardcore dudes'll even put the dog on a treadmill, and then they'll take a cat in a harness and they dangle it . . . "

"So, you're telling me Danny was training his pet to fight other dogs?"

"*No!*" Cricket broke in. "He was a guard dog, is all! *Jesus*, Dirt! Why don't you go get another drink? No, Thumb just wanted Tigger to be in good shape to protect us all. He trained him hard, and he had a knack for it, but he would never make him *fight* another dog."

Mom looked at Dirt, who was now holding his cigarette at eye level, staring at is trailing a corkscrew of ash as if willing it to break off and fall to the floor.

"Is that true?"

"Well," said Dirt, clearly offended by Cricket's interruption, "I never said nothing different."

Cricket shook her head in disgust. She said to my mother, "But what I *wanted* you to see was the birdfeeders. Even though they're all empty now, you can see that he had different types of them for different kinds of seeds and other food, and he kept track of all the different birds that came. Those long ones are thistle feeders—you can see one of them on the ground over there—and they're for the finches; the things that look like little cages there, is where he'd put suet, and those red ones, in summer he'd fill them with a liquid that brought the most beautiful hummingbirds around—they looked like fairies. Part of what we'll send to you in Florida are the notebooks he kept on the birds."

Dirt, having abandoned his apparent telekinetic experiment and flicked his ash to the floor, said, "And, if you knew what was good for you, you did *not* mess with Thumb's goddamn birds."

"*Dirt!*" said Cricket in a warning voice.

"Hey, Dirt," said Chef, and headed toward us from the kitchen. But Dirt ignored them both.

Looking directly at my mother, he began, "So, one day last summer, there I am sitting in the backyard having a cocktail and a little smoke, when suddenly this giant bird as long as my arm soars in from nowhere like a pterodactyl and lands *upside-down* on the trunk of that big tree right there. It don't even waste a second before it scrambles down and starts banging away on that big branch with its beak. Big red head and a mouth on it the size of a pickaxe. Thumb said later it was called a double-plied woodpecker, but in my state of mind, you know, I thought it might not even have a regular name, because I couldn't believe there might be another one just like it someplace."

Chef had moved in among us by then and he seemed eager to change the subject. But when he tried to talk, my mother, who had given me my first Peterson's *Field Guide to the Birds* long ago, cut him off. "*Pileated* woodpecker, you mean?" she said. "That's what

Danny would have told you. They're large—second in size only to the ivory-billed, which is now extinct, of course—but they're hardly as long as your arm."

"Whatever. Anyway, I'm sitting there watching all these huge wood chips flying through the air and showering down on the ground in like slow motion, buckets and buckets of them coming down like pieces of the sky, and that's when I start to get scared, like maybe I ought to *do* something. Like maybe, he's gonna peck right through that branch and make it crash down onto the house. Maybe even *kill* somebody inside."

"That's a very thick branch. And it doesn't look like it would fall anywhere near the house," my mother observed.

"Well, with *leaves* on it, it does," Dirt insisted. "But anyway, luckily I had my Glock lying right there under the lawn chair, and I was able to put a stop to it. He fell out of that tree and hit the ground in a big plop of feathers. Like watching a turkey fall face first out of a airplane."

My mother squinted as if she were having trouble visualizing such an improbable scene. She said, "You *shot* the woodpecker out of the tree? You were drinking alcohol and smoking marijuana in your backyard with a loaded handgun under your lawn chair, and you . . . "

"Next thing I know, Thumb comes busting from the house and drags my ass right out of the chair. Chair goes crashing away. I wasn't even ready for him, or I would've kicked his ass right then; I thought he was playing around, and I'm all like, 'Hey, Thumb, what's up?' But then he cracks the top of his head against my forehead, then he hits me in the stomach, and *then* the next thing I know, I got a mouthful of his knuckles, and I'm flying across the lawn. When I come to, I'm at ground level, staring right into the big red eye of that dinosaur-bird I shot. Out of the corner of my own eye I see the clip from my gun go sailing over the fence back there, and a second later a swarm of bees that turns out to be my bullets follows it over, and then the gun flies over, too. There's blood running down my chin, and then I feel something in my mouth, and when I spit it out and clean it off a little on my shirt, wouldn't you know it? It's my tooth." He gave my mother a mirthless grin and stuck a forefinger into the gap at the front of his mouth.

"Right *there*," he said in a sudden quaver, wiggling his finger as if she wouldn't have seen it otherwise. "The other tooth, I think the nerve is dead, and it might have to come out, too." He had begun to shake, anger and injured pride filling his normally empty eyes. He had never dared express those feelings to me while I was alive; instead, in his clown-like fashion, whenever the woodpecker incident came up, he played it for laughs. But now here he was, letting his cowardly rage glare through for my mother to see. Right then, if I'd had the power, I would have beaten the shit out of him all over again.

Visibly upset, my mother turned away from him and looked back out the window. "Well, he shouldn't have done *that*," she said. She drew a tissue from her pocket and lifted her glasses to dab the corner of an eye.

"No, he damn well shouldn't of," Dirt said, his fingertip still plugging the hole in the front of his face. "And, what a way to thank a guy who's only protecting your house." By then, Mantis had him by the shoulders and was pulling him away from behind. As soon as he was gone, Chef stepped in next to my mother. He placed his meaty hand in the middle of my mother's back.

"Of course he should of," Chef insisted. "When you got a drunken meth-head shooting randomly in your backyard, *some-body* has to stop him. That's what Thumb did. That's *all* he did. What else are you gonna do?" A few moments later, we heard Dirt's motorcycle bark to life in the driveway and go roaring off toward town. Mantis came back inside and closed the front door.

Cricket said, "Dirt doesn't have any sense. The real story is a little different than he told it, and anyway Thumb was just protecting the rest of us. He was a good protector."

"He was a good man," said Chef. "A good friend."

Mantis, who was standing behind them, added, "He led a good life." With that comment he once again went too far, and my mother snapped her head around to glare at him.

"I hope you don't really believe that," she said. She looked back at Chef, and Cricket, and then at Mantis again. "I loved him, of course; I'm his mother, and I gave birth to him and I raised him. And he did have some good qualities. But for your sakes, I hope you realize how wrong that is.

"You all must understand that his was a wasted life."

CHAPTER 5

A blood eagle is not a bird.

During the raiding and slaving days of the predatory Norsemen, it was a legendary form of gruesome torture and execution. The Vikings called it *carving* the blood eagle, and it supposedly involved holding a dude face-down on the ground, slicing the flesh from his upper back so that the ribs were exposed—and then hacking away the ribs and pulling out the lungs from behind. Those lungs, still attached to their tubing, were spread across the guy's bloody shoulders like a pair of stubby "wings." A blood-eagle sufferer who survived all the chopping and tearing would have quickly died of suffocation, since human lungs, hauled like trout from the sealed well of the chest cavity, can breathe no better than any other fish out of water. But it's more likely that by the time *any* of the dude's organs had been touched by the red light of a Nordic midnight, he would have already gone ghostward from shock and loss of blood.

If, in fact, anyone actually was killed that way; there is some doubt. At least a few historians say that while the blood eagle *was* carved—it was only on the backs of guys who were already dead, having either been killed in battle, or else executed in some less elaborate manner. Still other writers claim that the entire ritual was just a fantasy—something teenage Norsemen imagined might be cool to do to somebody, if only all that thrashing, screaming, and slippery, spurting blood didn't make it likely you'd slice off your own hand.

Anyway, *that* is where the Blood Eagles Motorcycle Club took the inspiration for their name as well as for the design of the insignia patches which, when stitched onto the back of a denim vest, comprise the "colors," or "cut," worn by any full-patch club member. Following are the specs for the Blood Eagles colors, as described in the original club charter:

Against a field black as death, a grinning death's head crowns a set of human ribs that sprout crimson eagle's wings from the shoulders. From the bottom of the ribcage, skeletal talons descend to clutch a sword. One talon clutches the handle, the other clutches the blade, and the one that clutches the blade drips blood. The eyes in the death's head are blue.

The Blood Eagles MC motto—cribbed, probably unwittingly, from the poet, e.e. cummings, by someone who no doubt picked it up in an otherwise long-forgotten high school English class—provides the final touch. Expressed in the form of an upward-curving rocker patch positioned beneath all the others, it reads:

MR. DEATH'S BLUE EYED BOYS

*

Attending the last part of my own memorial observance, together with witnessing Scratch's performance of a funeral fly-by "in my honor," seemed to provide just the shock I needed to help me recall many details of my final day as a breathing being. The next time I came around into the world, it was with the clear memory of having driven into Riverside and crossed the long, iron bridge to the southern bank near the river's mouth where the Blood Eagles MC—Maine Chapter—ran their operations out of a sprawling old ship captain's house. I had gone to the clubhouse to meet with Scratch in order to work out a deal for his group and mine to continue coexisting.

Yeah, I knew the Blood Eagles occasionally murdered people. In fact, that was part of the thrill. But, in going to visit them, I was not being suicidal or even especially reckless; I just did not judge the jeopardy in which I was placing myself as being especially acute. I was, after all, smarter than they were; I knew I could handle them, and I couldn't think of anything that would make them want to mire themselves in the risks and complications of killing me. Also, I already was acquainted and on friendly terms with most of the Blood Eagles, having spent time with them on their side of the river, drinking and shooting pool in the gin mills and strip clubs that stood among the warehouses and the abandoned factories. They all knew I was a producer and they were familiar with the quality of my product, which I was always happy to share with them. When Scratch invited me to their headquarters to talk a little business, I took it as proof that they trusted me.

The mansion stood on an isolated point of riverbank surrounded by a marshy no-man's land separating the city's old industrial zone from the residential neighborhoods that rolled down toward the seashore, the houses becoming larger and better-kept the closer they were to the ocean. I stopped my pickup truck before a closed wrought-iron gate that blocked the Blood Eagle's private road a good distance from their house. From both sides of the gate spread an iron fence topped with spikes and completely interwoven with trees and overgrown hedges, which made it impossible to see any part of the house except for random patches of peeling white paint and a slate-gray roof. It was no wonder the club had chosen this location; not only was it well concealed, but there were no neighbors close enough to complain about the inevitable noises—revving, inadequately muffled engines, howls, and the occasional gunshot—that would naturally escape from the outpost of a motorcycle gang.

I had always wondered how they'd been able to afford such a large and developable piece of property right on the river and so close to the coast. It certainly was true that times were hard and real estate prices were in the toilet—but then, Scratch and company had bought in at the height of the market, just before the big crash. In addition, while it also was a fact that the East Coast Blood Eagles enjoyed a decent cash flow from the sales of narcotics and firearms, most of which they laundered through a chain of bars and motorcycle repair shops back in the Midwest, I figured the big house would have set them back well over a million dollars. Lacking legal sources of credit, they would have had to pay most of it in cash.

A Blood Eagle I knew as Chimp stepped out from a concealed position and opened the gate for me. He waved me in, closed the gate behind me, and came to the window of my truck. Chimp was a blue-eyed, dark-haired man of about my age who was the best-looking of all the Blood Eagles; he was clean-cut for an outlaw, and he had a quick smile and an easy way about him that women in bars found appealing. But he was nobody to mess with. For one thing, I saw right away that he was wearing a semi-automatic handgun in a holster on his hip. For another, in spite of his easygoing nature I knew that the collection of patches on his cut included one very small but extremely significant one that read "ITCOB," which stood for "I Took Care Of Business"—an indication that he had killed someone on the club's behalf.

Chimp said, "Yo, Brains," which was his personal nickname for me. "How they hangin,' brother? Hey, I gotta ask you to step out so I can wand you down." After I had climbed from the truck, Chimp produced a metal detector and, in a brisk and businesslike way, he passed it over every part of my body. When the machine found my folding knife, my change, and the antique silver cigarette case in which I carried some of my product samples, he asked me to take them from my pockets and put them in a basket, which he then set on a nearby table. After that he wanded me again. On the second pass he inadvertently brushed my crotch with the antenna, and I joked, "Do that again." Chimp laughed and bobbed his head in appreciation.

"Okay," he finally said. "I'll call them and tell them you're here. Park right in front of the house; when you get to the door, knock four times and Fat Harold'll let you in."

As I was getting back into my truck Chimp, in a suddenly plaintive tone, said, "So, dude, you got anything for me?" I turned back to him, smiled, and drew a joint from the cigarette case, which I had not yet returned to my pocket. As I placed it in his hand I parodied the medical warning from the Viagra ads on TV by telling him, "Remember, if this gives you an erection lasting longer than four hours, you need to seek medical attention."

Chimp laughed again and said, "*Fuckin'* Thumb. I'm still on duty for a while, so I better save this till later, then." He added, "Thanks, Brains. Always good seeing you."

On my way to the front door, I took a better look at the house. It was apparent there would be twenty or more rooms in there, along with an attic like a cave and a cellar like a sinkhole. I could also see what a lot of work the place needed; most of the all-too-many windows were visibly rotted, a good third of the black shutters were either broken or missing, and the white paint everywhere was flaking away as if the building had a disease. Even so, the roof looked to have been recently reshingled, a long section of soffit had been replaced with new, not-yet-painted boards, and there was a scaffolding set up for some work on the highest line of windows. In spite of myself, I had grown a little nervous by then, and I found it somehow comforting to learn that the Blood Eagles were fixing up their place just as any normal family would do.

I was let into the house by Fat Harold, a three-hundred-pound albino dude with shoulder-length hair so blond it was almost white. His station was a small room to the left of the entrance hall that contained a desk, a chair, and, fastened against one wall, a pair of large televisions that served as split-screen surveillance monitors. On another wall was a gun rack that held a pair of pump shotguns, one a short-barrel job with a pistol grip, and an AK-47 assault rifle. From pegs at the bottom of the rack hung a holstered revolver with a six-inch barrel and a MAC-10 machine pistol on a green strap.

Fat Harold wanded me all over again, agreeably parrying my complaints about having to go through the process twice. When he

was done, he hit me up for a joint. Then, in the middle of my rep-
etition of the gag about the four-hour erection, something on one
of the monitors caught Harold's eye. "Just a sec," he said, before
stepping to his desk and picking up one of a half-dozen cell phones
spread across a blotter.

That was when I turned my own attention to the monitors.
Each television displayed six rectangular screens, three of which
were empty and gray, with the rest relaying different scenes either
within or just outside of the house. The only movement in any of
those rectangles came from a pair of girls dressed in what looked
like bathrobes who were sitting at a picnic table on a lawn, smoking
cigarettes and sipping from plastic cups.

Speaking into the phone, Fat Harold said, "Hey. Them two
bitches are hiding out by the barbecue pit, drinking I don't know
what. You might wanna have a word." Then he closed the phone,
which looked like a toy in his huge, pink fingers, and he grinned at
me.

He said, "Scratch got something to take care of. He'll be right
up to take care of *you* in just a minute."

A minute later, as Fat Harold and I reminisced about the last
time we'd seen one another, Scratch appeared on the screen we'd
been looking at, and the girls immediately stood up from the table
and began stubbing out their cigarettes. I saw then that both of
them were pregnant, one of them looking to be maybe seven months
along—although I've never been a good judge of that. Harold and I
stopped talking and watched.

Scratch, his cut-clad back to the camera, abruptly spread his
arms, and the less heavily pregnant of the two girls scrambled away
immediately; the other tried to follow her, but Scratch caught her
by an arm and then, when she seemed to speak, gave her a hard,
backhanded slap across the mouth which, witnessed even without sound, made me wince. Fat Harold shook his head as Scratch
released the girl and she staggered beyond range of the camera.

"Drunken whores," Fat Harold said.

When I had recovered enough to talk, I said, "Are those . . . uh, whose kids are those babies going to be?"

Fat Harold narrowed his colorless eyes. He said, "So, dude, *what the fuck were you telling me about a twenty-four hour erection?*"

A door opened then, and Scratch appeared behind me in the entrance hall, startling me in spite of the fact that I'd know he was coming. I imagine that Scratch's own mother would have been startled by the sight of him, no matter if she was expecting his arrival: He wore the Blood Eagles insignia not only on his back, but also inked onto his face. His cheeks were illustrated with a pair of blood-red eagle's wings that began at the inside corners of his eyes, and which were connected by the white stripes of a human rib cage that rippled across the bridge of his nose, his upper lip, and his chin. The skeletal eagle's claws curved beneath his chin to grasp a sword that seemed to slice into Scratch's own throat just above his voice box, sending "blood" streaming down to the collar of his t-shirt. The grinning death's head component of the insignia peered out from the middle of Scratch's forehead with bulging blue and bloodshot eyes and, touching the top of the white skull as if to make certain it would not be overlooked, was the tip of a lightning bolt that had been sculpted and styled from his dyed black hair. Except for this zigzagging Mohawk, which divided his scalp from nape to hairline, Scratch's head was shaved as naked as a newborn rat. A final cosmetic detail, and one with no apparent connection to Blood Eagles lore, was the set of pointed extensions he'd had permanently bonded to his eyeteeth. With these fangs he looked ready, at any moment, to bite a chunk out of somebody and swallow it whole.

I had heard gossip that even the highest-ranking Blood Eagles back at the club's national headquarters in Chicago had been awed, and maybe even unsettled, when Scratch returned from a trip to California sporting the club emblem indelibly imprinted on his face, and that he owed his presidency of the new Maine Chapter to the fact that he had been willing to demonstrate his loyalty in such a public and permanently disfiguring way. But I never believed it;

broad at the shoulders and standing at a height of around six feet, five inches, Scratch cut an intimidating figure even without the tattoos. Also, he was smart and ruthless enough to have risen quickly in the Blood Eagles ranks no matter what he did, or did not do, to his face. He had replaced his own face with a demon mask because that was the way he wanted to look, and for no other reason.

After giving me a scare by coming up behind me, Scratch made no move to shake my hand. He simply said, "Thumb. Follow me."

The entrance hall opened onto a room, big as a cavern, which was just beginning to undergo renovation. The gray ceiling was badly stained and even buckled in a few places from water damage—at one time, a pipe must have burst on the floor above—and, at the center of it, a wild nest of wires sprang from a gaping hole where a heavy light fixture once had hung. The legs of a tall stepladder positioned beneath the wires were surrounded at various distances and in no identifiable arrangement by a dozen or more pieces of furniture, all of them draped in white sheets that made them look like lumpy ghosts. The innards of a couple of partially disassembled motorcycles rested on beds of greasy towels; other paint-spattered sheets and towels also were spread here and there on the wide-boarded floor. As we crossed the room, every one of our footfalls not muffled by a swath of cloth echoed like a gunshot.

Without turning to me, Scratch lifted his arms and, in a mocking tone said, "This is called the *Great* Room."

On the far side of a shrouded sofa we passed three pit bull terriers lying shoulder to shoulder on the floor. These were fairly large, extremely muscular dogs of roughly equal size—perhaps only twenty pounds apiece lighter than Tigre. The outside two were a shiny, obsidian black, while the middle one had a coat of unbroken, snowy white I had seldom seen before on a dog of this breed. As we went by, the animals made no sound, but merely lifted their heads to fix me with eyes as cold as stones at the bottom of a river.

"Fine looking animals," I said to the grinning death's head on Scratch's back.

"They do their job," Scratch replied, again without turning.

In the middle of the far wall was a closed double doorway, with another couple of single doors to the right, and two more to the left. I followed Scratch to the right and through the door closest to the outside wall, which led us to a much smaller, freshly painted room so decently furnished it looked like the family room in a normal person's house. He closed the door behind us.

"Go ahead and grab that chair, right there facing the fireplace, Thumb." I could locate the fireplace only by the ridge that the mantle made in a heavy nylon tarp that had been tacked along the entire wall opposite the doorway through which we had just walked. Where it reached the floor, the green tarp curved away from the wall and the hidden hearth and spread partway across the room to touch the feet of the padded leather chair he had told me to take.

I sat and immediately noticed that the tarp, obviously fresh out of its package, was giving off the strong odor of an automobile straight from the factory. Scratch pulled two sweating bottles of beer from a small refrigerator next to the door. As he handed one of them to me, he pointed to the wooden coffee table that lay within reach between my chair and a matching leather couch, and he said, "Make sure you use a coaster." Then he sat down on the couch and, after a moment, kicked his booted feet up onto it as well.

After we had both taken a few sips of our beer, Scratch said, "So, what brings you around here, Thumb?" This annoyed me, because he and I had already discussed our agenda during the same conversation in which he'd invited me to visit him at the clubhouse. Nonetheless, I smiled and played along as if I this were the first time I was making my pitch.

I said, "Well, I thought it might be a good idea, since we're all operating out of the same town, for my group and your club to maybe figure out some ways to put our heads together. Business wise, I mean."

"Yeah? How do you see that working? Aren't we competitors?"

I said, "Symbiotic. There would be advantages to both sides. For instance, it seems to me that you Blood Eagles are trying to blanket the area, if not a good chunk of northern New England, with your distribution, and that's just not what my guys and I are about—at least not when it comes to weed. What we're into instead is creating a high-end, designer product targeted to a specific sort of client. Small quantity, *unique* quality—stuff that a certain sort of person is going to brag about, like, 'Hey, you *need* to try some of this shit.' Stuff they're going to pay a little extra for, because it was custom grown, and it's got that touch of magic to it." Scratch bared his fangs at me—though in what I believed was a friendly way.

"*Magic.* Yeah, I have to admit, your shit's pretty good. But then, a lot of people make that kind of magic, Thumb, and in larger quantities, too. In fact, it must not be all that hard, because I haven't run into any really disappointing smoke in a long time." It was a struggle to keep my irritation from showing.

But I kept smiling, and I said, "There's a big difference between 'not disappointing,' and something that's an actual experience—an *event* between your ears."

Scratch threw back his head and laughed, those ghastly false fangs chopping at the air. "An event inside your skull," he said. "I like that. Thumb; you're hilarious. Your talents are wasted in a business like this."

"Hey, marketing *is* important," I said. "No doubt about it. But you also have to have the quality to back it up. Speaking of which, I bet you could probably do with a little reminder of what my product is all about."

At this invitation, Scratch shrugged. "Sure," he said. "Why not?" He sat up and reached behind the couch to produce a bong that was already filled with water. As he set it on top of the coffee table, he said, "I've got a fresh head right now, so it's a good time for demonstration. Go ahead and load her up."

I took out a glass medicine vial containing a partial bud of some of my best material. As I was packing the bowl of Scratch's pipe, I worked him with my salesman's patter about this particular strain of smoke, which I called "Uma" (Thurman) or sometimes, "First Violin." I told him, "You're going to find this is somewhat different from what you're used to. It's an energizing high, rather than one that just dumps your ass in the dirt."

"Oh, an *energizing* high," he echoed, and grinned his predatory grin. After I applied a flame, he sat up to reach for the pipe and we smoked in silence, content to let the gurgling bong do all the talking. Then we both settled back to assess the results. I remember thinking that one benefit of getting high just then was that the smell of the dope covered up the odor of that damn green tarp.

His voice hoarse, Scratch finally said, "Uma Thurman. *First* violin. An *energizing* high. To tell you the truth, Thumb, I don't exactly feel like running a fucking marathon right now."

"A *fucking* marathon," I echoed. We both laughed long and hard. Helpless tears sprang to my eyes and I wiped them away with my sleeve. I said, "You need to just relax and let yourself be permeated by the spiritual quality of the smoke."

"Well," he said. "I *am* pretty permeated." We laughed again and I told myself that things were going well. It seemed to me that he and I were forming the same kind of bond that I enjoyed with Chimp and some of the other Blood Eagles, but which until now I had been unable to build with Scratch. At the same time, I found myself having to avoid looking directly at his face, because his tattoos had suddenly begun to seem cartoonish in a way that made captive laughter boil in my belly. Instead, I stared straight ahead at the shrouded fireplace and gnawed my lip. I remember thinking, *What an awesomely ridiculous life I've blundered into. I can't wait to start writing about some of these things.*

I said, "So, to get serious for a minute: You can see that we've got what some might call a 'boutique product' here—Hell, it could even help you get acquainted with a whole new clientele and start circulating in those sorts of circles. Opportunity is what I'm talking about. It's a whole thing, like they can brag that they got this special smoke from a Blood Eagle . . . it gives them something to say, something risky and sexy they've done . . . that they can talk about with all the other assholes. And it doesn't take away from your existing business, it only adds to it."

But Scratch waved that thought away and said, "What about the shit your fat boy, Chef, cooks up? Your little meth business, there?"

"Well you know, that's something separate to think about. To tell you the truth, working out of a trailer, we can't really produce a competitive quantity of that stuff anyway—and anyway, I don't even like the meth business all that much. It's filthy in a bunch of different ways. I'm sure we could come to an agreement about it."

"Yeah? Doesn't that leave Chef out in the cold? How's he likely to handle it?"

I thought about Chef's relatively subdued reaction when I'd taken Cricket away. I shrugged. "He'll be okay. We'll work something out."

At that point Scratch took a cell phone from his pocket, thumbed a message, and put it away way again. Then, seemingly out of the blue, he said, "Hey, you're a science guy, Thumb. A college dude. You can talk about symbiosis and shit. I hear you've even got a special place in your heart for woodpeckers. You know anything about coyotes?"

I started to laugh, but when I took a sideways glance at him, I saw that he wasn't smiling. "Coyotes; you mean, the animal?"

"I'm from Wyoming originally. A lot of people don't know that about me."

"*I* didn't know that about you, Scratch."

"Yeah, well, anyway, we got coyotes out there. And they can be a real problem if you're running a sheep farm."

"A *sheep* farm?"

"They're so hard to get rid of, coyotes. Guns, poison, traps—the faster you kill them, the more often and abundantly they reproduce. *Literally*; it's shoveling shit against the tide."

Impressed to be hearing an interesting natural fact that I hadn't known before—from a biker, no less—I said, "So, what do you do?"

"Well, there *is* a fail-safe solution, but most people where I come from are environmentally unenlightened and they don't want to hear it. But the solution is"—at this he bared his fangs again— "wolves."

"What do you mean?" I was starting to feel confused; I struggled to recall why we were discussing canine predators in the first place, but was having no luck.

"They're natural enemies," Scratch said. "You want to clear a hundred coyotes from a hundred square miles, you bring in *two* fucking wolves. That's all it takes."

"I get you now," I said. At the least, I understood the concept.

"Yeah; the wolves will either run the coyotes down and kill them outright, or else the coyotes'll get the message and leave on their own. Then the wolves have free range of those hundred square miles, with everything on it belonging to them. And in the long run, having a few wolves around is a lot healthier for everyone concerned than a whole shit-load of coyotes. Healthier for everyone but the coyotes, that is."

I was beginning to think that perhaps First Violin was not playing such beautiful music for Scratch, and that he might find one of my other strains more to his liking. "You know," I said, "I've got part of another bud here, of some stuff I call Sasha—Sasha Grey—or French Horn, take your pick. I'll leave it with you to try later, when your head . . . "

Just then I heard a faint noise, and Scratch's reddened eyes widened and lifted toward the door. I started to turn to see who it was, but Scratch froze me in place by saying, "Don't turn around, Thumb. Not unless you want a bullet in your face."

Time stopped and I remained unmoving in mid-turn, fixed on the thought that, no, I did not want a bullet in my face. My face was the *last* place I wanted a bullet. When another idea finally formed in my mind, it was that this was either some sort of hazing, outlaw-biker style, or else a straightforward "joke." One or the other but either way, it wasn't going to result in my being shot. Unless I turned around, which I had been fairly warned not to do.

My high evaporated, and when I turned back and looked full on at Scratch's comic-book-villain face I no longer felt like laughing. I relaxed, settled into my seat, and smiled at him. "Okay," I said. "What next?"

He said, "Bottom line: You and your little outfit, you're coyotes. The range is getting crowded and you've all got to go."

"All right. So, I guess we're *not* going to arrive at a business agreement? Is that what you're saying?" I kept smiling.

"No, Thumb, we are not going to arrive at a business agreement. And, by the way, we've already started to bust up your little pack; a month from now, your operation won't exist. In fact, that's not even a Blood Eagle standing behind you back there; that's one of your own posse holding the gun on you. I've agreed not to let you know who it is and I'm honoring my word."

When I started to turn again, Scratch said, "I've *seen* people get shot in the face with a twenty-two. It's ugly, and usually not immediately fatal; it looks real painful."

Whatever else I might have been, I was not a coward. If I truly believed I was going to be murdered, I would have turned and looked my murderer in the eye. But I was sure that, provided I *refrained* from turning, I would not be shot. After all, if Scratch were really going to have me killed, he wouldn't bother *explaining* it all to me. I thought it was possible, even likely, that in a minute or two Chimp and Fat Harold and a few of the other Blood Eagles would burst into the room roaring with laughter, drag me out of that leather chair, and begin pounding me on the back and praising me for having kept my cool.

I relaxed again, looked at Scratch, and widened my smile. After a moment I called, "So, who is it, back there?" When nobody responded, I said, "What's the problem? Lost your balls?" I heard nothing but a subtle rustling as someone shifted from one foot to the other, or stepped forward a bit. I shrugged at Scratch and said, "No balls."

Scratch said. "I am sorry about this, Thumb. We like you; all of us do. That's why I've let you go on living a couple extra minutes; that's why I'm talking to you. It's because I don't think a friend should die without knowing why—or at least as much as I can say."

At that, I allowed my smile to twist. "You're not killing me," I said. "It makes no sense. You guys are Blood Eagles; if you really wanted me and my group to go away, all you'd have to do is say so." But Scratch shook his head in a way that made me believe for the first time that my life really might be in danger. I felt my lips begin to twitch with the sudden strain of holding that smile, and all at once it occurred to me that the stinking green tarp covering the fireplace and part of the floor would make an ample and fluid-proof package in which to seal a leaking corpse. I began to feel afraid.

Scratch was saying, "In a regular coyote-and-wolf situation, you'd be right, Thumb. The wolves would say, 'You coyotes better get the fuck out of here,' and the coyotes would just fuck off. Problem is, here in the human world, there's more to it than that. There's other animals around—by which I mean the two other biker clubs who were here before us, and who would like us to leave what they consider to be their territory and go back to where we came from. Those two clubs, they're not yet sure us Blood Eagles are wolves at all; they're thinking we might only be coyotes just like you. It's a matter of life and death for us that we show them that we *are* wolves—and, not only that, we're badder wolves than they are."

I said, "And that's got what to do with me? In fact, I'm an ally of yours, not theirs, so taking care of business on me won't do anything for you." I turned my head as much as I dared and called, "What do you think back there, No Balls? You think killing me is going to help the Blood Eagles in some way?"

But again Scratch was giving me that worrisome headshake. He said, "Unfortunately, Thumb, the circumstances call for a blood sacrifice. Now, I could fairly easily kill a dude from one of those other clubs—but that would start a war, and a lot of good men would die. Some of those dead men would be Blood Eagles. In fact, we could even lose a war like that, because, as capable as we are, there are more of them than there are of us.

"If I kill *you*, on the other hand, especially since you're well known to all of the people I'm trying to impress, it gets the message out just as effectively that I'm willing to take a life. It gets the word across that I won't hesitate to kill any gangster who trespasses against me."

Mantis. He was likely the only one who would end up cooperating with the Blood Eagles—and probably the only one they'd trust to handle a loaded gun in their clubhouse. In fact, it made sense that they would make him do something like this as part of a membership probation—a condition of his joining their club. There was a good chance that, just as they wanted me to be uncertain whether I was going to be shot, Mantis, standing there at that moment, had no idea whether he would be ordered to do the shooting.

"Mantis," I called. "Isn't that gun getting heavy in your hand? I bet all that sweat is making it hard to hold onto. Careful you don't drop it."

Scratch grinned, but his eyes looked sad. "What's happened, Thumb, is that you've accidentally got yourself swept up in the big, three-dimensional chess game of outlaw-biker politics. Not really your fault; just bad luck. Wrong place, wrong time. But I really do believe that your sacrifice will save some lives, so rest assured it will not be for nothing."

I started to say something, but could not get the words to leave my mouth; it was as if I already were a ghost. My mouth was dry; my heart was galloping; my breath rattled through my pipes. At the same time, I somehow still believed it was all a play and that, at the last minute, they would take me off the hook. The man behind me, creeping ever closer, perhaps did not even have a gun. Perhaps once he stood close enough to touch me, he would jab a finger into my back and yell, "*Bang!*" I told myself that when it happened, I should try not to flinch.

Scratch, speaking now as much to that other person as he was to me, said, "There'll have to be some pictures taken—you know, for proof. But we will treat those with respect. They will only be shown when there's a need, and only then to people with a need to see them."

Scratch continued, "So, I guess now's the time to say thank you, Thumb, for all the good times, and especially for sharing your special shit with me today. I sincerely meant it when I said that really is some nice smoke, that Oprah Thurston of yours."

"No," I said. "It's Uma Thurman." It was then that Scratch must have given some subtle signal to the person standing behind me, because those were my final words before the darkness dropped.

CHAPTER 6

Over the days and weeks that followed my memorial service,
I dipped in and out of the underground river. Then one time I
returned from the depths to find my house stripped of everything I
had known. The furniture, the dishes, the rugs, even the curtains,
window shades, and light bulbs—all had been taken, and the building abandoned. The place was so completely empty that the crackle
of sleet driving against the naked windows made an ongoing echo
inside.

I went into the backyard where the trees were finally and completely shorn of leaves. A heavy lid of gunmetal clouds hovered just
above the roof, and frozen rain poured through me at a sharp angle.
The only remaining reminders of my life were the pile of wet ashes
and cinders from the torching of my generator shed and Tigre's forlorn tire swing, which twisted in the wind, its thick rope groaning
against the branch it was tied to. Even my bird feeders had been
rounded up and taken away—all except for one small suet cage,
which had fallen among the leaf-litter and been overlooked.

Things weren't any more hopeful at the front of the house,
where I found a Riverside realtor's crooked "For Sale or Rent" sign
sticking from the lawn to face an icy road so deserted it was easy to
imagine that no car would pass by until spring. By then, if I'd had

eyes, I would have cried. Imprisoned in and around an uninhabited house, how in hell was I supposed to find out who had stood behind me with that gun? As the sleet fell even harder than before, I began marching out from the abandoned house in all directions, trying to escape to anywhere I could. But each time I reached some arbitrary distance from the house—sometimes a little closer, sometimes a bit farther than before—I would suddenly find myself back inside, standing by the front door where I had started. In spite of what my first messenger had told me about moving up or falling below, I began to wonder whether this might be my private, final, and pathetic circle of hell: to spend eternity as a ghost haunting a ranch house in the middle of nowhere.

At one point I went out through the front door and gathered myself to make yet another useless dash at my metaphysical prison wall. But I stopped dead on the front steps when across the road I saw the disembodied figure of Professor Virgil Shallow, hovering as he had before between my mailbox and the shapeless, brown wreath that hung from the broken power pole. The professor glimmered with an eerie beauty as, amid the darkness of the wet storm, each wind-driven chunk of sleet that passed through him ignited with a meteoric streak of green light. I remembered his ember-like eyes and his worms and his crumbling skeleton, and my first impulse was to flee back to the river. But then I thought, *Here I am, in the depths of a canyon. What can a ghost do to me that hasn't already been done?*

The professor gave no sign he knew I was there. He kept studying the ruined wreath, the sleet lighting him from within like fireflies bouncing in a bottle. Finally, softly, I called, *Professor Shallow ...*

He seemed not to hear me, so I spoke more loudly. *Hey, Professor. A word if you don't mind.*

Still he ignored me, and finally, beginning to feel angry, I floated from the steps and drifted toward him. It was then that he snapped his head in my direction.

"*Stop!*" His scream tore through me and I stopped. I wanted to run, but I felt frozen to my spot. The professor lifted his hand and his arm unwound in my direction like a vine until his forefinger—the gray *bones* of his skeletal forefinger—was hovering before my face. In a matter-of-fact, almost pleasant tone, he said, "You criminal *filth*. Keep your distance." Then he disappeared.

*

I had no clock, no calendar, and it remained difficult to tell one day from another. After my second sighting of Professor Shallow, I continued to return from the river to haunt my abandoned home during times of sunshine, and during days and nights of further winter storm. After a while I began to find tire tracks in the driveway and footprints in the snow leading to my front door. This worried me, because I was not looking forward to watching a new set of tenants move into the house; not only did I value my privacy, but I hated the idea of having to overhear an endless chain of conversations on such topics as whose turn it was to take out the trash. I thought that *not* hearing such things was one of the few advantages of being dead.

One morning I arrived to find that someone had broken through the back door, ripped out the baseboard radiators, pillaged the basement, and torn open walls and flooring in order to steal the copper pipes. On one hand, this meant no one would be moving in anytime soon, which was a good thing, but on the other, even though my use for pipes and heating systems of any kind had ended, it seemed like a personal violation. Also, the house was a sorry-enough haunt under the best of circumstances; in this vandalized state, the place stood just a cut above a tool shed, and I felt that both my dignity and my position in the world had been diminished. Worst of all was my feeling of helplessness; I was a feeble ghost, no stronger than a shadow, and even if I had been at home when the vandals came, there was nothing I could have done to stop them.

After raging over the damage, I pushed out through the front of the house and into the yard, which was covered by a good two feet of new snow from yet another storm. The sun was shining now, the pure snow glittering beneath it, and if I'd been in a happier mood, it would have struck me as a beautiful scene. It took me a moment to spot Professor Shallow, who was hovering in his usual place. Fresh as it was, the deep, dry snow he was standing on was nearly as light as air and would not have supported the weight of a mouse—not a *living* mouse, anyway.

I gathered my courage and called to him: "Professor Shallow!" But he was no more interested in talking to me now than he had been during the first two times I'd seen him. His response was to crouch down with his arms stretched behind him and spring a backflip in the direction of town. He flipped again and then again, pausing each time with his feet seeming to touch the virgin powder. "Please!" I yelled, though I felt my cause was hopeless. He began to backflip faster and faster, whirling himself into a translucent blur as he traveled, and he was getting close to the point beyond which I knew I would be unable to follow him. It was then that my anger returned. I found myself yelling, "You're just as dead as I am, you bastard! *I* saw you die!"

The professor froze in mid backflip. After a moment he continued with a slow rotation until he was right side up, then he stretched his legs so that his feet were once again "touching" the snow. He stood looking at me, his face expressionless.

In a quieter voice I said, "I wanted to save you. I really did. I'm sorry."

He remained unmoving and I added, "Please. I *am* a bad man, but I'm not quite as bad as you think, and I'm in despair. I don't have anyone. I need your help."

After a long moment, he surprised me by ghosting across the snow in my direction.

*

You may remember I told you earlier on that there were a couple of living people helping me tell this story. Ben is one, but as you might already have come to suspect, he is not much of a writer, and of all the suspensions of belief I'm asking you to take over the course of this book, expecting you to believe he helped compose the text you're reading now is just too much of a stretch.

The other dude, the one who *is*, for better or worse, my true literary collaborator, is Fred, who published several novels under the more literary-sounding name of Frederick H. Muttkowski. Maybe you've heard of him. But it's likely you haven't; his most recent book, *Leaving Circe*, has been out of print for more than two decades. A few years ago, even the autographed first edition hardcover copy at the library in the town where he lives was sold for fifty cents at a clearance sale. Its purchaser was Fred himself, who, though distressed to discover the novel being disposed of, was too embarrassed to complain. It goes almost without saying that neither of the two clearance-sale volunteers who accepted his pair of quarters for the cash box recognized him or had even the remotest inkling that they were selling the unloved book to its own author.

But as Fred himself would say, *Boo fucking hoo*. He readily acknowledges that even without any but ephemeral success, his life has contained many moments of sweetness. In particular, there had been an especially delightful and fairly prolonged period during which the mere *illusion* of achievement had brought him a modest but gratifying amount of attention, including the admiration of a number of interesting women, along with a deceptively promising handful of paychecks healthy enough to fund a year of high living in South America, and a motorcycle trip across Australia. It was toward the end of those early years of happy ambition and giddy hallucination that he had gotten married and fathered a pair of beautiful daughters, identical twins named Hope and Iris who, at the time I first "met" him, were just shy of their twenty-second birthday.

Even after it had become excruciatingly clear that no publisher could be expected to gamble on yet another money-losing, ready-for-the-remainder-pile Muttkowski novel, his heavens only sagged slightly, and did not fall. He still had the best things, after all: health, wife, daughters, relative youth. After much discussion, his wife, Cici, convinced him that what he needed was to lash himself to the mast of a different dream. For instance, he'd grown up in the country, out in the Midwest; hadn't he always had a deep interest in the idea of rural life, and doing some organic farming? Why not give it a try? Who knew—perhaps a large garden, a herd of heritage-breed swine, and a handful of rustic neighbors who went around saying pithy things would end up providing rich material for that singular, watershed work of fiction the gods truly intended him to write.

However, as years and youth went by, his sky, though still more or less in place above him, did gradually darken, until one day Fred, whose nature it was to be a wary optimist, finally was forced to conclude that, while he'd been busy looking heavenward, wondering when it might get bright again, hell had grown up from the ground and woven itself around him. Nor was there a path of escape: By then, having long before relocated his family from Manhattan to Maine in order to pursue the rewards and romance of small-scale livestock husbandry, he was now mired, ass deep and seemingly for good, in an ocean of organic pig shit, every sloppy dollop of which came from animals that represented what had become painfully apparent was the only truly marketable talent he had. The pigs—anywhere from sixty to one hundred and fifty of them at a time—were pure-blooded Berkshires, a mostly black, piebald breed prized by chefs the world over, which, under Fred's intuitive supervision, bred enthusiastically and grew like happy weeds on the fifteen acres of electric-fenced, pig-pounded playground that opened out from the back of the insulated, ventilated barn in which they fed and slept.

Each organic Muttkowski Berkshire enjoyed six months, more or less, of indolent, oblivious pleasure at the farm, followed by a long, dark, anxious ride in the butcher's truck, which itself was followed by . . . Fred, at least recently, could not help but view the entire process as a metaphor for human life. Many human lives, in any case. His, certainly. He imagined himself at the truck-ride stage. . . .

You could say that after twenty years, he was burned out on pigs. But beyond that, an even deeper source of torment for him was his chronic failure in an ongoing fight to once and forever bury his earlier writing ambition, a fruitless addiction that made him feel like a bankrupt gambling addict who continued to chase his losses. The urge to play with words—that sickening cocktail of compulsion and desire—was as irresistible as it was frustrating, even maddening, and he was often helpless against it.

Fred's barn "office" was an empty farrowing pen before which curious pigs, pining for the reassuring taste of his rubber boots, would gather to observe him through the horizontal bars of a closed steel gate, but could not enter. Inside the pen, Fred kept a laptop computer and an old, rolling office chair. Whenever the wretched writing itch became too powerful to resist, he would take up the computer, sit down in the dusty chair and, after a pause, begin to spread words across the screen. For the next hour, more or less, he would type, pause, then type again, and all the time he typed, he would mindlessly, furiously, twirl in his chair, first clockwise, then counter, while during each pause, he would propel the chair around the pen using his booted soles to frog-kick off the gate and the cinder-block walls. After a few seconds, or a minute, Fred would stop kicking, give the chair a violent twirl or two, and type again.

Watching his performance, the audience of pigs would fall almost reverently silent, completely still save for the continual oscillations of their rubbery snouts. From time to time, there would come a mysterious outburst of muted grunting before a hush fell over them again. Mostly, Fred forgot the pigs. But occasionally, he would return to himself and remember them; he would look up, almost startled at the sight of so many expectant, twitching nose-disks with their nostrils like black eyes boring at him through the bars. Then, as a way of at once amusing and mocking himself, he would stop his twirling and kicking and writing and, with one hand gripping the laptop, the other gesturing in the air, he would read them a paragraph or two. When he had finished reading and, depending on his mood as well as on how he felt about the train of words he had excreted so far that day, he would either smile or chuckle, or just simply shake his head, or sometimes—rarely—burst into laughter. After that, he would resume his caroming and his keyboarding until he reached the point at which he felt completely emptied. Only then could he allow himself to set the computer aside and go back to doing useful work; slowly, feeling dazed and slightly displaced in time and space, he would release himself from the far-rowing pen, work his way through the dispersing throng of swine, and return to the uncomplicated but exacting algebra of organic pork production.

Every few years, after much revising, Fred would actually fin-ish—maybe "abandon" is a better word—one of his lengthy writing projects. At that point, at an hour when Cici was not at home—most days, this was almost any hour at all—he would carry his laptop into the house, connect it to one of the several printers that Cici used for her real estate business, and run off a single, several-hun-dred-page copy of his work. Once complete, the loose, white sheets of the pristine manuscript would cool for time on the kitchen table while Fred sat with his stocking feet propped on the cushion of a second wooden seat, staring blankly out the window and bending his forearm with almost metronomic regularity as he drank a glass or three of bourbon. Once back in the barn, he would return the computer to its case atop the rolling chair and add the manuscript to the tall pile of older manuscripts that he stored in the corner of his "office," with a flat rock from the river on top to keep the paper tower from collapsing. By the time I "met" him, the manu-script stack in the "creep," or piglet crib, of Fred's farrowing pen had grown higher than the steel rail beneath which the baby pigs would flee to avoid being crushed whenever their colossal mother crashed onto her side to feed them. The paper pile was enshrouded in pig dust and cobwebs, thereby all but ensuring that neither his wife nor his daughters would go snooping through it to find out what he had been up to.

After a writing project had been printed, bourboned, stacked, and stoned, and its fossilization in a sediment of pig powder had begun, Fred would promise himself that he had written his last—that he was once and forever free and that, from here on out, he would be content to enjoy the play of words solely in his mind, without the obsessive mania and the compulsive agony of having to squeeze them out onto paper or a computer screen. After all, what did it matter if words were impermanent, when there was no one to hear them but pigs?

But, of course, the computer and the chair would remain in the farrowing pen along with the dust-covered paper skyscraper—he would never quite get around to taking them away—and sooner or later, in a month, or a day, Frederick H. Muttkowski would find himself sitting down again as if out of nothing more than nostalgia. He would give the office chair an experimental twirl or two and, as rumor spread and pigs began gathering at the gate, he would kick himself playfully from wall to wall, the computer yawning on his lap. After a time, he would stop kicking long enough to type a glowing line, and then another—and then delete it all and replace it with something else. Twirl, write, ricochet, replace—and occasionally, recite; meanwhile, from beyond the metal bars, a periodic wave of grunted gossip seemed to relay and reconfirm the tragicomic news that Fred Muttkowski, recovering writer, had fallen off the wagon yet again.

*

By now you must be wondering whether I am able to tap directly into Fred's unedited thoughts. After all, I do appear to know him thoroughly, inside and out. Well, the answer is I can't; more than that, no ghost, as far as I'm aware, is able to read anyone's mind. Many ghosts, like most people, aren't able even to read their own. In fact, I have never spoken to Fred and, not only has he never spoken to me, but he doesn't believe I exist.

One reason I know so much about him is that I've got the interest. Along with the fact that I don't have access to many other living people—my spirit paths tend to lead me into bleak and abandoned places—Fred, as a writer, even a failed specimen of the genre, is something I've always aspired to emulate. In spite of Fred's own ambivalent feelings about his often-excruciating writing compulsion, it heartens me, even strikes me as heroic, to watch him continuing his work in the face of almost certain rejection. I especially love it when he reads to us—to me, and to his pigs—his voice rich with poetry and quavering with defiance and wounded pride. In this doggedness, this angry insistence on *doing* and *being* with little hope of any payment beyond further discouragement and humiliation, I find comforting parallels in my own struggle to make a place for myself in the seeming senselessness of the afterlife.

From a practical standpoint, since I've got nothing but time on my hands most days, during the brief months I've haunted Fred's farm I've enjoyed more opportunities for undetected observation, and for overhearing private things, than Fred's own daughters have had in their entire lives. In some ways I already know him better than they ever will. For just one example, I understand that when Fred stands behind his barn waving his arms and shouting to himself about being in hell, he is thinking about much more than a withered writing dream and a business he no longer cares for; these together constitute no more than a passable purgatory. He is distressed at least as much by the steady, unstoppable fade of his family life, which is nearly complete now that his daughters have moved out on their own. Though they still drop by occasionally, both twins—once enthusiast farm girls—are vegans now, as well as city women with a strong distaste for dirt, and an almost pathological intolerance for odors.

Cici, for her part, about five years before I "met" her husband, had herself abandoned farm work and taken up real estate not just as a way to pay some bills, but also to escape from the muck and the blood, of which she had finally gotten her fill. She was good at the new job, she enjoyed it, and it did not bother her a bit that it required her to buy, and to wear, fine clothes, a little jewelry, and to smell nice, as well. Hers was now a world of meetings and restaurant meals and socializing. Fred often was asleep by the time Cici returned home at night; she was usually still sleeping when he arose at first light. In order to avoid disturbing one another with their conflicting schedules, they now slept in separate beds, Fred, a few months before I knew him, finally having moved into one of the girls' abandoned rooms. But that apparently had not been a complicated decision as, even prior to Fred's relocation, it had been as least two years since he and Cici had last exchanged any touches more intimate than a dry kiss.

I should clarify here that this last is a piece of information that I would rather have done without; it is something I can never look at Fred without thinking about, and if there were some way of unknowing it, I would. And it is also important for you to keep in mind that any highly personal facts about Fred that you read in this book are not just gossip on my part; they had to have been approved—or at least overlooked—by Fred himself. After all, he's in control of the editing, a soul-crushing process that I, as a helpless creative spirit, have been altogether defenseless against. In fact, there is no guarantee that anything you read here was not put in by Fred, rather than by me. Passages that should especially inspire your suspicion at times are any of the ones containing rhymes, or a lot of alliteration.

*

Sometimes, in the morning, Fred would stand at the yawning rear entrance to the barn, his gaze traveling up and down that daunting length and, as an adoring mob of pigs gathered to gnaw his rubber boots and chew the legs of his jeans, he would feel like weeping. But then, a part of Fred's mind would squirm loose, and fly free, and it would rise into the sky past the tops of the trees. His mind would make dizzying circles with the eyes of a bird, looking down on his life, grown so sublimely absurd.

Rather than crying, Fred would begin to laugh. His laughter would start with a couple of gasping hiccups that took him by surprise and, as his shoulders shook with increasing rhythm, it would quickly build to a gusty, obscene gale, at the height of which Fred would throw back his head and yell, *Boo fucking hoo!*

Often, his laughter would become convulsive and he would end up staggering about, dragging pigs from his legs as he went, sometimes even having to sit down on an overturned bucket—a risky thing to do, because on more than one occasion, while he was nearly helpless with self-mocking mirth, a scrum of swine had nudged and tugged him off his seat, and into the dirt.

CHAPTER 7

"What do you mean, you saw me die?" The edge on *Professor* Shallow's voice suggested that he thought I was lying. Arms across his chest, his face twisted with an emotion that might have been anger or disgust or perhaps the onset of horror, he stood staring at me. But having been silent for so long, I suddenly found it hard to talk. It was as if I were so full of words struggling to escape, they had all tangled in a writhing, misfiring heap. As he waited for me to form a sentence, his upper lip curled back and his eyes began to glow like the cracks in a furnace. I was afraid he would try to repel me with another of his gruesome explosions, or worse yet fly off into the sky and abandon me again. But suddenly the flames in his eyes dimmed and his expression softened. He surprised me by saying, "All right. You're new at this, I know. Let's just take our time then, shall we? Let's sit down somewhere."

"Okay," I managed to say.

He looked up into one of the bare maple trees that rose high above my back roof, and he pointed. "How about up there?" Before I could answer, he had sprung to the middle of the tree and settled his ass against one of the more horizontal branches. Without looking down at me he said, "Come up. There's no reason to confine yourself to the ground anymore." So I rose into the tree and took a spot facing him on another branch.

"It's odd," Professor Shallow said, once we were sitting across from one another, "That even though we are absolutely weightless, with no need to sit, we still feel like sitting."

"That's because we miss everything we did while we were alive."

He gave me a crooked smile. "Is that what you think? In any case, please finish the story you started to tell me."

I said, "I thought you remembered. Your accident, I mean. The way you acted, I thought you were blaming me. You died right there." I pointed to the broken power pole. "Just about a year ago, in fact. That's why there are two power poles together; your car cracked the first one just about in half—it was bent over your roof like a boomerang—and later they had to saw it off and set another one in right next to it. The road was icy and you were going fast; that's why it happened."

After a moment he shook his head several times and in a near whisper he said, "I'm not dead."

"You don't think you're dead? What do you think that wreath is for? You stare at it every time you're here. Someone who knew you came by and put it up there a few days after you were killed."

"It's just a snarl of vines, and I don't know *what* it was for. I have wondered, but I never thought it had anything to do with me. This is only one of a number of places I seem compelled to revisit in my dreams."

"You think you're *dreaming*?"

"Did you see the person who put it up? The wreath?"

"No, I didn't."

"Well." He looked across the road to the snow-mounded marsh grass. His face was troubled. "I can believe there was a car crash. Serious injury would explain this twilight world I find myself in. But I'm *not* dead; if I were, I would have no consciousness." He looked at me. "I don't believe in those sorts of things. Spirits and . . . "

"Look, like I said, I was the first to find you. I heard the crash and I came out of the house, and you were already gone. Your window was shattered, and I stepped up onto the snow bank to feel your throat and you didn't have a pulse. I couldn't bring myself to look at your face, but I never have forgotten the awkward way your arm was sticking through the steering wheel. The wheels of your car were still spinning in the air and I had to reach across your chest to turn off the engine." I added, "I'm sorry. I wish there had been something, you know."

He seemed to shudder. Then, speaking more to himself than to me he said, "Other ghosts I've dreamed of might call you a 'messenger.' A spirit meant to tell me something I needed to hear. But I don't buy into messengers anymore than I believe in ghosts of any kind. Of course, I've heard from a few, but I don't necessarily swallow everything they tell me. Often, not anything. And I've got no reason to believe your story—or to think you're any more real than any other ghost."

"I don't know about being a messenger. No one's told me to tell you anything. I haven't even talked to any other ghosts except for a messenger of my own, one time. And I thought I needed *your* help, not the other way around. But I'm no dream—I can tell you that. I'm at least as real as you are, from where I sit. Listen, though; these other ghosts you've seen. Tell me about them."

The professor was looking down at the snow that swirled at the base of the maple tree.

"A terrible car crash," he said. "That *would* make sense. It's likely I *am* dying."

"My name is Thumb Rivera."

"Your name is *Thumb*?"

"It's a nickname. I prefer it. My real name is Danny. I was murdered."

"You were *murdered*?"

"I was hanging with some bad people. I always looked at it like I was doing research for a book I wanted to write but, in reality, I don't think I was that good of a person to begin with. I guess I got carried away with the role I was playing."

"What kind of book?"

"I don't know. A novel, maybe. Anyway, I was shot in the back of the head. I never saw who pulled the trigger, or even heard the shot; they told me it was one of my friends. My messenger said . . . "

"*Who* told you that you were shot in the back of the head? Your messenger?"

"No, the guy who wanted me killed. Just before I was. He told me not to turn around to see who was going to kill me, but I should have done it anyway. My courage failed me, I guess. Now it's eating me up, not knowing."

"Extraordinary," Professor Shallow said after a moment.

"So I was hoping you could help me, Professor, because I've got this thing my messenger told me I have to do, this investigation into my murder, but I can't even get away from my own house to start working on it. I need to move around in the world. Like you can, apparently."

He said, "Do you want to know why I wouldn't let you come near me, those other times you called to me? Even though this is all a dream in which I know nothing can do me any harm? It wasn't because I blamed you for my 'death.' It was because I used to see you here sometimes—you and your sketchy-looking friends, going in and out of this house. It was clear you weren't up to any good— that you were a gang of lowlifes and criminals. My guess was that you all were dealing drugs. And I certainly never pegged *you* as any kind of undercover novelist."

"My disguise must've been pretty good," I said ruefully.

"I always did feel bad for that young woman. She looked like she could have done better than a bunch of thugs like you."

"Cricket," I said. "My girlfriend. Her real name is Claire."

"And, were you the one who convinced her to throw her life away for the false romance of thuggery?"

"Not really; when I met her, she was already hooked up with one of the other thugs. But you saw her; she was a few steps above his level, and I ended up seducing her away. So, yes, I was less than a good influence."

Professor Shallow pursed his lips and shook his head at the shame of it all—and suddenly I felt a flare of anger.

"Hey, Professor," I said. "What about you? I've admitted I haven't been the best of people. But you must've done something wrong yourself, otherwise you wouldn't be in the same situation."

"What situation is that?"

"I figure I'm not resting in peace—whatever that really means—on account of all my sins, of which I have a shitload. So I have to assume you're not here just to keep me company."

"Oh, I see," he said, nodding his head a single time. "You think you're in hell."

"Maybe. It's probably more like we're in purgatory."

The professor almost smiled. "Purgatory! Perhaps I should have written some popular fiction of my own, if this is the way my imagination works. Horror novels, with murdered motorcycle-gang members thinking they're in purgatory. Oh, my; all that time I spent writing analysis and criticism was wasted."

"I'm real, Professor Shallow. And I'm dead. And so are you, whether you want to believe it or not."

The professor was quiet for a minute. Finally he looked at me and said, "*Thumb*. Is that your colorful name? What's happening to me is pure physiology. The way it goes is this: The neurons of a dying cerebrum, starved of oxygen in their last moments, eventually explode with a burst of electrical activity that, for a brief but glorious interval, creates an extraordinarily vivid hallucination in the mind of the expiring person. People see angels, hear music, imagine visits from departed loved ones, are pursued by ghosts—myriad wonderful and terrible things. Think of it as the grand finale to a fireworks display, just before the sky goes dark."

"Dead," I repeated. "Already. Like a doornail."

"Of course, part of the story you told me probably parallels reality, which is why I'm imagining it now. Likely I *have* had a car accident—struck a power pole—much as you've described. Right now I could be sitting behind the wheel of my car, my life trickling away as I wait in vain for help to arrive. But it's also possible that I'm lying in a hospital bed somewhere. In any case, it's clear to me that I remain alive, but barely, and probably not for long."

I said, "It happened a year ago, like I told you. And time-wise, you're not making much sense; how is it you can think you're living your final moments when you must know you've been a ghost since last winter?"

"Because it only *seems* like I've been a ghost since last winter. That's another trick of the dying mind; a full year's worth of halluci-nated experience has been telescoped into what may have been just a few seconds. In fact, it wouldn't astonish me if I experience what feels to be another twenty years of afterlife when, in fact, I'm going to die within the next twenty *minutes*, if not sooner."

"I think I mentioned that I *saw* you die? I felt your throat for a pulse and couldn't find one. You were gone."

He flapped a dismissive hand at me. "You're a hallucination. Why would I believe anything you say?"

I stared at him. Meanwhile, all the time we had been talking, the wind had been gaining force, and now it was rocking the tree around us and causing the dry snow to twist up from the ground. The branch the professor was sitting on kept lifting and dropping; whenever it rode skyward, it appeared to slice right through him until it was protruding from both sides of what would have been his ribcage, and when it bent out from beneath him, it left him hover-ing in the air. Through it all, he himself remained unmoving.

Suddenly he said, "Thumb. I have to go."

"*What*? Wait! I have more questions. I need . . . "

"I can't. I'm feeling weak. I have to get back to the river."

"The river! *You* go into the river!"

The professor nodded. "All ghosts do that—at least all the ghosts I've imagined. It's the most obvious metaphor. But it's *only* a metaphor. Goodbye Thumb. Your last name by the way—it's Spanish, isn't it?"

"I need help. How do I get away from here?"

The professor began to fade until he was translucent. A tall column of airborne snow came swirling along to dance inside of him. "*Hasta luego*," he told me.

"There won't be any fucking *luego*. You won't come back here; you don't even think I exist."

"Come to think of it, you're probably right." Then *snap*, he was gone.

*

I waited for him to return; there was nothing else I could think of to do. As winter wore on, I would spend entire days in doglike vigil on my front steps, hoping to see him, and I would not leave my place until I grew so faint I needed to return to the river for some rest. Often it was snowing as I sat, and fresh snow would pile up inside of me and all around. At other times, freezing rain sliced through me as if I were not even there—which, actually I wasn't. My situation was absolutely pathetic.

It was around this time that I had my second, brief encounter with the ghost named Angelfish (Ben has been nagging me nearly constantly about her; finally it's the right time to tell him a little more). She came upon me as before, while I was tumbling in the underground river. Her greenish lights whipped around me. She sounded like she was out of breath as she said, "Thumb! It's Angelfish! Thank God! Help! *Oh* my God! The baby! The *baby*!"

"The *baby*?" I was horrified. "*Your* baby? Is he living, or is he . . . one of us?"

"She's in between. She's in danger. You need to help us!"

"Where the hell *are* you, even?" But that was all; she was gone as quickly as she'd come.

Ben stops when he hears this. He lifts his shaking hands from the planchette. No doubt he's thinking about his own little half-brother and -sister, far away and possibly endangered by their own parents. After a moment he asks, "So, what happened? Did you help Angelfish save a baby? Her baby or some other one?" Before I can answer, I have to wait for him to remember the planchette. Finally, he does.

HW CD I WN I DNT NO WR SH WZ
4 ALL I NO SH CD HV BN N ANTHR PRT F T CNTRY R T WRLD R
EVN N ANTHR CENTURY
(How could I when I didn't know where she was? For all I know she
could have been in another part of the country or the world or even
in another century)

"I doubt that," Ben says. "If she said you were the one who could help. Why would it be you unless that baby was in trouble in the here and now? Unless it was someplace close to here?"

ITS G SHT B U DNT UNSTND IT
(It's ghost shit Ben you don't understand it)

"You don't either," Ben says—and he has a point. The he adds, "You told me you heard from her three times. What happened the third time?"

But I refuse to talk about her anymore—I'm still worried about him scrambling my story. Ben retaliates by taking an unannounced and extended work break. He gets up, goes to the kitchen, makes and eats a tuna sandwich on white bread, goes out for a walk. He doesn't return to resume his amanuensis duties for another three hours.

*

So winter continued and things kept happening to the house I haunted, seemingly whenever I was away. The first thing was that the landlord, or someone he had sent, nailed boards over the back door, which the scrap-metal scavengers destroyed when they had broken in. The house's plumbing remained unrepaired, and the "For Sale or Rent" sign in the front yard vanished and was replaced by two hand-painted rectangles of plywood, fastened to the outside wall on either side of the front door, that said, "Keep Out! Police Take Notice!"

But if the cops ever acted on this request, they, like me, must have come around at the wrong times, because it was not long before I found two back windows smashed from the outside in, with blade-like shards of glass shining on the floor. I also found cigarette butts and beverage bottles littering the kitchen; a few of these empties bore the Twisted Tea label, a sight that ignited a strong memory of the hatred I'd seen in Dirt's eyes that afternoon when he told my mother about how I had beaten the shit out of him for shooting the pileated woodpecker.

As part of my landlord's reactive war against the vandals, plywood soon was affixed over the outside of every window—broken as well as not. After that, and in spite of the fact that I had no trouble "seeing" in the dark, the house seemed even more depressingly crypt-like than it had before, without so much as a puff of living air moving through it—which was another reason I preferred to sit out on the steps rather than remain inside. In addition, the landlord installed a hasp with a heavy padlock on the front door, and also attached an array of bright, motion-activated floodlights all along the overhang of the front roof; I did not notice these until one starless night when they all flashed on at once to temporarily paralyze a laser-eyed porcupine shuffling across the snow-covered driveway.

When I finally saw the professor again it was almost spring, and every new snow had begun to melt within a day or two of falling. I was in my usual place on the steps when he appeared. Without hesitation, I rose and ghosted toward him.

"Thumb, isn't it?" he said. "You're still here."

"You promised you'd come back." There was accusation in my voice.

"Well, I don't think I said when. And I'm here now, am I not? *And*, in fact, it's not always my choice where I go and when I get there. Much of the time, I seem chained to my old office at the college—which, by the way, is now occupied by someone I've always hated."

"Can you show me how to get away from here? I've got things I need to do." In fact, I was worried that my killer's trail already had grown irrecoverably cold.

"Maybe I can," he said after a moment—though he seemed reluctant. "I myself learned much of what I know during a dream I had of an older ghost whom I met when he was passing through campus. He wasn't actually older than I in mortal years; he'd just been dead longer—although, as I've explained, I'm not actually dead. I've always thought of him as the 'post-graduate ghost,' and while I only dreamed of him that once, he was able to help me with some of the mechanics of this imagined afterlife. It seems that common decency, if not karma, might demand that I share what I've learned with you."

"That's good to hear. Now is not too soon."

Professor Shallow frowned. Then he said, "All right. Well, the thing that will be of most use and comfort to you is the knowledge that, although as supposed ghosts we start out nearly as helpless as we do in our mortal life, we gain abilities with time and experience. You must have discovered some of that yourself, since you're here talking to me in the shape and shade of a man, and not still trapped in a floor crack beneath a bathmat, or looking out at the world from the inside of a dust bunny."

"It was cobwebs, in a corner."

"For my part," said the professor, "I started my imagined afterlife in an electrical wall socket, behind a bookshelf. It's still my gateway back to the river."

"Yeah, that all sounds familiar."

"You already have more mobility than you're aware of—but what you haven't yet discovered is that almost nothing goes in a straight line. The world, for us, has become a maze; there are ghost routes that connect one place to another, but they're all crooked, and most of them are hard to find because they are invisible to us, at least at first. I've gotten so that I can see the outline of them sometimes—faintly, but I can. And the post-graduate ghost told me he could see most of them, and that he could visit hundreds of places, some of them very far from where he died. In fact, he had originally started out in Montreal and was planning to travel as far south as he could go, perhaps all the way to Antarctica. But he also warned me that he had been unable to find paths leading to many of the places and people he most wanted to visit—which to my sorrow has been my experience as well. In this dream I'm having, the people I truly care about have all been out of my reach."

"Purgatory. That's just part of our punishment," I said.

The professor shook his head and continued talking. "Another aspect of the maze in which we travel is something that the Post-Graduate Ghost called 'wormholes.' We usually run into them by accident—they're *always* invisible—and a ghost who steps or falls into a wormhole jumps directly from one place or time to another. They suck you right in and shoot you somewhere in a flash, and you don't always know where you are when you arrive. And the ends of wormholes can be treacherous: they often slide around so that once you've emerged from one of them you can't always find your way back in.

"Wormholes are also uncanny. By this, I mean that sometimes the places they take you to will seem to have some sort of personal significance to you, but the connection often is rather enigmatic—kind of like that wreath, hanging from the pole, whose supposed meaning I didn't know until you told me. Other times, the wormhole just seems to dump you in a random spot, sometimes among living people who are not in the least bit interesting. For instance, you'll find yourself with some lumpy-looking family in a fast-food restaurant, all of them chewing with their mouths open. Then you have to find your own way home."

When he finally stopped speaking I said, "I used to grow weed that made people talk like that."

The professor's laughter seemed to surprise him as much as it did me. He quickly became serious again and said, "I fought in Vietnam. I could tell you about a dance or two with Mary Jane myself—though not recently. But Thumb, let's try traveling now. Stay right behind me; ghost pathways are narrow, they twist, and they're easy to lose."

He tipped forward until he was hovering in the air with his face to the ground. Then he rose a few more yards toward the sky and began soaring up the road in the direction of Riverside. I did my best to copy his movements, but at the point where I had always been stopped before—on the side of the street, less than fifty yards from my house—I once again found that I could go no farther. The professor, meanwhile, kept sailing along until he was almost around the curve and out of sight. As I watched him vanish, my despair grew so great that I nearly screamed his name; fortunately, just before I gave in to that shameful impulse, he stopped and returned to me, feet first.

"Right on my heels, Thumb. You're about half a meter above the path; you must not have noticed when I changed my altitude. Remember; it's a maze in several dimensions. Shall we try it again?"

After that, I found myself flying far beyond my former boundaries. The professor soared above the tops of the trees and I stuck right behind him, awed by our view of the muddy, snow-blotched, late-winter landscape that passed below. On the edge of the marsh not far from the house, a gliding seagull cut right through both of us with a startling *whoosh*, then kept right on going, none the wiser and not the least bit put off its course by our unsensed presence. For the first time, I thought, *It could be the Professor is right; maybe I am having a dream in my final seconds of life.*

Virgil guided me on a zigzagging route that led over woods, brown hayfields, and housing tracts, and we ended up high above the city, looking down on our college. We paused side by side to watch as scores of students crossed campus during a change of classes.

"I love that place," Virgil said. "It makes me sad to be leaving it."

Directly below me a man and a woman, both of them carrying backpacks, stopped to kiss before heading their separate ways. The sight gave me a pang that I felt through my entire being.

"I wish I was back there myself," I said. "I wish I had never left." Suddenly it occurred to me that I might be able to travel all the way to the Blood Eagles' clubhouse, which stood only about three miles away as the seagull flies. I could almost see it from where we were. If I were able to eavesdrop on conversations at the clubhouse I might learn who had stood behind me with that gun.

I said, "Can we go across the river? The above-ground one, I mean?"

"I haven't been across that river since I've been dreaming," Virgil said. "Crossing bodies of water is difficult for us and I've never found a path, though I have searched a time or two. Bridges are of no use to us. However, as I think about it, there must be a way, or the Post-Graduate Ghost would not have been able to continue traveling south, as he said he was planning to do. And, if he hadn't made it across, I'm sure I would have seen him again." After a moment he added, "In my dreams, I mean."

"How would I find the path?"

"You just have to keep looking. The more you look for them, the more skilled you become at finding them. But now, Thumb, I have to tell you that I'm feeling tired. It's time for a tumble in the *other* river—the metaphysical one. My office is right down there. That's my home haunt." He pointed to a brick building on the edge of campus.

"Aren't you going to take me back to my place first?"

"You can get there on your own. In fact, it'll be good for you to do it yourself. Practice makes perfect. If you get stuck anywhere, just *feel* your way through." He tipped toward the ground and began to descend.

"See you again?" I called.

"Maybe," he answered, without turning around. "If I don't finally die for real between now and then."

I did find my own way back home that day, but not without a few moments of confusion and a few others of stark panic. And when I was once again "standing" among the piles of snow melting into my front lawn, for the first time since I had died, I felt hope.

CHAPTER 8

The motion-activated lights on the front of the house failed to discourage the vandals. They smashed all the lamps within days of their installation. Then, before my landlord could take action, they pried the plywood from the back door, invaded the house again, and scrawled graffiti all over the living room walls in a combination of spray paint and permanent marking pen. Rather than any kind of semi-artistic or self-expressive tagging, these messages were mostly made up of swear words, accompanied in several spots by primitive illustrations. Also, I found further, abundant evidence of boozing and smoking—of cigarettes as well as the flower of my former life's work—along with strong hints of some chemical-solvent abuse. It was clear that the original profit-minded scrap-metal foragers had been replaced by teenagers seeking relief from the boredom of their own pointless lives. I was mad about the damage but, as a ghost, there was nothing I could do that wouldn't threaten my own continued existence, such as it was. My afterlife was haunted by humans and there seemed no way of exorcising them.

The landlord reacted to the latest break-ins by replacing the bulbs in most of the motion-activated lamps, by restoring the plywood barrier over the back door using even more eight-penny nails than before, and by installing a cheap, battery-powered alarm system which, if set off, would make a noise likely to be heard by no one but the vandals themselves, owing to the isolation of the house and the nighttime near-desertion of the road on which it sat.

*

Although the repeated invasions and ongoing deterioration of the house were upsetting, everything else in my afterlife continued to improve: Early spring had arrived, and the surge of green growth cheered me even though I could neither touch it, nor smell it, nor feel the warmth of the sun that drew it from the earth. Also, not only could I now leave the house whenever I wanted and follow Professor Shallow's ghost path to the college but, as a result of a lot of blind, persistent thrashing around, I had blundered onto a couple of short ghost paths of my own. One of these routes dead-ended at a stretch of rocky, wave-pounded ocean beach, while another wound me through an adjacent town to Fred Muttkowski's organic pig farm.

I first came upon Fred in his writing pen, the soles of his shit-caked rubber boots propped against the cinderblock wall and a black laptop computer balanced on his knees as he tapped away at the most recent of his many unpublished novels. Seemingly spellbound, an audience of porkers watched him through the horizontal bars of the latched gate. It was not long before I realized Fred would make the perfect ghostwriter for the story I wanted to tell—though I almost immediately gave up on the idea because I had no means to communicate with him and did not yet know I'd eventually find one, as my first meeting with Ben was still a long way off. During most of my early visits to the farm, Fred served me as little more than unsuspecting company and a source of scarce amusement. His life and frustrations were both my inspiration and my entertainment.

*

During this same stretch of time, I had begun visiting Riverside, unsuccessfully haunting the sidewalks for any sign of my former housemates and desperately searching for a path across the river to the Blood Eagles' clubhouse. Then, a day or two after the graffiti attack on my home, I ran into Professor Shallow. By coincidence we met above our college among low clouds that streamed past like a herd of phantom buffalo—and he actually smiled when he saw me. It occurred to me then that I was not the only lonely ghost in the world; Professor Shallow just made more of an effort to hide his sense of isolation.

He said, "Thumb, come with me. There is someone who wants to meet you, though I really don't why."

"A ghost, you mean? Another ghost?"

"Of course a ghost. How could he be anything else?"

He led me on a long journey of many bends, twists, and changes of altitude. Sometimes we doubled back to circle a landmark we'd gone past once or even twice before; at other points the path took us directly to the ground, where we "walked" by swinging our legs even though we could have drifted along like fog if we'd wanted.

At last, we descended to a gravel road that wound through dense woods ten or so miles north of my house. This thoroughfare was badly rutted from the earlier spring rains and snowmelt runoff and its only dwellings were a scattering of forlorn trailers set among the permanent shadows of the forest. We glided on and soon, beside an ancient cemetery enclosed by a wrought-iron fence, we came upon a single-story church building set a short distance from the road among thigh-high dead thistle and the dry stalks of goldenrod. A heavy chain and padlock sealed the double front doors, while the lines of windows along both sides of the structure were shuttered with plywood. Hanging from the wall next to the entrance was a transparent box, which during better times would have displayed orders of worship and other important messages, but which now held only an inhospitable warning similar to the ones my landlord had nailed to my house.

"Oh, too bad," I said.

"Good for us, though," Professor Shallow said. "It makes for a peaceful haunt. Gib found it."

"Is Gib the person I'm meeting?"

"He'll be here soon I think. I first ran into him at the end of a wormhole a few weeks back; we began talking, and he brought me here. An older man. Owned and ran a small machine shop while he was alive. Let's go in."

Because of the boarded windows, the church was dark as dusk inside—though as ghosts, our ability to see was undiminished by the lack of light. After prickling our way through those thick front doors, we crossed a narrow foyer and entered a sanctuary divided by twin rows of a dozen wooden pews, all of them bolted to the green-and-white tile floor. The altar had been removed and the chancel was just a blank, stage-like space, save for an enclosure with some benches at the back that no doubt had served as the choir box.

Professor Shallow said, "This emptiness appeals to me. The silence. It feels like home. If I could, I'd move out of my office—did I tell you I can't stand the woman who's moved in since my departure?—and start haunting here for the remainder of my dreaming time."

Just then a third voice joined our conversation. In a Maine accent the unseen spirit said, "Don't forget who found this place, Virgil. If you're planning on moving in I might have to charge you some rent." A moment later a white-haired ghost materialized on the front steps of the church and coasted inside. My first impression was that there was something out of kilter with his appearance. Although the depth of the channels in his broad, ruddy face suggested that at the time of his death he'd been close to as old as a person can get, the rest of him seemed to date from an earlier era—one in which he'd been healthy and strong in spite of carrying nearly three-hundred pounds on a frame no more than an inch or two over six feet tall. It appeared that he had assembled his ghostly avatar from the bodies he'd inhabited during two separate periods of his life. He was clothed in the illusion of a yellow polo shirt, jeans, and the sort of navy-blue, canvas slip-on sneakers that old people buy in department stores. He gave me a wide smile.

"I never introduced myself the last time you and I talked. I'm Gibbous Waxing; everybody calls me Gib." His words confused me.

"The *last* time we talked?"

"Yes. And did you find out who murdered you yet?"

I stared at him until finally he laughed and, in the stony rasp of that first voice I'd heard at the bottom of the underground river, he said, *Thumb Rivera. Did you find out who murdered you yet?*

"Jesus!" I slid several steps back from him.

"It's a simple question," he said in his ordinary voice. He was no longer smiling. "And please don't be taking the Lord's name in vain."

"You're the . . . under the water, the . . . "

"I was your messenger, yes. So, did you, or not? Find out?"

"No. And who gave you that message? To give to me?"

Gib shrugged. "The words just came to me at the bottom of the river—almost like I was reading them off the rocks—and I somehow knew I was meant to say them to you. That's how it goes with messengers, I think; we don't always know the why or what of the message."

"Well it must have come from someone. The message must have."

"Maybe," he said. "Who do you suppose it was?" He was smiling again.

Professor Shallow said, "You were *my* messenger, Thumb. About my car crash. Do you know who put *you* up to it?"

"But that was different. I was just telling you what I already knew."

Gib said, "I don't think that's so different."

The professor said, "And we can't expect anything that happens in a dream to make a lot of sense in any case."

Gib smiled at him—I wondered if his teeth in real life had been that perfect—and to me he said, "Did Virgil tell you he doesn't think he's dead? That he believes he's really in some kind of a brain-dead dream? That you and I and everything around us are just part of some hallucination he's having?"

"He has."

"I am," said the professor. "You are."

"He's coming around, though," said Gib. "He's nowhere near as certain about it as he was when I first met him a while back. I think it might have something to do with meeting you—but his certainty has been cracking lately; I can see it in his face whenever we talk about it. Good thing for him we'll be around to help put him back together when he finally crumbles like a brown-shelled Humpty Dumpty."

The professor gave him a humorless smile. "What will finally happen is that I'll *die*. And when I do, you and Thumb will die with me along with everything else I've ever thought and never bothered to write down."

Gib nodded at him. Then to me he said, "Anyway, you and I still haven't met *properly*." He extended a meaty-looking hand, which struck me as weird because ghosts are no more capable of touching than two beams of light. When he saw my hesitation, he said, "What's wrong, friend? Put her there," forcing me to play along by lifting my own illusory hand. He then waved his hand through and through mine several times, at the same time saying, "This is the way we do it here in heaven. It's the angel's handshake—get used to it." My thoughts scattered once more in confusion; I looked at Virgil, who nodded but said nothing.

Gib said, "It's polite if you wave your own hand, too; you and the other soul make a blur of your hands and it shows the good will you feel toward one another."

Still looking at Professor Shallow, I finally asked, "Do you think we're in heaven, Mr. Waxing?"

"Call me Gib. And absolutely that's where I think we are. It's just that heaven is a more complicated place than we ever thought when we were alive."

"Even after that message you delivered to me at the bottom of the river? About falling through to a blacker death, and all? Not to mention . . . just take a look at your surroundings. We're in a boarded-up building on a dirt road lined with trailers. Heaven? Seriously?"

Gib said, "Of course it's heaven! You can fly, can't you? That makes you a fucking angel. Sure, there's a bunch of levels. This would no doubt be one of the lowest ones, and you probably wouldn't want to fall any lower than you are right now. But still . . . "

"Yeah, I can fly, sort of," I argued. "But not to where I want, whenever I want. And in a heartbeat I'd trade flying for being able to see the people I care about, and have them see me. Do *you* get to see the people you want to see?"

"I haven't managed that, no."

"Well, what's flying compared to that? And if we're angels, like you say, where the hell is God? Or Jesus? Or anybody? Where is all the goddamn information?"

"God will come in his good time," Gib said. "He will come when we truly need Him to come. And the 'goddamn information' is right under your nose, if you're willing to accept it." He was still smiling as he said this.

"Okay, maybe this is not actually hell, even though it feels like it to me. But if it's not, it has to be purgatory."

Gib said, "I don't know anything about any purgatory. But in my life I think I've probably gotten a lot closer to hell than you have, and this ain't it. Go through a war like I did over in Europe and hear your buddy lying with his leg blown off and screaming for his mother. See a child lying dead in a ditch. Or even without war—try moldering in a nursing home for a decade before you die. That's what I went through. I'd had a stroke and nothing worked anymore. Next to any of those things, all of this is a fucking piece of cake.

"Listen, Thumb: We're dead, yet we can move around; we fly. Best of all, we think, and we hope. And nothing on earth can hurt us anymore. Not for the rest of eternity. What a miracle that all is. How can you or Virgil or anyone say that God isn't looking out for us?"

I said, "What about your family? In a real heaven, you'd get to look down on them somehow."

"You think so? Why? Just so I could feel terrible about all their earthly sorrows, which I'd be helpless to do anything about? That would be cruel. No; I'll see them sometime after their own days of suffering are over. All rivers run to the sea; all waters meet. You just need to have some faith, my young friend. I will help you with that, if you like. But of course, only if you're interested. I'm not a preacher, or anything."

I looked at Virgil. "Does he convince you?"

"You know he doesn't. But I enjoy hearing what he has to say—which of course is only an expression of thoughts rattling around inside my own mind." Then he added, "For now though, gentlemen, I'm starting to feel a bit weak; I think it's time to head back home for a dip in the river."

I felt exhausted myself. "You're right, I think. It's almost time to swim with the dark fish."

Gib said, "Not me; not yet. I'm going to stay right here for as long as I can; I just can't stand that nursing home. I live in an air-conditioning duct in my old room, and my place in bed has been replaced by a wheezing corpse a lot like I once was; I don't care for his company. It does get lonely here, though, with no one around. Here in the church, I mean. When will I see you two gentlemen?"

"When I can," said Virgil. "And *if* I can. But for now . . . " Before he could finish, Virgil faded and disappeared.

I smiled at Gib. "When I can," I said, echoing Virgil. I couldn't resist adding, "I bet you never imagined paradise would be such a lonely place." As soon as I had spoken, dusk descended, and I fell into the river.

*

One day not long after my first visit to the abandoned church,
I was haunting my vandalized house when I heard the distant, flub-
bering roar of a Harley-Davison. I drifted through the front door
to wait by the road and a couple of minutes later Mantis's Softail
rounded the curve. When he coasted to a stop at the mouth of my
driveway, the raked front wheel of his machine was cutting through
my right shin at an angle. Boots against the ground to balance the
bike, Mantis sat staring at the house as the idling engine popped
and grumbled, his whiskered lower lip bulging, ape-like, with a wad
of chew. After a moment, he bent his head to the side and spat a
brown puddle onto the blacktop. Then he returned his attention to
the house.

Although my ghostly vision allowed me to see all sides of him
at once from right where I stood, out of long human habit I felt the
need to look him over from every physical angle. I drew my leg from
his chrome spokes and began to circle him slowly, all the while
resisting the urge to scream in his ear. The consequences, whatever
they might be, would almost have been worth it. Not only had Mantis's old cut been re-colored with the complete Blood Eagles insignia—they had made him a full-patch member in a shockingly short
period of time—but there, almost hidden beneath the long braid in
which he had tied his hair, was a tiny but significant black rectangle
bearing the white initials ITCOB.

I Took Care Of Business. And, who had that business been?

Just as I came back around to face him again, he spat another
stream of filth that passed through me on its trajectory to the
ground. I placed my face so close to his that the tips of our noses
intersected, and in my ghost voice I asked, "So who was it you
killed, Mantis? Was it *me*, you bastard? Weren't you the one standing behind me with that gun?"

He didn't answer, of course. His blue eyes were a snowfield,
and his face remained as blank as the moon. I saw not a clue as to

what ghosts of feelings might be flickering inside of him; in all likelihood, there was nothing turning in there at all.

"Where's Cricket, you son of a bitch? Is that why you did it? Or was it just so you could become a one-percenter again?"

Even though I knew he couldn't hear me, I had by then worked myself into a rage, and his lack of a response only infuriated me even more. I was giving serious thought to actually speaking—sacrificing my afterlife to give him a scare he would never forget—when suddenly he twisted the throttle, popped the bike into gear, and rolled right through me as he roared off down the road. I stood watching after him until the rumble of his machine had completely faded away.

*

After that I flew off to the abandoned church on the same twisting route the professor and I had taken the time before. When I reached the gravel road, I hurried along it as quickly as I could. As I was passing one of the battered trailers, a yellow mutt barreled toward me barking, the hair spiking from the nape of his neck. It was obvious the dog sensed my presence, and his attack scared me at first. But after he had run right through me, whirled, and passed through me again without stopping, it became clear he didn't know exactly where I stood; it was likely I registered as nothing more than a vague but threatening vapor drifting past his yard. A shirtless, black-bearded man appeared at the screen door of the trailer as the dog continued to turn circles in the road, barking wildly. "Toto," the man called. It was then that I got an idea.

"Toto," I said in my ghost voice. "You yellow piece of shit." At this, the dog lifted his head, backed up a pace or two and let out a frantic howl, proving that I had reached him with my tone if not my words. This made me wonder whether all dogs, throughout all of time, whenever they barked at "nothing," might actually have been reacting to the invisible shadows and dog-whistle voices of ghosts.

"Toto!" yelled the man. "What's the matter with you?"

"Yeah, Toto," I said. "What the hell?" The dog howled again, then stood with his rump to me as he snarled and snapped at the air.

"Toto!" the man called. "There ain't nothing there!"

"Listen to the man, Toto: They-ah ain't nothin' theyah." This pushed Toto to the edge of foamy-mouthed insanity, which further infuriated his owner.

"You jackass! Get over here!" In a rage of his own, the man threw open the door and stepped out, obviously intending to descend to the road and drag Toto back to the trailer by his collar. I didn't stay to watch this drama unwind to its ugly end. Suddenly I remembered how badly I wanted to see the other ghosts, and I continued on my way as the sound of barking faded behind me.

I found Gib and Virgil sitting in a pew, both of them staring down at what looked like a piece of paper that lay between them. They both said my name when I appeared, but otherwise ignored me.

I said, "Does either of you find that you get a reaction from dogs? Like they seem to know you're there?"

Without looking up, Gib answered, "I do, sometimes. Not all of them, though. But some dogs do go a little crazy; for some reason, most of those damn pit bulls seem especially touchy." Then, speaking to Virgil, he said, "I'm gonna move this pawn right here."

Virgil said, "That's not a pawn, Gib; that's your queen's knight." I saw then that the object of their attention was a wrinkled cocktail napkin, stained in a few spots with what looked to be barbecue sauce, which bore the printed image of a black and red chess or checker board.

"Where did that come from?" I asked.

"Lying right here the whole time, like a treasure in plain sight," Gib answered. "Now we've got something to keep us busy. You can play the winner if you want."

"How can you play chess with no pieces?"

"With great difficulty, apparently," said Gib, still keeping his eyes on the napkin. "Terrific training for the memory, though." He then placed his finger over one of the tiny red squares. "So, that's the pawn right there, then?"

"Yes, it is," said Virgil. "I'm certain of it."

"Well, I ain't moving *that*. I'd have to be crazy."

"Yes, you would. Take your time, we've got plenty of it."

"You got that right. We're the fuckin' King Midases of time."

I said, "I think I've figured out who killed me." They lifted their faces to me.

Virgil said, "You mean aside from the bad bikers—the fellow with the tattooed face?"

"The man who actually pulled the trigger—the one that Gib, when he was my messenger, told me I had to find."

"Who?" they both asked at once.

"One of my old housemates came by on his motorcycle earlier today. Mantis, his name is; he stopped to look at our house, and he was wearing the full patches of the Blood Eagles. They almost never patch a dude in that short a period of time, and yet, there he was. Not only that, he was wearing an ITCOB, which stands for, 'I Took Care Of Business,' which means he killed somebody for the club. I'm thinking that somebody was *me*—the puzzle pieces all seem to fall into place. I came *this* close to making myself visible to him, and screaming right in his face. That's how furious—"

Gib said, "ITC . . . *what*?"

"ITCO—"

"Jeez, Thumb," Gib said, not waiting to hear the rest. "How did a smart cat like you get involved in such a bunch of extreme bullshit as that? What kind of a way was that to spend a life—especially one that ended up being as short as yours?"

"Don't think it doesn't haunt me, Gib. You know, like I told Virgil before, I was sort of fooling myself into thinking I was doing research for a book, which is what I most wanted to do in the world . . . "

"It's not him," Virgil said.

"*What?*"

"The charmingly named Mantis. He's not the guy."

"How would you know that?"

Virgil laughed. "I'm omniscient," he said. "This is my end-of-life hallucination, after all."

"Yeah," I said with sarcasm. "I almost forgot about that."

"But, aside from that, it seems it's a mystery novel you're writing."

"*I'm* writing a mystery novel?"

"Yes; you've mentioned several times now that you were writing a novel. And from what you just told us, it would seem to be a novel about solving a murder—your own, in this case—which would make it a mystery. An offbeat one, but a mystery, nonetheless."

He continued, "Now, I'm far from an authority on the conventions of genre fiction, but I do recall that, in the case of mysteries, the killer is almost never the first person the detective suspects. The detective, in this case, being you."

"*That's* your reason? That Mantis is the first person I suspected? Because it's not the way they do it in mystery novels?"

"One of them, yes."

"But this is real life—or real afterlife, at least."

"Well, you already know we've got a difference of opinion about that."

"And what I said was I had been planning to write a novel while I was alive. Not a *mystery* novel. And not *now*. In fact, if I wrote something now, it would be biographical—my autobiography as a ghost."

"Oh," said Virgil, his amused expression unchanged. "My mistake."

"I mean, how would I write it in the first place? We're ghosts; we can't even pick up a pencil; we can't do anything at all."

"I suppose you're right," Virgil said, looking back down at the napkin. "Gib, while it's true we've got eternity here, you don't have to spend it all deciding on your move."

But Gib still had his eyes on me. Gib said, "We can fly, Thumb. We can walk and see through walls. We can think. That's a lot to be able to do."

Again with sarcasm I answered, "Yeah, I forgot, Gib; we're in heaven. Only you'd think that in heaven, they'd at least have a real chessboard for you guys to play on rather than a napkin that some kid used to wipe his mouth."

Gib laughed. "Thumb is taunting me," he said, looking at Virgil. Then he gave me a broad smile. "You're taunting me. But I like you, anyway. At the bottom of it, and in spite of all your errors, you're a good soul, and you've got a good future ahead of you. I think you should go ahead and write a mystery novel if that's what you want to do, and if you can find a way to get it done. Just don't drive yourself too crazy with the *real-life* mystery—this ITCO-whatever business. Your idea about making yourself visible and screaming in his face—that would be a bad mistake.

"Remember what they had me tell you in the river—that you'd have to come to terms with what you found? I not quite sure what that all meant, but I'm betting it wasn't a suggestion for you to lose control of yourself if you discovered something you didn't like. Find out what you need to know in order to move on in this afterlife, of course—and also to write your story. But don't go getting yourself into deeper trouble over anything that happened while you were alive. Because none of it really matters now. You're dead, Thumb; learn to live with it."

*

Another night, another break-in at my haunted home. But this most recent crew of vandals was craftier in several senses of the word. For one thing, after gaining entrance by prying the plywood from the back door, they replaced the boards on their way back out in order to conceal the fact that they'd been there in the first place. They also had apparently disconnected and then reconnected my landlord's sound alarms, because the contraptions all seemed to be working when I examined them. Inside the house, their creative destruction was of a higher caliber as well. Apparently among them was someone called "Ed," who tagged every remaining bit of unmarked wall with an artistic and multi-colored rendering of his own name. This group left not a single obscene illustration or four-letter word anywhere in the place; instead, it was all *Ed* spray-painted and marker-penned with nearly as much detail and care as if it were destined for display in an art gallery. And painting walls wasn't the end of what they did: I also found evidence that, while Ed was busy working toward fame as a graffiti artist, the others in his group—two of them, at least—had entertained themselves with a little weed, some halfway-decent red wine, and a couple of bouts of protected sex on the kitchen counter, after which they'd thrown their condoms in the sink. Rather than merely feeling resentment at this latest intrusion as I had with all the others, I found myself burning with envy over all the things they did that I could no longer do.

Meanwhile, at around the same time I was suffering so greatly from both my impotence against the graffiti-tagging vandals and my deep grief over the loss of my own carnality, I found that Fred Muttkowski was going through a similar, almost parallel, period of internal torment. I arrived at his farm one afternoon to discover that he'd emptied out the farrowing pen he had used as an office. Gone were the rolling chair and the laptop computer, and in their place stood a huge, and hugely pregnant, Berkshire sow who chewed, shit upon, and stepped through the toppled tower of Fred's old manuscript pages.

Fred apparently had finally accomplished it, then: he'd rid himself of the compulsive writing habit that had caused him so much misery. I congratulated him and, although of course he could not hear me, I hoped aloud that he would find satisfaction in his life as it was, and not as he once wished it would be. He certainly seemed, on that day, to have made peace with his lowly, pig-producing position in the world. As he went about his work he was whistling; he was singing snatches of old rock tunes to the pigs; he was muttering to people whom I could not see, and who I therefore knew were not ghosts, but were merely the children of Fred's own imagination. Apparently their mere companionship was sufficient for him now, these invisible friends at large in the air; he no longer felt the need to capture and imprison them in cages of words. I was happy for him then—but I also found something a little sad in his sudden and cheerful acceptance of defeat.

I should have realized, however, that Fred's newfound tranquility was not going to last. When I returned to the farm several days later, Fred, his bearded face tight as a fist, was no longer whistling, no longer singing. But he did continue to spit strings of half-pronounced words as if addressing an audience that was by turns hostile and infuriatingly stupid, and every so often this running dispute would draw him back to the paper-strewn, pig-fouled shambles of his former office, where he would stand gnawing his lip and staring not at the gravid, grunting sow the pen now housed, but at the spot on the floor beneath her bulging belly where the wheels of his rolling chair had once rested. He'd stare and he'd gnaw and he'd mutter, and then, before pivoting sharply away on the squealing rubber heels of his barn boots, he would suddenly shout, *No*!, or sometimes something more elaborate such as, "We've been through all this, you asshole! So, no, and no again!"

This struggle was painful to watch, especially since I was dealing with so much unhappiness of my own, and finally I forced myself to abandon him to his anger and his misery. When I returned to check on him a few days later, the now deflated sow was in another farrowing pen, nursing a squirming litter of eleven, while Fred was back in his office with the gate closed and the laptop balanced on his knees. The thousands of manuscript pages, looking far worse for the wear, had been restored to their stone-weighted pile. But Fred's battle was far from over.

For a solid hour, he sat drumming his boots against the floor without writing a word, without giving so much as a single twirl or spin of his chair. Finally he gently closed the computer, placed it on the chair, and set about cleaning the barn. Things went the same way the next day, and the day after that—plenty of sitting and not a word written—and then finally one afternoon I arrived to find that the computer was gone again and in its place Fred sat holding a ballpoint pen and an open, spiral-bound notebook.

And still no words came to him, though he stared so hard at that first blank sheet of blue-lined paper that it almost seemed possible he'd burn holes through it with the focused heat of his eyes. By the time he stood up from his chair, he'd gone pale and there was a look of real panic on his face; he was like a man in a wilderness without even the sun in the sky to guide him.

"I believe I may have fucked myself," he said, his voice barely above a whisper. After a moment, he dropped the notebook and pen onto his chair and shambled back to the house, returning a few minutes later with a bottle of bourbon and a coffee mug. Out in the pig run, he seated himself on an overturned bucket and proceeded to drink in silence for the rest of the afternoon.

I worried about him then. When I made my way back to the farm after another two mornings had passed, I fully expected to find him a drunken wreck, crawling among pigs on hands and knees. Instead, I encountered him deep in study. Next to his rolling chair stood a pile of books, four hardcovers and three paperbacks, all of which dealt with the topics of hypnosis and self-hypnosis. As I kept him company, he leafed through those books one by one, dog-earring, as he did so, the first pages of some passages, completely skipping others, and then dropping each book back to the dusty floor once he'd extracted the information he was looking for. By noon, he'd been through them all at least twice, and after a quick lunch at the house he returned to the barn ready to put his newfound knowledge to work.

He sat in the rolling chair, squirming until he was completely comfortable and, staring straight ahead, began concentrating intently on his breathing. After a couple of minutes, he slowly let his eyes fall closed, and for a while, as I watched his eyeballs tracking restlessly beneath those tired eyelids, I wondered what marvels he was beholding back there. But soon his eyes stopped their restless searching, and Fred's head settled forward onto his chest. He began to snore.

I laughed and said, "So much for that."

After his nap he gave it another try, however, and this time, for an impressively long while, he sat completely upright with his eyes closed—not sleeping, it seemed, but relaxed and breathing deeply, evenly, and intentionally. He remained, for the most part, entirely unmoving, although at one point his right arm lifted slowly and hesitantly into the air until it was even with his shoulder, his hand dangling limply from his wrist. Then the arm settled back and a minute later the other one rose in a similarly mysterious way, offering the illusion that it was under the control of some invisible force rather than that of Fred himself. Even to a ghost, this was eerie.

When Fred finally awoke and looked around, rather than immediately attempting to write, he stood and let himself out of the farrowing pen. Moving slowly, as if he were still in a trance, he shuffled out the back of the barn and onto the pig run. At first he squinted against the brightness of the sun, but momentarily his eyes widened in an expression of astonishment.

"Well now, look at *you*," he said to absolutely no one. "I'd have thought you'd be skinnier, as much crap as you give me about my appearance." Then he turned his head slightly to one side and said, "And *you*. You look ridiculous, although I assume you already know that. Is that beret ironic, or are you wearing it because you really think it's cute?"

He paused at that point, stopped smiling as he appeared to be listening, and then he said, "Fuck you. Bet against me if you want, but I'm pretty sure I've got the problem solved."

It was likely he was addressing the same people he normally muttered to as he went about his work. The difference was that, through his self-hypnosis, he seemed to have given himself the ability to see as well as hear them in his head. I found this at once fascinating and worrisome, because I suspected there was a fine line between vivid imagination and insanity, and I wasn't sure either Fred or I could be certain when he'd finally stepped across it. Weirdly, as soon as this thought entered my mind, Fred reacted as if I'd just posed it to him in the form of a question.

"Yes," he said, with acid in his voice. "Of *course* I know you're not real, any of you. You used to be nothing but auditory hallucinations. Now I can see you as well—big fucking deal. A bunch of nagging, translucent holograms. I just wish you all were better looking."

He couldn't see *me*; of that I was certain. Because I *was* real, and therefore really invisible, while the ones he saw and talked to were merely figments of his mind. That he *seemed* to hear me, and answer me, just a moment before . . . that had to have been a coincidence.

The next day Fred attempted to write while in a hypnotic trance. I arrived at the barn to find that he'd placed a card table in the farrowing pen. He was seated at the table, on which burned the twisted stub of a candle, and his spiral-bound notebook lay open to a blank page, a pen resting next to it. In one of his new hypnosis books, he was reviewing a chapter called "Automatic Writing"— which was illustrated, I noticed, with an ink drawing of a Ouija board planchette.

When he reached the end of the chapter, Fred clapped shut the book and dropped it to the floor. He placed his hands on the table, concentrated on the candle and, breathing evenly, he eventually let his eyes slide closed. A few minutes later, he looked down at the table and picked up the pen. As his hand slid onto the notebook page, Fred observed it in curious expectation as if it were someone else's appendage rather than his own. Soon—a minute or three later—his hand twitched and the pen tapped a dot of ink onto the paper. After a moment there came another spasmodic tap and then another, and then the pen was madly jabbing its way all up, down, and across the sheet. When the entire paper was almost completely darkened with dots, the pen and the fingers that held it seemed to freeze. Fred then used his left hand to nudge the right one onto the next blank page, where after a few seconds it pecked out a half-dozen more dots before starting to scribble. These scribbles were not words, but rather circular, swirling doodles such as a child might make with a fisted crayon, and in this way Fred filled up that second sheet, and then with his left hand he flipped the page so he could complete a third and a fourth. This went on until he'd used up half the notebook, then he set down his pen and carefully thumbed his way through the "work" he'd done. Neither he nor I could make out a single letter, much less a legible word.

He took a break, did some farm chores, relit the candle, and tried again in the early afternoon. But the results were no better than they'd been in the morning, and it quickly became clear that, rather than writing for him, his autonomous hand would give him nothing but a few dozen more pages of swirling childishness. That was when I decided to step in, thinking that I might somehow be able to influence the way his pen moved against the paper.

"Fred," I said, my head hovering next to his, "Try writing what I tell you." In what I hoped might be an affirmative response, the pen shot to the top of the page, then back down to the bottom.

"Good," I said. "Let's try a word, now. That word is . . . " Fred's fist clenched so tightly his knuckles turned white, then it shoved the pen to the middle of the page, where it scrawled in a tight circle with such pressure that the paper tore beneath it. The pen drilled down through five or six sheets and then, in a sudden jerk, his hand punched backward through my unseen face before flying forward again to launch the pen through the air, shattering it against the cinderblock wall of the farrowing enclosure.

Empty, Fred's hypnotized hand thumped to the card table, where it lay as limply as a bird blasted from the sky. Fred stared at it in astonishment before carefully flexing his fingers. After a moment he gave a snicker and said, "Clearly, my subconscious is every bit as fucked up as the rest of me."

I would have thought he'd give up on writing after that. Even the most determined person can't endure failure forever. I was also worried he'd start drinking heavily, and that was why I returned to the farm the following morning—where I found him preparing to give it another go.

The card table and candle were gone now, as were all the books on hypnosis. The rolling chair remained, and the laptop computer had made yet another return; Fred was clutching it as he stood next to the chair. A moment after I arrived, he turned to the gate of the farrowing pen and began to speak—though whether he was addressing the throng of pigs that had gathered there or a group of human hallucinations standing among the swine, I could not tell.

"The job is actually quite simple," he said. "No more complicated than shoveling pig shit off of concrete. Get words on the screen. One word at a time, one shovelful at a time. From this point forward, I declare my writer's block to be at an end."

He settled into the chair, stared at the screen, tapped out the word, "Once." Gave a single twirl of his chair, deleted the word—and then in seeming paralysis, spent ten minutes staring at the laptop while his fingers slowly writhed above the keyboard.

Finally, still peering down at the empty screen, he muttered, "Well, let's see. When the work is going well, I always do *this*." He scooted his chair to the closest wall, placed his booted feet against the cinder blocks, and pushed himself off. Then he twirled and pressed his boots onto the wall next to which his rolling chair had come to rest.

"And when it's going *really* well, I do this"—giving himself a more forceful shove that barreled him across the farrowing pen.

"And when it's going really, really, *really* well . . . " He cocked his legs, planted his soles, and gave a kick so forceful that as the chair rolled, its front wheels lifted from the ground, tipping it out from behind him and launching him backward and headfirst into cinderblocks, where his skull making an audible *clunk* against the gray concrete. He then slid down the wall and crashed heavily to the floor where he lay unmoving, his legs entangled with those of the overturned chair, the back of his head propped awkwardly against the filthy lowest line of cinder blocks, and his soiled baseball cap pushed down so that it covered his face. There he remained, looking as if he'd been shot, as two dozen pigs squealed in ear-piercing panic outside the gate of the farrowing pen.

If I hadn't been able to hear his heartbeat, I would have worried that he'd killed himself. As it was, I thought it likely he'd fractured his skull, scrambled his brain, reduced himself to a vegetable. And there was nothing I could do for him—not even call for help.

But after a couple of minutes, he groaned. A moment later, a shaking hand rose to lift the hat from his face and adjust his glasses. After yet another minute, he pushed himself to a sitting position, squinted out at the pigs, who had continued their high-pitched vocalizing, and shouted, "Pigs! Shut the hell up."

The squealing died down almost immediately. Most of the pigs fell to grunting instead, their dripping snouts protruding through the bars and oscillating enthusiastically in seeming hopes of sniffing out Fred's prognosis.

Fred pulled off his glasses, rubbed his eyes, put his glasses back on. He then stared for a long moment at his laptop, which lay open against the floor with a diagonal crack across its screen—a mockery of black blankness.

Aloud, in a voice containing neither humor nor irony, Fred said, "This is like death." After a moment, he amended himself with a sigh: "It *is* death. I'm nothing but a fucking ghost, now. A ghost is all I am."

I waited there in the barn until he climbed to his feet, righted his rolling chair, and began moving around again. When I was sure he was okay—physically, at least—I flew home—where I found my road and my yard crowded with black-helmeted firefighters and their flashing vehicles, and my house fully engulfed in flames.

CHAPTER 9

The fire crews knew the house was abandoned, so they watched it burn until it had completely collapsed into its basement, after which they hosed down the blazing embers. When they went away, ghost-like wisps of smoke still crawled toward the sky. After that, all that was left was the foundation, heaped with charred debris, and the blacktop driveway—which had partially melted then rehardened like lava, and now led to nowhere—as well as the concrete front steps with their two wrought-iron handrails, both of which had been weirdly twisted by the heat. No longer did it require a ghost's x-ray vision to see into my backyard from the road; the big red maple tree closest to the house—the one from which Dirt had shot the pileated woodpecker—was scorched on one side, most of its fresh, new foliage having disintegrated. But the wooden fence had survived, and the other two trees remained undamaged. Tigre's training tire still dangled from one.

With walls no longer surrounding it, my special spot above the front door was now a point fixed invisibly in midair; nevertheless, it continued to serve as my canal of birth and death, leading me to and from the dark river, and it didn't matter a bit that its man-made framing was gone.

For many days after the blaze, I didn't feel like visiting Fred or talking to the other ghosts, so I stayed home and sat on my steps. During this time of sitting, my road experienced a brief upsurge of traffic as people drove past to take in the results of the catastrophe. A few even got out of their vehicles and walked around the yard holding their phones in front of their faces. The day following the fire was the busiest: the county fire marshal stopped by and took some photographs, a ragged-looking reporter for the local weekly newspaper and its website did the same, and then my landlord and his insurance adjuster showed up. After the insurance woman had filled out her forms and driven away, my landlord took a half-dozen vinyl "Keep Out" signs from the trunk of his car and staked them along the front of the property, where they immediately caught the breeze that rolled up out of the marsh and began to flutter like an array of plastic pinwheels. Then he too drove off.

After that, it poured rain for two solid days, during which I continued to sit there on the steps, the wind-driven water slicing through me in sheets. At the start of the storm, I heard an occasional hiss as the rain hit one of the remaining hotspots in the gaping hole behind me, but within minutes all hissing had stopped, and then the only sound was the continual and rapid thudding of large raindrops as they punched through the cooling ashes.

Finally, in the late morning of the third wet day, the sun emerged and began drawing a thick mist from the marsh across the road. It was then that a car pulled up in front of the house, and a heavy-set man stepped out to release a dog from the passenger seat. It took me a few moments to realize that the man was Chef, and the dog, Tigre. In fact I recognized Tigre first, because Chef was dressed completely unlike himself: He wore dress slacks, a button-down shirt, and a tie, and on his pocket he wore a blue pin-on plate that identified him as "Charles," which was his given name. Clearly, Chef the meth cook now had a regular job of some kind, and had entered the straight-and-narrow.

"Good for you, Charles," I said in my ghost voice.

Tigre came right to the steps and ran up and down them and through me and through me, madly jerking his stump of a tail.

"Hey, buddy," I said. "You're looking good. It's so nice to see you." In fact, he had gotten a little smooth for my taste—quite a bit less like the chiseled block of granite he had been under my care and training. He carried a bit of extra padding now. But he looked healthy; that was the important thing. He was alive, and he seemed well fed and happy. I stuck out my hand and passed it over the top of his big, square, devil-horned head every time he swung it within my reach.

After a minute, as Chef stood watching with his mouth slightly ajar, Tigre scrambled off the steps and ran two complete circles around the cellar hole, front yard to back. During his third circuit, I couldn't help saying—again in my inaudible, ghostly voice—"Hit it, boy."

He responded, or seemed to respond, by launching himself into the air and latching onto his tire swing.

"I'll be damned," Chef said.

Tigre hung there, whining; undoubtedly this exercise was harder for him than it used to be. But he also seemed determined not to let his lack of conditioning deter him from fulfilling his life's purpose for a final time.

"Shake it boy," I whispered, "Give her a shake." His groaning whine of unaccustomed exertion shifted to a keen of eagerness as he began dancing in the air and snapping his head from side to side in an attempt to tear out a chunk of steel-reinforced rubber.

"I'll be *damned*," Chef said again. Then he and I both heard a car door open, and when I turned my attention toward the road, I saw Cricket struggling to ease herself from behind the wheel of her father's white Lexus.

"Oh, jeez, Claire," Chef said. He rushed down to the road to help her, and as he awkwardly drew her from the car by her elbow, I saw that she was hugely pregnant. The world stopped spinning.

When I was able to think again, I counted the months and determined that the kid could well be mine. At once I recalled all the many occasions, just before my death and then afterward, when she would refuse to drink, would merely play with her cigarettes, and would take only a token puff of pot. So, it seemed likely she had known about this baby back then—although if that were true, why hadn't she told me?

Of course, there was no guarantee it belonged to me; there had been times when she was out of my sight, sometimes for days at a stretch. I was either a fool or a father-to-be. But, the latter seemed most likely: Even though Cricket enjoyed flirting—was skilled at it, in fact—once she left Chef's futon for my bed, I never got the sense she was seriously tempted to sleep with anyone else.

"Look what they've done to it," Cricket said as she viewed the remains of the house. Then, carrying a bundle of flowers—a much nicer one, containing tulips and irises, than the bouquet of carnations that had decorated the kitchen table on the day of my memorial service—she made her way toward where I sat. Chef moved with her, stretching his arm protectively and a little possessively across the small of her back.

"Did you see him, Claire?" said Chef, lifting his chin in the direction of Tigre, who was still whining, swinging, and squirming in his game attempt to demolish the tire. Cricket looked up and stood staring at my dog.

"Oh my," she said after a moment, with a catch in her throat. "It's like . . . it's like . . . " Then she was sobbing. With the flowers clutched in one of her hands, the other hand grabbing at a fire-warped iron rail, she sank from beneath Chef's arm and settled to her knees in front of the steps. Slowly, like a flower wilting, she bent forward until her forehead rested on the second step only inches from my foot. It was then that I noticed the engagement ring on her hand—the tiniest chip of a diamond set in a modest band.

Shuddering and gasping, for a long time she continued rolling her head against the concrete as Chef hovered helplessly above her, his empty arm hanging in the air. His lips twitched with words that he was unable to speak; in the end, he said nothing and surrendered to his helplessness, letting his arm sink to his side and bending his own face toward the ground.

I reached down and placed my hand on top of Cricket's head—although of course, I could not feel her hair, and she could sense neither my touch, nor even my presence. At last, she pushed herself back to a kneeling position, unwittingly passing my fingers through the top of her skull as she did so. She wiped her face with the back of her wrist and, without looking at Chef, asked him for his handkerchief. After she had scrubbed her face of smeared makeup and tears and had blown her nose, she gave a sigh, set her jaw, and placed the flowers on the bottom step.

"Goodbye," she whispered. Then out loud to Chef: "Help me up."

They stood silently for a minute more, watching Tigre at his exercise. Finally Cricket said, "We need to go before a Blood Eagle rides by and spots us here. And you need to get to work, anyway. Call him; I'll take him home with me."

"Tigger. Down boy," Chef called. But the dog ignored him.

Cricket waited a moment, then she clapped her hands and sang out, "Come on, pal." Still he continued to growl and swing.

But when I said, "Tigre! *Suelta!*" he dropped to the ground and lay there gasping.

"Delayed reaction," Chef joked. "The words have to kind of rattle around in his brain for a while before they fall into the right slots."

"I hope he didn't kill himself there," said Cricket. "Look how exhausted he is. *Let's go, buddy!*" At this, Tigre climbed shakily to his feet and staggered around the foundation into the front yard, the pink necktie of his tongue dripping and yo-yoing.

They all walked to the road together, and Cricket opened the back door of the Lexus so that the dog could crawl inside. Then she turned to Chef and smiled.

She said, "You know what? I've got a psychic feeling."

"You do? What is it?"

"You're gonna sell a car this afternoon. Some lady customer's not going to be able to resist that sweet Alabama accent."

"Oh," said Chef, and laughed. "I hope so. And my boss does, too."

They exchanged a dry little kiss, then Cricket squeezed herself behind the wheel of her dad's car. Just like that, she was gone.

Chef remained a minute longer, surveying the wreckage of our former home, his eyes squinted and his hands on his hips. It was impossible to tell what he might be thinking.

Finally, aloud he said, "Danny Starbird Rivera. *Adiós*, Thumb." After a moment he added, "I'll take care of her. She's my girl now." Then he, too, was gone.

*

*Ben, his urgent tone warning me that he's slipping into full would-*be-rescuer mode, is on me immediately once I've finished dictating this episode. He blurts, "So, Cricket was pregnant! All along, she was pregnant."

YES

"So, dude, weren't you worried? Didn't you see, like, a possible connection between what Angelfish said—about a baby being in danger and the fact that Cricket was going to *have* a baby?"

IM NO STPD B
(I'm not stupid Ben)

"But, like, you weren't worried?"

DUDE I WZ FCKN WORRIED

"So, like, the third time, the *last* time you talked to Angelfish, what did she say? You have to tell me now—you tell me, or I pack up this Ouija board and never touch it again. Did she say any more about the baby?"

NO MO ABT T BBY

(No more about the baby)

"Dude, then what was it?"

ALL SH S WZ KP LKN 4 ME I CN HLP U FND WHO KLD U

(All she said was keep looking for me I can help you find who killed you)

"That's it? That she could help you find your murderer?"

TSIT

(That's it)

"And after that you never talked to her again, there in the dark river or whatever?"

NO

Ben hops up, paces back and forth in the little room, scratches his head with both hands, sits down again. "So you wanna know what I think, dude?"

NO

"I think Angelfish was another one of those messenger ghosts. And I think she was trying to warn you that whoever killed you wants to hurt your kid, too. Doesn't that make sense?"

After a moment I made the planchette skate up to the left corner.

YES

"And even after it's born—I figure it must be born already, isn't that right?—the dude who killed you may still be making bad plans against it. Don't you think so, Thumb?" When he realizes I'm not going to answer, Ben adds, "So dude, you got to do something." *Sure, Ben. But what?*

*

After my house had burned and cooled, and my landlord, my woman, my dog, and the man who passed for my best friend all had come and gone, I frequently found myself stumbling into those distance-warping openings that Professor Shallow liked to call wormholes, and that Gib, who did not care for them, always referred to as "pecker tracks." Usually, I happened across them while I was traveling to one of the handful of places I was able to go—to Muttkowski's farm, for instance, to hear what Fred might say that day to his pigs and his imaginary friends. As I moved along my spirit route, I would unexpectedly crash through a seeming "soft spot" in the space that surrounded me—this felt like a plunge through river ice, though without the feeling of wetness, or cold—and then I would find myself shot headlong to another place, and, occasionally, to a slightly different time.

Just as Virgil had described to me about these experiences, sometimes my destinations made an echo of seeming sense. For example, when I kept ending up at the funerals of strangers, standing shoulder to unknowing shoulder with the bereaved at their gravesides, I imagined that "someone" was trying to teach me a lesson about death that I had not already learned. At first, I guessed that some ghostly duty might be expected of me; perhaps I had been sent to serve as a messenger to the flickering, emergent soul as it rose out of its diseased, broken, or worn-out body. But over the course of a dozen or more burials, and although I often stayed behind after the mourners had all driven away in order to continue my watch even as the cemetery workers lowered the coffin into the dark rectangle of its eternal hole, I never once encountered another ghost, nor even the vaguest hint of an afterlife other than my own.

I sometimes also ended up in graveyards without even a funeral to attend. A number of the cemeteries I visited lay upon abandoned and overgrown farmland hidden deep in the Maine woods, and were themselves buried in alders, burdocks, and wild raspberries; they seemed to have been entirely forgotten. Rather than prayers and quiet weeping, the sounds I would hear in these places were the calls of the crows (*Corvus brachyrhynchos*), and the laughter of woodpeckers. One of these lost resting places haunted me more than all the others because, on some Christmas during the previous several years, a living being had cared enough to make his or her way through the December snow in order to decorate each of two dozen ancient graves with a wreath. Yet, no one had ever come back to recover the wreaths once their greenery had gone brown; nor had they returned to replace them on any subsequent winter solstice. The result was a sad, tree-shaded still life of faded ribbons, bare, twisted wire, and skeletal fir branches that seemed far more suggestive of eternal darkness and hopelessness than ever did the leaning, barely legible, lichen-covered gravestones they had once adorned. It depressed me terribly to look at them.

Whenever I found myself in a cemetery of any sort, I would always call out in the not entirely unreasonable hope of getting an answer from another ghost. I would shout, "Yo," or "Hey, dead people!"—and, not hearing a response, I would add, "Anybody home?" No one ever was.

Whenever I felt I had stayed long enough at one of these mournful destinations, it was usually fairly easy to find the entrance to the wormhole that had taken me there, and then jump through it to the place along my maze where I had first fallen in. But occasionally, the invisible tunnel would have shifted while I was out and about, and when I returned I would find no sign of it. This would force me to drift around for hours, and sometimes for as much as a day or more, searching either for that wormhole opening or for a ghost path that would allow me to return home. If I found neither, my only option was to wait until I grew so weak that the underground river sucked me back to send me for a tumbling swim. Then, the next time the river spit me out again, I'd find myself hanging in midair just above the gaping foundation to my former house, rested and ready for another dark adventure.

Eventually I began dropping into the scenes of other people's final moments—in hospitals and hospices, and once in a materni-ty-ward delivery room. Another time I fell onto a battlefield where fresh blood soaked dirt that was already red, and I said to myself, *I must be closing in on the climax of it all; something important is about to be revealed to me.* But I was wrong, just as I had been wrong so many times before. In total, I saw perhaps two dozen people draw their final breath, and at no time was I any more aware of a newly freed spirit on the move than were the awe- and grief-struck mortals who often witnessed them with me. I might as well have been alive, for all the good death did me.

One night a wormhole spilled me out beside a steel-railed hospital bed, parked in the center of a suburban living room, in which a grievously thin and pale old man, wearing nothing but a diaper, and surrounded by his wife and three grown sons, gave a soft rattle, and passed away. The family, all of them dressed in sleeping-clothes, their hair in scribbles and their eyes sunken with sleeplessness, retreated from him after a minute or two—not out of fear, but as if to give him his privacy.

I felt like an intruder here but, as a helpless ghost, there was nowhere I could go. I was able to do nothing in the middle of that death-dark evening except stay and watch as the three unshaven men, the oldest of whom might have been in his late thirties, assembled a number of dusty liquor bottles and a case of warm beer and began to drink. Within a short while, they were laughing about something the dead man had once said to one of them.

The mother, meanwhile, sat at a kitchen table mounded over with piles of official-looking papers, with stacks of ragged envelopes containing still more papers, and with plastic tubs full of prescription medication containers. Following a long moment of perfect, unblinking stillness, she lit a cigarette. She took a few sharp puffs, practically spitting out the smoke, after which she shoved away some of the papers to make room on the table for an old-fashioned rotary telephone, which she slammed into place and began using to make calls, one after the other.

"Hello," she would say, in her hoarse voice. "It's Elizabeth. I'm sorry to tell you, but Tom's gone. Just a few minutes ago." There would be a pause, during which she listened and smoked with a trembling hand and a tormented expression that edged toward impatience, and then she would say, "Yes, thank you." Another pause, and: "No, that's all right. My boys are here, so I'm okay for now, but thank you anyway. All right. All right, then. I will. Good-bye." Then she would take a puff of the cigarette, fire angry smoke from her nostrils, and climb the same steep hill all over again.

A heavyset nurse with a Slavic accent eventually arrived and spent a minute hovering over the corpse in the near-darkness of the living room. Her final ministration was to press his eyes closed and cover him to his neck with a sheet. After that, she moved to the harsh brightness of the kitchen where she hugged the mother, filled out some paperwork that she had pulled from a briefcase, and downed, in three gulps, a jelly glass half-full of vodka that one of the boys had handed her. She hugged the mother a second time before heading out into the night again.

An hour after the nurse had gone, two sleepy-looking men carrying a wheeled stretcher arrived at the front door. That was when the sons halted their laughter and their conversation and silently gathered in the living room to observe as the stretcher was telescoped into a rolling table, and their father, after being settled into the dark cocoon of a heavy vinyl bag, was lifted from the hospital bed and gently placed on top of it. The bag's zipper, closing, was as final a sound as I had ever heard.

They wheeled him out into the night, and the front door thumped shut. The sons exchanged glances before turning their eyes in different directions.

Not long afterward, the mother, having finished her phone calls, stubbed out her final cigarette, hugged each one of her sons, and walked into her first-floor bedroom, where she closed herself inside. For a time after that, the three men tried to resume their party, but an edge of desperation had crept into their mood; much of the humor now seemed forced, and the laughter hollow. Then a sort of collapse—a sudden, palpable, and irresistible weariness—set in, and first the eldest brother excused himself and retired to an upstairs bedroom, then the middle brother, after first making a terse, choked telephone call to a wife or girlfriend, went upstairs as well.

That left the youngest son, a man of about my age who, carrying a glass of bourbon, began wandering the empty first floor of the house from room to room, his exhausted eyes blazing feverishly and his mouth slightly agape, as if he were astonished by all he had experienced during the past several days. His gaze traveled up and down the walls; he stared hard at everything, seemingly trying to fix this moment and this place in his mind forever. At one point, in the room where his father had died, he stopped before a framed watercolor of a wooded mountain landscape. After a second or two, he nodded, and his hand rose and rested against the side of his face.

"*Yes*. That's *just* what it's like," he whispered to himself. "It's like watching . . . the tallest tree fall over in the forest." Then, as if he'd scared himself with the sound of his own voice, he stepped quickly away, paused to take a deep gulp of his bourbon, and resumed his solemn march around the house.

A short time later he and I both began to notice the moths. He stopped to look at a white moth that clung to a hallway wall, and then we spotted several more moths circling the kitchen light fixture. There were many airborne moths in the bathroom and, when we returned to the living room, there were three or four of them fluttering on the sheets of the empty hospital bed, apparently having appeared from nowhere.

The son broke into a smile that was at once goofy and wise. He threw wide the front door, set down his glass of whiskey and, traveling the house, he started gathering moths in his cupped hands one by one and carrying them to the door, where he released them into the night. He stood in the doorway as each one flew off, watching wide-eyed until he could see it no longer, and then he would turn and hunt for another.

When the son had allowed the final moth to flutter off his fingertips, I was at once struck by the anxious feeling, bordering on panic, that I was being left behind. They were on their way somewhere, all of them, and perhaps it was someplace that I also needed to go. This last moth ascended to the height of the rooftop; I was sure the dead man's son could no longer see it even though he seemed to imagine that he could. I, in spite of my ghostly nighttime vision, was also in danger of losing sight of it.

Finally, as the moth continued toward the stars through the moonless sky, I could no longer hold myself back and I flew off in yearning pursuit. Up we went, the moth and I together. At one point, she paused and circled back for a moment, seeming to look me over, before continuing her spiraling rise. We moved ever higher above the lights and the streets and the endless clusters of buildings, and the moth began to look larger than she had in the house, at the same time taking on an almost magical luminosity whose intensity increased with altitude. I was certain she and I were headed somewhere important, and I was overflowing with excitement and awe. It was at that point that the air around us became filled with a delicate clicking that I imagined might be the wing-beats of angels.

I saw the first bat out ahead of us; it was a little brown bat (*Myotis lucifugus*), and it rapidly snapped its wings as it zig-zagged through the sky. Before I could react, a second bat sliced right through me, entering at the soles of my feet and passing through my nonexistent stomach, chest, and throat without even suspecting I was there. She emerged from my face—from the near dead-center of my gaping mouth—and, with an audible crunch, she crushed that glowing moth between her needlepoint teeth. Without a pause, she twisted, and quickly dove away.

*

After witnessing all that, I found that I no longer looked forward to wormholes and the places they took me to. I began to agree with Gib that a wormhole adventure rarely was worth the anxiety it caused and that for the most part it was best for a ghost to avoid them when he could. Eventually, after much trial and error, I learned how to detect a looming wormhole before it could grab me—but the skill came too late to spare me from an experience that added a new possibility to the story of my murder.

I was headed to Fred's farm when I sensed a hungry wormhole lying just ahead—though by the time I realized it I'd gone a step too far and was already falling in. I flailed and fell and then I found myself in a tight, dust-choked attic room where my old housemate, Dirt, white as a ghost, lay unmoving with his back against the thin, bare mattress of a narrow cot. Close by I heard the thump of a door followed by the sound of boots descending a wooden staircase—someone was leaving the room just as I arrived—but Dirt looked so ghastly that I didn't want to take my attention from him in order to investigate.

Wearing nothing but a pair of filthy jeans, he sprawled with one bare foot against the floor and one arm hanging stiffly over the edge of the cot, a wobbling syringe sticking from just below the inside bend of his elbow. He was gazing toward the ceiling with unfocused, unblinking, half-lidded eyes, and above his blue-tinged lips the hovering dust swirled with his breath, but just barely. In his mouth, half open and leaking a goatee of grayish foam, I could see the dark space from which I'd knocked out his tooth; I also could see that, true to his prediction when he'd bitched to my mother, his other front tooth had also died and darkened. On the floor not far from his foot lay a dirty spoon, a lighter, an empty glassine bag, a couple of tufts of grayish cotton—that sorry still life of loserdom.

Below the room somewhere, I heard a motorcycle roar to life, and it was then I realized it might be important to my own investigation to know who had been there. I concentrated and peered down through the wall—we were at the top of an old, three-story house that stood along some city street—and I saw a Harley pull away from the curb and go thundering up the road. The rider's hair was hidden beneath a baseball cap turned backward, and rather than a cut with patches he wore a plain leather jacket; he could have been almost anyone. Then he zoomed over a hill and was gone. I returned my alarmed attention to Dirt, whose breathing now stirred the dust with even less force than before. I suddenly found myself pitying him almost as much as I'd disliked him when I was alive; it occurred to me that with some better friends—people who felt concern rather than contempt—he might have stood a chance. It was also possible I myself might not have died if I'd treated him with a little more respect.

"Dirt," I said. "Snap out of it, dude." There was nothing I could do for him, and within two minutes, though his eyes remained open, he disturbed the dust not at all. I waited without much hope to see if the spark of a ghost would come out of him, but his death was as ordinary and as seemingly final as all the others I'd seen.

Finally I said, "Well then, what the hell. Rest in peace." But I had no idea whether he really would—or whether he deserved to.

*

Of course Ben—non-hero and the world's worst detective—has a theory about Dirt's death, which he insists on sharing with me. After scribbling down his version of my account he declares, "So this means we can rule out Dirt as the dude who killed you and is threatening your kid."

NO IT DNT

"Don't you get it, Thumb? He was murdered because he knew who *your* murderer was. The dude on the bike—*that's* the dude you're looking for. Too bad you weren't smart enough to pay more attention when he was running down those stairs—use your x-ray vision to see who he was. I bet he killed Dirt to make sure he wouldn't talk."

HUGE LEAP NO PRF DRT WZ EVN MRDRD
(Huge leap no proof Dirt was even murdered)

"What do you mean, no proof? They shot Dirt up with some bad dope; they OD'd him on purpose. Why else would the dude run off and leave him there like that while he was still alive?"

BCS SCRD HPNS W DRUGGIES ALL T TME
(Because scared happens with druggies all the time)

Of course murder *is* a strong possibility—although even if someone did snuff Dirt, that wouldn't necessarily mean there was a connection to me. After all, lots of people, for a lot of different reasons, might want to kill a dude like him. In any case, none of this is anything I feel like debating with Ben. I just need him to keep writing while I figure it all out.

CHAPTER 10

So, Mantis had risen rapidly in the Blood Eagles organization and been made a full-patch member—one whose cut advertised the fact that he had "taken care of business" for the club. Chef, for his part, had apparently turned his life on a dime to become a respectable car salesman and was engaged to my woman—a dentist's daughter—and to all appearances was prepared to raise my unborn child as his own. Meanwhile, Dirt, who had real reason to hate me, in the wake of my death had tumbled deeper into drugs, and was himself now dead—possibly a victim of murder. I was sure that one of them had stood behind me on the day I died, and I believed there were clues, if not complete answers, at the scene of my death inside the Blood Eagles' haunted mansion on the south shore of the wide river-mouth that divided the City of Riverside. But hard as I tried, there seemed no way I could cross that tidal flow; in the sky above the college, each time I came across a new path through the spirit maze, it always led either to the North or to the East, with no openings to the South or West.

When I at last returned to the abandoned church, it was after being away for what must have been several weeks. In the meantime, summer had started and I often found myself thinking about Cricket and the baby to whom she had doubtlessly given birth. I wished I could know whether we'd had a boy or a girl, and what she had named it—and based on what Angelfish had told me, I desperately hoped it was safe. I came in upon Gib and Virgil playing imaginary chess as they hovered above their cocktail napkin; they seemed happy to see me, though not particularly surprised. In addition to my two friends, I noticed another ghost—a severe-looking gray-haired woman who was sitting quietly at the end of a pew a short distance away.

"Boo!" Gib boomed in greeting as soon as I appeared.

"Boo to you," I said.

Professor Shallow looked up and said, "There's the wandering soul. I bet you have some stories to tell."

"Oh," I told him. "Such sights I have seen."

Gib drifted over and insisted on giving me one of his angel's handshakes, which involved blending our illusory hands together. He then tried to hug me, which made a big, Gib-sized blur out of the two of us; it looked as if he had gulped me whole like a python with a pocket gopher.

"Thumb's been pecker-trackin' it," Gib said, and laughed.

"That I have."

"Well, we want to hear all about it, but first, I need to finish beating the professor's pants off, here."

"Be careful what you wish for," Virgil warned him. Then he lifted his chin in the direction of the new ghost. "By the way, that's Alice there. You two need to get acquainted. Alice, Thumb." Following this surprisingly informal, almost rude, introduction, Virgil and Gib returned to their game.

I went over to the woman and said, "My mother named me Danny. But Thumb is what I go by."

"I'm Alice Poe-York," she told me, without smiling. "I'm from Cairo, not far from here."

"I've been to Cairo," I said. In fact, one of Chef's and my best distributors lived in that town. Alice pronounced it "Kay-ro," as did all the town's natives.

"Born there. Grew up there. Spent *all* of my life there."

"I always enjoyed it. In Cairo."

"I was the head librarian in town for twenty-six years. My husband and I raised two girls in town. Now both of them have their own children, and one of them even lives in Cairo, right on the same road we do. She and her two little boys, Zack and Carl."

"Oh, nice," I said. "Have you been able to see them at all since you, uh, *passed*?" From the way Virgil and Gib looked at me then, I knew that this was the worst question I could have asked. Alice Poe-York's eyes narrowed to slits and her lower lip began to quiver.

"No!" she said. "I haven't! I can't reach them. And it just is not fair."

"It doesn't seem fair," I agreed. "A lot of this afterlife stuff. And you're never quite sure who or what to be angry at, or whether you even have a right to be angry in the first place."

"Oh, I have a *right* to be angry. And I know who to be angry at, too." As she said this, she was staring at the two chess players as if they were the ones at fault.

Gib and Virgil ignored her; they focused on their cocktail napkin, and after a moment Virgil said, "I suppose I'll have to take the knight."

"It's your funeral," Gib responded.

Alice kept glaring at them until at last she blurted, "The fat one there told me I shouldn't even *try* to visit them. That I should just give up on seeing my grandsons and my daughter and my husband *ever again*. Can you imagine?"

Gib looked up then, smiled at her, and in as mild a voice as he could manage he said, "It was *advice*, Alice. You're free to take it or leave it. In any case, I meant no harm or disrespect by it."

Alice aimed a finger at Virgil. "And the black man there is an egomaniac. He thinks my family and I are nothing but a dream he's having."

Virgil looked at Gib. "Did she just refer to me as 'the black man?'"

"Yes she did," Gib confirmed.

"Why, what did I say that was wrong?" Alice asked in a tone of offended astonishment. "Isn't that what you people call *yourselves*?"

Virgil met my gaze and gave me a rueful smile. "I've changed my mind," he said. "I agree with Thumb now—and with Sartre, too, come to think of it: We *are* in hell."

Gib said, "Alice is just upset. She's lost a great deal—as we all have, of course—and she hasn't yet gotten used to the afterlife. We need to be compassionate."

"Oh, be quiet, Fat Man!" Alice said. "You don't know *anything*."

"I know that God loves you, Alice," answered Gib. Then he returned his attention to his cocktail-napkin chessboard.

"That's a lie too!" said Alice. "I was a regular church-goer, and I used to think that way myself. But all I need to do is look around me here to know it isn't true."

Gib, still focusing on his game, said, "Maybe you need to look with a different set of eyes."

"Maybe *you* need to shut up, as I asked you to do."

"I'm shutting it," Gib said. Still without looking up, he lifted his holographic hand to draw an imaginary zipper across his non-existent mouth. He then mimed the turning of a lock, and the tossing away of an invisible key. He and Virgil laughed.

To my horror, Alice returned her attention to me. She was quivering her lip again. "I'm only fifty-five years old," she said.

"That is kind of young," I agreed. "But look at me; I'm only twenty-two. I won't be twenty-three until August, whenever that is."

"But I didn't *deserve* to die," she protested. "I had cancer. I was even in remission at one point. I *fought* as hard as I could; I did everything they told me to do; it just wasn't fair!"

"I'm sorry," I said. "But I don't think any of us deserved to die. It's just what happens, sooner or later. And, the professor there was only sixty."

"I was fifty-nine," Virgil said.

"Your obituary said sixty, Virgil."

"*Fifty*-nine," he insisted. "There was no obituary, and, in any case, I'm reasonably certain I can remember how old I am."

Alice said, "No matter how old he was, he died doing something stupid—driving like a bat out of hell on an icy, winding road."

Virgil and Gib looked at one another. Virgil said, "The black man got his just deserts." They laughed again.

"What a couple of hyenas!" Alice said. She looked at me and added, "And you, for your part—you did something stupid, too."

"I sure did," I agreed. "A *bunch* of things, each one stupider than the one that came before. In fact, the word stupid falls way short in most cases. But still I didn't deserve to die." Then I said to Virgil and Gib, "I think you two have been talking about me behind my back."

"We're sorry, Thumb," said Gib. "We had no idea what it would lead to." At this, there was a fresh outburst of laughter from them.

Alice was relentless. She told me, "And I can tell, just from looking at you, the kind of life you must have led. For instance, how many trusting young women did you bamboozle, just to get your way?"

"Checkmate!" Gib yelled. "Time to tell us about those pecker tracks, Thumb."

"At last," I told him. As I was rising to go over to them, I said to Alice, "The answer is, all of them. In different ways, I bamboozled every single one of them. And I feel terrible about it."

*

I didn't need to go into a ton of detail about my house burning down: Virgil had been there, had seen for himself, and had reported back to Gib. He told me, "That seems to be what happens to abandoned buildings these days. Kids and social misfits have nothing better to do. But I wasn't worried about you, Thumb; I knew it was about time for you to be out traveling, and that we would see you soon enough."

"And here you are," Gib said, with unmistakable fondness in his voice. It occurred to me then that they had become like a couple of uncles to me—and this was something I valued a lot, since I'd had no dependable men around me when I was growing up. I was the product of women who were suspicious of, and even feared, what I would become.

Nor, in my story of the fire's aftermath, did I tell them how helpless and depressed I had felt. Instead, I skipped ahead to the visit by Cricket, Chef, and Tigre, and I told how they had left their flowers and then moved on to avoid being spotted by a Blood Eagle riding by. I also told them about every one of the graveyards and deathbeds and other places I had visited. Once, Gib interrupted me to say, "She's gone, thank God." I saw then that Alice, apparently tired of being ignored, had slipped out of the church without saying goodbye.

"She'll be back," said Virgil. "It's too bad; when I first met her, she seemed like she'd be a good addition to our group. She was smart and well read. But a bitter ghost is bad company."

Gib asked him, "So, if this is all your dream, why did you dream Alice up in the first place?"

"I suppose you always have control of *your* dreams?"

"Point there, professor," said Gib after thinking about it for a moment. "Except, I don't dream anymore; I'm a spirit. I guess I sort of miss it, too." Then he looked at me. "Sorry, Thumb. I just needed to point that out to the prof. So you were saying, the kid was scooping up moths and making them fly...."

I wrapped it all up by telling them about finding Dirt with the dirty needle in his arm, dying silently in an attic. When I was finished, Gib made a whistling sound. Unexpectedly he said, "The guy who they got to shoot you. It was your friend, Chef, the meth cook."

"You think *Chef* shot me?"

"He had more reason than anybody. You stole his woman; he wanted her back. Not only did he love her, but because he was nothing but white trash and her parents were well off, she was his golden ticket to a life that didn't have jail or an early death in its future."

"Gib, I'm surprised at you. I thought you disapproved of my dwelling much on the subject of who my killer was. You told me to forgive and let it go."

"But you're dwelling on it *anyway*," Gib pointed out. "So I might as well help you with it. Plus, Virgil keeps telling me you're writing a book about it all, and that's got my interest going. I've always wanted to write a murder mystery myself."

"Chef, the meth cook!" Virgil said suddenly, with unusual enthusiasm. "It's *Hamlet*, don't you see? With Thumb as the *ghost*! Could it fall together more perfectly?"

I didn't mind being cast as the ghost in Hamlet—I *was* a ghost, after all—but I didn't like the idea of my kid as a madman or mad-woman, wasting his or her precious life on avenging my stupid death, so I decided to ignore him. I said to Gib, "The thing about Chef is that of the three of them, he's the one I would say who doesn't have it in him to kill *anybody*."

"I've been through a war," said Gib. "We *all* have it in us. We just need the reason."

"I'm still leaning toward Dirt," I said. "It would be like him to shoot somebody from behind. He sure wouldn't have wanted to look into my eyes while he did it. But then there's the ITCOB patch I saw on Mantis's cut. He had a thing for Cricket, too, you know; for a while, it seemed like they were going to get together, after I was out of the picture. And speaking of golden tickets, Mantis really wanted a ticket back into a one-percenter club. Now he's there."

Gib looked at Virgil. "So, Professor, who do *you* think killed Cock Robin? If you really like the meth cook for this murder, that makes two of us."

"It's not that I *like* him—or anyone, for that matter," said Virgil, who now seemed annoyed. "I really am not at all interested in the whole whodunit angle; I was just pointing out a plot similarity. If you must have my opinion, it could still be that the killer was none of the three; my soundest idea is that the evil biker fellow said what he did to Thumb because he's a sick person and because he wanted to add another dollop of anguish to Thumb's final moments. But it hardly matters now; knowing won't bring Thumb back." Virgil added, almost to himself, "And, what am I even talking about anyway? It's not like Thumb is anywhere to come back from to begin with. As for the book he's writing, this is all a cliché, you know. The story of the ghost seeking its own killer."

"*Is* it a cliché?" I was both curious and worried. "Did you read a lot of mysteries when you were alive? Were they part of your curriculum?"

"Certainly not," Virgil answered in an offended tone. "But I have a strong sense of what's out there in the world of literature. And your idea has been done before."

Gib said, "I thought *everything* had been done before."

"You're right about that," Virgil told him. "But, some done more than others—with some done better, some done worse, some done to death. All there really is now in literature is borrowing and rearranging. That's why I myself finally gave up on my own youthful ambition of writing fiction."

"Well," I said. "I'm not really writing a book. That's just your fantasy, Virgil. For one thing, I've got no way of writing one even if I wanted to. But just like you, I'm kind of a snob, so even if I did write a novel, it wouldn't be a mystery."

After sitting silently for a few moments, Gib said, "You guys *are* a couple of snobs. What the hell is wrong with a good mystery?"

*

The next time I returned to the church, Alice seemed to have been waiting for me. While I was talking to Virgil and Gib she interrupted us and said, "I've decided you're not such a bad young man. Not like these two, anyway. If you would like, I'll show you the few paths I've found for moving about this part of our state."

Gib looked up from the chess napkin and said, "I think that's her way of asking you on a date."

"Be quiet, you big lump!" Gib and Virgil snickered like a couple of boys.

"Do you know how to get across the river?" I asked. "I mean the above-ground one?"

"No," she said. "And no interest in doing so. I go back and forth to Cairo; that's about all. But, once in Cairo, I can travel widely. There's only one small corner of town I've been unable to reach."

I said, "Well, it's possible that route might be useful to me some day. Besides, I'm dead; what else have I got to do? Let's go." We set out on our midsummer, midday hike to Cairo. For some reason, as we traveled I suddenly made up my mind to confide in her my story about Cricket and the son or daughter I likely would never see. After I'd talked she seemed to further soften her attitude toward me, and she told me more about her own family. They all did sound like awesome people; if I'd known them, I no doubt would have resented being torn from them myself.

She also told me that she did not care at all for Professor Shallow, who she complained "thought a great deal of himself." But she especially hated Gib because of the fact that he was constantly "preaching his religion" at her. "I'm done with all that nonsense," she said. "He would be too, if only he'd quit being such a Pollyanna and take off those rose-colored glasses."

"Could it be that all of this ghost stuff is a test for us?" I asked.

"*Life* was the test." Alice said bitterly. "*Cancer* was the test. I passed them both. Now give me my damn diploma already!"

We traveled through woods, across fields and swamps, and along a weed-choked stretch of abandoned railroad track, moving mostly at ground level, but sometimes also levitating above the tops of the trees. Before long we ended up in the small but sprawling town of Cairo. Alice pointed out the white-clapboarded library where she had worked, as well as the hospice only a short distance from the library where she had ended her days. Her entryway to and from the underground river lay just inside the after-hours mail slot at the front of the brick post office building, which stood about halfway between the library and the hospice. As she was leading me past the little supermarket where in life she'd done most of her shopping, I asked, "Don't you ever see your family here? Or walking around town? It seems like all you'd have to do is stake one of these places out. Somebody would have to come by, sooner or later."

"I'm not stupid!" Alice replied. "Don't think I haven't thought of that. But none of them is ever here when I am, and vice-versa. It's like an infernal conspiracy."

"Wow," I said.

"Wow, indeed," she agreed. "And yet, the Fat Man thinks we're in paradise. Here, come with me; I want to show you something."

Alice lifted off her feet and started to fly, and I followed her. She finally settled to the ground at the top of a ridge where a narrow road plunged into a wooded valley. "We can't go any farther than this—at least, I haven't been able to find a way to do so. But, you can just make out the top of the chimney from here. Do you see it? You have to use your special vision to look through the trees, but when you do, you'll notice the red chimney poking up from behind a little hill."

Just then a black pickup truck whooshed right through us going downhill at about fifty miles an hour. When we saw the backs of the people's heads through the rear windshield I asked, "Do you know those dudes? They could be neighbors of yours."

"I don't know; I might. But they're not my family, so what does it matter? Anyway, the chimney. Have you spotted it?"

"Yes, I see it. It looks like a nice one."

She lifted her hand and pointed. "Well, that's my daughter's house." Her hand rolled forward and she added, "Two houses north of it is *my* house—mine and my husband's."

"Oh," I replied, because I could think of nothing else to say.

"Down there, for me, is the Promised Land," said Alice Poe-York. "I don't need anything else. I don't *want* anything else. No heaven in the sky will ever compare to it."

*

When I next went to the church, it was two days after my trip to Cairo with Alice. A ghost—a thin chick with plastic-framed glasses and a long, horse-like face—was standing by the double doors as I drifted through them. When I said hi and told her my name she only nodded and gave me a weird smirk. I went over to the pew where Virgil and Gib were sitting, thinking they might introduce us. But Virgil only looked up and said, "Thumb! How's the novel coming?" Gib watched me, grinning, to see what I would say.

"I think I've told you I'm not writing a novel."

Virgil shrugged. "If I believed you, I would say good for you. As an art form, it's moribund anyway; why waste your time, even if you have eternity?"

I tilted my head toward the front doors. "Who's the new dude?"

Gib answered, "Take another gander at 'the new dude,' Thumb." I looked, and after a moment, I realized it was Alice. She'd made herself about thirty years younger.

"Alice!" I said. "You look . . . good."

"Thank you, Thumb," she said, not bothering to conceal the skepticism in her voice.

"It'll take some getting used to, though."

"That's not my problem," she replied.

After that, Alice—her behavior along with her appearance—became erratic. The next time I saw her, she'd transformed into someone completely different—a slightly plump but still paralyzingly beautiful and somehow familiar young woman who Virgil and Gib reminded me was the actress, Marilyn Monroe. She was wearing a dress, and as she walked around the church, she kept making the skirt flutter skyward as if a strong breeze were coming up from beneath her. Virgil and Gib both thought this was hilarious—Virgil, especially, kept laughing about it—but the disguised Alice did not crack a smile.

The following day, there was another "new" ghost—a man in a wide-lapelled, long-out-of-fashion business suit who somehow also looked familiar.

"I'm Thumb," I said.

"I know who you are," the man said in Alice's voice.

Both Virgil and Gib were irritated by this latest transformation.

"Please, Alice," said Virgil at one point. "This gender switching. It's just very disconcerting."

Alice said, "Aren't you the one who's always telling us we're needlessly attached to mortal ways of doing things?"

"Yes, but there are limits to everything."

Gib suggested, "Why don't you just go back to being Marilyn Monroe?"

"Fat chance, Fatso."

Then Alice changed her avatar yet again. One night a large, blue-and-white plastic beach ball bounced soundlessly through the front doors and hovered, slowly rotating, above Gib and Virgil as they played chess. The ball was complete in detail down to its little blue air valve.

"Alice?" said Virgil, with dread in his voice.

"Yes, it's me," she said.

Virgil sat back in his pew. "Well, this, finally, is too much. I think we've got an agreement among us here at the church that we are to at least maintain a human form."

"I never entered into any such agreement."

"Come on, Alice," said Gib. "Things are hard enough around here."

"But you keep saying we're in heaven," Alice reminded him. "So, just make believe this is what an angel looks like. In fact for all we know, it is."

Both Virgil and Gib continued to be disturbed and seemed ready to go on arguing with her, but I knew it wouldn't do them any good. I decided I should try to mediate.

"Why a beach ball, Alice?" I asked.

"The last really good time I had with my grandchildren was when I took them to Popham Beach. We were playing in the water with a beach ball and having a wonderful time, when suddenly the wind took that ball out past where I could swim to get it back, ill as I was by then. The children were upset and I tried to distract them, but every time they looked up and saw that ball growing smaller and farther away, they knew that it would soon be gone for good, and they cried."

Alice added, "It's probably still out there somewhere, riding across the ocean. Maybe it will ride forever."

I said, "That makes some sense. But, will you go back to being Alice again, sometime?"

"I *am* Alice," she said. "This is me, now. And it's the most comfortable I've felt since I've been dead. As the young people say, deal with it."

Alice stayed a beach ball for the rest of the time we knew her, which was not for very long. One evening, not many days after she had gone spherical on us—it was by then late enough in summer that crickets chirped in the grass both morning and night—I arrived at the church to find the other three ghosts examining the high wall at the back of the chancel above the former choir box, where the entire space all the way to the ceiling had been turned into a mural of elaborate, multi-hued graffiti. As soon as I joined them, Virgil told me, "They pulled the plywood off of one of the back windows, and then smashed in the window. There is broken glass and splintered wood all over the floor of the minister's office. After they left, they replaced the plywood so that no one from the outside would know they'd been here."

"Were any of you around when they came?"

Gib and Virgil shook their heads, while round Alice wobbled. Gib said, "I guess it was bound to happen sooner or later. The building's abandoned, after all."

"And, now that they've gotten in, they're almost certain to come again," said Virgil.

When I looked more closely at the graffiti, I saw, at the center of those maze-like whorls of pigment, something that in life would have turned my blood to ice. "We're screwed," I said.

"What is it?" the three of them asked at once.

"Right there, you see—all the rest serves as camouflage for it— you can read the name 'Ed.'"

Virgil asked, "Is Ed one of your former associates? Some gang member?"

"I'm pretty sure that's the bastard who burned my house down. He and some other people broke in and tagged my walls with spray paint and marking pen. Then the next time they came around, they torched the place. I got home to find myself haunting a pile of ashes."

"Oh, no," Virgil said.

"Oh, shit," said Gib. "So that means . . . "

Alice, now spinning so fast that she had become a baby-blue blur, interrupted him. "We shouldn't have to stand for it. There must be something we can do."

"And what might that be?" Gib asked her. "We're dead. Remember?" Then he turned to Virgil, and with sarcasm he said, "Here's your chance, Professor. If all this really is your dream, I think you ought to change it. Make shithead Ed go away for good."

"The subconscious mind doesn't work that way. In any case, we've already discussed this several times and I keep telling you, it's not exactly a *dream* I'm having; it's a hallucination, and within that hallucination, I am just as dead, and just as powerless, as you are. I control nothing but my own actions.

"And, by the way, Gib—while we're mocking one another's beliefs—if this really is your heaven, why don't you just ask God to intervene? It'd be a fairly small favor, as those things go. After all, it's not just any abandoned building they're vandalizing—it's a *church*."

Gib answered, "Well, there's certainly nothing to stop me from praying for help. But God doesn't work that way, either."

As I studied Ed's mural, I said, "It could be that we still have some time. Sure, my place burned right after Ed signed his name in a few spots. But by the time he started tagging there, every wall and most of the ceiling had been tagged by somebody else, and he had no more room left to work. This place still is almost untouched, though, and what he's done here already may only be a start."

"There *is* a lot of wall space in here," Gib said, hope creeping into his voice. "This place could end up being an entire Sistine Chapel for an asshole like that. It could take him months to fill it all—and, by then, maybe he'll get caught and arrested. Or, at the least, we'll have had time to find ourselves another building."

"We shouldn't *have* to find another building," said twirling Alice, in her low librarian's growl. "This one is ours. We've made something of a home here."

"Nothing's ours anymore," said Virgil. "Our houses will always be haunted by the living."

At this, Alice stopped spinning and hovered for a moment, unmoving except for a silent and volatile-seeming vibration. Finally, she said, "*Phooey!*" and suddenly shot skyward, passing right through the ceiling.

*

After dark that night, Ed and company came around again. The four of us heard their car approaching on the rutted gravel road and watched the rise and fall of their headlights for a long time before they arrived. They parked toward the back of the cemetery where their vehicle would be difficult to spot from the road, and they pried the plywood from the broken window. Then, hauling knapsacks and shining flashlights, they came crawling into our sanctuary. There were three of them: A muscular, shirtless dude with a black beard and a ring in his nose like a bull, and two girls. One of the chicks was tall and slender, dressed all in black—black jeans, t-shirt, and high-top sneakers—with straight, dark hair cut and combed so that it covered her face like a lampshade. A narrow gap exposed a strip of pale skin, a single blue eye heavily underscored with eyeliner, and one side of her full lips, which gleamed with red gloss. The color of her fingernails matched her mouth. The other chick wore overalls and was shaped like a cinderblock. On her head perched a Red Sox baseball cap turned backward, and both of her bare forearms were sleeved in elaborate tattoos.

Gib was standing by to greet them as one by one they squeezed through the window and thumped to the floor. "Boo," he said to each of them in his best ghostly voice—but they only swept past him to set their knapsacks on a front pew. The woman in the baseball cap began aiming a flashlight into one of the bags as she dug through it in search of marking pens and cans of paint, and I realized with a shock that *this* was Ed; somehow, it had never occurred to me that the person who had done me so much harm would turn out to be a girl. While Ed prepared for her night's work, Cyclops Girl and the Minotaur dipped into their own knapsacks to produce a pair of powerful electric lanterns, which they switched on and set on the front corners of the chancel.

"It's like a stage!" Cyclops Girl cried out, her shrill voice echoing in the empty church. The other two shushed her, and she did not speak again. Working by the light of the nearest lantern, Ed attacked a strip of white wall between two plywood-covered windows with a set of marking pens.

"Oh, yeah," Gib said in a satisfied voice as he watched her. "She's got plenty of space to cover. And I don't see anything dangerous in those knapsacks, not even a lighter or a pack of matches. I don't guess we've got much to worry about for a while. By the way, Thumb, I thought you said Ed was a fellow?"

"Still," said Alice, before I could answer. "They have no business here. They're a bunch of nasty vandals."

"Some people would consider Ed to be an artist," said Virgil. "She clearly is very serious about what she does. I actually find some merit in her work."

"Yes, a *great* artist," Alice said with sarcasm. "A real Georgia O'Keefe. And I suppose you consider arson to be an art form, too."

As Ed's markers squealed against the wall, the other two intruders uncorked a bottle of wine, kicked off their shoes, and began skipping around the church in their bare feet. By the time the wine was finished and they'd opened another bottle, they were giggling, snapping photos of each other with their cell phones, and chasing one another through the rows of pews like a couple of kids. Eventually they ended up on the chancel, laughing, tongue-wrestling, pulling off one another's clothes, and tumbling to the floor in a sexual tangle. Both Virgil and Alice made exclamations of disgust and retreated to the front of the church. But Gib surprised me by sitting down next to their knapsacks to watch them. After I had settled in beside him, he glanced at me and said, "Young." Then he returned his gaze to the chancel.

I said, "This doesn't bother you? The location of it, anyway? A church, and all?"

Gib shrugged. "It's really just a building, Thumb. Wood and nails like any other."

A few moments later I said, "She's a little small. Up top. For my taste." As I spoke, I was aware that, speaking with a younger dude—or a younger ghost—I would have chosen different words.

Gib said, "They're all beautiful to me. That set there—I'd cry right now, if I could." At that, he blew Cyclops Girl a ghostly little kiss; afterward, his hand remained in the air. A moment later, the hand rose to his forehead.

"Speaking of proportions, will you get a load of *that*! That widget's about as large as they come—and as a former Army medic, I speak with some authority."

"Lengthwise, you mean? Because, for all that, it's a fairly narrow utensil."

Gib looked at me and grinned. "You're telling me you're a bit more girthy?"

I didn't speak for a long moment. Finally, I said, "Like a beer can—and it has been ever since I died." Gib laughed in appreciation.

Hearing him, Alice called out, "Gib, you're nothing but a filthy old man and a religious hypocrite!"

But Gib continued to smile. Then he winked at me and yelled back, "Why pick on me? What about Thumb, here?"

"Thumb is not always going on about religion the way you are. And he's young; that's almost to be expected of him. But then again, my son-in-law . . ."

"God invented sex," Gib informed her. "In *all* its remarkable variety. And Thumb is just as dead as I am. *And*, don't kid yourself; if your son-in-law is a man, he would be sitting right up here with us." Then, in a lower voice, he added, "Or at least, he would be unless Alice was haunting him from the other end of the room."

It was then that Ed stepped up onto the chancel and began tugging off her work boots and unsnapping her heavy overalls so that they collapsed to the floor. She sank down and joined the other two, with a seemingly powerful preference for the girl over the Minotaur. In fact, she eventually shoved him out of the way and forced him to wait, kneeling nearby, as she completed an excruciating crawl of Cyclops girl: Up between the pale legs that pedaled against her back, and slowly, lingeringly over the other girl's arching, twisting torso, until finally she was thrusting herself through and through those full, chirping lips. Even after Ed was finished, the Minotaur acted at her direction as she commanded the couple in a hoarse voice, sometimes insisting that they stop altogether so that she could reposition them to her liking, or pose them for a cell phone shot.

I joked, "Well, this removes any doubt about whether Ed really is an artist."

Gib said, "So, what we're seeing here now . . . it would qualify as an orgy, would it not?"

I laughed. "Well, I guess maybe it would. Technically . . . does your ancient vocabulary include the term 'three-way?'"

"In all the time I was alive, I never saw one. Nor participated."

"No?"

"You mean you *have*? Young as you are?"

"Once or twice." He gave me a look of disbelief, so I added, "Gib, I led a weird life. I hung out with bikers and people like that."

"Well, you little son of a bitch!"

At last, with a half-dozen squeaking barks and a limb-flailing fit from Cyclops Girl, followed by a bellow from the open throat of the Minotaur, their performance shuddered to a close. The Minotaur flung his open, leaking condom against the church wall opposite the one Ed was painting; it stuck there for a moment, slug-like, before rolling off and plopping to the floor.

"Beasts!" cried Alice.

"Well, maybe they'll leave now," said Virgil. "And, if we're lucky, they won't come back for a while."

Alice said, "Who is going to clean that up?"

The lovers dressed and the Minotaur scrambled out through the broken window in the minister's office, returning a minute later with a red, five-gallon gasoline can.

"Uh-oh," said Gib. By then, Virgil and Alice had rejoined us from the front of the church.

"Thumb, you told us this wouldn't happen!" Alice spun rapidly in her beach-ball shape.

"It was a guess Alice, not a guarantee."

The Minotaur splashed the entire five gallons of fuel onto the chancel, from where it immediately began cascading and running across the church floor in snaking streams that gleamed in the light of the electric lanterns.

"Stop that, you bastard!" Alice shouted.

The Minotaur tossed away the empty can. "I got some on my pants. Right near my junk. Somebody else better light it."

"Shall we leave?" said Virgil. "A childhood filled with infernal imagery makes its mark, even on an atheist."

Ed said, "I'll do it. First, though, I want a few pics in front of my new piece. A little video." Cyclops Girl and the Minotaur obediently took out their phones and began recording Ed as she stood beside her newly tagged patch of wall.

Ed said, "This is Ed, of Ed's Posse, bringing you the conclusion of Defiance Art, Work Number Seven. As you can see . . . "

Meanwhile, Alice was yelling, "Do something! Somebody do something to stop them."

"Alice, it's sad, but there's nothing we *can* do," said Gib. "We'll just need to find another haunt."

"We *could* do something," Alice said. "All of us, or any one of us. If we really wanted to, at least for a few seconds, we could make them hear us, or even see us. Tell them to get the hell out."

The Minotaur complained, "Edna, the fumes are getting my eyes. I think we should spark her up, and leave."

I said, "Yeah, but something happens to us if we do that, and we don't know exactly what. All we know is that we probably won't come back from it."

"We're *forbidden*," Gib added. "As far as we know, it's like another death. Maybe a darker one, at that."

"What do you care, Gib?" said Alice. "God will protect you, won't he? Maybe that's how you'll finally get to heaven."

Gib shook his head. "I don't tempt the Lord, Alice. Not in life, and not now."

"One minute," said Ed. "I'm almost done. Keep recording."

Spherical Alice spun toward Virgil. "Virgil! You don't even believe you're a ghost. What have you got to lose? Make yourself visible; say something to them!"

Virgil looked miserable. He said, "I am still alive, yes. And, it's irrational, I know. But I get the sense that if I did that I really *would* die. Eternal blackness . . . I just can't."

"*Thumb*?"

"Come *on*, Edna!" said the Minotaur. "We could get trapped in here, the way the gas is running everywhere."

"Alice, if I already knew who killed me, I'd be ready . . . "

"*Cowards*!" Alice yelled, not waiting for me to finish. "You men are all complete cowards! I can't believe you're willing to let this human sewage have their way!" At once, she launched herself at Ed and passed herself through and through Ed's oblivious, nattering, backwards-baseball-capped head. Then, twirling madly, she settled just off of Ed's left shoulder and seemed to gather herself for a moment before bursting into earthly visibility as a roaring, spinning ball of flames. Ed glanced at her, dropped her jaw to let out a wordless sound I'd never heard from a person, and threw herself against her doomed mural, her eyes wide and her fingers scrambling at the painted wall behind her. A dark stain bloomed in the crotch of her overalls. At the same time, Cyclops Girl and the Minotaur gaped and cringed as they stared at Alice; their bodies were shaking. The Minotaur seemed oddly detached from his own arm, which was still holding up his cell phone.

When Alice's flaming face took shape in the center of her fireball, I felt like cringing myself; I was terrified. Virgil and Gib had moved away, their ghostly hands stretched before them as if to shield them from the heat of her fury. Alice screamed, "So you kids want to *burn*?" When none of them was able to answer her— their white lips twitched, but no words emerged—she said, "Well all right, then, I'll *burn* you. I'll burn you till your souls are cinders. I will burn . . . " Alice was cut off in mid-sentence as she suddenly and silently disintegrated, her fireball imploding to a pinpoint of darkness. But by then Ed was splashing her way across rivers of gasoline as she ran for the broken window, Cyclops Girl and the Minotaur following close behind. They hurled themselves through the window, one of them scoring some skin on the way out and leaving a dash of blood on the window frame. They thrashed their way through tall weeds to dive into their car. The car started and immediately backed into the iron fence surrounding the cemetery, crunching the bumper and springing the trunk. With their yawning trunk lid flapping, they scattered gravel as they fled toward the nearest blacktop, their headlights against the tops of the trees growing increasingly faint until they vanished altogether.

CHAPTER 11

Not long after Alice Poe-York had sacrificed her afterlife to save the church, we began to receive further uninvited company. Our new, mortal visitors were neither artists nor arsonists, but were probably the next-worst thing: a group of people obsessed with the idea of making contact with the dead. They must have gotten permission to enter the abandoned building, because on their first visit they arrived in broad daylight and parked their shiny white van in plain sight along the edge of the gravel road. They came with a key to the padlock that linked the ends of the heavy chain fettering the handles of the two front doors. Their long vehicle, on either side, sported elaborate murals of a haunted house, complete with airborne bats, and large lettering that said:

GHOST HOUNDS: Paranormal Researchers of New England
(ParanormalResearchersOfNewEngland.org)

Virgil and Gib stopped playing chess when they arrived, and the three of us watched through the walls as they piled out into the late-summer growth of waist-high weeds—there were six of them, including two young women—and walked to the entrance. The chain rattled and clanked as they removed it and dropped it to the ground, and Virgil said, "Sounds like the Ghost of Christmas Past, coming for a visit."

One door groaned open and, carrying a white candle burning on a white china dish, in stepped a bearded young dude in a leather jacket whose blazing brown eyes darted above a sharply pointed nose. He tip-toed across the vestibule and stopped just inside the sanctuary to gather in as much of the scene as his flickering candle could illuminate and then, in a dramatic gesture, he pushed his open palm into the air and declared, "I am sealed from all imperfect energies!"

Gib, who had risen and moved toward the front of the church and was now hovering about an arm's length from the guy, looked back at us and said, "Oh, shit. I'd almost rather they just go ahead and burn the place down."

Speaking loudly enough for his friends outside to hear, the man in the leather jacket said, "In the name of all that is good, we beg safe passage!" This request was echoed by his five companions who then, carrying their own white candles on white dishes, all but the first of them gripping the shoulder of the person in front, single-filed into the church, together murmuring *Safe passage! Safe passage!* as they shuffled, caterpillar-like, through the vestibule. They continued chanting this hopeful mantra until they had assembled in the sanctuary and formed a circle by pinching thumbs and forefingers against the edges of one another's candleholders.

"Let us pray!" said the man with the beak-like nose, and they all fell silent and bowed their heads. He then recited:

"Saint Michael the Archangel, defend us in battle. Be our protection against the wickedness and snares of the devil. May God rebuke him, we humbly pray. And do Thou, O Prince of the Heavenly Host, by the Divine Power of God, cast into hell Satan and all the evil spirits who roam throughout the world seeking the ruin of souls."

Gib said, "I'm pretty sure that last part was all about Virgil. Don't you think so, Thumb?"

Virgil frowned and said, "This is funny now, but it won't remain amusing for long."

"All right," the praying man said when he was finished. "Headlamps and gloves, everyone."

"Peter," said the darker haired of the two chicks, addressing the man in the leather jacket. As soon as she'd spoken, all of them but Peter looked at her, and then all but one immediately glanced away again. The fellow who kept his eyes on her was a curly haired, lumpy-looking dude whose face still bore traces of acne, and whose name I would soon learn was Ben—the same Ben who would shortly become my amanuensis.

Peter, rather than acknowledging the girl who has called his name, said, "Place your candles in a circle on the floor."

The candles were circled, after which the six "researchers" slipped on white gloves and switched on the battery-powered lamps that were harnessed to their heads.

"Peter," the dark-haired girl repeated.

"We'll do our walk-through now," said Peter, "in order to allow any spirits who may be present to get acclimated to our presence, and so that they may learn we mean them no harm. Choose a partner, and hold hands at all times. Don't take any photos or video just yet. Walk slowly, and remember: no laughing or other forms of disrespect. We are here as guests."

Peter then turned to the other girl, the blonde girl, and he said, "Amber, I'd like you to come with me." Only then did he answer the girl who'd had been calling him: "What was it you needed, Melody?"

"Nothing," Melody whispered, sagging a little.

"Good, then," said Peter. "Let's walk."

Amber stepped over to him, took hold of his hand, and pressed her shoulder against his arm. The other four people then paired up as well. Ben turned his gaze to the floor, puckering his mouth as if preparing to whistle, and slowly oozed a few inches in Melody's direction. Until then, the young woman had been more or less frozen in apparent disappointment over Peter's rejection, but Ben's movements sparked her flight response, and at once she stepped to the side of the taller of the two remaining men. That left Ben and the other man who, after another pause, joined gloved hands while staring at opposite sides of the church.

The three teams strolled through our building, the beams from their headlamps climbing the walls and hopping between the pews. Virgil, Gib, and I all trailed Peter and Amber as they went about discovering, and in muted murmurs discussing, the discarded red gasoline can lying on its side in an aisle, the electric lanterns at either end of the chancel, whose batteries days before had faded and finally gone dead, and the random, river-delta pattern of gasoline stains in the finish of the chancel floor. The two of them spent several minutes studying the ambitious mural of graffiti with which Ed had tagged the high wall behind the choir box, and after that they moved on to the shorter and narrower work of art between the two plywood-covered windows.

Peter dropped his voice to a whisper and said, "This is where it happened. Right *here* is where the orb appeared to them, and where they saw and heard the apparition."

"It feels cold here," said Amber. She gave him a quick look. "Doesn't it?"

"Yes," Peter whispered. "Yes it does. We'll have to take some temperature readings in here to verify, but it seems like we've detected a cold spot."

At that point Ben, who was up on the chancel staring at the big mural, and whose hand and that of the other man were still entwined in mutual distaste, began to whistle. The sound he made was tuneless and shrill, the echo of each note ricocheting through the place like a shrieking bullet. Peter turned and shushed him.

"Don't whistle!" Peter said. "Are you *stupid*? Don't you know how dangerous that is? *Hum*, if you have to make noise. My God, Ben, think of the consequences . . ."

"Sorry," said Ben.

"We discussed this in training."

"I know," said Ben. "I forgot. Nervous, I guess." At that, he laughed nervously.

"Just stop *talking*, Ben!"

Melody, on the other side of the church, called out, "Peter! You need to have a look at this!" The other two teams hurried over to her, and all six Ghost Hounds focused their trembling headlamp beams on a contraceptive still life made up of the Minotaur's condom, lying there like a sliver of colorless road kill, and its partially spilled contents, which were flaking against the linoleum floor.

"They never mentioned this when they called us," Peter murmured. "And that was unbelievably irresponsible of them, because they've placed our lives in jeopardy. There's nothing more provocative to spirits than this—not even trying to burn the place down would make them as angry."

I looked at Virgil and said, "Any clue how they come up with this shit?"

Virgil rolled his eyes and shook his head, and Gib said, "Never mind where they get it. What it *means* is I don't guess they're planning on giving us another live performance."

Peter said, "We need to purify. To make amends for the disrespect that's been done here. Ben, go out to the van and get incense and holders. And bring our cameras in. Quickly."

"You want the digital cameras, or the film ones?" Ben asked.

"Both. Sometimes one will pick up an image that the other misses. And bring a couple of rolls of infrared film. And both of the camcorders, too. Hurry."

"How about the EMF meters?" said Ben.

"EMF . . . *what*? We can't do anything that intrusive just yet. Go, would you? Stop asking questions."

"EMF?" I said, and looked at Virgil.

Virgil said, "I would guess electro-magnetic field."

"For what?"

"For detecting *us*. Apparently, they think we're magnetic."

Ben brought back sticks of incense, which were lit and placed in ceramic holders that they set at the four corners of the church, as well as on the chancel.

"It's too bad we can't smell anything," Virgil said.

I told them, "My girlfriend, Cricket, used to light some incense once in a while. She'd pick them up whenever we went to a head shop. I'd kind of like to smell it if I could." At that, Gib made a motion as if to comfort me with a pat on the shoulder.

Ben retrieved several cameras from the truck, and the Ghost Hounds began wandering through the place individually, seemingly intent on documenting every inch of the walls, floor, and ceiling. Peter recorded the scene with a video camera, while the two with the digital still-cameras—Amber and the man Ben held hands with—carefully checked each image they captured for things that might not have been visible to their own eyes. From time to time, one of them would call out in excitement, and the Hounds would all huddle around the camera; but in every case, the possible "visual manifestation" was determined to be nothing more than a reflection or a shadow caused by an errant headlamp beam. After a while, Peter walked over to Ben and handed him a hundred-dollar bill. "We need something more than the incense," he said. "Go to the nearest florist's shop—*not* a supermarket—and buy us a nice arrangement in a white vase."

"That would be about fifteen miles from here," Ben said.

"What's your point?" said Peter.

"It's just a long way."

"Something nice," Peter said. "Like for a funeral. If you don't know what 'nice' is, ask the sales person. No carnations. Spirits hate carnations."

Ben sighed, then called out, "Anybody want to go for a ride?" When there came no answer, he repeated, "*Anybody?*" They continued to ignore him until he left. It was well over an hour before he returned to the church carrying the flower arrangement.

"Look at *that!*" said Gib. "It is quite beautiful. I for one am touched."

Without meeting his eyes or speaking to him, Melody took the flowers from Ben and placed them on the front of the chancel between the lifeless electric lanterns. They all gathered to look at them.

"Ben," said Peter after a moment.

"Yes?" Ben said, hope and dread mixing in his voice.

"Did the flower shop give you any change for that hundred?"

Shortly afterward, they extinguished their circle of candles and left the church, replaced the chain that held the front doors closed, and snapped the big padlock back into place.

*

The Ghost Hounds returned the following night, but instead of coming directly into the building, they spent a long while working among the weeds between the road and the front doors as they set up and adjusted a squad of aluminum tripods, each supporting either a bright light or a video camera. They ran electric cables from the tripods through the weeds to the back of the van, where they connected them to an array of large batteries. Ben, when he wasn't being ordered to do something else by one of the others, wandered aimlessly around with a microphone attached to the end of a silver boom and connected by a long cable to a black sound board, covered with tiny switches and jumping needles, that rested on a card table beside the van. Wearing a set of headphones, the tallest Ghost Hound—the one who had held Melody's reluctant hand—hovered over this control panel, making fussy adjustments and snarling at Ben.

Virgil, Gib, and I drifted out of the church to get a closer look. We watched as Amber, wearing makeup and a pretty red dress, minced around on the uneven ground in a pair of crimson heels, all the while balancing herself with open hands held in the air, her freshly lacquered nails gleaming beneath the camera lights.

Once the illumination and the electronics had all been calibrated to Peter's satisfaction, Peter and Amber took turns standing in front of the church, making sweeping gestures at the padlocked doors and explaining to some future audience why the Ghost Hounds had come to this place, what they had discovered, and what they hoped to find over the following days and weeks of their investigation. Ben stood close by, holding the microphone above each of them in turn, his arms stretched over his head in an awkward and uncomfortable-looking pose that pulled apart his pants and his t-shirt, exposing a smile-shaped protrusion white belly.

"*Weeks*?" said Virgil. "Did she say weeks? Oh my God."

After staring at Amber for a few moments, Gib said to me, "Boy, she cleans up nice, doesn't she?"

"I like the other one," I said. "Maybe it's a hereditary preference, but I prefer a girl who looks like she could soak up a little strong sunlight without turning into a giant blister."

"Speaking of, where *is* your new girlfriend?"

I looked around and found the other five Ghost Hounds: Peter and Amber taking their turns in front of the camera, Ben grimacing and exposing his stomach, the tall guy wearing earphones and fiddling with the sound board, and the short guy sitting behind the wheel of the idling van, smoking a cigarette and looking as if he'd rather be almost anywhere else. But Melody seemed to have disappeared. Then, using my ghostly vision to peer all the way through the church, I spotted her at the rear of the building, holding a flashlight and standing near the back corner of the fenced-in cemetery. Unlike Amber, she wore jeans and a flannel shirt; clearly, she had come tonight not to flutter before a camera, but to get down and dirty, hounding ghosts.

"There she is," I said. "I think I'll go see what she's up to. Want to come?"

"No," said Gib. "I'm enjoying the view from right here."

I drifted back to where Melody stood, and I watched as she stared off into the lightless woods behind the church, gnawing at her lower lip. I said to her, "I think you're way hotter than that other girl. You could stand to work on your personality, though." At once her eyes narrowed, and a fierce emotion crossed her face like a gunmetal cloud sliding over the sun. After a moment, she pulled a cell phone from her pants pocket and calmly snapped a couple of photos of the cemetery.

"It's too dark," I told her. "And you don't have a flash."

When she had finished her photography, she lowered the phone, drew a breath, and screamed. I wasn't startled—that's a physiological reaction—but I *was* astonished. "Dude," I said. "What the hell?" She screamed once more and began walking quickly toward the front of the church. Led by their headlamp beams, Peter and the tall ghost hunter met her halfway, with Ben stumbling behind.

"I saw!" Melody said. "I *saw*!" She grabbed the lapels of Peter's jacket with both hands and buried her face in his shoulder.

"What?" said Peter, his open hands lifting into the air behind her. "What was it?"

"Are you all right?" said the tall man—but he went unanswered.

"Peter. Oh my God," she said, gasping as if to catch her breath. "I know you told us not to go anywhere without a partner, but I needed to pee."

"What did you see?" Excitement, worry, and impatience were mixing in Peter's voice.

"It was—he was—an old farmer dude. Standing on the other side of the fence. In the cemetery."

"Do you mean an *apparition*?"

"I think so. It just . . . happened."

"What did it look like?"

"He had white hair, and bright blue eyes that never blinked, and he was wearing overalls." She pressed a trembling finger against her forehead just below her hairline. "There was a black hole above his eyes, like maybe from a bullet. Something black was leaking out and . . . running down his face."

"This is incredible," said Peter. He put his hand on the middle of her back. "Did he seem to have risen from any particular grave?"

"I couldn't tell. But I took a couple of pictures with my cell phone."

"You *did*? Can . . . could I see them?" By then Amber and the short man had also made their way along the dark cemetery side of the church. Amber had removed her heels to walk through the weeds in her stocking feet, and she was looking angrily unhappy as well as uncomfortable.

"What is it?" Amber said. "I've got burrs on my dress. What's going on?" Nobody answered her.

Virgil and Gib had come floating back as well. Virgil said, "It's good you're still here, Thumb. For a second we thought you might not have been able to resist the temptation of making yourself visible to a pretty girl."

"No. She had no idea."

"So, what was it then?" asked Gib. "All the hubbub?"

"As far as I can tell, you two aren't the only people interested in playing chess."

By then Melody had temporarily unmuckled from Peter and was bringing up the photos on her cell phone as he eagerly peered over her shoulder. "Here's one," Melody said. "But, oh no, there's nothing there. And here's the other. Nothing." She looked up at him with tears in her eyes. "I'm *so* sorry, Peter. I took them. I tried. I really did. It doesn't seem . . . "

"It's okay," he said, putting an arm around her. "It's all right. Don't worry; they don't always show up in photos. And sometimes they'll show up on film, but not in an electronic image. You kept your head; you did what you could. You're a hero."

Amber was staring at the two of them with her arms crossed. She said, "Excuse me, but so, it went down like *this*? Like, you saw this dude, and then you, like, took his picture, and *then* you screamed?" With one cheek pressed against Peter's leather jacket, Melody wore a slight smirk as she lifted her face to Amber.

"I didn't scream until he pointed at me," Melody said.

"He *pointed* at you?" said Peter.

"And he *talked* to me! Oh, God!"

"What did he *say?*" all of them but Amber asked at once.

"He said . . . *You look just like her*. And then he disappeared."

They did not go into the church that night. Instead, they took hundreds of photos in the cemetery, many of them incorporating Melody in their composition. After that, they all donned night-vision goggles and wandered among the old headstones as they stared down at variety of handheld electronic devices—fancy thermometers, EMF meters, several types of audio recorders. Every so often one of them would call out a report of an "anomaly," and they would crowd together to study the instrument that had registered the reading. Peter would scribble a few things onto a notepad, then they would again separate into two-person teams and continue their walkabout. Finally, as dawn began throwing streaks of light into the sky, they moved their video equipment into the graveyard and recorded Melody as she told the tale of her eerie encounter. Four times, standing in four separate locations among the worn stone markers and using four slightly different tones of voice, Melody told her future audience, "He said, *You look just like her*. And then he disappeared."

*

They spent the next two nights in the cemetery, awaiting some sort of repeat performance by the "old farmer dude" with the oozing bullet hole in his forehead. Melody, claiming still to be "extremely freaked out," stuck as close as she could to Peter during most of that time—something that he at first encouraged, then tolerated, and then, as disappointingly quiet hours continued to pile upon one another without further communication from the spirit, increasingly avoided. By the end of the first full, fruitless night among the ancient graves, he had begun to make tactical use of tombstones as a means of maintaining space between them; by the middle of the second, dead-in-exactly-the-wrong-way evening, it was the hips and shoulders of a resurgent Amber that served to keep Melody at a distance from him.

On the third night, the Ghost Hounds reluctantly gave up on Melody's Halloweenish will-o'-the-wisp, pulled the chain from the double doors, and reentered the church where, after replacing the faded flowers on the chancel with a fresh arrangement, they paired up again—Peter and Amber, Melody and Tall Guy, Ben and a disgusted-looking Shorty—and spent the better part of an evening walking up and down the aisles, in and out of the vestibule and the back offices, and threading their way through the pews with the same set of hand-held instruments they'd used in the cemetery.

The following evening they returned with yet another heap of expensive-looking electronic equipment—different sorts of sound recorders as well as a dozen tiny video cameras on telescoping tripods—which they set up all around the church. They then spent the next several nights scattered about the floor in sleeping bags, only to wake up each morning to stiff backs and—after reviewing the data from all their devices—disappointment. Gib, Virgil, and I kept waiting for Melody to experience another encounter with the headshot farmer, but she let us down; apparently she had used up all of her courage on her first and only performance. Finally one morning the Ghost Hounds gathered in the pews for a meeting. Peter said, "It seemed so promising when we started. And, it's not like we haven't gotten results. We're *clearly* getting results; we're just not getting *consistent* results."

The tall man said, "Dude, we're not getting anything we can document. Nothing. That's the real problem. And that's as bad as no results at all. So it's probably time to pack it up and move on, wouldn't you say?"

Ben said, "I found a Ouija board the other day. In my gram's trailer. Maybe we should try it." No one paid him any attention.

Amber said, "We could always come back here if we wanted. But for now maybe we should drive down to Connecticut and check out that haunted swimming pool. That sounded like it might work out."

"Anybody mind if I just *try* the Ouija board? I brought it with me."

"Dude, a Ouija board is nothing but a toy," the short man said.

Peter pushed his hair back and left his hand on his forehead. "All right. Let's take a vote. How many for the haunted swimming pool?"

"I can't go to Connecticut right now," Ben said. "I'm broke."

"All in favor?" Everyone but Ben and Melody immediately put their hands up. Then, reluctantly, Melody raised hers as well.

"So moved," said Peter. "Let's break it down."

The Ghost Hounds carried dozens of vinyl cases and nylon bags into the old church and began packing their gear. Ben, after making a few trips to and from the van, came in with a broken-sided cardboard box and made his way to the chancel. He sat down on the edge of the chancel and with shaking hands removed a masonite Ouija board from the box and opened it in front of him. Melody was walking by just as he set the heart-shaped, plastic planchette in the middle of the board, and he called out to her.

"Hey, Mel! This really takes two people. You want to do it with me?"

She stopped and narrowed her eyes at him. "You're the last person in the world I'd want to do it with, Ben. And, don't you know that's dangerous? Peter says people have become demonically possessed by fucking around with Ouija boards." Then she walked away.

After a moment, Bern curled the corners of his lips and hissed to himself, "*Peter says. Peter says. Fucking around with Ouija boards.*" Virgil, Gib, and I gathered around him as he hunched over the board and settled the tips of his plump fingers onto the planchette. After a minute had passed with no movement from that felt-footed plastic puck, he started to look worried.

Gib winked at us and said, "Maybe I'll take pity on the little puke." He bent forward so that his mouth was next to Ben's ear and he said, "Our father, who art in heaven."

The planchette stayed where it was and Virgil said, "You probably have to spell it."

"O-U-R F-A-T-H-E-R . . . "

Still the planchette did not move, and Virgil said, "Let me try." He stepped right through Gib to bend himself to Ben's ear and he spelled, "D-E-A-R H-O-W-A-R-D." But Virgil was no more successful with Ben or the planchette than Gib had been.

"Who's Howard?" asked Gib. Virgil only gave him an enigmatic smile. Then Gib said to me, "Thumb, before this bubblehead gives up on us, you might as well take your turn."

I shrugged, stepped through both Gib and Virgil, and began to spell. To my astonishment, as soon as I opened my mouth the planchette slid a few inches to the left and hovered with its round window and brass pointer directly above a letter.

P

I glanced at Virgil before continuing, and the planchette wandered the board like an obedient insect, pausing over each letter I suggested.

PETER IS A DICK

When we were finished, Ben sat back for a moment with his mouth half open.

"Well now," said Gib, with a touch of envy in his voice. "Looks like you've got the magic touch."

"It has to be a coincidence. He and I were just thinking the same thing at the same time."

Just then Peter walked past and said, "Ben, why are you sitting on your ass? Do some work." At that, Ben plunged forward again and returned his hands to the planchette, and I resumed spelling.

A minute later Ben let out a laugh and shouted, "You and your friends are assholes!" The other Ghost Hounds all glanced at him and then continued packing their equipment.

Virgil said, "Move over, Thumb. This isn't fair. I want to try again." I stood aside and watched as Virgil repeated his greeting to Howard and the planchette remained still. After that, Gib tried several different phrases with the same lack of result.

Gib said to me, "You're up again, you bastard. Seems you have some kind of connection with him that nobody else does."

By then, Ben again had begun to look worried, perhaps suspecting that his moment as a medium had come and gone, never to return. But I spoke to him, and soon he was yelling, "*Thumb!* Dudes, his name is Thumb! Isn't that awesome?"

I asked him where he lived, and he answered me aloud saying, "I live right here in Maine, in a little shithole called Cairo."

I smiled at the other two ghosts. I said, "Alice showed me how to get there. That's where she lived. She showed me how to go almost anywhere in Cairo I wanted."

"How nice for you," Virgil said. He seemed irritated.

"Ben!" shouted Peter from the back of the church. "If you *were* communicating with a spirit, which you *aren't*, you'd be getting yourself in deep, deep trouble there. You could end up possessed for the rest of your life. Maybe for longer than your life." That was when Ben stopped looking so completely delighted with himself and his hands began to tremble once again. He held his hands over the planchette for a minute without touching it. Finally, even as he seemed to resist, his fingers curled downward until they were touching plastic.

I NEED UR HELP WITH A COUPLE THINGS WILL U HELP ME

He didn't immediately answer, so I continued.

I CAN HELP U 2

Still he did not respond, so I spelled out

I KNOW WHERE THERES MONEY I KNOW WHERE THERES BURIED TREASURE

Ben sat up stiffly. His eyes were wide and he was breathing hard. He looked around at the other Ghost Hounds; he pushed his fingers into his hair; he gnawed his lip. A drop of sweat slithered from beneath the hair on his temple. "Come on," I said, "Come on," but he didn't get that message because his hands weren't touching the planchette.

Finally he whispered, "I don't know. Maybe. I gotta go." Abruptly he packed up the Ouija board and hurried out to the van. He didn't come into the church again.

*

After they had removed all of their things and had replaced the plywood over the rear window through which Ed's Posse had entered, Peter insisted that rest of the Ghost Hounds wait outside in the idling van while he made one last inspection of the church. Carrying nothing but a flashlight, he slowly and methodically stepped his way through our haunt, from the front doorway around one sanctuary wall to the small offices in back, then out again, across the chancel, and up the other side. After he had finished pacing the perimeter, he began to go through every row of pews, using his light to inspect both floors and seats.

When Peter arrived at the place where Virgil and Gib sat playing chess, he paused and let his flashlight beam linger on their checkered cocktail napkin, which lay there on the pew.

"Hark!" said Gib in a mocking voice. "The mighty nimrod spots his quarry." But Gib's tone turned to one of alarm as Peter stooped and reached right through his back and belly to pick up the napkin. "Hey, you bastard! That's ours. Put it back!"

Peter seemed to study the napkin for a moment. Then he opened it, brought it to his face, and loudly blew his beak-like nose into it. Gib and Virgil roared in helpless rage as Peter squeezed the now-soiled napkin into a marble-sized ball and flicked it off into the darkness.

Then he went out the double doors, closed them, and padlocked the chain behind him.

CHAPTER 12

His full name is Benjamin LeBlanc. It didn't take me long to find him again after he and his companions called it quits and drove away from our church. There were just two convenience stores in Cairo, and I spent no more than a couple of days ghosting from one to the other before he made his inevitable appearance. He arrived on foot, wandered up and down the aisles casting wistful glances at the plumpest of the three young women who worked behind the various counters, and finally bought himself a slice of pizza and a bottle of Moxie. Then he hiked back home with a ghost hot on his heels.

Ben's bedroom in his grandmother's trailer overlooked a back-yard littered with derelict cars, tires flat and dented hoods gaping, a half-dozen discarded appliances, and the rusted, wheeless frame of an old Harley-Davidson, to which a lethargic black billy goat stood tethered by a rope. His bedroom's limited space was fur-ther constricted by its own heaps of clutter: layers of clothing flat-tened against the floor, crusty dishes and toppling stacks of empty Moxie cans, cardboard boxes full of old toys and broken electronic devices. But I was happy to see that the room also contained a card table, and that on the table lay the vintage Ouija board with the planchette resting at its center. This meant he had been hoping— and probably trying—to hear from me.

As Ben ate his lunch, he watched part of a game show on the tiny TV that shared the table with the Ouija board and a laptop computer. Lunch finished, he flipped through the channels for a couple of minutes before flopping onto the bed for a nap. Finally, just as I was beginning to lose my patience with him, he got up from the bed, sat down at the table and, after a moment's hesitation, settled his fingers onto the planchette. I let him chill for a few seconds and then, to grab his full attention, I shouted, "*Yes!*" which sent the pointer on the longest trip it could take.

Ben's eyes opened; his Adam's apple rose and fell. "Thumb?" he whispered. I made the planchette back off and then hit YES again.

"I was starting to think I wouldn't hear from you."

R U READY

He sat back. After a moment he turned his eyes to the ceiling and answered, "I don't know. How do I know you won't hurt me? How do I know you'll go away when I want you to?"

I JUST NEED U 2 WRITE SOMETHING WHEN ITS DONE ITS DONE

"Writing? That's all?"
I hesitated, because I don't like to lie.

YES

"What about the money? You said there was money."

YES AFTER

"What if I need some now?"

AFTER

He sat back again, blinking. Finally he asked, "How much money is there, Thumb?'

MORE THAN U HAVE SEEN

When he didn't immediately respond, I repeated myself.

R U READY

Ben took his hands from the planchette and lifted them to his head. He pressed his palms against his temples as if he were trying to keep his skull from flying apart.

*

It was autumn, probably a few days past the first anniversary of my murder, when I sent Ben to visit Fred Muttkowski at his farm. Under his arm Ben carried two spiral-bound notebooks—in all about three hundred hand-written pages, representing about half the story I intended to tell. Though most of it was just as I'd dictated it to him, I'd come to realize that this draft was not much more than raw material; it badly needed reorganizing and revising, and there was no practical way for Ben and I to do the job together. For one thing, revising an entire book was a monstrous chore, and since I'd never done it before, I just didn't have the insight or the skills. For another, it would take forever, and I knew that Ben sooner or later would run out of patience—in fact, he was showing signs of it already.

A further problem—one I knew would make it difficult to enlist Fred's assistance: the manuscript was damn near illegible because Ben's handwriting and spelling both were awful. In spite of my repeated requests, he had stubbornly and consistently refused to switch to a computer with a spell-check program; apparently—and in spite of the fact that he spent roughly half his waking hours playing games on his laptop—the mere idea of actually *writing* something on the machine invariably brought on a traumatic high-school flashback that threw him into a panic attack.

Ben's feet crunched through fallen leaves as together we traveled the length of Fred's long barn. He seemed rock-steady until we reached the back of the barn and he saw the pigs; then he froze. There were perhaps three dozen porkers milling around behind the electric fence, all big as barrels and outweighing Ben by a good hundred pounds. The black-and-white swine reacted to his appearance by wheeling in his direction and stampeding to the wire, where they stopped in a scrum and tilted their snouts at him, their nostrils oscillating as they attempted to determine whether he might have brought them something to eat, or might himself perhaps be edible.

"Dude," Ben said under his breath as he gazed out over the backs of the pigs, afraid of looking directly into their pea-sized, nearsighted eyes. He was probably considering bolting back to his grandmother's old station wagon at the bottom of Fred's driveway. I was "standing" at his shoulder then, but without the Ouija board, there was no way I could encourage him to brace up and hold his ground. At that moment, I might as well not even have been there.

I think Ben would have given up in a moment or two if we hadn't suddenly heard Fred's voice coming from inside the barn. Fred was talking, or singing—perhaps a bit of both—and it was unclear whether he was communicating with his animals, or merely keeping himself company. A minute later he stepped out of the barn holding a rake in one of his rubber-gloved hands, and as soon as he stood beneath the open sky he thrust the tines of the tool high into the air, lifted his chin to the heavens, balled his empty hand into a fist, and howled, "I am Ulysses!"

Still aiming their snouts in Ben's direction, most of the pigs grunted in seeming agreement. Then, as Fred lowered the rake, he caught sight of Ben out of the corner of his eye, and he turned to face him fully. Several seconds passed during which Fred stared expressionlessly at the young man who gripped spiral-bound note-books in both of his pudgy hands. Finally he said, "Who the fuck are you?"

"My name's Ben."

"Well if you're looking for Iris, she doesn't live here anymore. But to be honest, from the looks of you she's way out of your league, anyway. And believe me fellow, your wardrobe is the least of it."

"No, I'm not," Ben said.

"What, then? Come to ask about working for me? Got the passion for pigs? Because I've been thinking about hiring somebody. The successful candidate will be a person with a strong back, no sense of smell, and not much of a brain. You look like you might fit exactly one of those criteria; I'll leave you to guess which one."

Ben's eyes widened. "Not pigs, no."

"Then why *are* you here? I've got shit to do, and I mean that literally. So, either use your vocal cords to produce some meaningful vibrations"—at this, his gloved right hand rose beside his head and snapped the air like a mouth—"or get the hell out of here and let me do my job."

Ben stared out over the pig run, obviously at a loss for words; I wanted to slap him. After a moment, Fred narrowed his eyes and seemed to consider stepping forward to give him a poke with the rake handle. But finally Ben said, "You're a writer."

Fred glared. "Who sent you here?"

"You're Frederick H. Muttkowski, the writer."

"I will not ask you again. I will just start kicking your ass."

Ben took a step back from the fence. He turned one foot in the direction of Fred's driveway and the safety of his grandmother's car. Knowing Fred as well as I did by then, I had instructed Ben to avoid at all costs admitting that he was running interference for a ghost; instead, I had supplied him with a few credible lies, which now, disastrously, seemed to have gotten log-jammed in his throat. At last, to my relief, he was able to say, "Nobody sent me!"

"I'm waiting," said Fred. "But not for long."

"Dude!" said Ben. "You're on the internet! I just Googled you, is all." He lifted the notebooks in Fred's direction and continued, "I got this . . . I got this thing I wrote. I need some help with it from a writer. That's all I want."

"Go ask your English teacher to help you with it. That's what they pay them all those millions for."

"I'm not in school anymore. And the job needs a professional."

Fred turned the rake so that the teeth rested against the hard-packed ground. He placed both gloved hands atop the rounded end of the handle. After a moment he lifted his chin at the notebooks.

"If I look in there, what am I going to find?"

"What do you mean?"

"What is it? Your 'thing' that you wrote?"

"It's . . . I don't really know how to describe it. It's kind of a murder mystery."

Fred grimaced and shook his head. "I am not the least bit interested in reading any kind of half-baked genre bullshit. Not that I'm a snob, or anything."

"Well, it's really more of a ghost story."

"Strike two, buddy. Go home."

Ben drew a shaking breath. "Well it's . . . could you just please have a look?" To my distress he added, "If you don't like it, I will never bother you again."

Fred thought for a moment before stripping the gloves from his hands and tucking them beneath the arm that held the rake. He lifted the rake and wordlessly kneed his way through the mob of pigs to stick his free hand across the fence. Ben gave him the notebooks. Fred opened the topmost one as he stood with the rake handle resting against his shoulder and huge pigs jostling for the privilege of nibbling his boots. He spent five seconds scanning the first page before handing them back. Peering over the tops of his glasses to look Ben directly in the eye, he said in a quiet voice, "Son, you aren't even literate. Now, go away."

*

If legitimate mediums—people able to talk to the dead—were anything but rare, I never saw the evidence. In my entire afterlife I only "met" one other living person aside from Ben who could communicate with a ghost, and that person, a biker mamma named Pickle, was at least halfway out of her head. Because of my connection with Ben and the ability he gave me to transmit messages to the living world, I imagine that most other ghosts would have envied me a lot.

But the truth is, I was unhappier and more frustrated after meeting Ben than I had been before. The problem was that having a psychic hunchback at my beck and call presented me with certain choices I had not previously faced—choices that were so completely miserable I would have felt relieved not to have had them at all. For instance, after Ben came along, I could have dictated a letter to Cricket and poured out my heart, telling her finally and clearly how I had felt about her and how great it was that she'd had our child— our boy, or girl, who would now be well over six months old. Of course this really was not much of a choice, because it would have been such a monstrously selfish thing to do—something that not only would have literally spooked Cricket, perhaps even driving her and our baby back toward her old, downwardly mobile way of life, but also no doubt affecting her relationship with Chef or whatever man might now be serving as our child's stand-in father. Still, it was a course of action I was forced to consciously reject and, in rejecting, had summoned a tide of regrets that until then I had pretty much held at bay.

But the most painful decision I had to make was one that was not as mad-makingly obvious. Without the slightest danger of alerting or alarming Cricket, I could have coached Ben through some elementary research to find out whether we'd had a boy or a girl, and what name Cricket had given our child. *His* name! *Her* name! And there was a good chance that without much effort Ben could have gotten me a photograph as well. How I longed to know; how I longed to see, regardless of how painful knowing and seeing would be.

But the rub was in what I already knew about myself. In life I'd had a genius not so much for making bad decisions, but for rationalizing or ridiculing away all of my good choices until nothing but the bad ones remained. If my vague, and vaguely unreal, son or daughter out there in the near world somewhere were to take shape in my mind as a specific person—a human being with a sex, a name, and a face—there was a strong possibility I would begin to feel the irresistible tug of a thousand reasonable-seeming and toxic pretexts for haunting the lives and meddling with the minds of those I cared most about.

No. It was far better for me not to know.

*

It was lunchtime on a warm fall day, and Frederick H. Muttkowski came to the screen door of his house with a half-eaten hard-boiled egg in one hand, a brown bottle of ale in the other. He peered down at Ben, who after knocking had retreated with his notebooks to the lowest step, and he said, "You disappoint me. You and I had an agreement that you wouldn't come back."

In the words I had insisted he rehearse while looking in a mirror, Ben said, "Sir, if you would just have one more look. The story is the thing, once you get past my bad spelling. And, if you *can* get past the spelling . . . and the punctuation, too, I guess, the writing isn't half-bad either."

"If you do say so yourself," said Fred, and took a bite of egg. "I told you no before, and I'm running out of polite ways of telling you to get lost. I have absolutely no interest in reviewing any more of your moronic scrawlings."

"I can pay you," Ben said.

"Well, good for you. Come back with a bag of gold and maybe we'll have a conversation." Then Fred closed the inside door and faded back into the depths of his house.

*

About two years earlier, I had made a couple of remote caches of cash and other supplies as a precaution against a law-enforcement raid or other catastrophic event that would make it necessary for me to leave the Pine Tree State in a hurry. Post-death, I had not yet figured out a way to reach the locations of those buried stashes on my own, but I was able to give Ben detailed directions to the nearest one, which lay beside a stone wall at the wooded edge of a hilltop blueberry field. I remembered that the view from the field, of ponds and forests, was spectacular, especially in the fall.

Although I had promised to give Ben money—I had no further use for the stuff myself—I had been reluctant to send him off on a treasure hunt because of the fact that, enclosed within the moisture-proof box among my two changes of underwear, three-thousand dollars in worn twenty-dollar bills, and a few other items I thought would be useful to a man on the run, there lay a Beretta Tomcat .32-caliber semi-automatic handgun with a seven-round clip and a full box of ammunition. It was my strong belief that what the living world needed least was one more fool with a firearm. In fact, I still believed it possible that if that other idiot, Dirt, had not had his Glock close at hand on the day the woodpecker came knocking, I might still be alive.

But now I had no choice, given Fred's stubbornness so far. At sundown, I sent Ben skulking up the blueberry hill along a vague foot trail, his grandmother's garden spade and a pickaxe he had borrowed from his next-door neighbor clutched in his hands. After dark, several hours later, he returned to the trailer with my treasure box, which he immediately carried to his bedroom, locking the door behind him. Over and over again, he riffled through the stacks of twenties with shaking hands; it was obvious he'd never expected to handle that much money at one time. He then removed all the other treasure-box contents, spread them onto the grayish sheets of his unmade bed and, to my dismay, spent a considerable amount of time pointing the handgun at the mirror above his dresser. I was worried that he'd see it as a substitute for the heroic sword he'd always felt belonged in his hands.

When finally—*thankfully*—he cracked a warm can of Moxie and sat down at the Ouija board, I told him that while the other items in the box still belonged to me, the cash was his to keep in partial payment for taking my dictation. I suggested that he open a bank account and deposit two hundred dollars a week until all of it was in. Of course, by then we had long before worked out our code:

RMBR T GUN Z MINE I WNT U 2 THRW IT N T NEAREST POND

Instead however, he wrapped the pistol in one of my t-shirts and stuck it beneath some of his own clothes in his bottom dresser drawer. After that, whenever I mentioned the Beretta and what I wanted him to do with it, he always pretended not to have understood me.

*

The next time we visited Fred, it was another relatively warm day in either late November or early December, and we found the old man reading a dog-eared paperback edition of *Under the Volcano* as he sat behind his barn in a lawn chair, his booted heels propped on the spine of a sleeping swine.

"No," said Fred, when he saw Ben come around the corner.

Ben carried our notebooks in one hand and a paper Dunkin' Donuts bag in the other. He held out the bag and said, "Here you go, Mr. Muttkowski."

"Is that a donut?"

"No; it's what you said you wanted." I felt proud of Ben then; he was learning to stick his ground.

Fred sighed, took his feet from the pig, which reacted with a lazy grunt, and walked to the fence. He accepted the bag, opened it, and peered down into it as if he thought it might contain a snake. Then he reached inside to remove a small velvet box that, until recently, had lain buried beside the blueberry field along with three thousand dollars, my underwear, and a gun. He popped the hinged lid and spent a moment studying the gold coin that lay nestled in the box before looking up at Ben with a grim expression and saying, "Did you hurt anyone in the house you broke into to get this?"

Having already rehearsed this part—in the mirror, while holding my Beretta in his hands—Ben said, "I didn't steal it. It was my gramp's; my gram gave it to me after he died."

"You're fucked, you little freak; I'm going to call the police."

"The coin is from Denmark. It's one of four of them they made for the two-hundredth birthday of Hans Christian Andersen. Gramp sent for it. This one's from *The Shadow*—you can see the illustration thingy on the back." Ben dug into his pants pocket for a wad of paper that he painstakingly unfolded, smoothed against his thigh, and then squinted at for a moment before reciting: "A word is a shadow, said the shadow, and as such, it must speak." He looked up and added, "That's my favorite line. From *The Shadow*."

As Fred continued to stare at him, he dropped his gaze again, and in a softer voice he said, "That's your bag of gold, Mr. Muttkowski. That you asked for. Will you help me with my book, now?"

When Fred finally spoke, it was to say, "Kid, do you think you're in some kind of fucking movie?"

"Wait—w*hat*?"

"Are you fantasizing that I'm actually some sort of beautiful old man who, though grumpy on the outside, secretly aspires to help you turn your life around? Help you gain confidence and competence and coach you maybe to win the girl of your dreams?"

"Uh . . ."

"Because I'm not. I am the furthest thing from that person, especially where you're concerned. I don't care about you or your so-called book, or your gramp, or any of your trailer-trash problems. Nothing. Not one mother-fucking bit of it."

Ben edged back from the fence. "You told me that if I brought you a bag of gold you would help."

"You only brought me *one* coin, you cheater. And what I said was we would talk. What I want *now* is some dope. They still call it that, don't they—dope?"

Ben widened his eyes. "You mean weed?"

"Pot. Mary Jane. *Mota.*"

Ben let out a surprised laugh and nodded. "They call it dope sometimes."

"I *want* some. I haven't been high in twenty years and I think I'm overdue. Is it still sold by the ounce?"

"It is, if you want that much. That's a lot, though. . . . "

"Jesus! I sound like Rip Van Winkle, don't I?" He barked out a laugh. "And, aren't you a knowledgeable and helpful young man all of a sudden. Bring me an ounce of it. Something good—and keep in mind that, while it's been a while, I can still tell the difference."

"For real, dude?"

"Don't forget a couple of packages of rolling papers. Zig-Zag, if they still exist." He stuffed the bag containing the gold coin into his jacket pocket. "Take off now, fellow. I've got work to do."

*

Fred's marijuana wish was an easy-enough one to make come true; Ben knew a friendly dealer who lived three trailers away, and even after shipping some expensive presents to his out-of-state toddler siblings, he still held plenty of my ill-gotten cash with which to buy it. As soon as his grandmother's car was once more available for his use—two days later—Ben drove back to the farm and triumphantly passed a second Dunkin' Donuts bag across the gate in the electrified pig fence.

"Papers are in there, too," Ben said with a touch of smugness in his voice. "I even bought you a lighter."

Fred took the bag from him without opening it and said, "Great. Go away now." When Ben stayed at the fence blinking and not moving, he added, "You didn't think I was going to invite you to smoke some of it with me, did you? That would hardly be appropriate in a mentor-mentee relationship. Come back in three days—and when you do, make sure you're wearing a suit and a tie." With that he turned, paper sack in hand, and walked into his barn without looking back.

Once we'd returned to his grandmother's trailer, still in possession of the notebooks with my story scrawled inside them, I tried to encourage Ben.

HE CLD HSLF YR MENTOR W R MKN PROGRES W ND 2 KP TRYN

But I could tell that not only was he getting tired of dealing with Fred and his eccentric, seemingly endless, demands, but now that he had a little money in his pockets the novelty of having an invisible friend—me—was starting to wear thin, and his mind had begun wandering in some different directions. The next day, he deserted me right in the middle of a writing session, went out in the station wagon with a wad of my cash, and came back with a new flat-screen television and an Xbox 360. He set up all of this equipment in his room and he began to play a loud video game in which people killed one another with a variety of weapons. As he played, it started snowing outside, but Ben was so busy he barely noticed.

The heavy snow continued on and off for the next several days, piling up against the sides of the trailer and icing the coat of the sluggish black goat in the backyard, and all the while Ben entertained himself nonstop with his sophisticated new electronic toys. He was so preoccupied with his gaming that he missed his appointment with Fred and completely ignored the Ouija board. In fact, at one point during the long snowstorm, I arrived in his room to find that the planchette had somehow gotten knocked to the floor and partially buried beneath a mound of dirty clothes—where it remained for the next several weeks as Christmas approached and Ben, in the animated role of various muscular and tough-talking demigods and demi-demons, electronically shot, stabbed, hacked, and blasted his way through an endless assortment of anti-heroic Xbox scenarios.

Christmas and New Year's came and went with a glassy-eyed Ben barely leaving his room at all, except to boil a pan of ramen noodles or to say hello to the occasional relative who stopped by. He did not once attempt to talk to me, and I began to consider giving up on him and going back to the abandoned church to hang out full-time with Virgil and Gib. Finally, however, a dark accident worked in my favor—though it also came with some unintended consequences.

One day as the oblivious Ben single-mindedly thumbed his gaming console, I saw a dog emerge from the woods behind the trailer. A lop-eared mongrel, it stood just beyond the scope of the black billy goat's long rope and waited. Dog and goat stared at one another until finally the dog gazed over his shoulder to watch as a pack mate stepped out from the trees. The second dog was long-legged and hyena-like, with a bowed back and a head it held close to the ground.

Other than the nervous, unceasing twitch of its tail, the staring goat seemed paralyzed. Both dogs began slinking forward over the snow, and I thought somehow to alert Ben; I bent to him and said his name, but he merely gave his ear a brisk, irritated swipe before continuing on with his game. I did it again, and again he waved me away.

The dogs separated and slowly circled. Then, as if by agreement, the large dog froze while the smaller one crept closer. Finally, the goat lowered his horns and committed to a charge. The goat leaped, the smaller dog wheeled away, and the larger dog, the hyena dog, rushed in and closed its jaws on the goat's belly, just ahead of the haunch. The other dog jumped to take the struggling goat by the throat.

I'll spare you the worst of the horrors here, except to say that a goat can make a scream that sounds remarkably human. That noise pulled Ben to the window, where he slapped at the wall and yelled, "Stop it!" As if in obedience, the goat fell silent—but the dogs did not even glance toward the window.

Ben dropped to his knees and jerked open the lower drawer to his dresser. He took out my shirt-wrapped gun, laid it bare, stared at it a moment. I told him, "Don't shoot yourself, asshole," though I knew he couldn't hear me. He ran from his bedroom and down the hallway to the kitchen, where he kicked open the backdoor. Both dogs lifted their heads at the slap of the door against the vinyl outside wall of the trailer; they were covered to their eyes in blood, clouds of frozen breath boiling from their mouths. At Ben's appearance, they began fading toward the woods.

Ben lifted the gun and squeezed the trigger. Nothing. He looked at the gun—his hand was shaking badly—and he clicked the safety off. He raised it and squeezed the trigger. Again nothing. Then he remembered that he needed to chamber the first round and he clumsily, tremblingly racked the slide. Once more he sighted down the barrel—but by then the dogs were gone. The woods had absorbed them like ghosts. Ben fired anyway. Toward the ghostly woods he shot again and again, flame spitting from the barrel until the gun was empty. Then he stood panting and staring out over the yard and its snow-mounded metallic debris and the carcass of the goat whose blood continued to color the steadily falling snow.

Two hours later, his hands still trembling, it finally occurred to him to return the planchette to the Ouija board; he was shaken and he wanted to talk. By then I'd come up with a plan to use the tragedy to my own advantage. I didn't want to do it—I felt bad about it—but I didn't see any other way to get him working again. So I let him sit at that card table for a good long while; I wanted to make him beg. Finally, when I saw tears forming in his eyes, I sent the planchette sliding to spell out my message.

YES I MD THT HPN
NOW FNSH YR JOB JKASS B4 SMTHN RLY BAD HPNS
(Yes, I made that happen. Now finish your job, before something really bad happens.)

After that, Ben did go back to work. By pretending I'd been responsible for the killing of his grandmother's goat, I succeeded in bullying him into resuming our task. And he was better at the job than ever: he'd sit for hours without even his usual and frequent food and bathroom breaks, taking my dictation. That's what I gained by scaring him, and I believe that if I had not done so, he might never have returned to writing.

But I also lost something of value as well, because there were some unintended—though in hindsight, entirely predictable—consequences to my deception. Ben never said a word, but I could tell that his attitude toward me had shifted, that the innocence of our association was over. Now when he worked his Ouija board and scrawled my words into his notebook, he no longer drove me to frustration with childish questions and ridiculous digressions; instead he said very little at all, keeping his lips pursed and his eyes on the table, working with the concentration of someone who looked forward to getting finished and moving on. It was apparent he no longer viewed me as his special invisible friend; instead, I'd become a spirit of ambiguous intention—a gray and possibly sinister presence around whom he needed to watch himself, for fear of inspiring further violence.

Following an initial glow of satisfaction, I began to find this change to be almost unbearably sad—and I also learned that there was no going back to the way things had been. Whenever I'd pitch him a peace offering in the form of a joke or a compliment, he would just nod and say "Okay, that's cool," and then he'd wait for me to move on with my story.

IT WZ JST A FKN GOAT B ID NVR HRT U

"Oh, don't I know it," he quickly replied. "I never thought that for a minute. It's cool, Thumb. It's totally cool"—a response that made me think of a cringing boy hoping to forestall the fury of an abusive father. I found this image so upsetting that a couple of days later I ended up fully confessing that I'd been just as much of a spectator to the killing of the goat as Ben himself.

I JST USD IT 2 GT U 2 QUIT PLAYN GMES N GO BK 2 WRK

"No shit? Well you sure had me fooled! Thanks for telling me that."

RLY B BLEV ME

"I do believe you. Now, what were you saying?" Then, his fingers spidered against the planchette, he sat without speaking as he waited for me to continue my story.

Even more troubling than the loss of Ben's trust, however, was a new and wild slyness that I sometimes detected in the sharp movements and unaccustomed narrowness of his eyes. I was sure that inside his head he'd taken a crafty turn; that he was rebelling against me somehow; that he was scraping together some kind of treachery. I wanted to find out what it was, but I couldn't think of an effective way to go about this discovery. It would be almost impossible to trick him into telling me, because my cruelty had made him continually wary of anything I said. For probably the first time in his life, Ben was always thinking hard before he spoke. And I certainly couldn't scare it out of him, because that card was already out of my hand. He was prepared for me now, and no matter what nightmares I menaced him with, he'd merely deny that anything at all was afoot. In fact, Ben was able to keep his secret until the next time we visited Fred.

*

Following the absurd instructions Fred had given him when we'd last paid him a visit, Ben went out to the farm wearing black dress shoes, a dark suit, and a black overcoat. He was visibly relieved to find a well-beaten path through the snow alongside Fred's barn. Even so, he walked on eggshells because the shoes were new and their leather soles extremely slick, and he was afraid of placing his full weight on a snow-covered patch of ice and flying into the air. When we finally reached the electric fence, there was not a pig in sight, probably because it was so cold outside; I looked through the wall and saw them all lying or milling about on the concrete floor. There were many fewer pigs than there had been the last time we'd come by, which meant Fred had sent a bunch to the slaughter-house. I also saw Fred himself, clad in a blood-smeared vinyl apron as he walked to the wide doorway with something cradled in both of his calloused hands. When he emerged into mortal view, we saw that he carried a limp and nearly shapeless lump from which stuck a twist of umbilical cord and four little legs tipped with tiny trot-ters. As soon as it hit the cold air of the outdoors, the still bundle of black-and-white flesh began to smoke.

Fred's eyes were red, probably from tiredness—although it occurred to me it was not impossible that he also felt sad. He had to stare for a moment before he recognized Ben in his good clothes, but he did not seem surprised to see him. He said, "You haven't come at a good time, friend. I've still got seven sows that are ready to farrow." Vapor boiled out of his mouth and mingled with the wisps dancing up from the dead newborn. He nodded at the Dunkin' Donuts bag Ben carried and added, "Is that for me?"

"Yes," replied Ben, his eyes still glued to the lifeless creature Fred was holding. "I thought . . . "

"I've got my hands full right now. I'll get it later; set it down right there and put a little snow on top so it doesn't blow away. Far enough from the gate so a pig can't reach through and grab it."

Ben did as Fred had asked, bowing toward the snow to weight the paper bag. Then, as he stood again, brushing melting snow from his pink fingers, I saw that his mouth was a bloodless line and his eyes were narrowed in the same suspicious way that recently I'd so often noticed.

"I have something to tell you," he said to Fred—a declaration that was not part of the script we'd worked on together. Whatever he'd been plotting, it seemed like he was ready to unleash now, and there was nothing I could do to stop him.

"To tell *me*?" said Fred. "What might that be?"

"The thing, the manuscript I want you to help me with. I'm not the one that's writing it."

"No? Who is, then?"

"The guy, the dead guy, the ghost. Thumb. He's the one that's really writing it."

I immediately understood what Ben was up to. Telling Fred the truth about me was guaranteed to piss the old man off. He would think Ben was completely crazy—or worse, making fun of him—and likely chase him off his property with a rake. Order him never to come back under pain of a beating—which would make it useless for Ben and I to continue our work together. He'd then be off the hook. He'd be free of me, the demanding, goat-murdering ghost. I had to admit, Ben's assumptions seemed sound; in fact, his plan would be admirable if it weren't so infuriating.

Fred gave a little snort and said, "Your character is writing his own story? Well it certainly seems that way sometimes, doesn't it? It's happened to *me*, in fact."

"No, dude, I mean he actually is. He's a ghost, and he's really writing it." How I yearned to give Ben a kick in the ass. If only I had a leg, and a leather-booted foot. . . .

Fred stared at him. After a moment his jaw tightened, and color began building in his cheeks. The explosion of obscenity that Ben counted on was working its way through the pipes. And I'm sure it soon would have arrived all on its own if Ben hadn't gotten smug and decided to prod it along.

"I just write it down for him. That's all I do. Thumb spells it all out on the Ouija board, and I put it in my notebook."

A few heartbeats passed, and Fred audibly exhaled, his mouth staying parted. His eyes widened and his shoulders settled. After a moment, in a quiet voice he said, "You use a Ouija board?" I remembered then, the Ouija board illustration at the start of the automatic-writing chapter in one of his hypnosis books.

"That's how I talk to him. That's how Thumb writes the book." A slight smirk was pulling at the corner of Ben's mouth. The little asshole was enjoying himself.

Unexpectedly, Fred said, "Well, I'd like to hear more about that . . . Ben. That's very interesting. But first, I need you to do me a favor." He stepped to the fence and said, "Here, take this." He still had the dead piglet in his hands, though it no longer steamed in the cold.

"Wait—w*hat*?" Ben's smirk vanished and he began backing away. "No fucking way."

"Come on. I've got a whole litter in there to take care of. I need to get some heat lamps set up before I lose more of them." He lifted his bearded chin toward the back of his property. "See that hill, with the tall pine trees on it? There's an old cemetery up there; when you reach it you'll see the tops of the slate gravestones sticking up. Take her up; lay her out on the snow. The ravens will do the rest. By tomorrow, there won't be anything left. You and I'll be the only ones who know she ever existed."

When Ben remained statue-still, Fred said, "Get it in gear, sunshine. If you're going to be a writer, you can't be squeamish."

Ben, almost in spite of himself, wobbled forward and received the cooling mass in his cupped hands. As he was trudging toward the hilltop through knee-deep snow, Fred called out behind him. "I'll be waiting for you."

Ten minutes later, Ben set down his small burden, vomited a short distance away just like he had after disposing of the dog-savaged remains of his grandmother's goat, and scrubbed his hands and lips with fresh snow. When he reached the corner of the barn again, Fred reemerged to open the gate in the electric fence.

"Come in," he said. "I made some coffee. Let's have a talk."

For a minute Ben stood wavering, his palms, now stained the color of rust, open before him as if he expected Fred to pass him the carcass of another tiny pig. Up on the hill, ravens were already descending, just as Fred had predicted.

"Come in," Fred repeated. "Quickly, before they figure out I've opened the gate." From the flash of confusion that crossed his face, I could tell that Ben was at first uncertain who Fred was talking about. Then he realized it was the pigs. The pigs would figure it out.

And still he hesitated. This was the opposite of what he'd planned. Instead of chasing him off the farm forever so that he'd never have to see Fred again or write another word for me, Fred was trying to pull him deeper in. I caught a look in Ben's eye and realized then that he wasn't used to being invited anywhere; it was difficult to resist. After a moment his entire body twitched beneath all that new, dark clothing, and then he took a step, and then another. Fred closed the gate behind him, and warily he followed the old man into the barn.

The two of them wove a path among the massed bodies of sleeping pigs, past cinderblock enclosures full of pregnant sows and sows with piglets to an open pen that contained two chairs and a card table, on which a candle burned. Next to the candle rested a spiral-bound notebook and a pen. Ben froze, obviously wondering what it was Fred wanted from him, and seemed to consider retracing his steps back out into the snow and the sunlight.

"Want some coffee?" Fred said. "I've got a little kitchen in the front room. It's up there."

"No," Ben said. He shook his head. "I'm good. You know, I really . . . "

"Tell me about that Ouija board."

Ben shrugged. "It's, uh, you know, a Ouija board. My gram had it."

"Yeah, so what about it? What were you saying about it before?" Now that he had Ben in the barn, Fred could afford to let a little of the old sharp impatience return to his voice.

"Well, like I said, that's how I talk to Thumb. He spells out the words, and I write them down."

"And you're telling me in all honesty you actually believe that Thumb exists?"

"I don't *believe* he exists—He *does* exist. He's here right now, in fact; he and I came here together." As Fred was looking around him, his eyes wide and a smile tugging at the corner of his mouth, Ben added, "In fact, he's with you more often than I am. He hangs out and watches you, and when we write, he tells me what you've been doing. You'd know that if you read our manuscript."

"He does?" said Fred. "What does he tell you about me?"

"He says you talk to yourself." Fred looked surprised for a moment, then nodded and grinned his lopsided grin.

"Yes, I do. More than a little. But that wouldn't be hard for you to imagine, since my only company here is pigs."

"I used to like Thumb; I used to want to help him. But he's been a prick lately." At this Ben's eyes darted around guiltily; I'd told him my story about the beating I'd given Dirt, and he looked as if he expected me to materialize in front of him and fill his mouth with my knuckles.

"What else did Thumb tell you about me?"

"I don't know. You're a writer, but not a successful one. And you're not very happy." Laughter exploded from Fred.

After a moment Fred said, "Sorry, I'm laughing at myself, not at you. And Thumb sounds like a very observant young man. See, though, the thing is, there *is* no Thumb. But the truth is even more interesting than a ghost. Thumb is your subconscious mind *pretending* to be someone named Thumb. All the writing you've done up to now? It's all your own work even though it feels to you like you've been taking dictation from somebody else. We're talking scientific fact here; it's a well-documented psychological and creative phenomenon."

"Nope," said Ben. "He's real. And he's probably standing right here, all pissed off at me for telling you about him. He probably wants to kill me."

"Okay," said Fred. "All right." He lifted his hands to show that he wasn't interested in arguing. "It doesn't really matter whether you believe what I say or not. Maybe it's even better if you don't. So let's just move on to the mechanics of the whole thing. Tell me: writing with your Ouija board—having to wait for every word to be spelled out—how is that working out for you as a . . . as a"—Fred fought to force the word out—"as a writer?" Ben shrugged again.

"It used to be okay. We have a system worked out to make it go faster. I didn't mind it. But now I'm kind of sick of it. It's slow, and boring. And like I said, I'm not that happy with Thumb anymore. He's been nasty; that's why I told you about him in the first place. Just because he didn't want me to. Fuck you, Thumb, if you can hear me."

"Well, look, I've got something I'd like to show you. It doesn't work well for me, but I'm interested in seeing if it would be effective for somebody like you. It's a technique—something that might work *instead* of the Ouija board. It's *like* the Ouija board—same principle—but a lot faster. It's called automatic writing. So how you do it is, you hold a pen in your hand, and your subconscious—the invisible spirit, whatever—uses you as a tool to write whatever it has to say on a piece of paper. No spelling it out letter by painful letter and then scribbling it down afterwards. In fact, back in the early 1900s, entire novels were written this way by people who thought they were taking dictation from spirits. Mark Twain—the *Huckleberry Finn* guy—supposedly even wrote a novel from beyond the grave." Ben looked into the farrowing pen at the flickering candle and the notebook. His seemed to relax; automatic writing was obviously less worrisome than many of the other things he imagined that Fred might propose.

"The thing is, Mr. Muttkowski, I was thinking about not having anything more to do with Thumb at all. Like I said, he's a prick."

Fred stared at him. After all the pleading for writing help that Ben had done on my behalf, Fred couldn't have expected this sudden lack of motivation, and he clearly was wracking his mind for something he could use as leverage. Finally he said, "I understand. I understand. But you know, I hate to see a couple of friends—you and Thumb, for instance—part on such bad terms. Why don't you sit down here—" he swept his arm in the direction of the table and the candle—"and have a last conversation with him, then? A good, long one via automatic writing—much easier than you could ever have using your Ouija board. Tell him how you feel, and give him a chance to answer. Clear the air, why don't you? Then, if you still don't want to have anything to do with him, you'll never have to talk to him again."

"What if he threatens me?"

"Isn't he more likely to threaten you if you just refuse to talk to him again? But anyway, if he menaces you, we could end the conversation. What really could he do to you? And, aren't you curious? I certainly am. Aren't you full of curiosity to see whether automatic writing would work for you?"

Following another minute or two of urgent salesmanship on Fred's part, Ben finally shrugged, drifted into the farrowing pen, and settled into Fred's rolling chair. Fred took the folding chair on the opposite side of the candle.

"All right, so hold that pen in your hand. Make sure you've got a comfortable grip. Let your hand rest on the open note pad, there. Good. Now I want you to stare into that candle."

"Are you trying to hypnotize me?" Ben's eyes widened, and there was a note of alarm in his voice.

Fred's voice was quiet and even. "It *is* a hypnotic technique. But all it's going to do is help you write. You can't be made to do anything but write. Except for the hand you use to write, you will still have full control over every other part of your body. No one can make you do anything you don't feel like doing. You'll just feel very relaxed all over, and then when you're ready to write the pen will begin to move."

"So, like, stare into the candle?"

"Look into the candle, take a few deep breaths, and just watch the candle flicker. Concentrate on taking deep, even breaths. That's right; just relax. Feel your neck relax, and your shoulder relax—all that tension going out of them—and down through your arms . . . and your chest . . . and your shoulders and your hips . . . and your legs. Feel your feet relax. Even your toes. And keep taking those deep, even breaths. That's it; just like that. Keep looking into the candle, and then when they're ready, when your eyes feel ready, when they're tired enough, you can let them decide to close all on their own."

Ben's face had gone slack. He blinked slowly, he swallowed, and then his eyes slid closed, his head tipping forward.

"Good," said Fred. "Your eyes decided to close all on their own. Now, concentrate on your hand—feel the pen *in* your hand. What will your hand decide to do? Just concentrate on your hand and your arm. *Feel* your hand and your arm—how light they are. Your hand and your arm are so light that if they wanted to, it would take almost no effort for them to lift into the air all by themselves." Ben's shoulder twitched, then his elbow lifted a couple of inches from the table.

Fred said, "That's right. Your arm, your hand, your fingers can move all on their own, independently of you. If Thumb spoke to you now, his words, each of his words, could go right through you and down through your arm and your wrist and into your hand to the nerves in your fingers, and your hand could write them on the paper. Just like electricity moving through the wires of a safe and helpful machine. So easy." At this Ben's forearm and hand lifted a little, then his fingers twitched and tightened. The pen Ben was holding made a zigzag scribble on the blank, blue-lined paper.

By then I was curious myself about whether the whole hypnosis thing would work, so I leaned forward and put my mouth close to his ear just as I had that day in the old church, the first time he'd sat before the Ouija board.

"Ben," I whispered. "Hey, Ben." His fingers squirmed, and he scrawled out onto the paper exactly what I'd said. No punctuation, no capitalization, but all the words. Fred grinned and silently clenched his fists in the air while I continued to speak. I spoke for about a minute and then I stepped back and waited. Soon Ben opened his eyes, blinked, and looked down at what we'd written:

ben hey ben i wasnt lying when i said i didnt kill that goat i wouldnt have killed that goat im sorry those dogs killed it i really am your friend and id never hurt you either id try to protect you in any way i could and i need your help i need to get this thing written please help me finish it signed your friend thumb

Ben stared down at the page. "Wow," he said after a moment. He looked up at Fred. "He really does seem sorry, doesn't he? Maybe he *didn't* kill my grandmother's goat. . . . "

Fred said, "How long would all that have taken you with the Ouija board?"

"Five minutes, maybe," Ben answered. "Or more. Depends."

"And you'll be able to do that any time you want, now. Automatic writing. Anywhere, any time. The candle is just a prop; you don't even need it. Just sit down with a pen, get relaxed, and invite Thumb to come along. Take a few deep breaths and close your eyes, if you like. That's all it will take. No more Ouija board."

"Huh," said Ben. He nodded. "It *is* kind of cool. I guess I'd at least like to try it again."

"Great," said Fred. "A successful experiment, then." He looked around as if suddenly realizing where he was. He slapped his knees in a gesture of finality and stood up. "Good job with the writing, friend. I'm actually envious that it works for you. I'm sure you've got places you need to be now. . . . "

Fred moved toward the gate to the farrowing pen and began unlatching it. Ben watched him, his face clouding at he realized the old man had merely been using him to satisfy his own curiosity and was now finished with him. He looked down at his hands for a moment, then stood and shuffled toward the now-yawning gate. He was halfway through it when he stopped, stood still for a moment, then slowly lifted his shoulders.

"You guys do nothing but fuck me over," he said.

"What?"

"You and Thumb. You treat me like a piece of shit. I'm tired of it." He turned around and looked Fred in the eye. After a moment, Fred looked away.

"Son," he said, "I never asked you to come here."

"Not the first time. But then you had me bring you dope, and a gold coin. I could have kept that coin for myself, and I didn't charge you anything for the dope. That's a few hundred bucks, right there. And I bought these new clothes after you told me to, even though I knew it was just because you thought it was funny. . . . "

"All right," Fred said, lifting his hands. "I still have the coin; I can give it back to you. You want me to repay you for the other stuff?"

"I *want* you to do what you said and look at the writing." Ben's voice was shaking.

Fred sighed. He lifted his eyes toward the ceiling. "To be honest, that's a huge ask. A less-than-half-baked, hand-written book. I think I'd rather just repay you for the smoke."

Ben stared at him, not speaking. Finally Fred said, "Ah, shit. Do you have it with you? The so-called book?"

"It's in my gram's car. I can get it."

"I hate to break it to you, but I'm likely to be unimpressed by it."

"The whole thing, Mr. Muttkowski. I think you owe me to read the whole thing. At least look through it all. Then if you think it sucks, just tell me, and I'll never come back."

"All right then," Fred said. "Get it. If I don't like it, I'll feed it page by page to the pigs."

After a moment, Ben nodded slowly. "I'll come back next week to hear what you think."

Fred hesitated before saying, "Make sure you're dressed appropriately."

*

There were now two full notebooks and half of a third filled with my story, as transcribed by Ben. It took Fred a couple of days to overcome inertia and open the first one, and as he did, he cringed, as if expecting a harsh sound to hurt his ears. It was early morning and the strong eastern light, filled with swirling dust, was pouring straight through the open barn and over the backs of piebald pigs. Fred stood outside his farrowing-pen office, apparently not even planning to sit down. After he'd flipped through the first dozen or so pages his face unclenched and he stood up straight and began to hiccup with laughter—a bad sign for me, it seemed, since I couldn't remember dictating anything funny.

But while he kept laughing and spitting out little blasts of incredulous blasphemy, he also continued to read. After ten minutes or so he let himself into the farrowing pen and settled into the rolling chair. A short time later he muttered, "Bikers. This kid does seem to know a little bit about them." Fred's computer and the notebook he'd shared with Ben were back at the house, but he scrounged a leaking pen from the floor, grabbed a wad of his old manuscript pages from the stone-weighted pile, and began to scrawl across the backs of them. Over the next couple of hours, he made several more trips to the manuscript pile, dipped in and out of my first notebook a number of times, and kept on writing until the bleeding pen died in his ink-stained fingers. At that point he got up and burst from the farrowing pen, his knees thudding against the rumps of slow-moving porkers as he rushed out to the pig run, where he stood looking around him, wide-eyed and seemingly out of breath. When he spoke, I knew he was addressing his gaggle of imaginary friends and adversaries.

"I'm actually writing," he said. "First time in months. Ghosts, bikers, and other complete bullshit, but I'm writing. This stupid, half-assed manuscript the kid brought—somehow it opens me up. It's . . . I don't know *what* it is, but"—he turned his eyes toward the sky—"thank you, whatever the hell you are, for giving me another chance."

He made a brief trip to the house and returned with Ben's other two notebooks, a ream of clean, white paper and, instead of his laptop computer, an old manual typewriter. After setting all these things on the card table in the farrowing pen, he spent another half-hour flipping through the first notebook. Then he cranked a sheet of paper into the typewriter and began hammering away. He worked like that—moving from my story to his, pausing only to swear and separate type bars when they jammed—until sunset. When he was done for the day, he'd banged out a good twenty-five double-spaced pages.

I have to admit that at the beginning I was dismayed at what I saw in this new draft. Fred was taking my autobiography as a ghost—what actually *happened*—and fictionalizing it in a way that, while still recognizable, was not exactly the way it had gone down, or what I'd wanted to emphasize. I'd done my best to relate history, facts, and details in just the order they happened, and now here was Fred, imposing a *movieness* onto the whole thing, with whole parts left out, other parts distorted—I suppose to give the book what he considered to be a better structure. For just one example, in my version, before I got to my death and my transformation into a ghost, I'd dictated a lot of important stuff about my father's early years in Caracas, and how he gotten his start in the cartel, material that Fred seemingly had elected to ignore—so much so that my dad, rather than being central to my story the way he was when I'd started writing, now was no more than a ghostly presence at the beginning of the book.

But Fred also was making me sound older and, I have to admit, smarter, than I actually was, and it was hard not to be flattered by that. In the end, I decided that since there was nothing I could do to change the way he was going about our business, I might as well try to appreciate the result.

Fred finished working his way through Ben's notebooks in about four days. He stopped writing, then—apparently *couldn't* write, no matter how long he sat at his card table, staring at the typewriter. That was the closest I'd ever seen him to crying.

When Ben returned at the end of week, Fred ignored the fact that he was dressed in his ordinary clothes, and not in a suit and tie as he'd been instructed. He met him in the driveway and yelled, "Great to see you, son. Did you bring me something to read?"

*

As for Ben, he was also newly inspired. He put away the Ouija board, and through automatic writing he and I churned out pages at nearly five times the speed of the past. A few weeks later, in the early spring, he traveled to the farm once more, two new spiral-bound notebooks riding the passenger seat of his grandmother's car, and when he arrived Fred again seemed delighted to see him. As soon as Ben drove into the dooryard, Fred burst from the house clutching a thick sheaf of papers. Ben stepped out of the station wagon grasping our spiral-bound notebooks.

"So, did you finish it?" asked Fred.

"Not yet. I think we're about two-thirds of the way through."

"*We?*"

"Me and Thumb."

"Oh, yeah. Thumb."

"I brought you a bag of donuts, too."

"Fine," said Fred. "I've been working on your story as well—just some light editing. And I also wrote an entire nonfiction book just for you; you and no one else. Let's swap." He relieved Ben of the notebooks while simultaneously shoving his own loose manuscript into Ben's hands. Ben looked at the top sheet, which was a title page that read, "*Practical Organic Pork Production: The Muttkowski Method.*"

"What's this?"

"I've got to go someplace. Where *is* my donut?"

Ben reached back through the window of the car, came out with the Dunkin' Donuts bag—he'd purchased the contents with a portion of my second, largest, and last buried treasure—and handed it to Fred.

"Okay," said Fred. "So, we're all squared away, then. I've got to go back in and change my clothes, and then I have to leave. People to visit. I'll see you in four or five days. Everything you need to know and a few things you don't are right there in my textbook."

"*Wait . . .*" Ben started to say. But Fred kept talking.

"I've made things easy for you by reducing my herd to a minimum. There are only thirty head remaining: my two boars, Kilgore and Falstaff, eighteen sows, and ten nice gilts that I kept back for breeding. I'll probably end up selling the gilts, but you never know.

"As you'll read in my book, you don't have to worry about water, because I've got an automatic system, and they can get a drink any time they want. Just make sure you feed them the recommended amounts—no more, no less; you'll find complete directions for taking grain out of the hopper and mixing in the diatomaceous earth, so they don't get worms. Also, make sure you keep the main floor of the barn as clean as you can.

"But don't even *think* about trying to clean the boars' pens; I'll do that when I get back. As breeders go, they're both easygoing boys, but they'd make mincemeat out of a tyro like you. Just feed them and—I shouldn't have to tell you, but, just in case—do *not* let either one of them out of his pen. *Ever.*"

"Mr. Muttkowski . . . "

"You can't leave until I get back. Not even for an hour. There's a cot just for you in the kitchen. Also a small refrigerator I put in there that has some cold cuts in it—a good variety, I must say—some bread, and a bag of carrots. Mustard and mayonnaise. Candy bars, because I'm a thoughtful guy. You'll also find a sink, a roll of paper towels, and a bottle of hand sanitizer. You'll need all of that. There's a first aid kit somewhere in there, too."

"Mr. Muttkowki . . . "

"When I come back, we'll spend some more time talking about this." Fred gave the new stack of notebooks an enthusiastic shake. "I found some real promise in what you've already given me, so the future's looking bright for us, my boy." At that he turned and ran back into the house, leaving Ben standing stunned in the driveway. He reemerged some twenty minutes later looking clean-shaven, wearing a jacket and tie, and carrying a large suitcase. As he whooshed past to throw the suitcase into the bed of his nearby pickup truck, Ben detected a whiff of cologne.

"Mr. Muttkowski," said Ben. "I can't . . . "

"Yes," said Fred. He fixed Ben with narrowed eyes. "It's for the sake of our writing project. There's a couple of people I need to talk to about it.

"So, you can do this. You *will* do it. You're a highly capable young man. I've got your . . . *thing* right here in my suitcase now." He climbed into the pickup truck, started it, and rumbled out of the driveway.

*

At first, the sows and the gilts seemed disgruntled about having a substitute caregiver, and they hazed Ben unmercifully by shredding the legs of his pants and eating the tops of his sneakers. Luckily, before he was completely barefoot, he found a pair of Fred's steel-toed rubber boots in one of the farrowing pens, and he made a swap. After that the pigs, apparently appeased by having Fred's boots moving among them again, seemed to settle down.

Halfway through his second morning at the farm Ben received a visit from Cici Muttkowski. She wore high heels and a long skirt whose fabric she clutched in her fingers, and she seemed ill at ease standing outside the pig fence. "Who are you?" she asked when he walked out of the barn.

"I'm Ben," said Ben.

"Where is Frederick?"

"I don't know. He told me to take care of the pigs while he was gone."

"He *told* you to?"

"He's helping me with something I'm writing."

Mrs. Muttkowski seemed upset. "This isn't like him at all," she said.

Ben, whose own experiences with Fred had taught him to avoid making predictions about the man's behavior, merely shrugged.

"When is he coming back?"

"He said four or five days. Which was yesterday, when he told me." I could tell by Ben's expression that it had suddenly dawned on him there was no guarantee Fred would ever return at all.

"Aren't those Fred's boots?"

"Yes, they are. Only because the pigs ate my shoes." Cici stared at him for a minute without speaking; finally, she turned and walked back to the house.

The next day, he received another visit, this time from two beautiful young women, both of whom, in addition to bearing the same vague resemblance to Fred, were also nearly identical to one another in every other way except for the fact that one of them had black hair while the other was a blonde; Ben could not tell which color, if either, was the natural one. The blonde girl wore a knee-length tartan skirt and a frilly white blouse, a golden locket dangling from her neck, while the dark-haired twin had on pants made of tight-fitting black leather, with a many-zippered jacket to match.

Her face was a celestial map of metallic piercings. Ben would later write that he immediately fell in love with both of these girls even though, as they stood outside the gate to the electric fence, they were furrowing their perfect foreheads in seeming fury.

"Where is our father, you freak?" asked the blonde twin. Her voice was like music.

Ben said, "I wish I knew so I could tell you."

"If you did something to him, I will fucking kill you," said the pierced and black-haired sister. She sounded like a rock star; Ben thought he would like to hear her sing a song.

"I didn't," said Ben. "I'm helping him, is all."

But the black-haired sister seemed not to have heard him. She said, "I'll come right in there and rip your ears off. That's how I'll start." Ben found himself almost wishing that she—or better yet, both of them—would do just that. Being pummeled, scratched, crushed against the ground—perhaps even bitten—by such a pair of angels was as fine a death as Ben could imagine.

*

During the handful of days Fred remained away—six altogether, rather than the four or five he'd said—spring arrived for good, and the frozen ground had turned to bubbling mud. Cici was not home when he pulled his truck into the driveway, so Fred quickly changed into his work clothes and walked down to the back of the barn carrying our notebooks.

He called Ben's name as he stood outside the fence. Their roles temporarily and weirdly reversed, Ben emerged from the barn wearing rubber gloves and carrying a rake.

"Did we lose anybody?" Fred asked.

"Wait—*what*?" said Ben.

"Are all of my pigs alive?"

"Oh. Yeah."

Fred nodded, "Well . . . well done, it seems." He lifted the note-books and gave them a couple of shakes. "So, I've spent some time thinking about all of this. Talked to some people, actually; showed them my edited version of what you've done. And I'm pretty sure now I can turn it all into a book."

"A real book? You mean like, that somebody would publish?"

Fred laughed dryly. "Well, we'll give it a fucking shot. My track record isn't good; I'm about zero for five at this point. But we can try."

After a moment, Ben nodded, paused, nodded again. His eyes swept the pounded ground of the pig run. Finally, in a voice barely louder than a murmur he asked, "Will my name be on it? If it gets published?"

The question seemed to catch Fred by surprise. His mouth opened, and for an instant it looked as if he were going to laugh again. He drew his hand across his mouth once, then once more. His fingers were still obscuring his lips when he began speaking.

"Ben, you're actually a *character* in this book, which is quite a landmark. Quite a special honor. What's a byline compared to that sort of immortality?" He stopped to assess Ben's expression, which was far from a look of delight, so he continued: "But . . . I kind of see your point. I kind of know what you mean. So tell me, do you know what an acknowledgments page is?"

"*Acknowledgments* page? I don't think so. But I have to tell you that lately I've been considering trying to go to college; I didn't do that good in high school, and I'm thinking my name on a book might help me get in."

"College!" said Fred. "Great idea. I'd write you a glowing rec-ommendation. As for the acknowledgments page, it's usually the first real page in a book. The first page by the author, anyway. It's certainly the most *important* page—one of them. It's where all the people who have contributed to the book are mentioned. Your name would absolutely go on the acknowledgments page. In fact, it would be the very *first* name on that acknowledgments page. Stellar. Just a stellar . . . kind of thing."

Ben stared at him without speaking. Fred stared back until the silence grew heavy. Then he looked down and scuffed his booted toe against the ground. Just as he looked up again and seemed about to make some further concession, Ben said, "That's not quite right."

"Well, so . . ."

"I mean, as pissed off as I've been at Thumb, it's really his story. *His* name should go first on the acknowledgments page. *Then* my name."

Fred's eyes widened. He smiled, his tongue touching his bottom lip. He gave a vigorous nod. "Thumb. Of course. Thanks for reminding me. Not just Thumb, in fact: Daniel 'Thumb' Rivera. His name will absolutely go first on the acknowledgments page. Then yours. Still stellar."

"What about money?" Ben asked.

"For the *book*?" Fred said. He laughed. "To be honest, the way I'm planning to go about this, there's not likely to be much, if any."

"But some?"

"Maybe. If there is, I'll give you some of it. And if you're really going to college, I might be able to help out there, too. Not out of my pocket, of course, but I bet I could help you find a scholarship or two. I used to know how to do that sort of thing."

Ben was undeterred. "How much will you give me, if you get any money for the book?"

Fred sighed and rolled his eyes. "Half. How's that? Fifty-fifty. Keep in mind, though, that half of nothing is nothing."

Ben seemed satisfied with that. He nodded. He smiled. Then he actually reached to shake Fred's hand.

As for Daniel "Thumb" Rivera himself . . . I guess I thought it was okay, too. It was my story—novelized, if it needed to be—that I wanted out in the world; I didn't really care who took credit for having written it.

CHAPTER 13

With the arrival of my second spring as a ghost and Fred Muttkowski's enthusiastic involvement in our project at long last— each day he was now spending two or more hours in his vacant farrowing pen with our notebooks balanced on his lap—Ben and I began a sprint to finish the book, often working through both morning and afternoon, with just a handful of quick breaks for him to eat, or shit, or attempt to appease his grandmother, who frequently nagged him about hunting for a job. We were more efficient than ever; not only were we much faster than we'd been with the Ouija board, but we even worked out a system whereby I could capitalize and punctuate without slowing us down excessively.

From the start of this new beginning, however, it was clear that things had permanently changed between us. In spite of his having held out for my inclusion on the acknowledgments page, Ben still carried something of a grudge against me over the death of his grandmother's goat—he didn't completely buy my claim of innocence, and he certainly no longer saw me as harmless. Our collaboration remained almost entirely businesslike.

When Ben and I weren't working, rather than flying off to the abandoned church as I formerly might have done, I spent my days and nights haunting the concrete stairway to my vanished former home and staring out over the marsh as I remembered, brooded, and wondered. By then my yard had become something of a dumping ground for people who didn't want to pay the fees at their local recycling center. My immediate surroundings now included several stacks of worn tires, a threadbare couch whose upholstery was bloated with rainwater, a heap of asphalt shingles, two piles of old lumber profusely fanged with nails, and a couple of shredded garbage bags whose former contents had been spread by animals through the unmowed grass. One afternoon when a shiny minivan pulled to the shoulder and stopped, I assumed this was someone with yet another bag of trash to toss, and I began to wish I could do something aside from just sitting there and fuming; I wanted to swear or throw a rock. But the driver turned out to be Cricket—and with her was a baby, a little girl, who slept in a car seat behind her. A *girl*!

I rose from the steps as Cricket, in jeans and a sweater, her hair shorter than I had ever seen it, stepped from the car and quietly closed the door. Almost faint with excitement, I was ready to rush over and get as close as I could to the child. But after looking warily around her for a moment, Cricket moved toward me, so I stayed on the stairs and waited. She crossed the feral lawn to stand before me; she was close enough to touch, and how I did yearn to put my arms around her and crush her to me and feel her against me—the deceptive strength of her thin shoulders, the firm push of her breasts, the beat of her heart against my chest, the heat of her internal fire. Her hands clasped before her, she stood staring through me for a long minute; I found the lack of direct eye contact unsettling. Eventually she murmured, "This place is so ugly now. But I feel closer to you here than anywhere else. I don't know why." She drew in a shuddering breath, and when she spoke again, she was whispering: "Anyway, I miss you. I wish you were here. I think . . . " but instead of finishing the thought, she pressed her fist against her lips and sharply shook her head. After she took her hand away, she said, "Goodbye again."

I groaned as Cricket turned to face the road once more. So soon, oh my God. But then she lifted her chin toward the car. She was whispering again: "That's Lizzie. She's asleep. She's beautiful. She has—" she paused to brush the back of her wrist against an eye "—She has Charles's last name. Chef's last name. Anyway . . . we just thought we'd stop by." She gave a little laugh, then walked to the car, got in, and began to buckle her harness.

I ghosted my way through the sliding passenger door. The little girl—Lizzie—was still asleep and breathing softly. She was a healthy-looking dumpling of a child with a pink bow in her still-wispy, light-brown hair. Her complexion was very pale—much more like Cricket's than mine. "Hi, Lizzie," I said. I wished she would open her eyes so I could see what color they were. I also wished I could pass on to Cricket my cryptic warning from Angelfish that the baby might be in danger—perhaps from the same person who'd killed me. Maybe I would have Ben write her that letter after all—although as I'd already figured out, a letter from a dead guy presented dangers all its own.

Cricket started the car. "Bye, Lizzie," I said. "I love you. *Te quiero mucho*." The car started moving; the rear bench seat passed through me followed by the lift gate, then I was hanging all alone in midair above the edge of the road.

The following day Chef showed up and stepped out of a convertible sports car bearing dealer plates. His blond hair was cut and combed, he was sporting a neatly trimmed moustache, and he seemed to have lost some weight—although this may have been nothing more than an illusion brought about by the fit of his fine suit. After looking around for a moment, Chef lit a cigarette—I'd never known him to smoke anything but weed—and he walked up to the steps where I was sitting.

"Dude," I said. "You're looking prosperous. What's going on?" It was only then that I noticed an unfamiliar hardness in his eyes. Though there was no telling what had caused it, the change was profound; these were almost the eyes of someone else, and it disturbed me to imagine him turning them on my daughter.

Unlike Cricket, Chef did not speak to me. Instead, he just smoked and glowered, and when he had finished his cigarette, he flicked the butt against the back of the lowest concrete step, where it lay smoldering beside my foot. Then he walked back to his car and drove away.

*

The next visitor I received was another ghost.

One moonless evening a dense fog rolled in from the coast and came flooding through the marsh, smothering the landscape for miles. With mortal eyes I barely would have been able to see the edge of the road from my seat on the steps a few yards away. It was through this fog, and seemingly from all directions at once, that I heard a man attempting to whistle. Over and over he squeezed out the same half-dozen broken notes as he seemingly struggled to master the beginning of a tune. I thought the whistler probably had company because every few seconds, even as he slid from note to tortured note, there came a separate timbre like the blat of a child's toy horn.

Eventually the spirit materialized out on the road and, still eerily whistling, came walking toward me from the direction of town. Fog swirling around him, he stopped before my stairs and stood glowering down at me and I recognized him as the ghost of Dirt. His face was unshaven and he was dressed in the same greasy-looking clothing he'd worn in life; after a moment he ceased whistling and spread his mouth in an angry grin. One front tooth remained missing, the other was still black. I was about to say something to him when I heard that horn again, after which I saw a flash of scarlet behind his ear—and suddenly the eye and long beak of a bird loomed above his shoulder. The bird clawed its way up Dirt's back until its feet were fastened to what would have been his collarbone had he been alive, then the amber eyes in its red and tufted head were watching me from beside his own. It was a pileated woodpecker. The bird studied me for a moment before abruptly swiveling its neck in Dirt's direction and stabbing its thick black beak into his ear. Dirt grimaced and a moment later the woodpecker drew out a beetle with wildly waving legs and swallowed it with a single toss of its head.

"Fucking bastard," muttered Dirt. I was unsure whether he meant me or the bird.

I said, "What's wrong with you? You're a ghost now; you could take any shape you wanted. What's with the bird, and why do you still look like a walking piece of garbage?"

Dirt sneered and shook his head. "No, Thumb, I *can't* look like anything I want. I'd look like fucking Brad Pitt if I could. Showing myself to other ghosts like this—it's part of my atonement."

"Oh. Well I guess you do have some things to atone for."

"Fuck you, and so do you. And I wouldn't be here talking to you if I didn't have to."

This was surprising to me. "You're a messenger? *You*?"

Dirt nodded. "Otherwise you can be sure I wouldn't give you the shit off my shoes."

I had a good, long laugh at this as Dirt stood gritting his awful teeth at me and balling his fists. The woodpecker, meanwhile, scooted over to his other shoulder and pecked a couple of times against the side of his head. Finally I said, "So what's your message, then, messenger? Are you here to admit you killed me?"

"Me?" It was his turn to look surprised. "No." Then he smirked. "Not to admit it, at least."

"Do you know who did?"

"I thought you knew. It was the Blood Eagles. They blew your fucking head off." I felt like punching him. But a ghost can no more punch another ghost than a shadow can assault another shadow.

"There was one of our posse there, too. Standing behind me with the gun. I never saw him. I figured it might have been you."

He studied me, and finally, in a tone that suggested he was impressed with his own cleverness, said, "I bet that's *your* atonement. To find out. Isn't it?"

"Part of it."

The smirk returned to his face. "Well, we all had reasons to hate you, Thumb. But right now that's not important 'cause there's a place I got to take you. Come with me."

Through thick fog we flew toward Riverside on the same ghost path Virgil had shown me long before. When we had almost reached the college, Dirt banked away and led me toward the river; a couple of minutes later, we were standing in a supermarket parking lot a stone's throw from the muddy, tidal shore. Fog crawled from the river and swarmed past us like a living creature.

"Really?" I said. "You mean after all this time I finally get to go across?"

"A dead lobsterman showed me this path a while back," said Dirt. "But I've only made the trip a couple of times. The route's a tricky little zigzag, like a lightning bolt, and it's easy to lose the way."

He led me out over the swirling tide. We turned upriver for a half-mile or so and then headed to the middle of the flow, where we changed direction yet again and began to cross a little island of seaweed-smothered rocks that lay exposed by the falling tide. It was then that we spotted two other ghosts gliding toward us over the water and through the fog, heading for the bank we had recently abandoned. They were the strangest spirits I had yet seen: young American Indian men who obviously had lived during a much earlier epoch, and who were dressed in buckskin leather elaborately decorated with shells and colored beads.

"Is this part of your message? Are we supposed to talk to these guys?"

"I don't think so. I never seen them before. Weird-looking fuckers, though."

At first we heard them speaking in their language, but they shut up as soon as they spotted us. We moved off to the edge of the fairly narrow spirit path in order to let them slide past without having to go through us. I said hello as they ghosted by but they didn't reply; they only stared at the pileated woodpecker, which was now clinging to Dirt's arm, tail pointing skyward. When they were gone Dirt said, "Couple of pricks, anyway."

"They've got their reasons not to like us, I think."

A few more zigs and zags and we reached the far shore, where we ascended a trash-strewn bank and emerged onto an industrial-looking nighttime street. I was excited to be there.

"Is this the place?" I asked.

"It's a little farther on," said Dirt.

We moved along the nearly deserted strip of potholed blacktop until we arrived at a highway overpass at the base of which sat a flat-roofed brick building that throbbed with music. There were blackout curtains covering the insides of all the windows, and between the curtains and the glass of each window flashed the garish neon outline—alternately pink or blue—of a shapely, long-haired woman sitting with her knees angled invitingly, her arms stretched behind her to support the weight of her arched torso, and her head thrown back in the anticipation of ecstasy. The pink neon sign above the front doorway identified the place as "The Magic Hat." A dozen motorcycles were angled along the front wall like horses at a hitching post, while the parking lot was half full of pickup trucks commingled with a handful of sedans and two or three out-of-place-looking mini vans. "The Hat," which was what its regulars called it, was familiar to me; in fact, I'd actually spent a considerable amount of time there, back in my heartbeat days.

"Is this our destination?" I asked.

"Yeah," said Dirt. "This is it. My job's done; I can leave you here now."

"It's a strip club."

"No shit, Thumb. You're supposed to go inside."

"But not you?"

"I think you're meeting somebody here."

"Do you know who it is?"

He hesitated. "Maybe I do. But you'll find out soon enough. Now *adiós*, asshole. I hope to never see you again." As he started back toward the river, the woodpecker let out a couple of sharp beeps as if to say goodbye. I called Dirt's name, and reluctantly he stopped and turned.

"I was there when you died; I don't know if you remember. In the rooming house. Needle in your arm and everything."

He seemed a little surprised at this but then he shrugged. "Okay. Whatever the fuck. I'm just as dead."

"It's not like there was anything I could have done, or I would have."

He shrugged again. "You finished?"

"Someone else was leaving your room just as I got there; I didn't get to see him. Do you remember who it was?"

After a moment he answered, "It was Mantis. Why?"

"Mantis was in your room when you OD'd?"

"He came to visit. He brought the shit I used."

"He brought you the shit? Did he use any himself?"

"I don't know what he did. We had one needle, and I went first. I don't remember anything after that."

I spent a moment trying to calm myself so that I wouldn't shut him down with a too-eager tone. "So you think maybe Mantis cooked up a hot load for you? Do you think your OD wasn't an accident?"

Dirt grinned, exposing his terrible teeth; he looked happy for the first time since he showed up at my haunt. He stopped slouching and jabbed a finger at me. "You know what? Fuck you, Thumb. I don't owe you nothing. I may *know* some shit, but I don't have to *tell* you shit. Other than bringing you here I don't have to help you work out your atonement, and I ain't going to. Go talk to that bitch in the titty bar; maybe she can help you. But for my part, the only thing I have left to say to you is *fuck* you." He turned again, began whistling, started walking, and suddenly looked back at me. "By the way, there's one thing I *will* tell you. Your old lady? Cricket? I saw her not long ago. She was pushing a baby carriage." He grinned again before turning for the last time and heading off through the fog.

*

The Hat looked about the same as I remembered it: A long bar
running down the left side as you entered from the parking lot, tables
filling most of the space between the bar and the far wall, and at the
back, a square, velvet-skirted stage with a pair of polished chrome
dancer's poles. At the moment I drifted through the doors, two girls
in thongs and high heels were twining themselves around those
poles to the thumping beat of a hip hop song as a dozen hunched
men seated around the cockpit at the base of the stage watched them
work. Though not completely packed, the place was busy; about half
the tables, half the bar stools, and two-thirds of the chairs in the
cockpit were occupied, and during lulls in the music, the air droned
with the murmur of men's voices. The female bartender was pouring
drinks nonstop while a waitress shuttled continuously between the
bar and the tables with her glass-laden tray.

I spotted the ghost immediately. She was a young woman who
perched as lightly as a cloud on a bar stool not far from the door.
This attractive spirit wore her blonde hair pinned back tightly
against her head, and she was attired in a white blouse and a
pleated skirt—not an outfit you would normally see in a downscale
strip club. As I nodded to her, she smiled and widened her brown
eyes.

"Well now," she said. "Look at *you*! You're a major improvement over the last dude who came in here."

"The last ghost, you mean?" Just then, a man in a leather jacket
stepped between us, plunged his arm to the elbow directly through
her chest, hauled from her breast a brimming beer stein that had
been waiting on the bar behind her back, and walked away. But the
gorgeous ghost paid him no more mind than if, of the two of them,
he, not she, were the invisible, immaterial being; she kept her eyes
on me the entire time.

"I hate calling us ghosts. Ghosts are too much like zombies;
they're mean. What we are is ethereal people."

I laughed. "Okay, then. We're ethereal people. My name is Thumb."

"I already knew your name; the other ethereal dude told me about you the last time he was here. He said he was supposed to bring you around. I'm Angelfish."

I froze. I stared at her. After a moment she began laughing; it must have been my expression. Finally I was able to say, "*You're* Angelfish? I already know you then."

"You do? I don't think so, dude."

"From the river?"

"*What* river?" I had called it that for so long that I'd forgotten other ghosts might have other ways of looking at it—other names for it.

"You know, the place we go when we're not haunting the world. You were my messenger down there. First you said you needed my help. Then you said you needed my help to save a baby. *Then* you said . . ."

"In the *cave*, you mean? No, I don't remember talking to you there. I don't remember taking you a message." Her eyes were bright with amusement and she was on the edge of laughing again.

"Give me a break. How could you not?"

She shrugged and bowed her mouth in a comical way. "Maybe it was a different ethereal girl named Angelfish. Maybe it was actually a *dude* who was *pretending* to be an ethereal girl named Angelfish. Or what if—" she blinked at me "—maybe it *was* me, but a *future* me, which would make it impossible for me to remember it *now* because it hasn't happened yet. Is that clear? Maybe that explains it."

After a moment I said, "You're just fucking with me."

She shrugged again. "You're gonna believe what you want to believe."

"So, the whole baby thing . . . "

"Or, maybe I'm being honest with you *now*, but I was fucking with you *then*."

"I'm not going to get anywhere, am I? You're a strange lady."

"Not you though," she said. "Not strange at all. You're straight up and down."

I stared at her. Finally I said, "Okay. You win. Angelfish, anyway; that sounds like a road name—but you don't seem like the type to have one. In fact, I'd peg you more for a Lisa, or a Wendy; you don't look very roady to me at all. Did you change your appearance, post-mortem, maybe?"

Angelfish's smile widened. "I shucked my tats, is all. Other than that, except for the clothes, I'm pretty much the same. People always did tell me I cleaned up well when I wanted to."

"I'd have to agree," I said.

"Here, Ethereal Thumb, I bought you a drink." She indicated two full shot glasses standing side by side on the wooden bar top. "Jack Daniels. Bottoms up."

I laughed. "What are you talking about? We can't . . . "

"We can do what we can do," she said. "Observe." She pretended to grasp one of the glasses and pantomimed lifting it to lip level; of course, the actual drink remained unmoved. "Cheers," Angelfish said, and with her pinky finger curved in the air she tilted her hand as if to swallow the whiskey. I was about to humor her by mimicking her motions when two fat dudes in dress shirts and loosened ties stepped into us, one of them passing his beefy shoulder right through Angelfish's face, and the other enveloping me almost entirely within his sweating frame.

"Hey, fuck off, jackass," Angelfish snarled at the man who had unwittingly invaded her space. The two of them picked up "our" drinks, clinked them together, and gulped them down. When they were done, they hammered the empty glasses back onto the bar top, grabbed the two fresh beers that the bartender had just set down for them, and turned to head toward the stage, where the pair of hip hop pole dancers were making their exit to a smattering of applause. The amplified, disembodied voice of DJ Dave broke through to announce that it was time for a straight set of tunes by

ZZ Top, along with a Texas "hoe down" by cowgirls Crystal and Tiffany, to which the clientele clapped with increased enthusiasm.

"Go, Crystal!" yelled Angelfish. She whistled as she made devil horns of the fingers on both her hands and pumped them into the air.

"Do you know her?" I asked, watching as the opening chords to "La Grange" twanged through the sound system and two girls in denim mini-skirts, red suede waist-jackets with fringes hanging from the arms, and white cowboy boots and hats strutted out one behind the other through a set of curtains and down a short runway onto the stage, where they began to dance as the men in the cockpit howled.

"Yeah! That's what *I'm* talking about!" Angelfish shouted, alternately poking one set of devil horns higher than the other to the beat of the music. "Thumb baby, why don't you buy us another drink?"

"We're ghosts; we don't get to buy drinks anymore."

"You're no fun."

"And I asked, do you know her?"

"I used to work with her. In fact, she's the last of the girls I knew. All the rest are new." I should not have been at all surprised by this, knowing as well as I did not only that appearances were almost always deceiving, but that a ghost's appearance was never anything *but* illusion—deception by another name—no matter how innocently intended.

"So you were a dancer. And you worked here." It occurred to me then that I might have seen her perform at one time or another. However, it was no wonder that she did not look familiar: While some guys would get all hung up on individual girls in a place like this, I'd always considered exotic dancers to be entirely interchangeable. In addition, most of my Magic Hat time was spent conducting business and networking, rather than watching the performances.

Angelfish lowered her hands to her lap. "I was. I did. I was good, too."

"Of that, I have no doubt."

"Would you like me to dance for you?" Although her eyes were still flirtatious, her smile had taken an ironic tilt.

"I think there's plenty of dancing going on in here already. And what would be the point of that, anyway? A private dance for another ghost? It's not like we can even touch ourselves, never mind each other, so it'd end up in nothing but frustration."

"*Ethereal*," she said, correcting me. "I'd never dance for a nasty *ghost*. And like I said before, we do what we can to keep our spirits up. Now, how about that dance, lover boy? Do you want it, or not?"

"Did Dirt mention that I was murdered?"

"Who?"

"The other ghost. The ugly guy."

"Dirt!" she said, and laughed. "Dude had the dumbest parrot on his shoulder; it couldn't say a word. Yeah, *Dirt* did tell me that, actually. By the Blood Eagles, he said."

"Do you know the Blood Eagles? I used to come in here with some of them."

She hesitated before saying, "I did know some of them, yes."

"So, how about you? You're young; how did you happen to . . . get here?"

"How did I become ethereal? It was easy: I stopped breathing, then I made a noise like this—" here, with her eyes bulging and her mouth stretched in an O, she gave a ghastly, unnerving impression of a death rattle "—and then my heart stopped beating."

"Okay. I don't blame you for fucking with me now. It's a personal question, I know. I'm sorry."

"Then I tumbled in a river until it poured me out through a crack in the wall of the dancers' dressing room."

"A river? You said it was a cave before."

"Did I? It's kind of like a river *in* a cave."

"Anyway, so this is your haunt? When you're not bouncing along the bottom of the river?"

"So to speak. This place can get depressing during the day. Nights are lively though."

"I am sorry about getting all nosey on you. Even ghosts like to keep some things to themselves." The second song of the ZZ Top set, "Pearl Necklace," was now ending, and except for boots, hats, and thongs, Crystal and Tiffany were already entirely nude and completely a-jiggle. The next song was "My Head's in Mississippi," which, as you may know, is the one about that naked cowgirl who was "floatin' across the ceiling."

Angelfish pursed her lips and began bobbing her head in time to the music. She said, "This is kinda my song. I made a *lot* of money on this song. The dance, baby. The dance is the thing. If you'll excuse me." She rose from the bar stool, twirled around, and suddenly was no longer dressed in her relatively prim attire. Instead, she was costumed like a revved-up version of an 1800s dancehall girl in a low-cut, lace-frilled red corset, black heels, and fishnet stockings whose garters climbed beneath a black leather miniskirt. She wore bicep-length black silk gloves from which her fingers, with red-painted nails, popped through, and on her head was a bowler derby that sported a scarlet ostrich feather sticking up from one side.

"Dude," I said. "Whoa. Wait a minute."

But Angelfish ignored me and swung directly into her cocky dance. Swaying from side to side, she would prance toward me on those snapping heels and then quickly spin away. In one moment, she was giving me a direct and hungry look as she flicked the hat from her head and freed her hair from its prison of imaginary pins to cascade down the middle of her back; in the next instant, she had turned away to bend her supple upper body halfway to the floor, a single, smiling eye peeking back at me across the top of her shoulder as she lifted her skirt. After the surprise wore off, I found myself shaking my head.

"That's great, but do you mind stopping now? I've got a few more questions."

The fingerless gloves quickly went the way of the hat and then, after tousling her hair and flipping it all around so that it veiled most of her face, she teasingly loosened her corset, one by one unsnapping the black garters from its bottom fringe and slowly peeling it up her well-toned torso and over the top of her head. She then tossed the illusory corset, which disappeared as soon as it left her hand. Naked from the waist up—and quite breathtaking, I have to say—she was no longer smiling; her mascaraed eyes were fiery slits, her lips were peeled back in a gleaming snarl, and her dance movements had become abrupt, combative rather than sensual.

"Really, this is weird," I said. "Can you just talk to me?" I had by then lifted a hand to my forehead as if to shield my eyes.

Her response was to laugh—a sound like breaking glass—and she didn't stop, not even when the song ended and another ZZ Top number began. She danced toward me until she was almost touching my knees with her own—I was by then hovering on a bar stool with my back against the bar—and she began unzipping her skirt, inch by teasing inch drawing it down over her hips.

"That's enough, now, right?" I said. "Come on."

After a moment, as the leather skirt continued its mesmerizing, disturbing southerly slither, I saw the tops of some blue-ink letters emerging on the taut skin of her lower belly.

"What's that?" I said. "I thought you told me you got rid of all of those."

"Did I say all? I meant all but *one*, which I kept as a reminder."

"A reminder of what?" She just grimaced and kept lowering her skirt. In a moment there appeared a line of two blue words tattooed on her in a Gothic font:

Property of

I glanced at her face, and as soon as I looked back down, Angelfish let go of the skirt, which plunged past the waistband of her thong and vanished against the floor. Suddenly she was no longer dancing. The remainder of the message said:

Blood Eagles, MC

Unlike the rest of the text, the "C" in "MC" was neither Gothic nor blue, but was tapered at the top and banded in black, red, and yellow like the tail of a coral snake, and instead of ending at its bottom serif, the semi-serpentine letter continued on and curved away to bury its unseen, reptilian head beneath the thin, string-strapped strip of Angel's thong.

"Holy shit," I said. She seemed unembarrassed to be standing before me, naked.

"What's the matter, Thumb? Lost your wood?" When I did not immediately respond, she said, "Thing is, I wasn't always a dancer. It wasn't exactly my greatest ambition, you know? But when hard times hit, we needed some new flows of cash because of the big mortgage Scratch had taken out to buy the clubhouse. Almost a million and a half dollars, with no way of selling it again for anywhere near the same amount, and the people holding the note weren't any ordinary bankers; they were some Chinese dudes not even a biker on bath salts would want to fuck with. So, among other things we all had to do—and dancing was by far the least of it—I started working here."

I looked up at her again. "When was all this?"

"Nearly four years ago, now. Almost as soon as we moved into Maine to get the new chapter started. Funny thing about the dancing, though; as you could probably tell, I got so I almost enjoyed it."

"Listen. Do you know a ghost path to get to the clubhouse? I've got to go there. Can you show me?"

Instead of answering she said, "That tattoo down there—you can't imagine how funny it looked when I was pregnant, all stretched out and distorted, like words on a balloon. Everyone thought it was hilarious."

It seemed like maybe she was finally finished hiding behind her own smoke. I found myself nodding. "*You* had a baby."

"A little girl. Chelsea—although I don't know what her name is now; her new parents probably call her something else. She just turned two and a half. I can keep track, because the girls always have a calendar tacked to the wall back in the dressing room." Suddenly, Angelfish was no longer nude, but was wearing the same

modest clothes she'd had on when I first came in. Her hair, however, continued to hang down past her shoulders.

"That's terrible. I mean that you . . . oh, my God."

"It *is* terrible," she said. "Thank you. I mean, there are worse
things, but not many."

"So, how long ago did you die?"

"I think I just told you it was two and a half years ago."

"You told me you had your *baby* two and a half years ago."

"Yes. That's right."

"So, you must have been . . . were you *sick*, or something?"

"No, I wasn't sick."

"So, what happened? Some big complication? I mean, I'm sorry
to pry like this, but my girlfriend had our baby about a year ago,
quite a while after I'd already died. It's such a huge coincidence."

"You, a baby too?" said Angelfish, not exactly sounding surprised, as she watched me through narrowed eyes. "Yeah, what are
the odds of that?" Then, nodding but not smiling as she echoed my
words, she added, "And yes, you're right; it was a *big* complication.
That sure is one way of putting it."

"Well, I'm sorry. But, you say she was adopted by some people.
Do you know, are they *good* people, at least?"

"I think so," said Angelfish. "No reason for them not to be. I
know they've got a lot of money, anyway. They didn't know."

"Well, that's . . . something. But *what* didn't they know?"

"It *is* something. I'm glad your girlfriend got to keep her baby.
No matter what else happens, Thumb, you should always be thank-
ful for that."

After a pause during which Angelfish turned to watch her friend
Crystal finish her final dance and exit through the curtains, I said,
"Are you going to keep claiming you never talked to me before? In
the river? About saving a baby?"

She was staring at the curtains, which continued to ripple in
Crystal's wake. She said, "There's not much we can do for *my* baby,
now."

"What about that spirit path? To get to the clubhouse. Can you help me out?"

She looked back at me. "There's somebody else I think you need to talk to first. She's got a story you'll find helpful."

"Really? A real person? Or a . . . an ethereal one?"

I was relieved when Angelfish cracked an unambiguous smile. "Pickle? Sometimes I think she's somewhere in between. But she is alive—at least for now. Come back here tomorrow night, and we'll go see her."

CHAPTER 14

The next night I returned to the Magic Hat at our appointed hour, more or less—we ghosts carry neither watches nor cell phones— but I failed to find Angelfish waiting in the parking lot as we had arranged. Rather than scanning the building with my freakish x-ray vision, I entered The Hat and ghosted around, searching for her in the public area as well as backstage, in the dressing rooms and offices. I had finally seated myself in the cockpit to watch the performance when I sensed her presence back outside on the blacktop, and I walked through the wall to meet her.

"I think you're late," I said. She was wearing jeans and an untucked plaid shirt with the sleeves rolled up, and a long braid swung down the middle of her back; the overall effect made her appear quite a bit younger and far more innocent than she had the day before, when she'd alternately tricked herself out as a business woman and a stripper.

She said, "Did you really think I was going to get here first and wait for *you*?" She came over and pretended to kiss my cheek, momentarily making me forget not only that our meeting was taking place outside of a strip club, but also that we both were dead, and the otherwise earthly normalcy of our situation—we, a man and a woman, smiling, bantering, kissing, just as any living couple might do at the start of a first date—nearly overcame me with a dizzying sense of strangeness.

"You look nice," I said, falling almost helplessly into the role the circumstances had assigned to me.

Angelfish said, "Let's fly," which immediately broke the disorienting spell of otherworldly mortality, because I knew she meant literally for us to take to the sky. Pointing upward toward what in a moment I realized was the planet Mars, she added, "The path from here runs almost straight toward that really bright star; can you see it? We go a little bit to the left of where the moon is now, then we make a downward turn and head for the shore. It's almost like following a rainbow from end to end—a rainbow with a kink in it, except there won't be any pot of gold." As she spoke—and for the first time ever in my afterlife—I was able to see a faint, milky glow that marked part of the spirit route she had described. After nearly two years of death, apparently I was getting to be a "mature" ghost who could find his way around the ghostly world. This idea was at least as unsettling as it was liberating, because I had long before figured out that the more skilled I became at negotiating the afterlife, the less attachment I would have to everyday matters and the faster my cherished humanity would trickle away—to be replaced by only God knew what.

The aerial path was wide enough for the two of us to travel on it side by side without our avatars intersecting. After we made the turn she'd told me about, I was fairly certain of where we were headed.

"We're going to the clubhouse after all, aren't we?" I asked.

"We are. Are you scared?"

Strangely enough, I was a little afraid. But I answered, "I'm a ghost; what can happen to me?"

"That's right. What *could* happen to you?"

"Now, if we were still alive, I'd have reason to be worried. You're one of *them* after all; you're a mamma for the Blood Eagles."

"Yes, I was."

"I'd have to wonder whether you were setting me up."

"You'd be a fool not to give that some serious thought."

"As it is, though, not only do I own an array of super powers, including 360-degree vision that comes with an x-ray option, but I'm already dead."

"That's the biggest advantage to being dead; nobody can kill you." After a pause she added, "They can still hurt you, though."

After that we didn't talk until we could see the clubhouse and the surrounding grounds below us and we began to descend. Then I said, "By the way—and, tell me if I'm getting too nosey here, again— but I knew most of those dudes down there. Do you know which one was your little girl's father?"

Angelfish narrowed her eyes and drew back her upper lip. "Asshole! Of course I know who Chelsea's father is." A moment later, just before we touched our feet to the lawn in front of the huge house—and although I was not expecting any further information from her—she said, "It was Scratch, if you have to know. Scratch is Chelsea's father."

We drifted together through the closed front door and into the entrance hall, past the little room with the guns and the video monitors—it was manned by a young Blood Eagle I did not recognize— and entered the vacant great room, which looked nearly the same as it had on my previous and only visit, except that there seemed to be even more partially disassembled motorcycles strewn about, and no longer did a ladder stretch toward the nest of wires that bulged from the ceiling; apparently they'd given up, at least temporarily, on replacing the missing light fixture.

"Why?" I said, as we stood looking around.

"Why what?"

"Why Scratch?"

"Oh, are you disappointed in me?" There was an edge to her voice.

"Kind of. That tattooed face and the fangs, and everything. The fact that he's a murderer a few times over. *My* murderer, come to think of it. But it's really not my business . . . "

"I fell in love with his strength. I was young, I had nobody, and I thought he could take care of me. I thought he *would* take care of me. And FYI, I was already dead by the time he killed *you*." For the first time since I'd met her, she sounded bitter.

"Like I said, it's your business."

"And don't you *dare* judge me. You made plenty of mistakes of your own."

"Yes," I agreed. "I sure did. That's why I've been so anxious to come here, in fact; I died here, and I need to get a more complete picture of the worst and last mistake I made. I never knew who pulled the trigger—he was standing behind me—and I've got to find that out."

"Like, as part of your atonement?"

"That's right. Yeah."

"Well, don't go spooking around on your own just yet. Like I said last night, there's someone you have to talk to here, and she's waiting for us now. That's the important thing; that's why I brought you."

"Hell with that," I said. "I can talk later to whoever. What I want is to get a closer look at Scratch, and see if I can find any evidence of anything. In fact, I think I see him back there now, in the same room where I died. My dying room."

At that point, we were interrupted by a chorus of barking so loud it would have been painful to mortal ears, and Scratch's three big pit bulls—two of them seemingly chiseled from black volcanic glass, and the third and largest with a hide of brilliant, unbroken white—rose together from behind a sheet-shrouded couch to trot in our direction. The click of their nails against the floor echoed in the cavernous room.

"Oh, hello boys!" said Angelfish, her voice as syrupy as if she were talking to a baby. "Big, strong, handsome boys, yes you are!" The dogs repeatedly passed through our legs as they milled about, growling in their throats and sniffing for the source of the atmospheric disturbance they sensed. Angelfish pretended to pet one of the black dogs on the head. After a moment, in her normal voice, she said to me, "This is strange. They come to greet me sometimes, and they sort of follow me around in a friendly way. But they never get riled up like this; they never bark or growl."

The Blood Eagle who was stationed in the entrance hall opened the door to the great room and bellowed, "Dogs! Shut the fuck up!"

"Shut the hell up yourself," I said as he was closing the door again—and the dogs, all three of whom had all momentarily frozen and fallen silent at his command, began scrambling around and barking again, louder than before.

"Shut *up*!" the biker howled, but he did not bother reopening the door.

"Interesting reaction," said Angelfish. "Probably because you're a dude? When Scratch attack-trains these guys on people in padded suits, the targets are always dudes. So maybe they just feel more of a threat from a male ethereal person than from little old me."

I laughed and said, "Too bad I make them feel threatened. So, where are all the other Blood Eagles right now? I'm x-raying the place, and I only see Scratch himself along with this dick in the hallway, that other jackass out by the gate, and a couple on the floor above us—they're in a bed, so one's a woman—and somebody down in the cellar. There should be a dozen or fifteen people here."

"They're bikers. They party. Knowing them, they probably all rode down to Portland to hang out in the Old Port. They do that two or three nights a week."

"Why didn't your fuck-buddy go with them?" Just then, the white dog snarled and lunged, snapping his jaws where they would have made me bleed, if I'd been made of flesh and blood.

"Ouch," I said—although, of course, I felt nothing at all.

Angelfish told him, "It's okay, boy! There's nobody there!" Then she lifted a finger toward my face and spent a long moment seeming to consider a number of different responses before she finally spoke.

"Are you going to keep doing that? Rubbing my face in my mistake?"

"I'm sorry," I said. "I won't."

"He never goes with them anymore. He's got business worries, so mostly he just sits back there in his office, tapping away on his computer."

"Well that just sucks that he's not able to get out on the town. I think I'll go have a peek over his shoulder and take a look around his room."

"Negative. What we need to do now is to go down into the basement and talk to Pickle."

"We can do the Pickle thing later. Like I told you, I've been waiting for almost two years to get into this place." I started walking toward the door to the room where I'd been murdered, and one of the black dogs moved along behind me, sniffing the floor as if to track me.

Angelfish called, "Thumb!" and I thought she would continue trying to talk me out of detouring in Scratch's direction. Instead, she said, "Look at *that*! Say something to that dog."

"Like what?"

"I don't know; something mean. Something loud."

"Bad dog!" I yelled in my ghost voice. "Bad, stupid dog!" The dog barked and snapped at empty space, a thick rope of slobber flying from its mouth and spinning through my knee. The other two animals raced over as if to see what the excitement was about.

"Happy now?" I asked.

"Yes," she said. "I couldn't be happier."

*

In my death room they had covered the front of the brick fireplace with a panel of white-painted plywood. On the hearth, with its back legs resting on the wooden floor, stood Scratch's black desk. The seat of his chair shadowed the spot where I must have lain bleeding on the floor. On the desk there were ledger books and piles of papers and a computer whose keyboard Scratch was punching with his long-nailed index fingers. A spreadsheet glowed on the screen. Cursing Scratch beneath my ghostly breath, I traveled through and through the desk as I circled him, looking at him from every angle. Although less than two years had passed since I'd seen him last, he looked as if he'd aged; he had put on perhaps fifteen pounds of doughy weight, and his tattooed face had begun to sag so that the red wings that spread from the inside corners of his eyes appeared as though they were drooping. On the bridge of his nose, just beneath the tattooed, blue-eyed death's head, perched a pair of black-framed bifocal glasses, the seam distinctly visible in each smudged lens.

I told him, "You're dying, you bastard, and you don't even know it. And, when I meet you in the afterlife, I will kick your ass from here to the end of time."

Just then Scratch surprised me by giving a sudden groan. "Oh, God," he said, his grimace exposing his cosmetically bonded vampire fangs. "The fucking insurance, on top of it. This *cannot* go on the way it is." He tore the glasses from his face and, before he thought better of it, seemed ready to throw them across the room. Instead, he closed them and worked them carefully into the tight top pocket of his weathered denim cut, after which he shoved the keyboard aside to make room on the desk for his folded arms. He buried his face in the crook of an elbow.

"Come on, Scratch," I said. "I was hoping for some action from you; a show of evil shit. But all you are right now is pathetic." He answered with a broken snore.

Able to draw neither satisfaction nor entertainment from the dozing man himself, I crawled inside his desk and nosed around. There were a few loaded handguns in there, a couple of .22s—no telling whether one had been the weapon that ended my life—along with more papers and notebooks. There was an entire drawer of drug paraphernalia, including pipes, rolling papers, lighters, a ceramic mortal and pestle, and a scattering of capped syringes. But I found nothing that shed light on the circumstances of my death: who it was who had shot me, and where they had hidden my remains.

I had high hopes for the contents of a combination safe that stood to one side of the desk, but when I stuck my head inside of it, I discovered only the most commonplace assortment of personal and criminal materials—an entire pound, more or less, of pot, some white powder in a glass vial, assorted pills in plastic bottles, yet another handgun—this one a tiny .22 automatic sealed in a ziplock bag—a modest stack of money, some legal documents that seemed to include deeds and other contracts, a few brightly colored, battery-operated sex toys, a wad of women's undergarments.

Disappointed, I spent a little more time looking around the rest of the room before I moved out and began exploring the remainder of the house—all of it except for the cellar, which I was saving for last because I knew that was where Angelfish wanted me to go. I went all through the first floor including the kitchen and dining area without finding anything interesting, and then one by one I cased the upper stories of the house. These were warrens of dark, messy bedrooms and ashtray-strewn sitting areas that together made up a set of particularly slovenly dormitories—the sort of quarters you might expect to find below decks on a pirate ship. Beyond the third floor was one more level of vacant space and storage rooms and, above them all, a low, unfinished, and dusty attic. On the whole, almost everything looked completely unmenacing and entirely ordinary, and nowhere did I see anything that might help me solve my mystery—and, really, why should I have? I'd been killed nearly two years before; my death was ancient history. How illogical it had been of me to imagine that at this point there might still be obvious evidence of the crime that had ended me lying around in plain sight.

When I had finally and completely satisfied my doomed curiosity, I drifted back down the four flights of wide, wooden stairs to where Angelfish was waiting. She was sitting in mid-air with her legs crossed beneath her.

"Hi, honey," she said. "Did you find your dead body?"

"Stupid, wasn't it? I don't know what I was really looking for anyway. A written confession posted on the wall? A gun still smoking?"

"I know where your bones would be, if that's a comfort."

"Really? Where's that?"

"With all the rest of everyone's they've killed. The property here, one of the reasons it was so expensive is that it's got a piece of frontage on the river, with its own boat dock."

"So, you're telling me I'm sleeping with the fishes? In my green plastic shroud?"

"You are, no doubt, sleeping with the fishes. Either in the river or out under the ocean. In your heavily weighted plastic shroud. Instead of a teddy bear, you're cuddling a cinder block."

I nodded. "That makes sense, I guess."

"They'd of been careful to put you down someplace where a fishing boat wouldn't trawl you back up; maybe out among the lobster traps near a big pile of rocks or construction debris, or a sunken barge or something. That would be the kind of place to look if you were still obsessed with finding yourself. Me, I'd just as soon let myself rest in peace. In fact, I think it's kind of nice to imagine you and me might be resting side by side down there somewhere. Maybe holding hands and sticking starfish all over each other like badges."

I stared at her as she hovered there, smiling her ironic smile. After a long moment, a question began to form on my lips, but she forced me to put off asking it by saying, "You haven't seen the cellar yet. And we need to go down there right away; Pickle's been waiting for us, and she's getting more antsy by the minute; she'll be pulling her hair out in fistfuls before too long."

So I followed her as she descended directly through the floor. We ended up before a heavy steel door that was bolted from the outside, and through which I could see a person moving around in the space beyond. I tried to complete the thought I had been struggling to put into words a moment before. "So, why would they have wanted to kill you?"

As she seemed to do so often, Angelfish gave me an answer that appeared unconnected to my question. She said, "Scratch was brought up on a farm out West. He calls this area down here the 'farrowing floor.'"

"You'd just had his daughter. Why . . . " But at that moment, the person on the other side of the door let out a plaintive, quavering call.

"Earth to Angelfish," she said.

"Uh-oh," said Angelfish. "See, she expected us earlier, and now she's starting to lose it a little. Your fault entirely, Thumb."

At that Angelfish passed through the door, forcing me to follow her into what appeared to be the narrow central area of yet another dormitory. Compared to the rest of the house, the construction here looked fairly recent; Blood Eagles had probably done the carpentry themselves. The place was furnished with a couch, a flat-screen television tuned to a talk show, a half-dozen standing lamps, and a couple of coffee tables with their accompanying chairs. On either side of this lounging space were four doors leading to tiny bedrooms, and at the far end was a small kitchen and dining area.

The southern-accented voice that had cried out to Angelfish belonged to a thin, freckle-faced biker mamma dressed in slippers, pajamas, and an open bathrobe far too big for her, and whose reddish-brown hair was twisted and streaming in every direction. She was clutching a blue enamel hand mirror with a scrimshaw-like design etched in black on the back. A moment after we entered, she began speaking into the oval mirror as if it were a microphone.

"Earth to Angelfish!" she said. "Come in, Angelfish." She held the mirror at arm's length and began doing a bizarre dance in which she awkwardly twirled herself first one way and then the other, almost like a toddler trying to make herself dizzy.

"I'm right here, Pickle!" Angelfish called.

"Earth to Angelfish! *Please* come in, Angelfish." During one of her twirls, the bathrobe flew back and I could clearly see that beneath those baggy pajamas Pickle was pregnant. In a jolt I recalled the two pregnant young women I'd seen at the clubhouse the day I died. Then I remembered Angelfish in the underground river, telling me about the baby who was in danger.

Angelfish explained, "She can't hear me unless she sees me in the mirror, and she spins like that because she's trying to find me. The problem is, she *can't* find me unless she stops that damn spinning long enough for me to get behind her."

"Angelfish! Angelfish! *Come in*, Angelfish!" Angelfish stepped toward Pickle and began shadowing her movements as she tried to position herself behind her shoulder and in line with the mirror. Twirling and bobbing together in that poorly choreographed way, the two of them put me in mind of a pair of courting cranes, or an especially clumsy duo of ice dancers.

"That chick is with child," I said.

"Dude, you should be a detective." Angelfish continued gliding behind Pickle in what looked like an attempt to set her chin first on one and then the other of Pickle's collarbones.

"Come in, Angelfish! Are you here, Angelfish?"

"I'm here, honey! You can stop twirling, honey!"

I thought about Angelfish's story of her pregnancy, her childbirth, and her death. I thought about Cricket and our baby, and a sick feeling welled up in me. "What the hell's going on here, Angel? Is Scratch the father of *her* baby, too?"

"Oh! *There* you are! Oh my God!" Pickle placed her free hand on her breastbone. "Oh my *God*! I thought you weren't coming." Pickle stopped spinning, only to stagger with dizziness as she tried to stand still and stare into the mirror. It was amazing, but there in the glass, as clearly as if she were alive, I was able to see Angelfish's face; it was different—a little more full, a touch less symmetrical, and a great deal less blonde than the version I saw when I looked at her—but the differences, at least to my mind, were not significant.

"We got here late," said Angelfish. "I brought a friend, and he had something else to do. How are you, Pickle? How are you feeling? Are you still getting sick?"

"Sick? Oh, no. Not sick; not no more. Not for a little while, knock wood. Who's your friend? And, guess what? Guess *what*, Angelfish?"

"What is it, honey? What's going on?"

"Scratch said—*Hello*? Are you there?"

Angelfish slid to her right and said, "I'm right here, Pickle. Just stop waving the mirror around so much, okay?"

"There! There you are. *Whew*! Anyway, Scratch said if this baby's a boy, I get to keep it this time. Isn't that cool?"

Angelfish frowned. "Honey, I think Scratch probably already knows what the baby is."

"Well no, none of us knows. Because we told the doctor we wanted it to be a surprise."

I said, "So, Scratch . . . "

"Pickle, my friend wants to know if Scratch is your baby's daddy."

"Well, you know very well my baby daddy's Chimp. He makes the prettiest little girls—but his boy baby would be a handsome one, too, don't you think? After all, he'd look just like Chimp! So, who's your boyfriend, Angelfish? Is he a ghost dude, too? Is he hot? Is he here right now?"

"Hi, Pickle. My name is Thumb."

"She can't hear you. For one thing, you're not in the mirror. For another, I don't think the mirror works for anybody but me."

"So, what's going on with all the biker babies? Scratch is *selling* them?"

"They're private adoptions."

"What, Angelfish?" said Pickle. "What did you say?"

"Sorry, honey. I was talking to Thumb. He's asking me where the babies go."

"They go to nice homes," Pickle said. "In other states. Nice parents who give them everything and send them to private school.

They all grow up to be filthy rich and happy. Can he hear me, Angelfish?"

Angelfish intentionally moved so she was no longer in line with the mirror. She told me, "The Blood Eagles get maybe seventy thousand for each kid. Girls who pass all their medical tests are preferred, and bring a better price. Private doctors, private lawyers, friendly judges in friendly states; everything looks legal, at least on paper—everything except for the fact that the mammas are owned by the club and they don't really have a say. But that last part's a Blood Eagles family secret."

"Jesus. Is that what happened to *your* baby?"

"Angelfish! Where did you go, Angelfish?"

"It is. In fact, Chelsea was the first baby to go. Her adoption hit a few snags, but overall it went smooth enough for the club that they sometimes worked with a couple mammas at a time after that. Girls from shitty families or no families at all who would do what they were told for love of the Blood Eagles and the promise that they could one day keep a kid. The few that didn't fall in line and resisted signing the papers ended up like me—dead." She stepped back before the flashing mirror and said, "Yo, Pickle. I'm right here."

Pickle said, "Did you say his name was Thumb? I know Thumb." Angelfish looked at me.

"She's wrong. I never met her; I'm sure of that. Unless maybe she was another dancer at The Hat." Angel's expression changed in a way that told me she knew far more than she'd been letting on, and suddenly I imagined the earth opening up to swallow me.

"He says you never met him, honey."

"No; I never *met* him. I only know about him from Cricket. Did you ever know Cricket, Angelfish? Probably not; she was only here for a few days when I was knocked up with my first baby, my little girl who's in Texas now. I think you were gone by then, Angelfish. It was me and Doll, who had her baby first, and then they brought Cricket down here, but not for long."

After a stunned moment, I fought off the horror that threatened to hold me paralyzed and I managed to say, "When the hell did all this happen?" I wondered whether it was possible that Cricket had been imprisoned here shortly after my death, or perhaps even *before* I died, without my missing her—and, if so, in either case, had they taken her, or had she willingly, for some self-destructive reason, actually placed herself in their greasy hands? And what about Lizzie, in whom I'd taken so much hope—did this mean she wasn't mine? Or could it be that this obviously insane girl, Pickle, was just having a hallucination?

"Pickle, Thumb wants to know when this was."

"I don't know. Long time ago. Like I said, I was pregnant then; that's all I remember. Doll right away got pretty tired of hearing Cricket go on so much about Thumb, but she let it go. Otherwise, Crick was a pretty cool chick."

Angelfish said, "So what exactly was Cricket telling you about Thumb?"

Pickle shrugged and brought the blue hand mirror close enough to her face to fog it with her breath. "She told us this, and she told us that. She made him sound like an ordinary dude; you know how they all just think about themselves? It didn't seem like he took very good care of her—sorries, Thumb, if you can hear me.

"Then, the night before she left here, she told us she was gonna kill him. And I'm pretty sure she did, because we never saw her again—and here he is, a ghost."

CHAPTER 15

Angelfish and I stared at one another. She wasn't smiling. I said, "She's crazy, this chick. I think she's making that up. Some of it, anyway." Angelfish slowly shook her head.

"How do you know?"

"I'm a ghost." She lifted her face toward the ceiling and the floors above us. "I hang around and hear them talking. They say all kinds of things."

"Shit."

"There's more. . . . "

But I could not stand to listen to another word about how the woman I trusted had fired a bullet, maybe two, into the back of my brain. I rose through the ceiling of Pickle's dungeon, and as Angelfish shouted for me to return, again calling out that there was more I needed to learn, I continued straight up through the attic and the roof and into the nighttime sky.

Above the house, beneath the stars and in the open air, I was temporarily disoriented. Then I saw the faint glow of two spirit paths, one leading West, the other marking the route above Riverside on which we had arrived. I began to retrace our flight along the twisted arc that had led us here from The Magic Hat. Below me as I flew I could see a line of nine motorcycles with shining headlights weaving their way toward the clubhouse like a Chinese dragon in a New Year parade; the Blood Eagles were headed home from their night on the town, and I knew that riding among them would be Mantis, Chimp, Fat Harold, and perhaps one or two others who, along with Scratch, had co-starred in Cricket's betrayals. I found myself wishing I had the power to make every one of those bikes explode into spontaneous flames—which, of course, was nothing more than the impotent fantasy of a helpless spirit. I arrived at The Magic Hat, zig-zagged across the water to the eastern shore the way Dirt had shown me, and went back to my haunt, where I immediately extinguished myself in that other river, that rolling river of darkness and forgetting—the river known only to the dead.

I would have stayed forever, had I been able, in that disassociating flow, but the Great Whatever still had places she/he/it required me to go. After some days passed—it was now late summer; beyond that I didn't know the date—those waters cast me into the air above my hopeless concrete stairs. With little else I felt like doing, I descended to the top step, and there, for what could have been a week, I sat, hand under chin, like The Thinker at the Gates of Hell. Traffic rumbled by; rain fell; a couple of kids walking past swung for a few minutes on Tigre's old tire swing, and still I stayed, sitting fast.

One thing I thought about during that time was revenge for all that had been taken from me—fatherhood, love, life—but not against Cricket, who had fired the fatal round. Not only did I feel far more regret than anger when I thought of her, but I knew she had a child to care for, and I would not deprive a baby of its mother regardless of what she'd done, and no matter who its father had been. No, it was Scratch whose death I imagined, in a number of different ways. Under just the right conditions, for instance, I thought it might be possible to scare another biker into shooting him.

The Great Whatever seemed to get wind of my homicidal musings, and it was around then that a messenger bearing a severe warning visited me in the river—you might remember that I

246

mentioned this ghost at the very beginning of my story. He, or she, was the one with a voice like the gurgle of the river itself, the one who told me that if I ever caused the death of a person, damnation would be my reward. But at that point, I was not sure I really cared.

Thinking about Cricket's baby—and still my baby as well, perhaps—also put me in mind of that poor, crazy, pregnant girl, Pickle, trapped in the basement of the clubhouse. As soon as that kid was born they were going to take it away from her and sell it to someone—the most evil thing I'd ever heard of, and yet one more circumstance I was forbidden to act upon. In fact, saving that child would be more difficult than mere revenge, because while vengeance only required that I somehow kill Scratch, saving that baby from being sold off like a puppy would require killing several other Blood Eagles as well in order to prevent the sale from going through. I was helpless in every direction, and it was maddening.

It was then that my mounting anguish caused me to make a huge mistake. While in the wake of Pickle's revelations my enthusiasm for finishing my book had all but disappeared, I one day went to visit Ben, for no other reason than that I was lonely. I found him home and ready to work—in fact, he'd been both angry and worried about my long absence. Together we sat in his room and wrote, and although Pickle's story was a little ahead of the events he and I had so far reached in my afterlife biography, I nonetheless dictated it to him in a hopeless and misguided attempt to unburden my heart.

His lips pursed, Ben wrote all that I told him without pausing, or speaking. When I was finished, he sat back and cupped his pudgy hands against the sides of his head and stared at his bedroom wall. After a moment he said, "So that's the baby Angelfish told you about, way back when. Not yours. Not hers. *This* one. Pickle's baby. The one she needed your help to save."

I hadn't thought of that, but it was possible he was right. In spite of myself, I was impressed at his unexpected flash of inductive intelligence. When he picked up the pen again, I told him as much.

That could be. But I've thought about it, and there's absolutely noth-
ing we can do.

Ben said, "We? *You* couldn't, because you're dead. But I could at least call the cops."

That'd be useless. Dude, you have no proof that Pickle even exists.
And you don't know her; she's batshit crazy; even if the police
dragged her up from the cellar, she'd probably tell them she was
fine. That she was looking forward to being a mother, or that she
was giving up the baby of her own free will.

Ben sat stewing for at least ten minutes without touching the pen. Finally, he stood up from his writing chair, went to kneel before his chest of drawers, and drew out my Beretta Tomcat, which was now wrapped in an oiled rag rather than my old t-shirt. He returned to set the gun on his writing table, unwound the cloth from around it, then sat down to stare at it. The gun's blue finish gleamed with a sheen imparted by the oil from the rag. Several times he picked it up and turned it over and over in his hands; the oil stuck to his skin and made his fingernails shine. Then he placed it back on the table, and I waited impatiently for him to lift the pen.

When he was finally ready to write again I asked him what he planned to do.

Fuck are you doing?

"If nobody can help—I sure wouldn't drag old Mr. Muttkowski into this—I guess I have to do it myself."

I imagined Ben trying to shoot his way through the Blood Eagles clubhouse, and it made for a disturbing movie. Most likely, at some point he'd suddenly realize what he'd gotten himself into, and he would lose his nerve and run. It would take a lot of luck just to get back out and escape in his grandmother's car. Or perhaps, at the gate or inside the front door, if he managed to make it that far, they'd come in force to confront him, and he might end up actually squeezing off a shot or two. He'd doubtlessly miss—although it was possible he'd successfully wing somebody. In either case, the bikers would descend on him like bearded Furies, disarm him, take out knives, slice open his pants, hack off his little dick and toss it to the dogs. Then, as Ben shrieked in a flailing astonishment of agony, they'd carve up the rest of him until he finally gurgled, twitched, and fell silent. For the first time since I was a child, I found myself using multiple exclamation points as I wrote. In this case, they seemed entirely appropriate:

No! This is not a fucking video game! You'll just get yourself killed!!
I told you to throw that fucking gun into a pond!!!

"Yeah, but what am I supposed to do? Nothing? How is that acceptable? Who else is gonna help her?"

Not you! Not you!!! You wouldn't get anywhere near her.
They'd murder you.

"Maybe so, Thumb. But I don't think I can just let them do this to her. And anyway I think you underestimate how great video games can be to get you ready for something like this. That's how the Army trains soldiers these days."

Ben, you're crazy. They're killers, and you're not.

Ben sighed, picked up the gun again, slowly tumbled it in his hands. Finally he said, "Well one thing you're right about is that I won't do much good with this unless I practice." At that he stood up, tucked the Tomcat into his belt, knelt again to remove a box of thirty-two caliber cartridges from his bottom drawer, then walked from his room, out the back door of his house, through all the white-trash detritus of his backyard, and up a trail into the woods.

*

A day or so later, as I returned to my haunt from a short rest in the underground river, I was startled to find Cricket sitting in my usual spot on the steps. She wore her leather jacket, a baseball cap, and a pair of dark glasses. She had opened two bottles of beer; one bottle rested in her hand while the other—it was my usual brand, and I immediately knew she'd brought for me—stood on the bottom step. Her minivan was parked on the street; I looked through it and was disappointed to find that Lizzie was not with her. I had no idea why she'd come, but I hoped—desperately, unrealistically— that it was to tell me that everything Pickle had said was a lie.

Looking out across the marsh, Cricket took a couple of sips of her beer and set the bottle down. She reached into her jacket and drew out a package of rolling papers and a plastic vial of weed. She took her time crafting the joint, fussing over it as she always did until the taper was perfect. When she was finally satisfied with her handiwork she fired it with a lighter, took two short hits, and placed it on the top step. As soon as she turned to pick up her beer again, a freak gust of wind flipped the joint off the steps and into the weeds, where it lay smoldering. Cricket stared after it for a moment before saying, "Well, I guess you don't like to get high anymore. I don't either; not much anyway."

She sipped the beer and said, "So . . . it's been almost two years now, Thumb. I was gonna come talk to you on the exact date, but now I won't be able to. Charles, Lizzie, and I, we're all moving to Seattle two weeks from today." After another sip she said, "Fresh start, and all. Oh, and don't worry—Tigger's coming too."

Seattle? That alone was enough to fill me with despair. But something in her tone also robbed me of my hope that she was about to tell me what I longed to hear. Pickle had told the truth.

250

Cricket said, "But two years, like I mentioned. I think it's been long enough for me to stop feeling so guilty for what I did, don't you think? For what I had to do? For Lizzie's sake, I think it's time for me to forgive myself, so that's why I'm here."

Cricket, I said, *Jesus. Forgive yourself? Is Lizzie even my kid? Tell me that, at least.*

"Yeah," Cricket said, nodding as if she'd actually heard me speak. "Life's tough enough; the last thing a kid needs is a guilty, miserable, self-destructive mom. I knew you'd understand."

No, I don't understand . . .

"Thank you. Thank you, Thumb. I'm sorry about how it all turned out. For what I did, I'm sorry. I loved you, you know. In a way I always will." She took a long, last drink from her beer and poured out the rest. She tossed the bottle into the weeds, kissed her fingers and touched them to the stairs. Then she stood. "Bye now, baby." She tipped her face to the sky. "See you in the clouds sometime, maybe."

Just tell me why, Cricket. . . .

She walked down to her car and drove away.

*

After many more days of brooding about all the things that had been done, and all I could not do, boredom got the best of me again. Several times I went to Ben's trailer to try talking him out of his plan to confront the Blood Eagles, but I did not find him there. Each time I visited, I poked my head through his chest of drawers in search of my Beretta, and each time the gun was gone as well.

Eventually, I decided I would fly out to the abandoned church and visit with Virgil and Gib, whom I had not talked to for some time. I did not plan on sharing my despair with them; I would leave out what I'd learned about my death, and instead amuse Gib with some white lies about what I'd done with Angelfish, all the while allowing their honest happiness at seeing me to buoy my spirits.

Out I went into the sky, and by the time my feet touched ground on the gravel road that led to the church, I'd actually begun to feel eager to see to them.

But as I drew near enough to the abandoned building to see and hear inside, I could sense that things had changed, and I stopped to take stock. Most notably, along with my two friends I made out the figures of four other ghosts gathered in the pews; three women and a man, all of them older spirits—by which I don't mean spooks who had been dead for a long time, but rather people who had passed over only after turning white and withering, at least a little, with what the living think of as old age. The four "new dudes" were trading funny stories with Gib, and their repeated laughter rolled out from the church in waves. As I moved closer, I could see that Gib sat side by side with one of the three women, his arm on the back of the pew behind her.

"Gibbous Waxing," I said to myself. "Good for you."

I would have gone in then and allowed myself to be introduced, but the other new thing I noticed was that Virgil did not take part in the party; instead he floated at a distance from the others. He was moving about the church with a seeming aimlessness that was entirely out of character for him. It was just then that Gib also noticed the professor's peculiar behavior.

"Virgil," Gib called, and his new friends hushed then so that he could continue speaking. "Why don't you come sit with us?"

"No thank you," said Virgil, his voice sounding weak.

"What's the matter, pal? Are, you feeling okay?"

"No, I'm really not. I can't describe it, other than to say it's a *vague* feeling. I feel almost as if I've got one foot in some other world that I can't yet see."

"I'm sorry to hear that, Professor," Gib said with worry in his voice. "If I could, I'd bring you a glass of cold water."

"I know you would, Gib. Thank you, anyway. But don't be concerned; I think perhaps I'm finally about to wake up from my long dream, and that's probably a good thing."

I decided then against going in: If I entered, it would be unforgivable for me to ignore Virgil in favor of Gib and the other cheerful, joking older folks—and yet the professor and I, with our two heavy humors, rather than lifting each other up likely would only end up sinking one another like a couple of drowning swimmers. No, I would come back here only when and if I could actually serve my friend as something other than an anchor, a manacle, and a length of heavy chain.

Instead I flew off to Muttkowski's farm, where I found Fred seated in his farrowing-pen office. Heaped on the card table alongside his old manual typewriter were several half-inch-high stacks of manuscript which together probably would constitute nearly an entire draft of our book. Also on the messy table: an ashtray holding a blackened crumb of reefer pinched in an alligator clip and three of Ben's spiral-bound notebooks.

Fred was shuffling through his typewritten sheaves of manuscript, scribbling and crossing things out with a red Bic pen. For a while I stood at his shoulder and watched him work, and in this way I learned that he had already redacted Ben's and my version of events right up to the part where the Ghost Hounds showed up at the church. Although this was excellent progress, it still bothered me a bit to see the extent of the license he had taken with my story, both in its telling and in its larger meanings. Not only had he removed events and observations of importance to me, but there were places in the work where he'd dropped in literary references I could not come close to comprehending and—most painful of all— there were many passages describing actions I'd allegedly taken and thoughts I'd supposedly entertained that had been distorted or even wholly fabricated, apparently for no other reason than to suit Fred's offbeat, pig-farming fancy. But there was little I could do about any of that, beyond trying to feel grateful and lucky at being the first dead man ever privileged to tell a tale—regardless of whether the story was entirely my own. Best, I guess, to leave it at that.

*

I spent many more days on my concrete steps, around which the high, unmowed grass had begun to turn brown and die. One morning Angelfish appeared on the road and drifted over to settle herself next to me. We sat without speaking until she finally remarked, "You have a beautiful haunt here, Thumb."

"Yeah, they should dig it up in one big chunk and put it in the Metropolitan Museum of Art; you couldn't ask for a finer representation of American rural decay."

"I don't mean what's left of your house—although most people would think it's an improvement over the dressing room in a strip club. I mean the fact that it's so peaceful, and the view you have. The swamp, or whatever, is kind of pretty."

"It's a marsh. The difference is . . . never mind. And yeah; it is beautiful. It's full of wild things, and mystery."

"As for these steps,"—she pretended to pat the concrete with her hand—"I'm going to call them Thumb's stairway to heaven."

We both laughed, and I said, "I love a girl with a sense of irony."

Then she became serious. "Listen, dude, you didn't stay for the end of Pickle's story. There was more to it than you heard—some parts that would have helped you make sense of things."

"I heard enough—from Pickle, and from Cricket herself when she came here a few days ago. The woman I cared for killed me, and the baby she had probably wasn't mine—which means that when I died, I left behind absolutely nothing of value. My life, such as it was, was a waste."

"But it *was* your kid. That's what Cricket told Pickle and the other chick who was in the cellar with them. She had just figured out she was pregnant and was trying to decide how to break it to you when the Blood Eagles grabbed her off the street one night, and stuck her down on the farrowing floor with Pick and Doll."

"So, she really *is* my child? Lizzie?" I was almost afraid to let myself believe it. "And, they *kidnapped* Cricket? She didn't go there on her own?" As soon as I spoke, and in spite of the fact that I knew she'd somehow managed to get more or less safely away, I realized what a selfish thing this was to be happy about. Angelfish gave me a look that let me know she shared this thought, and I added, "Did they hurt her? Why did they take her in the first place? And, how could she have let herself shoot me? If our places were switched I would have willingly died before I harmed her."

"Other than to slap her some at the beginning when she'd yell at them, they didn't hurt her much. But they did threaten her. First, they put her down there with the other girls so she could learn from them all about how the baby business worked. Then they told her they were going to keep her there until she had a baby of her own—and if she caused any problems for them, they'd put her under the ocean afterwards. That was when she told Pickle and Doll she was already knocked up, and that the baby belonged to you. She talked to them about everything; she wanted to tell them as much as she could about herself in case she didn't survive. Then maybe someday one of them would be able to talk to somebody who knew her—talk to *you*, maybe—and her disappearance wouldn't be a mystery."

"So, Scratch wanted to sell *my* kid—Cricket's and my baby?"

"Well, he wouldn't of known it was yours until they took her to the doctor for her tests and found out how far along she was. But, I doubt that would of stopped him from selling it so, yeah."

"I only wish I was alive right now," I said. "I'd kill that fucker."

"Thumb, why they took Cricket, though, wasn't for your baby, or anybody's baby, but for you, so they could have her kill *you*. You were so different from most of the rest of us in that life—the rich dude's college, and all—that Scratch got the idea you might have family who could put pressure on the cops to keep looking for you, and also make a lot of trouble for the Blood Eagles, if you happened to vanish. So, instead of getting your blood directly on their hands—to help murky the water in case there was a serious investigation, and no doubt also because Scratch just thought it would be an entertaining thing to do—they came up with the idea of making somebody close to you do the shooting. And who closer and with more imaginable reasons as far as the cops would be concerned, than your own old lady?

"So after a couple of days, they brought your girl up from the cellar and they made her an offer. They told her, 'Thumb's coming here, and he's a dead man, no matter what—and you're a dead woman, too. But if you're willing to pull the trigger on him and then just hand the gun over to us, we'll let you walk out of here, and that way at least one of you will survive.'"

For a minute I sat swirling with rage and sadness. I said, "Okay. Maybe they did do that; it's possible. But, like I said, I couldn't have shot *her* if the tables were turned."

"But, you just said you'd give up your life for her."

"Willingly."

"Well, that's what you did, Thumb."

"But, it wasn't my *choice!*"

"So, the way Pickle tells it, Cricket was a smart chick, and a brave one. She kept hoping you would smell a rat and not come out to the clubhouse. But you didn't—you just weren't that smart—and you did, and once you were there, she knew you wouldn't leave alive no matter what she did or didn't do. She also knew what your choice would be, if anybody gave you one: that you'd give up your life in order to save the two of them. To save Cricket *and* your baby. So she let you make that decision without you knowing you'd made it. And because she was strong enough to follow through on her deal with Scratch, instead of the three of you being dead, or you and Cricket both being underwater, with your baby sold away to strangers, two of you are alive, and together."

I rose from the steps and ghosted all around my yard which, I noticed for the first time, was showing signs of slowly turning back into forest, whiplike aspen shoots popping up everywhere among the trash and through the grass. I felt the urge to run away again—to try to fly out over the marsh and disappear, but I fought the feeling and went to sit back down next to Angelfish.

"What you just told me is a fairy tale," I said. "At best, it was crazy thinking on Cricket's part. For one thing, how did she know they'd let her go once she killed me?"

"I guess she didn't, really. But, she must of figured there was at least a chance, and the smallest chance is better than no chance at all. Plus, their plan would of made some sense to her: To confuse the cops, in case they found your body or something, she'd be a more smoky smokescreen alive and walking around free than she would as a murder victim herself. Blood Eagles could just stash that gun, with her fingerprints and DNA all over it, someplace where the cops would find it and then start talking about how she'd been telling everybody she was pissed at you for one thing or another and planned on dropping you in the dirt."

I said, "And how, supposedly, would anybody believe that Cricket, by herself, would have taken me out and thrown me in the ocean?"

Angelfish waved a dismissive hand. "Dude, you're way over-thinking it; these aren't cops like the cops on TV; you're worrying about details nobody else would give a crap about. Besides, didn't you and Cricket live with another bunch of scummers, all of them with jail records? Maybe one or two of them helped her do it; they either hated you or wanted Cricket for their own old lady, or both, or who the hell knows, or even cares? The only thing provable, if police divers found you, or if your poor skull with a couple of slugs rattling around in it got pulled up in a trawling net, or if the club themselves decided to announce that they had an idea where you were, would be that Cricket fired the shots that killed you. Beyond that, do you really think anybody would spend a lot of time playing TV detective in order to drag the Blood Eagles into it? No; Cricket, still chirping her wild-ass story about how she made a deal with the devil to save her and her unborn baby, would end up going to prison."

I rose again, flew all around, went back. Holding a pretend pistol in my hands, I said, "What I would have done, if I'd had a loaded gun, instead of killing Cricket, would've been to turn and put a bullet right between Scratch's eyes."

"I'm sure you would of. And then you would of tried to shoot your way out of that clubhouse—but you wouldn't of got far, especially with only one or two more bullets in your gun. You, Cricket, and little thumb-sized Thumb Junior would of ended up in puddles of blood, and in a hurry, too.

"But Cricket is smarter and has a cooler head than you; I'm sure she thought of that, and it wouldn't of taken her long to realize it wouldn't work. Besides, knowing how the Blood Eagles do business, you can be sure that behind Cricket, when she had the gun, would of been a club member with *another* gun that he would of used to shoot her if she had made the smallest move to make him nervous. Then, after she did what they told her, that same dude would of stepped up next to her and said, 'Good job, sugar; we'll take it from here. Just drop that gun into this plastic bag, and you can be on your way.'"

After a long silence I said, "It's . . . " But I could not continue; there just were no words that would work. I shook my head.

"I know," Anglfish said.

"I can't . . . "

"I know it, honey. It can't fit in you all at once. Not yet, anyway." She made a patting motion against my knee.

"I need . . . "

"I absolutely understand. It'll take some time. Don't forget, I've been through something like this myself. I'm gonna leave now and let you think. If you need me, you know where I am."

Angelfish pretended to kiss me on the cheek. Then she disappeared.

*

After I'd given it some time, it was all easy to imagine. Though Cricket would have wanted to close her eyes before she squeezed that trigger, she would have realized that she owed it to me to bring down the darkness as swiftly as possible. She would have opened wide her sighting eye, willed her shaking hands to hold steady, and taken careful aim. If I were slow in falling over, she would have fired a second shot without their having told her to.

Having finished, she would have fought the urge to run to me—she knew I was no longer there—and she definitely would not have let them see her cry. Instead she'd have turned, given them the gun, and walked straight out through the great room to whatever vehicle—car, truck, or scooter—they had waiting out front to carry her back to town.

As I sat thinking about all those things, it occurred to me that I now knew Cricket in ways I hadn't while I was alive—how strong she was, for one—and what a pity it was I hadn't recognized her strength and learned to love it long before. For another instance, I was suddenly certain that she'd held all her tears for me until that day she brought me flowers and set them on the stairs. It was only then that she released her hoard of grief.

And I forgave her then, of course; she'd done the only thing she could. I began to yearn to send her my message of forgiveness, and gratitude. Ben would have delivered it for me if I asked him to. But I also understood how harmful that would be to Cricket; how it would have turned her into a haunted woman for the rest of her days, her mind wandering partially and prematurely in the afterlife, when there was so much work left for her in the living world. Better for me to stay silent, and give her the time she needed to forgive herself truly and completely. And I hoped she could forgive me as well for not encouraging her to do better for herself than to accompany me down that low road I had chosen. We'd both gotten snared in the darkness there, but she had not deserved it. For that, no matter how many millennia go by and how many stars I see born and die, I don't think I will ever entirely forgive *myself*.

Nor would I forgive Scratch, the author of so much suffering—mine, Cricket's, Angelfish's, and of so many other innocent and partly innocent people. Scratch was a monster, and likely to cause further anguish in the future, to the naïve and too-trusting Pickle, and to Pickle's soon-to-be-born baby. I wished I could step forward to stop him, but I was, after all, nothing but a ghost; my footsteps left no impression on the living earth. Sitting on my stairs brooding about it all, I would have cried if I still had eyes.

CHAPTER 16

It was a windy late afternoon, probably past the middle of October and somewhere just beyond the second anniversary of my death. I was riding my stairway to heaven when I heard a vehicle coming down the road; a minute later Ben swerved to a stop in his grandmother's car.

"What fresh hell?" I groaned.

He marched directly to the steps and stood before me, wide-eyed and gasping from having moved so quickly across my overgrown lawn.

"I hope you're here!" he announced.

"You know how to find out," I said. But apparently he was too busy to sit down with a pen and one of his notebooks. Instead, when he reached into his jacket pocket, it was to produce my Beretta.

"Oh, for fuck's sake," I said. His finger inside the trigger guard, he gave the gun a dangerous wave.

"Time," he said. "It's time, Thumb. You're right that the cops would do nothing. But if I want to live with myself for the rest of my life, the only right thing to do is to help that pregnant girl escape."

"How about we discuss this?" I said.

"I don't want to argue about it with you." It was almost as if he'd heard me. "You'll just try to talk me out of it, and I've already made up my mind. I'll be back though; don't you worry. I'll have the element of surprise on my side." This last part he said as if he were trying to convince himself; in fact, he was shaking as he spoke. "And I've gotten pretty good with this thing." He held up the Tomcat, then slid it back into his pocket.

"So, tomorrow, Thumb. By tomorrow morning, it'll all be over, and I'll see you back at gram's trailer, bright and early. For work. Mr. Muttkowski says we're making great progress. With the money we make on your book, I'm going to college. And I'm going to make sure my little brother and sister have everything they need."

"Ben," I said, despairingly. "You won't be going to college. You won't be helping your brother and sister. Tomorrow bright and early, you'll be lying in the ocean wrapped in a green tarp, hugging a fucking cinder block. Your gram will never even know what happened to you."

He waved an energetic goodbye high in the air, as if I were floating in the sky rather than staring directly into his doughy belly. He then turned, walked back to the car and drove off toward Riverside. I had the strong urge to follow him; I was ready to rise from my concrete step, but held myself back. The painful truth was, I wouldn't be able to save him, and I didn't want the remainder of my afterlife haunted by the gruesome images of his almost-certain death.

Also upsetting was the fact that my book now would never be finished, unless Fred just decided to make everything up—but even as the thought occurred to me, I felt ashamed for thinking it. What was the importance of a book compared to a real-life tragedy, one that I was directly responsible for?

About twenty minutes later Angelfish, in a ponytail, jeans, and an untucked shirt, appeared at the roadside and came over to settle next to me on the steps for her second and last time ever.

"Hey, boy," she said.

"Hey, lady."

"What's up?"

"Well, this dude, Ben, just stopped by . . . "

"I was worried I wouldn't find you here. I need your help." I noticed then that her eyes were dark with worry—a lot of that going around all of a sudden.

"You know that I'm a ghost, don't you? My ability to help anybody . . . "

"Pickle's in bad trouble. I heard the Blood Eagles talking. A couple days ago they ran some tests on her at the hospital, and it turns out her baby's going to need heart surgery as soon as it's born. Its chances are good, but not a hundred percent, which means that the club won't be able to sell it as a premium product. They sure don't want to pay a bunch of money for a heart operation either, or have a sick, expensive kid around their place afterward. On top of it, Pickle said some things to people at the hospital that made Scratch nervous. Which, combined with them seeing her on the surveillance monitor, talking to her mirror all the time—my fault, guilty as charged—they've decided she's seriously cracked, and at least a liability to them, if not an actual danger."

I sat thinking. Finally I said, "I don't suppose they'd just let her go."

"Not when they think she's crazy enough to talk about everything she knows. Scratch is going to take her for a boat ride about an hour from now. Then, as soon as it gets dark . . . " Angelfish made a plunging motion with her hand.

"Oh, Jesus. It's gonna be an actual slaughterhouse over there. How I wish I was alive."

"We have to do something."

"Like *what*? In fact, we are *not* alive."

"You must of learned somewhere along the way that we can make ourselves seen, if we really want to."

"What I know is that we've got less than a minute of *boo* in us, and then we're gone forever. I've seen that happen before to other ghosts. How's that supposed to help?"

"We don't really know whether we're gone forever. No one's ever come back to tell us." After a pause, she asked, "Are you afraid?"

"You know, I might not be if I thought it would actually work. But I don't see how even the two of us together throwing a short scare into the Blood Eagles will save Pickle—or that asshole, Ben, I was starting to tell you about. After we disintegrate, they'll just conclude they must've gotten a little too high on whatever drugs they were using and seen some things that were never there. Then they'll go ahead and drown her anyway. Cut Ben into blue-fish bait."

"Well, I've got an idea. In fact, with the special talents each of us has—mine being my ability to talk to Pickle—it's possible we won't even have to show ourselves at all, and we'll live to *boo* another day. But we each have to be ready to do what we need to do, and when it needs to be done if it comes to that."

"And *my* special talent—the one that's supposed to keep me from having to commit suicide—what is that, exactly?"

"It's getting late," said Angelfish. "Our chance will come as soon as Scratch lets her out of the house to walk down to the boat dock. I haven't told her what they're planning—she'd just freak out and lose her shit—but I made her promise to keep checking her mirror whenever they're not watching her. I figure that once Pickle's out on the lawn, you'll be able to distract the Bloods while I get her to run to the nearest house and ask the neighbors to call the cops. If I have to, I'll use my big *boo* to block for her."

"*Distract* them? That doesn't sound like leaving me to fight another day." But by the time I finished speaking Angelfish had already taken to the air, heading for Riverside and leaving me with no choice but to follow. I was not able to catch up with her until we were past The Magic Hat and our spirit path had widened enough for the two of us to travel side by side without our avatars inter-secting. All along the way I scanned the roads below for Ben's car, but there was no sign of it. I said, "So, what are you seeing as my super-power here? What is it you think I can do to distract them without blowing myself up in the process?"

She said, "The dogs. It's good they hate you, Thumb."

*

I finally spotted Ben's vehicle when we were above the gravel road and almost to the clubhouse. It was sitting off in the woods with the driver's door yawning, and Ben nowhere in sight. He had either left it there to hide it, or the Blood Eagles had run him off the road and dragged him out of it. As far as the odds went, I figured it was a coin flip.

Angelfish and I touched down just inside the wrought iron fence. In spite of the wind, Mantis and Fat Harold, both of them on gate duty, were trying to play a card game as they sat on opposite sides of a weathered picnic table. Their weapons, a couple of AK-47s, rested against one of the wooden benches.

"They must be having trouble with another club," I said. "That's why the artillery's in plain sight, and why they're doubled up on the gate." I looked around; still no Ben.

"Tensions're high," confirmed Angelfish. "Somebody got stabbed last week, I'm not sure who."

We blew through the front door and past the monitor room, manned by Chimp, who was leaning back in a creaking office chair as he snickered and murmured into a cell phone. As soon as we entered the great room, we knew something was wrong. Although we could sense people all through the different levels of the big house, the two we were looking for were missing. "Pickle's not here," Angelfish said.

"Neither is Scratch." As soon as I spoke, the three big pit bulls rose from the floor and began barking.

"Fuck a *duck*!" said Angelfish. "We're too late. They must of got an early start. Let's head down to the dock; maybe they haven't gotten into the boat yet. Once they get out on the water, we can't follow

them. And even if we could, there'd be nothing we'd be able to do."
We flew through rooms and walls until we popped out the back of
the house onto several hundred yards of lawn sloping steeply to the
river and a long wooden dock that reached out through withering
sea grass past the point at which the low tide could strand a boat.
Scratch and Pickle were walking down the lawn toward the dock,
where a white, center-console skiff about twenty feet in length sat
bobbing. Scratch, carrying a couple of stout fishing rods rigged with
treble-hooked bass plugs, had almost reached the dock, while the
gravid Pickle—dressed in sweat pants and a nylon jacket which,
though buckled at her breast, was open and flapping on either side
of her bulging belly—straggled behind, the handle of a picnic basket
in one hand and in the other the beautiful blue mirror, which she
held in the air above her head.

"We have to get down there," Angelfish said. She swooped
toward the river, and I followed her closely.

"Earth to Angelfish!" Pickle called softly as she peered up into
her own reflection. Scratch stopped, stiffened, and looked over his
shoulder—but Pickle had shoved the mirror behind her back before
he turned.

"What'd you say?" he asked. It was apparent Scratch had not
shaved for several days; the tattoos on his face were receding
behind a dust of grayish whiskers.

Pickle answered, "I said, how come we're going fishing now,
when it's gonna be dark in a hour?"

"I told you, the big stripers don't start biting until the sun goes
down. But, that's not what you said."

"I thought I did."

"You said, 'Angelfish.'"

"I guess I did, yeah. I still miss her, so I talk to her sometimes."

"Well fucking cut it out. It gives me the creeps." Scratch turned
toward the dock again and Pickle brought the mirror out of con-
cealment. Just as Angelfish moved to line herself up with the glass,
Pickle began her twirling dance.

"Goddamn it to hell!" Angelfish yelled. She looked at me and said, "Thumb, fly up and get those dogs. Bring them down here."

"How do I . . . "

"When they bark at the door to the Great Room, the dude in the monitor room lets them out onto the front lawn. So, all you have to do is make them bark." She then glided behind Pickle and began mirroring her movements while calling, "Pickle, stop! Pickle! *Pickle*! Stop the fucking twirling!"

As I was heading back to the house, I was relieved to hear Pickle say, "*Oh*! There you are!"

"Bitch, shut up!" hissed Angelfish.

"*What*?" said Scratch.

"My comb!" said Pickle. "I found it in my pocket!"

"Pickle! Stand still! Listen . . . *Pickle*! Do *not* get in that boat!"

I flew through the back of the house and spun around above the three dogs yelling, "*Dogs! Dogs! Dogs!*" When I had their alarmed attention, I drew them toward the door to the entrance hall and I passed feet first through its wooden panels. I then hovered on the other side calling, "*Here boy! Come on, boy!*" as they lunged, and roared, and slobbered.

But Chimp, still caressing the phone with his lips, ignored them. "I'll show you *exactly* what it's good for," he assured the woman at the other end. "And you won't have to wonder anymore."

I stuck my head back inside—the dogs clearly sensed me there—and yelled a few curses at them. Raging, they threw themselves fully against the door, their combined weight threatening to pop it from its frame.

"Hey!" Chimp finally shouted, lowering the phone. Then, after putting the phone back to his mouth he said, "Darling, I'll call you back. These fucking dogs are going batshit here, and I gotta let them out before they wreck the fucking place." He stood, opened the door to the great room, and called out, "Easy! *Easy!*" as the three of them charged past him and into the entryway. I ghosted through the front door, and as soon as Chimp had released the dogs onto the lawn I lured them around the house and down the slope toward the boat dock.

Pickle, with Angelfish at her side, had moved back up the lawn toward the house. She was facing the river with the mirror behind her back as Scratch, the fishing rods still in his hand, stood glaring at her.

Pickle was saying, "You know, I changed my mind, Scratch. I really don't like the water. I'm really kind of afraid of it."

"I'm about out of patience with you," Scratch said. "Come down here and get in the fucking boat."

Meanwhile Angelfish, in a desperate voice, was saying, "Pickle. Look in the mirror. Pickle, don't go back to the house. They'll kill you if you go back to the house"—none of which Pickle could hear, because she was concealing the mirror.

Running behind me, the dogs swarmed past Pickle and Angelfish and rallied around Scratch's legs. Scratch said, "Why the hell are these dogs down here?" He looked down at them as the four of us circled him, the three dogs barking and growling in furious confusion. Pickle took advantage of his distraction to turn toward the house and peek into her mirror. Standing before her, Angelfish bent over the mirror with the top of her head just beneath Pickle's chin; this upside down view of Angelfish must have startled Pickle because she flinched when she saw it. Angelfish said, "Don't go back to the house. Go to the neighbor's house. Run, if you can."

Pickle stood straight, gave a moon-eyed glance toward Scratch, dropped the basket she carried, and began moving in the direction of the nearest neighbor's house as fast as her pregnant belly would let her move.

"Pickle! Get back here!" Scratch shouted. Toward the house he yelled, "Mantis!" When Mantis appeared at the top of the slope, Scratch called, "Come and get these fucking dogs." Then: "Pickle! Goddamn it!" He threw down the fishing rods and began loping toward her, the dogs scrambling alongside. He easily caught up with her, grabbed her by the shoulder, and spun her around. He drew back his arm, seemingly ready to club her with a closed hand, then saw that she was clutching the mirror. Instead of hitting her, he ripped the mirror from her fingers and pitched it out toward the river. Flashing, the mirror spun end over end as it arced down to slice into the black, rolling water and disappear. By that time, Angelfish and I were both standing near them.

"That means I'm all finished now," Angelfish cried out to me. "I can't talk to her anymore. The rest is all on you." Above us, Mantis and Fat Harold were walking down the lawn toward the dock, while Chimp stood up by the house, watching. Still no sight of Ben anywhere.

I stepped in beside Scratch and started shouting at the dogs, calling them names and using my Spanish to insult their mothers. They went wild again, barking and snapping their jaws as they pressed against Scratch's legs—though they showed no sign of wanting to bite their boss.

"Shut up!" Scratch yelled at the dogs. When he let go of Pickle in order to kick them away, she staggered off again, but he easily recaptured her a moment later.

"Got to do better, dude," Angelfish urged. So I screamed, I swore, and finally I ghosted right inside of Scratch so that whatever sounds or movements of mine the dogs detected would seem to be coming from him. This was enough to trigger one of the two black pit bulls; the dog launched and locked its jaws around Scratch's forearm, and as soon as its hind feet hit the ground again it began snapping its head as if hoping to tear the arm off.

Scratch let out a hoarse scream and let go of Pickle in order to pound the attacking dog in the ribs with his fist. The well-trained dog whined with each of his blows, but did not let him go; meanwhile the other two animals, in spite of my ongoing provocation, merely wheeled and barked but still held back from attacking. At the same time, Mantis and Fat Harold exchanged a glance, drew pistols from beneath their cuts, and began jogging toward Scratch and the dogs. Fat Harold paused for a moment to turn back to

Chimp, who remained at the top of the hill, and yell, "Chimp! The cunt!" Then he continued his waddling run toward the battle below him. Chimp took off across the slope in Pickle's direction, and it was obvious he would intercept her with little trouble.

Angelfish said to me, "It won't work if you don't stop them from killing the dogs."

"Okay," I said. "I will."

"I gotta go. Goodbye, Thumb," she said.

Scratch quickly gave up on beating the dog off of his arm and drew out his own semi-automatic handgun. After struggling to work the slide and safety with the thumb and forefinger of the hand that was being shaken by the pit bull, he placed the barrel just behind the dog's shoulder and pulled the trigger. The dog flopped down and lay twitching in the grass.

Pickle continued to make her awkward and painfully slow escape as Chimp closed in on her. Then, halfway between Chimp and Pickle, Angelfish blossomed on the hillside, fully visible to ghosts, mortals, and animals alike. In the twilight her naked body was blue-white and phosphorescent; her skin was puckered all over as if she'd lain for a week in a briny bath. Gleaming garlands of seaweed hung from her arms and her shoulders, and green crabs struggled in her matted hair.

"Hi, Chimp," Angelfish said. "Where're you going?" He stopped with his hands open before him and stood staring at her. "You're not on your way to murder your own baby, are you? Tell me you wouldn't do such a thing." She took a hop in his direction, and he turned and ran back toward Mantis and Fat Harold, who had almost reached Scratch and the two surviving dogs. Scratch continued to stand there without moving, gun in hand, seemingly in shock, blood from his shredded arm pattering onto the lawn.

Chimp yelped wordlessly at Mantis and Fat Harold, and they looked up to see the spectral Angelfish approaching them like a puff of wind-blown smoke. "Hi, Harold," Angelfish said. "Remember the time you told me that if only I didn't belong to Scratch? You can kiss me *now*, if you want." She paused to vomit a black eel onto the grass, where it writhed for a moment before vanishing. She wiped her mouth with the back of her hand and grinned. "We can do *anything* you want. And who's your tall friend there? He's kind of cute too; what do you think of a three-way, maybe?" By then I could tell she didn't have much time left; she was fading quickly.

Mantis and Fat Harold fired their guns at her. Then Chimp, Mantis, and Fat Harold all ran for the house, which was fortunate because no sooner were their backs turned than Angelfish silently burst into a rain of emerald sparks that almost immediately extinguished in the descending dusk.

That left the badly bleeding Scratch, the two remaining pit bulls, and me—along with the steadily retreating Pickle, who, although almost a hundred yards away, was still a good eighth of a mile from the nearest house not infested by a motorcycle gang.

"That fucking whore," Scratch muttered as he came back into himself. He took a step in Pickle's direction as if he were about to run after her again, but then seemed to reconsider. Wild-eyed, he looked around him, apparently bewildered at not finding any of his club brothers about; then he raised his gun toward Pickle, squeezing one eye shut as he aimed.

I did not stop to think. I shoved my face through his outstretched arm, made myself fully visible to both man and beast, and in a voice any living creature could have heard I shouted, "Hit it, boy!"

Everything after that happened within a handful of Scratch's final heartbeats: The second black pit bull flew into my eyes to snap its jaws around Scratch's elbow. Scratch screamed, fired a wild shot into the ground as the dog jerked his arm down, then fell to his knees on the grass. The gun dropped to the lawn, but Scratch had the presence of mind to lunge for it and cover it with his free hand, the hand on the arm that had been savaged by the now dead dog. I knew that if he picked up that gun he would shoot the black dog, and then probably the white dog as well just for safety's sake, after which he would go staggering after Pickle and put a bullet between her shoulder blades. With my last bit of living energy—I was fading, and it felt as if I were being devoured by flames—I knelt and pushed my head through the back of Scratch's skull until I masked his face with my own. Then I taunted the white dog.

The dog leaped at me, looking as if it would swallow my head. Instead it closed its maw on Scratch's throat, forcing his tattooed face skyward with his false-fanged mouth agape. For a moment, and seemingly inside of my own "ears," which were still buried beneath Scratch's skin and bones, I could hear the two of them breathing together in what seemed an almost obscene intimacy: I heard the man's desperate, strangled wheeze overlaid by the wet, insistent suck of air pulsing through the dog's flaring nostrils. A second later there came a muffled crunch, and Scratch stiffened and stopped struggling. After that the only breathing was the dog's.

Dying then, and on fire from the inside out, I stood up and drew away from them. Scratch, still on his knees with one dog gnawing his arm off at the elbow and the other hanging from his neck, followed me with his eyes. In his last moment, he lifted his shaking hand from the gun and raised it toward me. Then, his eyes glazing, he slowly lowered his hand, and sank.

Around me, as I continued to burn, the world was dissolving to water. Something drew my attention up the hill to the house; I looked and, as if peering through a liquid prism, I saw Ben silhouetted against the last light of the western horizon. It was likely he could see me, too, just as the dogs, and as Scratch, had seen me.

"Ben," I yelled. "Get the hell out of here. Go now!"

For a moment he stood without moving, and I was unsure whether he'd heard me. But suddenly he broke into a waddling run—not toward me, thankfully, but in the direction of the iron gate.

And that was, as they say, all she wrote. I, everything, the world and its surrounding sky, we all finished our watery dissolution and swirled off into the ocean.

CHAPTER 17

So here I am finally, beyond the end of my time as an earthbound ghost. It is dark, without even the illusion of light. It is silent. I see nothing, I hear nothing. There is no up, no down, no hot, no cold, no air, no movement, no sensation of any kind. And I am utterly alone. At this point, I don't know how long I've been here, but as promised by the first messenger who came to me in the underground river—Gib, pretending to be something scarier—I do indeed "feel the crawl of every moment," my apparent punishment for the specific transgression of having intentionally caused a death, which I was warned against by that other, much later, messenger. My ghostly hope is that there remains some mercy in the universe, some compassionate intelligence out there beyond the coldness of starlight that might consider the reasons behind what I'd done, and that in spite of what I've been told, my sentence will not last for eternity.

The only thing that remains to me—that remains *of* me—is imagination. I use much of my endless time to picture Angelfish in a better place than this. She was an authentically good person, a hero, even, and she deserves more of her afterlife than eternal darkness.

As for me, what do *I* deserve? I imagine Ben and Fred meeting in the back of Fred's barn to discuss that very question. For I am fairly sure that, undetected amid the chaos surrounding Scratch's death, Ben managed to escape and survive. Despite his clumsiness, he would have waddled right back out of the Blood Eagles' compound the same way he'd gotten in, however that had been, unscathed but not untraumatized. No doubt he still would have been disheveled and shaking a few days later when he went to talk to Fred, and Fred would have grown increasingly impatient at the way he stuttered out fragments of our story. And of course Fred would refuse to accept as literal any of the more fantastic parts—Angelfish materializing as a sea demon, or me stepping out of Scratch's dying body to yell at Ben. But he'd doubtlessly interpret these portions of the narrative as imaginative illusions such as he himself frequently experienced, and having heard the news reports of Scratch's gruesome death, he would believe that, not only had Ben actually witnessed Scratch torn to the ground by his own dogs, but that Ben himself had been in mortal danger from the other bikers. He'd be relieved that Ben had made it out alive.

The two of them likely would have a brief discussion about whether Ben should offer himself to the police as a witness—and they'd quickly decide that, not only was there very little that Ben could contribute to a justice that had already been served, but the fact that he'd been at the clubhouse in the first place would be impossible to explain without getting himself into trouble with authorities and the surviving Blood Eagles alike. Far better to let the dead dogs lie.

As for me, what would they decide? Fred would likely come to the conclusion that, in spite of the fact that the unholy ghost of Thumb Rivera was nothing more than the product of Ben LeBlanc's subconscious mind, readers of the book they were writing would not be satisfied until they were told what "really" happened to him. An ending was required, and my disappearing into thin air after killing Scratch just would not turn the trick. So the question remained, what would be a fitting conclusion for me? What did I deserve?

I imagine Ben saying, "Well, we can't just make something up. That wouldn't be right. But maybe if we look back over who he was and what he did, we can guess about where he probably ended up— whether after he died for the second time, he went down, up, or sideways.

"One thing good he did was, he helped save Pickle's life. And her baby. And he may have helped me by telling me to get away from the Blood Eagles' clubhouse before they killed me—but I think I would have figured that out on my own.

"Then again, I still think maybe he killed my grandmother's goat. And also he could be a real asshole, sometimes."

To this I imagine Fred responding, "Well, if being an asshole got you sent to hell, I'd be headed that way myself. You too, for that matter. But the way we've written him, he was a guy who all his life seemed to think mostly of himself. Back in the day when there really *was* a hell, that's one of the things they sent people there for.

"Beyond that, he also peddled drugs that must have hurt or even killed some people. Left some kids without their parents, no doubt. Not the pot he grew, necessarily, but the meth business and the pill repackaging he was a partner in. Plus, he stole his best friend's woman, which is no small thing—and he patronized that strip club where all the girls were little more than slaves."

By this point, I knew Ben would start to feel guilty about hanging me out to dry—literally helping to damn me. He might then try to rebalance the scales in my favor, but likely would be able to come up with nothing more persuasive than, "Well, he liked dogs." To which I imagine Fred snorting and shaking his head—a rebuke that would bully Ben into rejoining him on the "fuck Thumb" side of the argument. I imagine Ben getting legalistic about it then, saying, "Well, the answer's in the book. I think we have to go back to what they told him when he first started thinking about killing Scratch, and stick with that. Remember what it was? That if he scared somebody to death, or if he caused somebody's death by scaring someone else—no matter how much they deserved it—then he'd end up in a dark place forever. I think we can include scaring those dogs—making them kill Scratch by scaring them and pissing them off. Thumb has to follow the rules, otherwise his story makes no sense."

Fred, slightly annoyed and also not trusting Ben's memory of their collaborative text, would then want to be reminded of what, exactly, my messenger had said to me. He'd lift the typewritten manuscript from the card table in the farrowing pen and flip through the first few pages to read aloud the messenger's admonition to me as we tumbled together in the underground river: *I've been told to warn you. If you cause a death out of revenge, you will remain a ghost forever. A solitary ghost who wanders in the dark.*

I imagine Fred peering at Ben through his glasses and from beneath the brim of his filthy baseball cap. "Revenge. So you tell me now, genius—and I'll take your word for it, since you're the one who thinks he knows him: Did he do it out of revenge, or did he do it because he really wanted to help that girl? If it's the latter, we could probably let him off with a lighter sentence."

Together, they're quiet for a time, and in my imagination all I hear is the soft sounds of pigs snuffling and shuffling about the barn. Ben finally breaks the silence: "How could we know what he really was thinking? I don't believe it's possible."

"That's right," says Fred. "It's not—not unless you're willing to admit you made the guy up, that he's a creation of your mind, in which case you get to decide why he did what he did. Otherwise, as with anybody, you might think you know what was in his heart, but you *don't* really know. Bad things done for good reasons; good things done for bad. Sometimes that's the way it is even with somebody you're close to."

"So what if it's a mixture? What if he did kill Scratch partly out of revenge, but might have stopped himself if Pickle wasn't there to save?"

Fred gives him a crooked smile. "That's more likely than not. What you're describing there are the motivations of a human being—the way a human being ends up doing almost anything that matters, you and I included. It's a fucking mess."

"Well, so, what then, Mr. Muttkowski?"

Still smiling, Fred says, "I'll tell you what, college boy. He's your invisible friend, so I'll leave it up to you. All I care about at this point is that we get the book published, and I think the ending will work either way."

"I don't know," Ben says. "I don't know. Help me out."

"What I *can* tell you is that what you're trying to figure out, you'll never know for sure. All you'll ever have is this: Is the world now a better or a worse place because he was here?"

THE END

. . . I saw bright sky from which the sun was absent, and above which I could somehow make out every sharply glittering star. I seemed to be lying weightlessly on my back in the tall grass. Beyond me I heard the silky, timeless rush of a river, along with a strange thunder that rolled and trembled in a higher register than any thunder I had ever heard. I also made out a murmuring babble of human voices.

A pair of huge woodpeckers, male and female, flapped their way across my blue field of vision. I thought they were pileateds, but there seemed to be something not quite right about them. Soon another pair went over on a similarly flat trajectory, and I realized they weren't rising and dropping as they flew the way pileated woodpeckers would do. Then I noticed the white trailing edges on their wings.

"Those are ivory bills," I said aloud. "Which would mean this isn't earth anymore."

"So, like, are we on another planet?" It was Angelfish, speaking from nearby. I saw that she was lying not far off in the endless meadow. She wore jeans and a loose shirt, and she was barefoot, with her pink-painted toenails peeking above the grass.

I sat up and saw that not far off was the bank of the smoothly rippling river I had heard; it was so wide that its far shore could not be seen through the curtain of mist that rose from the water a far distance out. There was no way to know whether this was the same river in which I had so often swum as a ghost—just farther downstream, perhaps, and beyond the underworld's deepest shadows—or part of an altogether different drainage.

All along the riverbank, as far in either direction as I could see, ran two other broad streams, these made up of the spirits of people. Thousands of souls were eddying upriver, while about as many traveled with the flow. Still other spirits were leaving the river altogether, and in columns, threads, small clusters, and even on their own, they struck out across the green plain toward a distant forest and the still more distant mountains that defined the horizon. There was, of course, great variety among all these ghosts; almost none were as pale as Angelfish, and most were darker, even, than I. Many of them wore different types of robes, and some even walked naked along the bank of the river, or toward the far-off mountains. Meanwhile, out on the river were many small boats. They were being rowed by . . .

"Yo, Thumb," said Angelfish. "I asked you a question." She was now sitting up.

"Oh, yeah. Another planet. I don't know. Where the hell is the sun—or *any* sun? For all I know this could be the Elysian Fields."

"Elysian Fields. What's that?"

"It's just some ancient Greek stuff. Kind of like heaven, but underground."

"What happened to Pickle? I didn't get to see if she got away."

I smiled at her. "I'm sure she did get away. I think you bought her the time she needed. And didn't you scare the piss out of those three assholes?" I laughed. "Come here, Fat Harold, and suck an eel out of my mouth!"

"Oh, nice!" Angelfish said. "And, so, in my whole life, next to having Chelsea, that's one good thing to my credit—even though I had to die before I could do it."

"That's more good than most people do, I think."

"What about Scratch?"

"Scratch is dead, dead, dead."

"Shut *up!*"

"No, really. I was there to see it. That white dog got him by the throat and crushed his windpipe."

"Wow. Yuck."

"Yeah." I wondered if she would start to feel bad about that.

But after a long moment Angelfish said, "Well, isn't it just so awesome when every little part of a plan falls into place just like you planned it."

Now it was my turn to pause. "I didn't know that there *were* any little parts, other than to keep Pickle from becoming one of us."

"Yeah, you're kind of innocent that way. It's one of the things I like about you."

I went back to watching the small boats as they floated the river. They were piloted by wraiths in human form, their faces concealed behind grinning death's-head masks. These costumed beings oared their boats into view from beyond the curtain of mist, and once they reached our shore they rowed parallel to the bank, apparently offering rides to anybody who wanted one. After they'd collected a passenger or several—not everyone who walked the bank seemed interested in going out onto the river—they headed straight toward the other side until they again were swallowed by the mist.

"What do you think is over there?" Angelfish asked. "That other side?"

"Beats me. And those dudes with the masks look kind of sketchy; I wouldn't trust them to tell me the truth about it, either. Why? Do you want to give it a try?"

"Not just yet. Let's walk, can we?" We both rose from the ground.

"Upriver? Or down?" I asked.

"Which way is the beach?"

"The *beach*? I'm not sure there *is* a beach. But if there were one, it would be downriver."

"Let's go downriver, then."

"Or, we could go toward the mountains."

"Downriver, Thumb."

We moved to the riverbank and mingled with the throngs of spirits who were following the flow. Unlike on earth, ethereal people in this in-between place seemed not to mind walking right through one another; the result was a giant, sweet-natured swirl of souls. Now that we were in among the other ghosts, Angelfish and I began to see spirits who had chosen a vastly different appearance than they'd presented in life. There were human spirits in the form of birds, cats, flowers, and kites. I looked in vain for a twirling beach ball; I also searched the crowd for my father. I wondered where in this afterlife they might be.

Both above and below the murmur of human speech and laughter there continued that odd, tenor-sounding thunder I had earlier noticed. At almost the same moment I started paying closer attention to it, Angelfish said, "That's not thunder! That's a *voice!*"

We stopped to listen and, as spirits streamed around and through us, I realized she was right. Not only was it a voice we heard but, judging from its tone, it seemed to be reciting a litany either of warning or advice. The trouble was, not only could we not make out a word it said, but we found it impossible even to tell what language he, she, or it was speaking, and there was no way of knowing whether the suggestions being offered would do us any good. Angelfish and I asked several passing ghosts whether they understood the voice or could tell us what it wanted; no one did. However, one shaven-headed dude in an orange robe did pause long enough to say, "I think we must get closer."

"Which way is 'closer'?" I asked. The man only smiled, shrugged, and continued on his journey.

Suddenly, Angelfish said, "Thumb! I want to show you something!" She jerked the loose tail of her shirt to the top of her midriff, where she let it hover, then began unbuttoning her jeans.

"Hey!" I said. "I don't care what you see other people doing; keep your clothes on." But she ignored me and pulled her pants down far enough for me to see that her lower abdomen was now pure white and unmarked. There were no blue, spiked letters, and no banded snake slithered south to hide its head inside of her.

"Your Blood Eagles ownership tat is gone. Did that just happen on your way here, or did you make it go away yourself?"

"I got rid of it just now. I only kept it as a reminder, and I don't need it anymore."

"Good for you." We continued our walk downriver, and after what might have been several hours of earth time we began to hear the roar of a waterfall, and to see the wall of mist it threw high into the sky.

"That waterfall sounds huge," Angelfish said, with excitement in her voice.

"It does. I can't wait to see it."

"Thumb. If the afterlife is eternity, you have to figure that the life we've already led will start to seem smaller, and like a lot less of a *thing*, all the time."

"Yeah; I guess it would have to, as a matter of proportion."

"I mean, in ten thousand years, my whole life up to now will seem like one day in a regular lifetime—although, of course, I won't really be alive."

I did the math in my mind. "More like *two* days, more or less. But I know what you mean."

"And that confuses me, because even though I'm dead my life still is everything I am. So, what will I be when life is just a tiny part of all my time?"

"We'll be different then, I think."

"Maybe I won't even want to look like myself anymore. Maybe I'll want to go back to being nothing but a invisible spark, or a drop of water in the river, the way I was right after I died."

"Maybe. And, when you think about it, what do we need bodies for anymore?" Then I added, "But, if it's any comfort at all, a lot of scientists say that time is just an illusion, anyway. Everything that happened while we were alive has always happened, continues to happen, and always will happen."

"I don't really get it."

"No; I guess I don't get it either. It's a hard thing to wrap your mind around. But that doesn't mean it can't be true."

Soon, we were standing at the edge of the waterfall, which might have stretched the entire width of the river, although we could not see how far out toward the other shore it ran. The spray and mist it threw into the sky were so thick and rose so high that the water seemed to be falling in two directions at once. Most of the spirits traveling downriver were now moving out and away from the bank and floating like milkweed fluff down a steep, mist-shrouded trail toward the unseen base of the plunge. But as we stood watching, several souls surprised us by walking right out into the waterfall and disappearing.

After a moment Angelfish said, "That's what I want to do!"

I hoped she was joking. "Really? What about the beach?"

"No; this looks more exciting. And, it can't kill us; we're already dead. We could hold hands and step on out there."

I remembered Gib telling me not long after I met him, *All rivers run to the sea; all waters meet.* But I felt afraid, and I said, "We can't hold hands; we're ghosts."

"We can do what we can do. Let's mix our hands together; hell, let's blend our bodies into one and fly right off the edge."

So that, finally, was what we did: Angelfish and I came together in an indistinguishable tumble of color and motion—what would have been an embrace if we'd been alive—and we stepped out into the smoking emptiness.

Up we fell.